I'm Not the Hero

I'm Not the Hero

Book 1

SourpatchHero

Podium

For Sarah, who means everything to me.
You are my happily ever after.

And for Oliver and Milo, for reminding me how fun
telling stories could be. This book is for you … in a few years.

Cover design by Podium Publishing

ISBN: 978-1-0394-2536-1

Published in 2023 by Podium Publishing, ULC
www.podiumaudio.com

Podium

I'm Not the Hero

Chapter 1

Orrin walked behind Daniel, the same as he did every day after school. At least for the last two months, this had been the routine. His friend did not look back once as he jabbered away to his new girlfriend, Cara.

At least her house is on the way to our neighborhood, Orrin thought as he kicked a rock on the sidewalk. It skittered along for a few feet when he failed to connect fully.

Daniel and Orrin had been inseparable since elementary school. They had become friends due to proximity—as they had grown up next door to each other, their parents made sure they did all the same activities. Soccer, baseball, even martial arts, until everyone realized Orrin was terrible at any coordinated activity. Daniel had excelled at everything.

That continued into high school. Daniel was on just about every sports team, while Orrin just . . . existed. He had decent grades but wasn't anywhere near the top of his class. He had some friends, mostly people who would say "happy birthday" but nothing more. The entire cheerleading team had baked a cake and sung "Happy Birthday" to Daniel.

Despite his popularity, Daniel stuck around as Orrin's friend. He brought him to parties, where Orrin sat in the corner. He made him go to the homecoming dance, where Orrin sat in the corner. They played video games together and shot hoops at Daniel's house. During dinner, Orrin tried to be invisible while Daniel's parents talked to his sister and Daniel about their days.

Orrin's mom was an emergency room doctor, staying late into the night and working strange hours. His dad had disappeared years ago. No letter. No "going out for milk." Just gone. So Orrin ended up spending a lot of time at the Kaysons'. Mr. and Mrs. Kayson treated him like another son. Daniel's sister was a year older than them, a senior, and the unrequited love of Orrin's life. They had all played together when they were younger, but Orrin knew he didn't exist in her orbit anymore.

Orrin stood back as the trio approached Cara's house, letting Daniel get a minute of privacy. The street was pretty empty as he looked up at the old Victorian with the well-manicured lawn. *I should probably mow the lawn tomorrow before Mom gets off shift.*

The sound of metal on concrete tugged his attention away. He heard the mechanical grunt of a motor speeding up, the gears changing as the speed increased. He turned his head and saw a truck speeding right toward Daniel and Cara. It had already hopped the curb and was riding two wheels on the sidewalk. The sun glinted down, glaring across the windshield.

"Daniel! Cara! Look out!"

Daniel looked back to see Orrin waving frantically. Orrin threw his books to the ground and ran with all his might toward his best friend.

Why am I charging like I'm going to tackle him? Orrin thought.

Daniel turned toward the growing sounds of metal grinding as the truck got closer. Orrin watched his friend hurl his girlfriend through the air and prepare to dive himself.

He's not going to get out of the way in time.

Orrin was close enough now. He went low, just like his coach had taught him in peewee football years ago. His entire lanky frame hit the solid mass of Daniel as he pushed his friend out of the way of the swerving vehicle.

At least, that had been his intent.

Orrin hit Daniel just as he jumped after Cara's body flying through the air. If Daniel's feet had been on the ground, Orrin would have bounced off him like a ping-pong ball hitting the wall. With his feet already in the air, Daniel lost all momentum as Orrin slammed into him. As they fell, the truck seemed to correct its course, as if it was TRYING to hit them. Orrin scrambled up in front of his friend. Daniel started to crawl frantically toward the house, but the truck's front bumper was too close.

Orrin didn't have time to say "Shit" before the crash and pain.

> Interface Loading . . .
> Error
> [Unknown Essence Found]
> Rerouting . . .
> Error
> [Changing Parameters]
> Loading . . .
> Error
> [Two Entity Essences Entered]
> Rerouting . . .
> Initializing Sequence 427 AB
> New User Interface Loading . . .
> 58%
> 74%
> 99%
> Enter Name_

Where am I? His thoughts felt slow and distant. Orrin turned his head to . . . his head didn't turn. Or maybe it did, but the floating prompt in front of him was all that remained in the darkness around him.

O. R. R. I. N. He thought then, and the letters appeared one at a time before merging back into his name, ORRIN.

> ORRIN accepted.
> Loading Creation Table . . .
> Error

Multiple Essence Error
Debug
Debug
Debug
Rebooting . . .
Class Table Mainframe Loading . . .
Error
Administrator Access Granted
Class Table Loading . . .
Select your class _

The blue screen in front of his eyes scrolled by with thousands of options, using words from every video game and tabletop manual Orrin had ever seen or heard of . . . and more.

There didn't seem to be any sort of order to the selection list, but he found a few he recognized.

Fighter
Mage
Rogue
Sorcerer
Dragoon
Paladin
Wizard
Priest

And some he didn't.

Bloodfinder
Stalwart Wall
Knife in the Dark
Spade Jester
Glassfiend

Even normal-sounding jobs appeared.

Farmer
Farrier
Cook

I'm dead. I'm dead, and I've been isekai'ed. This isn't real. I have the day off tomorrow, and I'm going to play video games with Daniel until Mom comes home. Wake up. Wake up.

Orrin felt himself begin to hyperventilate. He hadn't had a panic attack since his end-of-year presentation in eighth grade, but he felt it happening now. He tried to take deep breaths and close his eyes, but the boxes remained.

Error
Anomaly Building
Source Overridden
[Mind Bastion] GRANTED

Orrin felt as if he'd been dunked in a tank of cold water, then blasted dry with hot air. Suddenly, he could think clearly again.

I died. I really died. I was hit by a truck and died. This is either the afterlife or I'm about to meet a goddess who will give me a giant sword to kill the Demon Lord. I know how this story goes. No use panicking. I can find a way home if I try. The hero usually gets a wish at the end of the story. Right? Okay, so . . . He started looking over his options again. Slower this time. His options took up hundreds of lines of text.

Fighter and straight melee are out, since I'm never going to get that right and don't want to stab myself. As he had the thought, the list shrank to about half its earlier size. *Convenient!*

I've played with magic before in Dungeons & Dragons, *but I don't really know what kind of world this is. I'm going to guess that anything named different is a specialized magic class . . . and that sounds like a lot of pressure. I don't want to be the special one getting targeted. I want to be of help for sure, but I want to be in the background, quiet and away from any main battles. Able to control fights with precision but also have some options to do big damage or escape if I need. Maybe something with healing? Not like a priest—I don't want to be worshipping some god or gods . . .*

Amazingly, the list responded to his thoughts again. Orrin watched as the list became smaller . . . smaller . . . just a few . . . then two . . . one . . . wait, WHAT?

The entire list disappeared. *SHIT!*

Initialing Custom Class Creation with Administrator Access

WHAT THE FUCK?

Creating Custom Class based on given parameters . . .

Hold on. Wait. Let me see the list again. I'm sure something is . . .

Class Created Utility Warder. Welcome, Orrin.

Blackness engulfed him.

Name: Orrin
Class: Utility Warder (New Class)
Level 1 (0/100)
Ability Points: 10
HP: 80
MP: 120
Strength: 8
Constitution: 8
Dexterity: 8
Will: 12
Intelligence: 10

Abilities: Mind Bastion—Individual is able to control his own mind and therefore part of his body.

Orrin woke with a start, scrambling back along the ground and digging up tufts of grass with his hands before his back hit something hard. Rubbing his neck, he looked back and up to see an eighty-foot tree towering above him.

A forest? He looked around. *And no starter pack or flaming sword of doom? Lousy isekai . . .*

Orrin spotted a pair of legs sticking out from behind a tree a few yards away. A low groan emanated from the body. He crawled forward to find Daniel facedown . . . and very naked.

Orrin realized his clothes were also very, very gone.

"Fucking hell?"

At Orrin's outburst, Daniel seemed to come around. He sat up. Looking dazed, he peered at Orrin, then turned away.

"Dude, what the hell? Put your clothes back on." Daniel started to pull his covers over his body. He had been having the weirdest dream about . . . He looked at his empty hands. No blanket. This was not his bed. He looked over his own body, turning red all over.

"WHAT THE HELL IS GOING ON?" Daniel started to stand up but ended up in a half squat, covering himself and looking around with frantic eyes. "There was a truck, and I think it tried to hit me. Why are we in a forest? Where the FUCK are my pants?"

Orrin turned to face away. "Daniel. Dude, we obviously just got hit by Truck-kun and are in another world. Take a look at your status screen."

"What the hell is a status scr— WHAT THE FUCK? There's a blue box in front of my face with my name and it says [Hero]. Orrin, what did you do, man?"

Orrin was so shocked to hear Daniel's class that he turned and, after getting an eyeful of his friend again, quickly turned back. "I didn't do anything. I think . . . I think it was just supposed to be you that got hit by the truck and sent here. I got a lot of error messages and had to create a class and . . ."

Daniel interrupted, "Listen, I don't give a shit what you think right now. I've got a game tonight and a date tomorrow. I have to finish my homework and see my parents. Orrin, how the hell are you so relaxed and WHAT THE HELL ARE YOU DOING?"

As Daniel continued to flip out, Orrin decided to give him some time; he had started playing with the blue box. A row of icons in the corner he had missed before was blinking. A small square with a triangle on top, almost like a little house, lit up twice as Daniel had gone into his tirade.

> **Welcome to the Store**
> **AP: 10**
> **Spells !**
> **Skills**
> **Abilities**
> **Misc.**

He clicked the blinking Spells ! cursor.

Attack spells, defense spells, buff spells, debuff spells, healing spells—the list grew and grew as he watched. This would take him years to get through.

It responded to my thoughts last time . . . maybe . . .

He concentrated on the blinking cursor, watching the list scroll faster and faster until the words were a blur.

PLINK

> **Spell Selection:**
> [Calm Mind] Negates mind magic to a degree.
> Calms the target, reducing stress, anger, or sad-
> ness. Increases peacefulness and allows logical
> thoughts. 5 MP.
>
> **Would you like to purchase for 2 AP? Yes or No?**

Daniel was still yelling at him and crying now. *YES!*

Knowledge of [Calm Mind] filled his brain as he turned back to his friend and put his hand on his shoulder.

With a thought, the spell drained his MP by five. Four times. He was left with one hundred MP.

Daniel's eyes glazed over for a minute, and then he took a deep breath. He looked down, and Orrin watched as his friend found himself again. The trauma wasn't healed or gone, just reduced and pushed to the back. Probably not the healthiest thing, but they were standing naked in a forest that probably had some sort of monsters coming to get them at any point.

"Sorry. Thanks. What was that? A spell?" Daniel stood straight and watched the distance.

"No problem, D. Yeah, I bought [Calm Mind] from the store. Little house cursor in the top corner. You can use your ability points to get stuff, although I have no idea what options [Hero] is going to get you." Orrin replayed the list of options he had seen. He was 90 percent sure [Hero] had not been available. "So you picked [Hero]? Anything else? I'm at eighty hit points and 120 mana points . . . magic points? I think constitution must be a ten multiplier for health and will for magic. No idea what strength, dexterity, and intelligence do, though."

Daniel risked a glance back before keeping watch of the distance again. "Orrin, I didn't pick [Hero]. I woke up to it. And how are you only at eighty health? I've got three hundred."

"WHAT? You started with a thirty constitution?"

"No, that's at fifteen."

"What about your strength?"

"Same."

"Any abilities?"

". . . huh. Yeah. [Summoned Hero] gives . . . oh, that explains it. Gives me times two to all physical stats. So it must double my HP, my strength, and my dexterity."

During the back-and-forth, Orrin kept scrolling through the store. He tried to remember every web novel, comic, manga, and show he had watched or read that could help. He was creating a list in his mind of possible options to buy.

"So, I'm guessing you're going to want to take a look at the miscellaneous section of the store. There are some really great options for weapons, but most are too expensive right now. I only have eight points left, but I think I could get a—"

"I have three hundred points, Orrin," Daniel almost whispered.

Must be nice to be the hero. Orrin regretted the thought and was glad he hadn't said anything out loud. He glanced at Daniel, glad he was too distracted reading his own blue boxes to notice any jealousy on Orrin's face.

"Okay. Well, then, I'll just get some of the things I'm eyeing, then . . . Can you get us some clothes? Some of the common clothes come in sets of ten for a point."

Daniel grunted and pointed at a pile that had appeared between them. He was already dressed. Orrin really needed to start paying attention to his surroundings. He grabbed a dark-green shirt and something that looked like jeans but with more movement.

Well, I'm going to have to wait for some of these things, but I think these are most important right now.

Spells:
[Heal Small Wounds] heal up to 10 HP. 5 MP. (0/1,000) -2 points
[Increase Strength] increases target Strength by +1 for 5 minutes. 5 MP (0/1,000) -1 point
[Increase Dexterity] increases target Dexterity by +1 for 5 minutes. 5 MP (0/1,000) -1 point
[Camouflage] melt into your surroundings. Increase ability to remain undetected for 5 minutes. Attack damage breaks the spell. 10 MP (0/10,000) -1 point

Abilities:

[Dimension Hole] place items into a container of your choice (pocket, bag, etc.) Store items in a dimensional chest. Retrievable from any empty container. UPGRADABLE -3 points
8 points used.

Orrin squatted down and started shoving the extra shirts and pants into his [Dimension Hole]. Daniel was still looking into his purchases. Occasionally, something would appear around him. A sword strapped to his back. A bracer of knives. Orrin blinked, and an entire set of leather armor appeared on his friend.

"D, don't spend all your points. We might need some for food."

Daniel looked down from his boxes.

"I think we'll be all right. I took [Map], and I think we are only a few miles from a town. Besides, I took [Hero Kit] for most of my skills. I still have about a hundred points left." Daniel picked up a small backpack from right outside Orrin's sight. "This one is yours. Just some jerky, water, and a bedroll. But at least you don't have to carry all the . . . clothes . . . Where did the extra clothes go?"

"[Dimension Hole]." Orrin pulled a shirt halfway from his pocket.

"That's not showing on my list. What else did you get?"

"[Heal Small Wounds], [Increase Strength], [Increase Dexterity], and [Camouflage]."

"Yeah, man. None of those are in my store. How do you have things I don't? What's your class?"

"Um . . ." Orrin pulled his status up again. "Utility Warder? I don't know what that means, but maybe I just get better options?"

"Better options than [Hero]?" Daniel frowned like he did when Orrin used a glitch in a game to win. "We can figure it out later. Have you looked at Quests?"

Orrin pulled his status back up. At the top were tabs. Status, the house that would open the store, and an empty circle. With a thought, the circle tab opened.

> **Quests: 0/0**
> None available

"Open right now. Guess we don't have to defeat the Demon Lord or anything, huh?" Orrin chuckled.

Daniel's frown deepened. "How did you know there's a Demon Lord?"

"It's a joke. You know, like one of those stories of getting hit by a truck or stabbed and having to defeat the Demon Lord before the world is destroyed?"

Daniel paled a bit. "Orrin, you know I never watched the same shows as you. I have a bunch of Quests and one of them says 'Defeat the Demon Lord.'" He put his hand into the air and moved it toward Orrin. "Let's see if this works," he muttered before a new blue box appeared on Orrin's screen.

> **Daniel, Hero Level 1, is sharing a Quest.**
> **Would you like to accept it? Yes or No?**

Yes.

> **Quests: 0/1**
> Defeat the Demon Lord—In the southern lands, the Demon Lord has risen. The dark armies have been assembled. Seek out and defeat the Demon Lord before the Dark Horde attacks.
> Reward: 1,000,000 XP and Dark Essence Unlocked

"Okay. That's just too cliché. How many Quests do you have?"

"Six, but I already completed [Buy Hero Kit]." Daniel started tossing them all over to Orrin. He spammed the yes response.

Quests: 0/5
Defeat the Demon Lord [Expand]
Defend the Wall—Help push back a Horde
Reward: Variable on participation percentage/
Horde Type
Defeat a Dungeon.
Reward: Variable

Obtain Level 10
Reward: [Hero Kit Level 2] Unavailable reward
Reach the Wall of Dey within 24 hours [23 hours
20 minutes 18 seconds]
Reward: +1 to all stats
Failure: No penalty

"Weird. The [Hero Kit] seems to be unavailable to me. Guess I won't be getting any help there." Orrin finished reading and watched Daniel pull the straps closed on his backpack.

"If I'm reading this [Map] right, we're only half a day from Dey. You ready to go hiking, O?" Daniel smiled for the first time since they woke up here. Orrin felt the pressure in his chest lift. His friend was here. He'd be fine.

"Yeah. We got this."

Daniel's smile widened. "I'm glad you're here. I really don't—" Something from the tree overhead reached down and wrapped around Daniel's leg, yanking him up into the dark foliage above.

Chapter 2

Orrin stared at the spot where his best friend had stood seconds ago. Blood dripped down from the tree above. Too much blood.

> New Mandatory Quest
> Save the Hero
> Reward: 100 XP and [Identify] ability
> Failure: Death of Hero. Likely annihilation of the world.

What the fuck? Orrin had no offensive spell. The only reason he hadn't been scooped up as well was [Camouflage]. He had been concentrating on his new spells and activated [Camouflage] in terror as he saw the vine-like appendage grab Daniel.

He looked up at the tree. He could see a form through the branches struggling, but it appeared to be moving slower and slower. Orrin searched the ground for anything to throw . . . He was definitely not climbing an eighty-foot tree. A few of Daniel's daggers had slipped out, or more likely Daniel had reacted and tried to stab the vine. Orrin found two and picked them up.

And what good is throwing a knife into the air going to do anyone? Orrin peered through the leaves and watched a second vine ensnare his friend. Even with a double increase in strength, two vines seemed to be more than enough to hold him tight.

Strength! That's it. Orrin locked his eyes on Daniel and started pushing mana into his buff spells.

[Increase Strength]
[Increase Strength]
[Increase Strength]
[Increase Strength]
[Increase Dexterity]
[Increase Dexterity]
[Heal Small Wounds]
[Heal Small Wounds]
[Heal Small Wounds]
[Heal Small Wounds]

Orrin lost fifty MP in the span of seconds. He didn't know how hurt Daniel was. He didn't know how much extra strength he'd need. Hell, he didn't know if the spells were touch only or ranged.

A third vine was snaking its way across the branches.

Orrin started casting again.

[Increase Strength]
[Increase Strength]
[Increase Strength]
[Increase Strength]
[Increase Strength]
[Increase Dexterity]
[Increase Dexterity]
[Increase Dexterity]
[Increase Dexterity]
[Increase Dexterity]

His MP bottomed out. He felt dizzy for a second and tried to push more mana into a healing spell, but nothing happened.

0/120 MP

Orrin tried to throw a dagger at the third vine, but it went wide . . . like ten yards wide. He clutched the last dagger and drew back his arm to throw again.

"SCREW THIS!" Daniel yelled from above. His friend finally had gotten a hand free and pulled his sword off his back. He swung drunkenly, with no balance. Luckily, one wild slash thunked right into the third vine as it neared his neck.

Orrin heard a scream from behind the trees. An unearthly, low, rock-on-rock scream. Daniel was swinging at the other two vines, his arm a blur as he chipped strips of plant life off each.

Orrin quietly stepped around the large trunk and squatted low, imitating every stealthy video game character he had ever played. Orrin realized his [Camouflage] was still active. A few yards away was a monster. It looked like a ball of vines, constantly wiggling around. Three appendages had reached up the side of a nearby tree, traversing branches to sit over where they had been chatting minutes before.

It's an ambush creature. Orrin did not know where the thought came from, but he trusted it. He'd always been good at figuring out strategies in games. More than once, he'd pissed Daniel off by coasting through a difficult part of some video game, pulling off something unexpected like running at the creature instead of rolling to the side or throwing a torch to distract an enemy. *If I attack it now, it might just run away.*

Yeah. All 130 pounds of me running at that thing with a kitchen knife is totally the way to survive. Guess this world is doomed. Sorry, Daniel. Even as his mind was second-guessing, Orrin was moving. He held the knife point up in his fist. He would stab it and then run. He was only about five feet behind it now. Sounds of Daniel's sword hitting the vines and the occasional thunk of wood as he missed and hit trees still echoed.

Almost there. CRACK.

Orrin looked down. So engrossed in his upcoming role as Jack the Ripper, he had stopped watching where he stepped and broken a long stick cleanly in two.

He felt the vine monster's attention turn to him. [Camouflage] obviously stopped working if he made too much noise. *Shit. Well. Good to know, I guess.*

Orrin lunged forward the few remaining feet, the knife hilt gripped in both hands as he pushed it toward the monster. He saw the third vine arm swinging down toward him. It would be close.

The knife hit something rough and hard. The tip snapped and turned the entire blade to the side. Then it stuck fast, and the monster howled again. The vine arm smacked Orrin in the side, and he was thrown ten feet, rolling and coming to a stop only when his left hip hit a tree. An explosion of pain blossomed from his rib and hip. The vine slithered along the leafy forest floor and gripped his foot, pulling him back toward the waiting monster.

The sounds of swordplay in the trees had stopped.

This is bullshit. I'm going to get eaten by Tangela. But the uglier, wooden vine version.

The vine had grabbed his left leg, so every pull jostled his hip and sent a fire throughout his body. Something definitely was broken. It hurt to breathe, too. *Probably a broken rib.* His mom's constant chattering about her job had caused a few bits of medical knowledge to get stuck in his head. He hadn't even thought of her since he'd landed here. Did she know he was dead? Would his body have been brought to her hospital? She'd be fine, right? They hadn't had a dinner together in two years, so her life wouldn't change that much.

The vine monster lifted him in the air by one foot. Orrin heard a thump as Daniel's body, still wrapped in vines, hit the ground nearby. He wasn't moving.

Orrin hung upside down, waiting to die. As the vine lowered him down, the wiggling mass slowed, and a hole appeared in the middle. A mouth filled with rocklike teeth, maggots, half of a rotting animal, and breath so pungent he gagged.

And there, just to the side of the lip, was the knife.

The vine let go, and Orrin fell into the gaping mouth.

When Orrin was nine, his dad had signed him up for soccer. Orrin had already proven at this point that anything involving moving objects and him were a recipe for disaster; however, his father was adamant.

So, Orrin laced up his new shoes and set up behind their house to kick a ball with his dad. Orrin faced away from the house, so anything he kicked would only get lost in the small wooded area behind the yard.

"Look, son, you don't have to be good at this. But you do have to try. Life is trying." His dad paused, looking for a laugh to his dad joke. "Now set your feet and just kick when I roll it to you." His dad never pressured him to succeed at anything, just to try everything to find his "passion," as he called it.

The ball rolled slowly and stopped a few feet behind Orrin. He picked up the ball and rolled it back to his dad. He hadn't even tried to kick it the first time.

His dad let out a sigh and nodded. Readying himself, he tossed it again. This time, Orrin had the speed down, and when his raised foot came down to kick the ball . . . he missed completely and was looking at the sky.

His dad laughed as he bent over to help his son up off the ground "Really whiffed it there, huh? Don't worry, you'll get it."

They spent an hour trying before Orrin connected with the ball with any meaning. He fell more times than he could remember, missed nearly every easy roll, and when he finally kicked the ball . . .

The light in his dad's eyes had stopped shining as brightly, but his dad never gave up. That was one thing he always remembered. His dad never gave up. Until he left.

"Okay, you'll get it this time."

Why his dad thought the hundredth time would be any different was beyond Orrin, but as his foot moved, something clicked. He launched the ball. All his strength was in that foot. The soccer ball blasted off his leg, and WHACK! it hit his dad right in the face, ricocheting over Orrin's head right through the dining room window.

Orrin had never played soccer again.

As he fell, Orrin remembered his dad and that soccer ball. The handle of the knife was so much smaller, but with nothing to lose, he turned his body as he fell and punted the knife as hard as he could.

Of course, he missed. He kicked the side of the monster instead. But his right shin connected with the knife, driving it through the meaty part of the monster's mouth. It must have been a poor-quality knife, too, because it shattered even more, shards of metal penetrating deep into the open maw of the monster. It shook its head in pain, which meant Orrin landed only half in the mouth. The pain in his left hip reached new heights as his left leg crumpled in the meaty mess of rotting flesh and blood.

He tried to lift himself out gingerly, but the monster finally had had enough. It shook his head and launched Orrin into the air. He landed near the still body of Daniel.

The monster retracted its vines and rolled off into the forest, keening as it went.

Quest Complete
Save the Hero
Reward: 100 XP and [Identify] ability

Level 2 Obtained!
+10 AP
+ [Identify] You can see

Orrin looked at Daniel. He was breathing, but those breaths were ragged. His right arm was snapped in two places, with bone sticking out and blood running. The entire side of his face was bruised where a vine had slapped him.

0/120 MP

This is too much. Why?!? He's the hero! He's my friend! Orrin felt tears sting the cuts on his face.

He opened the store. "Listen here, asshole. You do not get to die. We are going to solve all the Quests and get back home. You are going to go on your date with Cara. I'm going to make my mom stop working so much. Can you hear me?"

Orrin kept rattling off whatever popped into his mind. He went through spells, skills, and abilities. He almost bought a [First Aid Kit], but he wasn't his mom. He didn't know how to set a fractured arm or what to do about internal bleeding.

I need more mana, he thought.

His blue box gave him the options.

> [Meditate] regenerate mana at 1 MP per minute
> (5 AP)
> [Mana Pool] increase MP by 100 MP (onetime purchase) (10 AP)
> [Blood Mana] exchange HP for MP (one-to-one)
> (5 AP)

Orrin took a breath and thought. [Mana Pool] sounded like the best idea, but he didn't know if it would actually give him MP now or just increase him to 0/220 MP. Plus, with that cost, he'd have no other options if it didn't give him one hundred MP to use.

He purchased [Meditate] and after a moment went ahead and got [Blood Mana] too.

HP 35/80
MP 1/120

This is taking too long. Orrin hesitated for a long second . . . and dropped twenty-four health for mana.

HP 11/80
MP 25/120

Orrin cast [Heal Small Wounds] on Daniel four times in rapid succession. Then, on a whim, Orrin used his last spell on himself. He pulled up his status and [Heal Small Wounds].

HP 23/80
MP 0/120
[Heal Small Wounds] 45/1,000

So [Heal Small Wounds] heals twelve HP but only costs five? That seems broken with [Blood Mana]. Did I really find a loophole here?

He pushed fifteen health into his mana and then healed himself three times.

HP 59/80

All the while, his MP ticked up one every minute. *Okay. Let's figure this out, then. Five MP for twelve HP. Turn the HP into ten MP and heal two times more, upping my health by twenty-four. Rinse and repeat. I should keep my health above ten if I can. This is totally broken!*

Orrin got to work. He dumped forty-five points of health back into mana and then used [Heal Small Wounds] nine times in row on his friend. That should be 108 HP, in addition to the forty-eight from before.

Daniel coughed and then breathed easier. His eyes flickered open.

". . . did we die again?"

Orrin laughed.

Orrin kept the healing up, cycling. He told Daniel what had happened, his ill-fated attempt to be a soccer player again, and the glitch he had found.

"So, you get to heal as much as you want . . . and regain your own mana from your health . . . at a rate of one to two?"

"Actually, I'm healing more than I should be. I think will is more than just my MP times ten. I haven't figured out the equation yet, but I'm going to. It definitely boosts the damage—or, in this case, the healing of my magic. It's like will also makes spells hit harder."

Orrin realized he was waving his hands as he walked in circles in front of his friend. His friend who was still cradling his broken arm. He started healing again. "Sorry."

"Nothing to be sorry about. You saved us." Daniel watched in fascination as the bone of his arm pulled back in and reset. "Yeah, I'm glad I haven't eaten anything. That was disgusting."

He cast his spell until Daniel told him his HP was topped off, then got his own HP back to full. He almost stopped but realized he could gain more XP by pushing his MP to full, too. He started [Blood Mana] cycling again. When he felt no more returns were really possible, he tried to pull up a smaller status.

Level 2 (0/200)

HP 74/80
MP 120/120
[Heal Small Wounds] 315/1,000

"Damn. I forgot [Identify]." He tried to use the skill.

Daniel
Hero Level 1

HP: 300/300
MP: 25/80

Strength: 14
Constitution: 15
Dexterity: 13
Will: 8

Intelligence: 10

Abilities:
[Summoned Hero] Gives x2 to all physical stats
[Hero Kit]
Sword Proficiency Level 1
Dagger Proficiency Level 1
Mace Proficiency Level 1
Axe Proficiency Level 1
Hammer Proficiency Level 1
Spear Proficiency Level 1
Bow Proficiency Level 1
Quarterstaff Proficiency Level 1
Unarmed Proficiency Level 1
[Hide Status]
[Map] See the world around you
[Stone Skin] Increase your vitality! Physical damage is halved for 5 minutes
[Identify] Attempt to peer into others' status
[Power Strike] Deal 2x damage on your next hit
[Eagle Eyes] See up to twice as far
[Edge of Death] You can fight on! When your HP is reduced to 0, find the burning life within

"Daaamnnnn, Daniel. Your abilities are no joke!" Orrin tried [Identify] on the trees, grass, and even the knife he had thrown and found again. Nothing appeared. "I guess it just works on people?"

"How . . . how can you see my abilities?" Daniel was looking down the length of his reclaimed sword. "I can only get your status to say your name and HP."

Orrin shrugged. They were going to have to ask a lot of questions when they got to the nearby town. They should really discuss their cover story. Too many stupid adventurers in stories ended up getting duped because they just loudly proclaimed, "I'm the hero!" without doing the smallest bit of reconnaissance first. "What did you say the nearest town was again? Day?"

"Yeah. Dey. D-E-Y." Daniel slid his sword back into the sheath holes near his shoulder. Orrin hadn't noticed it in detail before, but it was a big thing. A two-handed weapon for him for sure. Hadn't Daniel been swinging it with one hand in the air with ease?

"Right. Like the Quest one." Orrin pulled it up.

5. Reach the Wall of Dey [22 hours 5 minutes, 10 seconds]

"We should probably head out. You said it would take half a day to get there? I should probably get [Map] too. I used all my points from leveling to heal your sorry ass." Orrin bumped his shoulder into his taller friend's side. Daniel didn't budge.

"You leveled? How? We didn't even kill the thing. I got no XP for all the damage I did."

"Oh I got a Quest reward of one hundred XP for saving the [Hero]." Orrin drew the last word out sarcastically, wagging his eyebrows up and down.

Daniel shrugged again. "Well, savior of the [Hero], try to keep up. We're going to need to jog a bit—it looked like the sun was in the middle of the sky when that thing tossed me over the tree line. We should probably not try running in the pitch dark of night."

Orrin hated running.

The first ten minutes were bad. The following two hours were brutal. He could tell Daniel was trying to go slow for him. He even knew Daniel was stopping too frequently for rest breaks. But none of that mattered.

Because Orrin hated running.

"Wait . . . stop a minute." Orrin pushed himself off another tree and sank to his knees in the leaves again.

"Orrin. We just stopped twenty minutes ago. At this rate, we won't make it in time for the Quest. We've barely moved on the map."

Orrin didn't care. Logically, he knew the Quest rewards were worth the pain now. More health, more mana, more everything for running a few miles in the forest? He'd been all for that ... before the running.

"Unless you plan on carrying me all the way there, we need to set a better pace, D. I just can't run like you can."

Orrin breathed hard, trying to remember if it was "in through the nose, out through the mouth" or the other way round.

"... carry you ..." Orrin heard Daniel muttering.

"Orrin. How much do your spells increase my strength and dexterity?"

Orrin pulled up his spells. "Plus one for five minutes every cast."

Daniel grinned. "Does that stack?"

As it turned out, the spells stacked five times each. With Daniel's [Summoned Hero] perk, that gave him a plus-ten strength and dexterity. More than enough to let Orrin ride piggyback as Daniel dashed through the trees at a rate that left Orrin feeling a little nauseous.

They made great time. Daniel said they'd made almost the entire trek, but when the sun went down, the rustling they had heard as they traversed the forest turned into full-on growls. Branches swayed above them, and neither felt comfortable being a moving target. They discussed climbing a tree to sleep in the branches, until a large cat the size of a small car walked by above them. It ignored them completely, but the timing and the wicked intelligence in its eyes made Daniel pick up his jog for twenty minutes.

Then Orrin spotted a tree with a crack in the side.

"There."

The tree was dead. Hit by lightning in the past but still not fallen to time. A large crack stretched up fifteen feet, and a fire had obviously burned out most of the inside. The darkness was heavy now, as the sun had fully set.

"There's probably only five feet of space inside, Orrin," Daniel said hesitantly.

"Good thing you have axe proficiency, then. Get chopping, Paul Bunyan."

Daniel set Orrin down and sighed. He poked around on his screens, and a set of axes appeared in his hands.

"That cost two points . . ." He handed one to Orrin. "Watch my back."

"Of course." Orrin took the axe and turned toward the encroaching darkness. He pulled up his status as his friend used [Power Strike] after [Power Strike] on the dead wood inside the hole.

Three hours of running hadn't done much for Daniel, but Orrin had been soaking in the XP. He used [Increase Strength] and [Increase Dexterity] five times each, every five minutes. He'd also put [Camouflage] up just in case it helped. Then he'd done his [Heal Small Wounds] [Blood Mana] cycle to get his MP back to full before starting over . . . and over.

He had a blinking ! next to one of his abilities.

> [Heal Small Wounds] (1,000/1,000) ! Upgrade available. 4 AP (Insufficient AP)
> [Increase Strength] (970/1,000)
> [Increase Dexterity] (960/1,000)
> [Camouflage] (380/10,000)

As they'd been running, he'd watched as he neared the one thousand mark and was surprised when he realized he needed to buy the next level. No other healing spell had been available in the store, but he'd figured it would level. He just hadn't thought that it might cost points AFTER he had worked so hard to use one thousand mana worth of heal.

I need to level again and get that . . . and strength and dexterity are so close, too . . .

The chopping behind him stopped.

"Here's our home for the night." Daniel pointed his axe at the tree. He had hollowed out enough for them to sit comfortably on the floor. No standing room.

They pulled some brush up against the edge and sat down in the dark.

"I'll take first watch?" Orrin asked. Daniel had almost died earlier. And carried him. And just chopped down half a sequoia from the inside.

"Fine by me. Holler if something tries to eat me." Daniel pulled out his bedroll and covered himself, turning to the side.

". . . D. I'm glad it's you I'm here with. Thanks, man."

Daniel sat up and smirked at his friend. "Same, buddy. I know I said it earlier, but thanks for saving my life. Now, don't let that tiger-leopard thing eat my face. I'll carry you into town tomorrow and we'll find the local king or president and get set up for success."

Daniel was blinking hard as he talked. The day had taken more out of him than he was letting on. Orrin smiled softly at his friend. "Yeah. We'll kick ass and find a way home." He'd remember to get a good plan ready in the morning, because no way were they going to go straight to whoever was in charge.

Daniel nodded and fell asleep as Orrin held a sword way too big for him pointed toward the night.

Chapter 3

Orrin did not sleep. His friend snored gently and tossed occasionally. Daniel's parents had been strict with bedtimes for as long as he could remember, but Orrin had become his own guardian after his dad left. Spending all night reading or playing video games had become a normal occurrence.

He needs the rest. I'll sleep in a real bed tomorrow, Orrin told himself. This was all temporary. He would find them some way home. Until then, he was already piecing together a plan to survive.

Spells:
[Teleport] teleport to any known point within 10 miles. 50 MP per person (0/5,000) 5 AP
[Increase Will] increases target Will by +1 for 5 minutes. 5 MP (0/1,000) 1 AP
[Increase Intelligence] increases target Intelligence by +1 for 5 minutes. 5 MP (0/1,000) 1 AP

Abilities:
[Side Steps] 1% chance to evade any attack (0/100) (1 AP)
[Map] See the world around you (4 AP)
[Mana Pool] increase MP by 100 MP (onetime purchase) (10 AP)

Skills:

**[Merge] Combine Spells/Abilities for new effects.
Caution May lose original Spell/Ability (20 AP)**

If he could max out [Teleport], maybe there was some way to get all the way home. Orrin doubted it, though. It was probably a distance modifier.

The stat increase spells would round out his ability to buff up Daniel.

As they had run, Daniel had mentioned that all those spells had buffed him during the tentacle monster fight. So Orrin's spells were ranged to some point. If he could increase his own will and intelligence before a fight, he could do more. Plus, extra intelligence would mean a quicker [Blood Mana]–to–HP conversion. Orrin was beginning to believe MP reset during sleep, as other than his plus-one a minute from [Meditate], his MP never recovered.

[Side Steps] also would help him avoid taking damage. His HP was full, but he could still remember the feeling of the vine breaking his ribs. [Skills] seemed to be full of things like [Blacksmithing] and [Alchemy]. Nothing he really thought would be helpful short term. He'd scrolled right past [Merge] the first few times.

It's expensive . . . but maybe I could combine all four stats into one spell . . . or find something to merge with [Teleport] to make a universal teleport or something to go home with?

His first priority should be to level his healing. Then the stat increase spells, so Daniel could tank better. *We can probably take on most things with a little more preparation and a few more levels. I wonder if there are any other ways to gain XP besides Quests and killing monsters.* The lack of even partial XP for fighting had really pissed Daniel off the day before.

He spent the hours blood cycling, as he named the process. He quickly brought [Increase Strength] and [Increase Dexterity] up to 1,000/1,000. He also kept [Camouflage] running on himself. He had tried to cast it on Daniel, too, but nothing happened. At a cost of 120 MP, he could keep it running on himself for an entire hour. He let Daniel sleep for seven hours before waking him to talk.

[Heal Small Wounds] (1,000/1,000) ! Upgrade available. 4 AP (Insufficient AP)
[Increase Strength] (1,000/1,000) ! Upgrade available. 2 AP (Insufficient AP)
[Increase Dexterity] (1,000/1,000) ! Upgrade available. 2 AP (Insufficient AP)
[Camouflage] (1,220/10,000)

Orange and red light trickled through the treetops and lit up the ground as Orrin peeked through the hole in the brush he'd created. The frequent howls and crashes in the night had stopped an hour ago.

"D. Wake up. We should head out soon." Orrin pushed his bedroll back into his backpack, using [Dimension Hole] to make it disappear.

"No, Dad, I have a game. I need more sleep." Daniel turned over and pulled the blanket over his head.

"No game today. Just reaching the wall of a fantasy town before monsters eat our faces."

Daniel's breathing stopped. Then he sighed heavily. "Fuccc—I guess that wasn't a dream, huh?" He sat up. "Did you let me sleep the entire night? Damn it, man."

Orrin was busy pushing the brush out of the front hole in the tree. "You needed it more than me." He grabbed a branch and pushed. It stuck tight. He pushed again. Nothing. "Besides, you're the one who did most of the heavy lifting."

Daniel walked up beside his friend and kicked the limb. It snapped in two with a loud "crack" and fell to the side of the entrance.

"I can't believe you did that. You've been casting spells nonstop. I don't know how you do that. When my MP got low, it felt like I got kicked in the nuts. You should have taken the chance to get some sleep." Daniel grabbed the last of the tree branches and walked out of the tree. "Ahh. At least the temperature isn't too cold here. That sun feels good."

Orrin frowned as he hitched his bag on his shoulder. "I've gotten down to below ten MP a few times and haven't felt more than winded. Must be a class thing."

He pulled up the Quest box:

5. Reach the Wall of Dey [8 hours 18 minutes 34 seconds]

"Just over eight hours. Can we make it? I really need to get [Map], too."

"Yes, you do. It looks like we made it about three-quarters of the way yesterday. Should be fine with time as long as nothing jumps—"

"Shut it. Don't jinx us."

Daniel smiled and knocked on the tree as he adjusted his armor. "So am I carrying you again?"

It took two hours of Daniel running to reach the edge of the forest. Orrin got [Camouflage] to 1,460/10,000. Nothing jumped them, either.

Orrin squinted against the sun. He could vaguely make out a blurry mass in the distance. It was mostly wall shaped. "Is that . . . ?"

Daniel grunted and picked up his pack from where Orrin had put it down. "Yeah, that's gotta be Dey. I think we can probably walk from here. It's only like four or five miles."

Orrin frowned but didn't argue. Riding into town on Daniel's back would be too conspicuous. "Is there a road you can see, Mr. Eagle Eyes?"

Daniel pointed with his sword before he strapped it back in its sheath.

Orrin saw nothing but the hills and field. "Lead on, then, because some of us can't see that far."

They walked for twenty minutes before Orrin could make out the road in the distance. Little more than packed dirt and the occasional ditch along the side—it was no wonder he hadn't seen it.

Just as he saw the road, Daniel's hand darted out and grabbed Orrin's sleeve. Orrin opened his mouth to speak, but Daniel put his finger to his own lips and squatted down. Orrin did the same.

Orrin tried to see what he was missing, but it wasn't until he tracked Daniel's pointing finger that he made out the small smudge in the distance getting closer along the road. It was headed toward the city.

"A horse-drawn carriage?" Orrin whispered.

"Yes and no. About three hundred yards ahead of us, near that small clump of trees. There's a group of men holding swords and something else. I thought it was just a group of travelers waiting in some shade, but now I think they're bandits." Daniel slowly drew his sword.

Orrin groaned. "D. You can't possibly be thinking you are going to rush in and play hero. How many are there?"

"Just four. And I have to. Just got a Quest. Here."

Daniel, Hero Level 1, is sharing a Quest.
Quest: Defeat the bandits 0/4
Reward: 200 XP
Penalty: Lose 2 Strength for 14 days
Would you like to accept it? Yes or No?

Orrin hesitated to accept the Quest. He could just buff Daniel and stay out of sight, but if he did that and Daniel died . . .

Yes.

"Shit. Okay. What's the plan?" Orrin put five [Increase Strength] and five [Increase Dexterity] on both of them. He also topped off his [Camouflage], as it had ended while they sat and watched the carriage approaching. He also cycled his health and mana until he was topped off again.

Daniel gave Orrin a quick look and smirked. "Remember when Mark Lenoti tried to pick on you in middle school?"

Orrin moaned, "No. I'm not doing it."

Daniel's grin grew. "Got a better idea?"

The carriage slowed to a stop when two men walked in front with crossbows drawn.

"Move, vagrants. You do not wish to attempt a robbery here today." The man driving the carriage looked the part of a knight, but from where he stood, Orrin could tell he was outmatched. Crossbow bolts would probably punch right through the man's armor. The horse would have been dead already if he hadn't stopped.

Daniel had traveled toward the city and was supposed to come from behind. With [Camouflage], Orrin was able to get about twenty yards away from the men. Two held the crossbows pointed at the knight. The other two held their swords bare to the side.

"No need for names, sir." The larger man with the crossbow spit to the side. "Just have the lass throw some gold out the door and we can all be on our way. We know she's in there and what she's been doing. What's a few hundred gold to the Catanzanos?"

The knight's visor had gone down as soon as he'd spotted the trouble, but Orrin could almost feel the man shaking in rage. He quickly cast strength and dexterity on the man, hoping the added bonuses would help keep him alive.

". . . or if the lady would like to spend some time with us instead, I'm sure something could be arranged." The large man, obviously the leader, had a wicked grin as he watched the knight get angry.

Orrin could tell this was the moment. He stood up from his spot in the grass and walked to the road a few feet behind the carriage.

"Hey, guys! Do you know the way to the nearest rest stop? I've got to shit so bad and forgot to pack any toilet paper."

The two nearest the carriage door turned their swords on him. The leader kept his bolt pointed at the knight, but the second crossbowman wavered between the knight and Orrin.

The plan was for Orrin to distract them until Daniel blindsided them. The same tactic Daniel had used to teach Mark Lenoti not to pick on Orrin. The plan had worked great on a preteen boy not used to actual violence.

Orrin suddenly realized just how stupid they had been.

"Kill both the guards," the leader ordered. The crossbows released, and both bolts hit the knight, pushing him off the carriage. A quick scream from inside cut off in a quiet sob.

"Idiot." The leader tossed the crossbow to his comrade. "Two bolts, two guards. What if he's a [Swordhand] or something?" He drew his own sword as the three men surrounded Orrin.

"Um . . . listen, guys. Maybe you didn't hear me. I just need a bathroom. I didn't mean to interrupt or any—" Orrin started backing up and tripped over a small rock. He hit his ass hard as he landed.

He watched as the nearest man smiled in relief. "Nah boss. It's just some lost pup. Don't worry, son, I'll make it quick." He lifted his sword to strike.

When an axe lodged itself in the side of the man's face, Orrin blinked for a solid five seconds as the blood rained down on him. The man's body dropped like a doll.

Yelling and clangs of metal exploded around Orrin, as he sat staring at the dead man in front of him. The blood was soaking into the ground, but there was still so much pouring out of the cracked flesh of the side of the man's face. The wooden handle of the axe had been splattered as well, leaving the grain darkened as it, too, drank the man's life.

"Orrin! ORRIN!" Daniel was shaking him. Orrin wiped at his face and saw his hand was covered. The sticky feeling, combined with the metallic tang of the blood on his lips, was too much. Orrin turned and vomited on his friend's shoes.

"Is that your blood? Are you okay? You were only supposed to distract them, not get in their faces. What were you thinking?" Daniel was getting more frantic as Orrin didn't respond.

". . . fine. I'm fine," Orrin finally sputtered. He cast [Calm Mind] on Daniel, who visibly slumped. He pushed himself to his feet and looked around.

The bandit holding the two crossbows had been opened up from behind. Orrin spotted a dozen cuts on the second swordsman's arms, his body folded around a gaping stab wound in his chest. The leader's head rested by the carriage wheel.

"D . . . you butchered them." Orrin dry heaved, reminding him that they hadn't eaten since yesterday.

Daniel stayed quiet. He moved the axe stuck in the bandit's face with his foot and then left it alone. With his back to his friend, he whispered, "It was them or us. I'm not dying again, Orrin."

Orrin turned and walked to his friend. He grabbed his arm and pulled him around. "You did the right thing. You saved me." Orrin shivered. "I guess I shouldn't be surprised. Golden Daniel is good at everything, right?" He tried to smile, using the nickname he knew Daniel hated more than anything.

"Asshole." Daniel reached down and pulled the axe free with a squelching suck of air. "Go check and see if that guard is alive?"

Orrin scrambled around the carriage, remembering he could heal. Maybe the knight was still alive. He could still redeem himself and feel useful.

The armored knight was facedown, and Orrin couldn't turn him even with his strength still buffed. "D. Come help me turn this guy. I think he's breathing still." Orrin began spamming his heal and cycling his own mana and health. The knight's breathing evened and came deeper now. Definitely still alive—good.

"Stay away from him! I will give you one hundred gold each and you will leave. A [Message] has already been sent, and help is on the way," a female voice called from inside the carriage.

"We don't want your money," Daniel announced as he walked around the carriage to help Orrin, who had already dumped around 150 HP into the knight. His [Identify] showed the man's HP was still dropping even as he healed him.

Brandt Bennett
Knight Level 18

HP: 80/200
MP: 90/100

Strength: 15
Constitution: 15
Dexterity: 15
Will: 10
Intelligence: 9

Abilities:
[Sword Proficiency] Level 3
[Mace Proficiency] Level 2
[Axe Proficiency] Level 2
[Spear Proficiency] Level 1
[Unarmed Proficiency] Level 1
[Hide Status]
[Map]
[Identify]
[Power Strike]
[Defensive Fighting]

The man's abilities went on and on. Orrin had to stop reading and focus on healing. Daniel grabbed his arm and grunted as he lifted, turning the knight on his back.

"My father will kill you if you attempt . . . anything." The woman sounded scared.

Orrin looked at the two bolts that had pierced the knight's belly and chest. Blood seeped out from both wounds, and he could hear the pierced lung gurgling. Orrin looked at Daniel in horror. "I can't keep his health up. I think we have to remove the arrows before I can heal him." He turned to the carriage. "If you can't help, then shut up. We saved you, but your knight is hurt."

Orrin heard the door open and leather shoes dropped down. "Are you a healer? What are you doing outside a Hospital?" The lady from inside the carriage had come out. Orrin and Daniel saw a girl near their own age with dark skin and short hair. She wore well-oiled leather armor that looked expensive but comfortable. A single earring pierced her left eyebrow. and her brown eyes were on the knight.

"Uh, I can use [Small Heal Wounds]?" Orrin turned it into a question.

Tears streamed down her eyes. "Then he will die. We would need to rip the barbed bolts out and you will run out of MP well before small healing would make a difference." She stood straight and looked to the sky. "Please end Sir Bennett's suffering."

"Yeah, no. Fuck that noise," Orrin muttered and grabbed a bolt. He pulled hard and gagged at the noises. He pushed healing and cycled his own health. He had to rest every few heals on the knight and get his own HP back up, but the more he did his cycling, the quicker he got at the process.

"What are you doing? I told you it's hopeless. Under the banner of House Catanzano, I command you to—"

"D. Can you shut her up? I need to concentrate on this." Orrin took the second bolt, the one in the man's chest, and yanked hard. His HP dropped by nearly 150. He listened as Daniel used a gentle voice to push the girl back. Two minutes later, the knight coughed once. His eyes pulled open, and he vomited blood and something gray to the side.

"Daniel, he's back up to full, but I think that kind of damage might need some recovery time." Orrin pushed himself up and looked around. The adrenaline was fading, and the gore made him feel like he was in a dream. The ground was hazy, and Daniel was far away. Everything was getting farther away.

Orrin came back around to the bumping of the carriage on the road. Daniel was sitting across from him, talking with the girl they'd rescued.

"You're awake?" Daniel noticed his friend open his eyes.

"Nnrgghh," Orrin groaned.

The dark-skinned beauty turned to Orrin. "Thank you, sir, for saving my b— Sir Bennett's life. I should not have doubted a healer's own skills. We are in your debt."

Orrin didn't correct her. Let everyone think he was a healer and he wouldn't have to explain his class.

"Oh, Orrin's not a—" Daniel began

"Not one to keep another in my debt," Orrin cut in over his friend. Daniel's eyebrows went up, but he shrugged. "I'm Orrin. Nice to meet you. How's the knight?"

"My name is Madeleine Catanzano. Everyone calls me Madi. Sir Bennett was up and pulling those bandits to a ditch within ten minutes of you overexerting. He's driving now." She waved toward the front of the carriage.

"Overexerting?"

Daniel butted in, "Madi was just explaining that when someone uses the entirety of their MP multiple days in a row, they can pass out from mana-use exhaustion. I guess you doing that a few times in a row short-circuited you." Daniel laughed.

Madi looked at them strangely. "You used your entire mana pool more than once to heal Brandt? Did you have a MP potion? I will reimburse you for the use, of course."

Orrin had meant to talk with Daniel about a story to tell when they got to the city, but the bandits had ruined that plan. *Maybe we can use saving their lives to get information and get them to keep quiet about us being summoned here.*

"No, I have an ability that lets me swap my HP for MP. Then I just heal myself. I should have known I couldn't have found an un-limited mana cheat." Orrin watched Madi's face change from disbelief to shock to anger.

"You use blood magic?" Her voice was quiet. "And you brag about it?"

Orrin shrugged and smirked at Daniel, thinking she was joking.

"You dare . . . you . . ." She took a deep breath and sat back imperiously.

"Orrin and Daniel. I thank you for saving my life and the life of Sir Bennett. However, the laws of Dey are absolute. You are hereby under arrest for the use of blood magic. I will deliver you to the city guard, and you will be executed by the end of the week."

FFFFFFfffff—

Chapter 4

While Orrin's mind raced through different scenarios, from jumping out of the moving carriage to attacking Madi, Daniel started laughing.

"Leave it to you, O, to find the one thing these people have outlawed," he said as he turned toward a glowering Madi. "First off, I have no 'blood magic,' so you aren't arresting me, that's for sure. Secondly, I'm not even sure Orrin is actually using blood magic, or at least I've never seen anything using blood. I mean . . . the guy is basically just healing."

Daniel paused and watched Madi's face switch emotions several times. He asked in a quiet voice, "Madi, do you even know what ability he's using?"

Madi spluttered for a minute and then put her hand out to Orrin. "Show me," she demanded.

Orrin put his hand on her hand.

"What are you doing?" Madi flushed and pulled her hand back.

"I have no idea what you want here," Orrin lashed out. "We save your life, and now you want to kill us . . . me . . . for using some sort of magic, which, by the way, uses my own HP, to be able to heal my friends a bit more. Maybe we should have just completed the Quest and left you to the bandits."

Madi sat emotionless through his tirade, but when he said, "'Quest she sat forward with blazing eyes. "Quest? You found a Quest? For what? What type of reward is there? No matter, it's almost always worth it. Can you share it? Do you both have it?"

Orrin opened his mouth to tell her no, she could not share their Quest. But Daniel beat him to it. "No. We will not share our Quests

41

with you. Especially not after how you treated Orrin about the abilities he picked."

"QUESTS? Multiple?" Madi was near hyperventilation now.

Daniel smiled, crossing his arms and sitting back as the carriage hit another rut and jostled them all.

The three sat in silence for a few minutes. Orrin pulled up his status and noticed a lot of blinking exclamation points.

Quest Complete
Defeat the bandits 4/4
Reward: 200 XP

Level 3 Obtained!
+10 AP

He cleared the boxes with a thought and started rummaging through the store again. He should just buy [Teleport] and get out of here with Daniel. He hovered over the buy button but then stopped.

"Madi. If we share a Quest with you, what would that be worth?"

Daniel raised an eyebrow, but Orrin ignored him.

She looked at Orrin with a sneer. "Not enough to save your life, [Blood Mage]."

Orrin smiled at her and leaned against the shut door. "What if I told you I'm not a [Blood Mage]?"

"I'd call you a liar. The only classes that can use HP for MP are [Blood Mage] or [Vampire] and I saw you in the sunlight."

"Is there a way to show you my class? Or do you not have [Identify]?" Orrin asked.

Madi's sneer turned into a frown. "I have no need to waste the points on [Identify] that's for the guards or Guild. And to ask to see a person's class is rude . . . I should not have asked to see your ability, either. I apologize for that, even to a [Blood Mage]."

Orrin thought of how Daniel had shared his Quests before. He pulled up his status and pinched the boxes he wanted. He flicked his wrist toward Madi in a throwing motion, tossing the ability and his class boxes.

The shock on her face turned to puzzlement. "I've never heard of [Utility Warder] . . . and [Blood Mana] is a restricted ability to only [Blood Mage]."

Daniel finally spoke up. "Is [Blood Mana] or the class outlawed?"

Madi answered hesitantly, "[Blood Mage] is outlawed. Mostly because the spells of the class require sacrifices for fuel. I've read that [Blood Mana] is used to sap targets of their HP for the large mana requirements, but it's usually not the worst of what those who take the class do."

"Oh, shit! I didn't even think to try using it on others. Could I have drained those bandits?" Orrin fiddled with a loose string in the upholstery of his seat.

"You truly have never used your spell on another?" Madi asked incredulously.

"Only had it for a day, and the only person I've been draining is myself . . . That sounds dirtier out loud."

Daniel chuckled.

"But if I promise not to use that spell to do blood mage-y things . . . and we gave you a Quest we could probably overlook the whole thing, right?" Orrin was betting Quests were rare, based on her earlier reaction. "I mean, we did save your life, too."

Daniel had leaned back and closed his eyes, ignoring the entire exchange now. He knew Orrin could weasel his way into a good deal.

"The law technically only regulates the class, not the ability. And you did save the life of a noble going about the administration of the country's business."

Hook, line, and sinker, Orrin thought.

"If . . . if you give your word, I will not alert the guards. But if they check your status, I can be of no help. What is the Quest?" Madi tried to keep the excitement off her face, but her hands were clenched on her seat cushion.

Orrin pulled up the Quest

> Reach the Wall of Dey within 24 hours [3 hours 2
> minutes 54 seconds]
> Reward: +1 to all stats
> Failure: No penalty

He willed the Quest to her and leaned against the side of the carriage again.

"Plus-one to all stats?" Madi exclaimed. "To simply reach the city walls? This is the most ridiculous Quest I have ever heard of."

"What kind of Quests do you normally get, then?" Daniel chimed into the conversation.

Madi mumbled and pushed Orrin's hand off the upholstery string he had started pulling on.

"Sorry, I didn't hear you," Daniel insisted. Orrin waited for Madi to turn and then yanked the thread out completely at the base.

"I've never received a Quest before. Most people see one or two their entire life ... unless you find a [Hero], but we haven't had a true [Hero] in over sixty years." Madi frowned at Orrin. She had noticed the vandalism.

Daniel looked at Orrin and said nothing. Orrin could tell his friend was letting him take the lead.

"I haven't heard of that class," he gambled.

"Not surprising. Usually the nobles try to keep a [Hero] contained. Nobody knows all they can do ... They start off with ridiculous boosts and only grow stronger. I heard a visiting duke tell a story that a thousand years ago, one of them killed a Demon Lord and created the Sea of Fire!"

"So anyone who took that class would probably stay away from nobles, then. I guess that's why Quests are so rare."

"Well, that's only the nobles who don't care for the people. Someone with a [Hero] class can only be summoned, and that uses a lot of magical resources. Usually an entire country will pool the cost together in the face of a major threat. Most [Heroes] are treated like foreign dignitaries and given every comfort. Of course, they also have to defend against whatever evil arises, but most succeed."

"Just most? What happens to the rest?" Daniel asked with trepidation.

Madi appeared bashful again. "Um, I don't think I should be talking this much about classified classes. But thank you for this Quest. How did you get it? Meet any traveling [Heroes]?" She tried for a joke.

Daniel and Orrin glanced at each other. It was an instance of two friends communicating far more than an outsider would guess.

Should we tell her? Daniel wanted to trust her.

HELL, NO. Orrin didn't want to get tangled up with a noble family.

I'm going to have to defeat the Demon Lord eventually. Might be nice to have some backing and not have to buy clothes with my points.

Don't do it! We don't even know why she was out on the road. That bandit said something about "what she's been doing" outside the city. What if she's more than she seems or tries to imprison us?

Daniel let his easy smile spread on his face. "Nothing like that. We just got a Quest to reach the Wall and another to defend it when we were traveling nearby. We've never been this far . . . from home. Maybe we were just lucky."

"Defend the Wall from a Horde?" Madi sat forward on her seat again. "Does it have a countdown, too? Would you share it?"

"No countdown timer. Variable reward. And what's in it for us?" Orrin butted in before Daniel gave away the Quest.

"Hmm." Madi looked at the ceiling. "I could have my father give you knighthood for the city? Or one thousand gold each? That's about the price to purchase knighthood, anyways."

Daniel and Orrin exchanged another glance. Neither wanted knighthood, for sure. And while money was probably good to have, what they really needed was information.

"Only a thousand gold for us to split, but you have to answer every question we have until we reach the wall," Orrin offered.

"Deal! I can pay you that right now with the tax money . . ." She bit her lip. "Please ignore that I just said that. Nobody is supposed to know I'm out collecting on my father's behalf."

Madi pulled Daniel off the seat next to her and flipped the seat cushions up. Underneath, hidden below a false top, was an iron chest with a single keyhole. She made them both turn before pulling a key from down her leather chest piece and opening the lid. Inside were stacks of gold coins wrapped in cloth to reduce the jangling they made with the lid open. There were hundreds of gold pieces, thousands of silver.

"I may only be able to give you a little less than half now," Madi said sheepishly. "But you can find me at the castle gates and I'll get you the rest, of course. Or I can open credit for you at the Guild. Are you registered?"

Orrin and Daniel took 150 gold each from Madi and began to ask questions as she opened a small basket and handed out some bread and cheese.

Dey was the most western fortress on the continent, sealing the only pass of the Great Mountain Line, the impassable, impregnable mountain range that separated the civilized world from the lands of roaming monsters. The no-man's-land through the Pass was certain death to anyone below level fifty, and even then, most adventurers never returned.

Dey was governed by the houses of Dey. The Catanzano family, the Wendeln family, the Tarris family, and the Timpe family. Control of various parts of the city was cycled between the families to keep power out of the hands of any one person. The Catanzano family was currently in charge of the guard, the collection of taxes, and internal crimes.

The Wendeln family watched the Wall and would repel any Hordes that arrived. The city saw a Horde every other month, with the occasional surprise Horde as well. Scouts in the Pass usually gave a few days' notice before any attack.

The Tarris family was in charge of dungeon eradication. The various dark energies that allowed monsters to form in the first place could occasionally fester, even on this side of the Great Mountain

Line. Those energies would create dungeons that would grow until ripe. Then they would pop like a festering wound and open their doors to the world. A newly appeared dungeon was hopefully defeated within the year. If not, they grew exponentially harder to end. Luckily, only two dungeons in the area had ever been able to evade total subjugation. The Tarris family kept those contained.

As Madi answered their questions about ruling classes and dungeons, she only gave a few odd looks at how little they seemed to know. Orrin waved off her concerns by saying, "Yes. That's how we were raised, too, but Mom always said it's best to find out how the locals think before you say something stupid." She seemed to buy it.

They didn't ask the more pressing questions in their minds, like *what is the Guild*, although Orrin had a good idea. They also steered away from more class or ability talk. Best to not have her dwelling on Orrin's near–[Blood Mage] ability.

The horse pulled the carriage to the side of the road and stopped during Madi's explanation of the last Horde attack, something that sounded like "ghost panthers the size of a small carriage."

The crunch of boots on the ground alerted them to Brandt hopping down. He opened the windowless door. "Lady Madeleine, should I approach at the commoners' gate as planned, or should we abandon pretense and announce ourselves?"

"Huh?" Orrin asked elegantly.

"Our original plan was to travel incognito and retrieve some taxes that local lords had been . . . late on paying, without alerting anyone that I was gone from the city. But we only have . . . an hour left before the timer runs out, and customs and guard checks will take at least that." Madi's brow furrowed as she considered. "Abandon pretense. Don't announce my name, just the house. And for goodness' sake, don't tell anyone we were attacked."

"Lady, I must report my near failure to protect you! I am sworn to it and have lost honor enough already." The knight's helmet was in his hand. His dark-brown hair contrasted with his bright-blue eyes and pale skin. The pain he felt was etched across his face.

"Sir Bennett, if I might," Daniel chimed in. "You failed at nothing. In fact, you have brought much more into Lady Madeleine's life to-day . . . and your own. Keep her secret as she requested and"—Daniel made a hand gesture—"you can join us in getting some free stats."

Madi and Brandt looked aghast, but for different reasons. Brandt was fumbling over himself thanking Daniel for sharing a Quest with him. He hadn't been able to hear the conversation from outside the carriage, and the shock of a Quest was obvious. Madi looked pissed that Daniel had shared the Quest so easily with Brandt.

With Sir Bennett's cooperation settled, Madi continued to answer questions about the best and most affordable inns and shops, and even the general location of the Guild, for twenty minutes before a ding rang in Orrin's mind.

> Quest Complete
> Reach the Wall of Dey [35 minutes remaining]
> Reward: +1 to all stats
>
> Name: Orrin
> Class: Utility Warder
> Level 3 (0/300)
> Ability Points: 10
>
> HP: 90
> MP: 130
>
> Strength: 9
> Constitution: 9
> Dexterity: 9
> Will: 13
> Intelligence: 11
>
> Abilities:
> [Mind Bastion]

[Dimension Hole]
[Identify]
[Blood Mana]
[Meditate]

Spells:
[Calm Mind] 5 MP
[Heal Small Wounds] 5 MP
[Increase Strength] 5 MP
[Increase Dexterity] 5 MP
[Camouflage] 10 MP

All three of them were reading and not paying attention to each other or their surroundings. So when Sir Bennett opened the door that Orrin was leaning on again, nobody could react. Orrin fell out bodily and landed hard on the dirt.

"Sir! Are you all right? I apologize for—" Bennett picked him up by one arm and stood him up, brushing his pants off while he continued to sputter.

"Brandt, it's fine." Orrin tried to back up. "It's fine, really."

Daniel stepped out, laughing. Madi followed behind. Daniel looked as if he was going to rib his friend, but his eyes widened as he noticed his surroundings.

"Wooowww." Daniel turned a slow circle. Orrin followed his gaze.

They had ridden through the Wall, which looked even higher from inside. But the city itself was classical fantasy brick with towering spires, paned and stained glass everywhere, and street vendors selling everything from meat on a skewer to weapons.

The smells were fascinating. Orrin watched a little girl drag her father to a man holding tiny balloons. A quick exchange of money, and the girl walked off with a blue balloon the size of a tennis ball floating behind her. Orrin let out a quick yell when she pulled the balloon down and stuffed it into her mouth and swallowed.

"That girl just ate a balloon! We have to tell her—"

"What's a ball-une? Do you mean the little girl in the green dress? That's just a willowpuff." Madi oversaw a set of guards taking the hidden compartment out of the carriage. "Have you never had a willowpuff?"

"Uh, no. What . . . no." Orrin shook his head and spotted Daniel talking with Bennett as they looked in another chest at the back of the carriage.

"I love the purple ones." Madi held her hand out, and Orrin noticed a glimmer of coins. "Get three, please. Brandt hates them."

Orrin watched Daniel pick up a crossbow and turn it over. *They're going over the bandit loot*, he realized.

Madi coughed politely. He took her coins and walked over to the balloon man.

"Can I have three, uh—willowpuffs?"

The man turned and smiled. His teeth were stained multiple colors, but not like a rainbow. Instead Orrin was reminded of an artist he'd done a report on who just threw paint on canvas.

"Colors? Three for three coppers, sir." The man continued grinning his crazy and colorful grin.

"Purple?"

Orrin returned holding three balloons. They floated slightly in front of him, defying the wind.

"O. What the heck is that?" Daniel appeared next to him. His backpack had more bulk, and Orrin saw one sword handle peeking out.

"Edible balloons." Orrin handed one to Daniel and held the other out to Madi. She pulled the string down and inhaled. The purple circle distorted and turned to smoke as she did, swirling into her mouth. She chewed and smiled. Her teeth were purple.

"Thanks. It's been a while since I've had one."

Orrin and Daniel shrugged at each other and tried the floating food.

Although the willowpuff turned to smoke, it filled his mouth like melted chocolate, but with a nutty spice that warmed his mouth, then his throat, as it flowed into him. *Delicious!*

Daniel smiled. "That's good." He looked around. "We might need to go try some more food."

They left Madi to her work, promising to find her the next day at her home. Walking along the stalls, the boys quickly figured out the conversion rate of the currency. Ten coppers made one silver, and there were ten silvers in a gold. None of the food cost more than a copper or two. The meat on sticks was actually two fully loaded sticks with veggies for one copper.

They ate five of those each.

Nothing was familiar, and yet, Orrin already felt more at home here than he ever had in high school. With his junior year ending soon, Orrin hadn't started planning for college or anything after high school ended. He knew Daniel was already getting scholarship offers, but they never spoke about that stuff in detail. But as they walked along the aisles toward an inn Madi had suggested, the smells assaulting his nose and the sounds of multiple instruments floating in the air, Orrin felt comfortable. He felt free.

Chapter 5

Daniel pointed out that the architecture looked advanced. "I mean, it's not like I expected steel frames and huge walls of glass, but this looks nothing like anything from *Lord of the Rings*."

Orrin shook his head at his friend. "I definitely wasn't expecting . . . this, either."

Three main gates on the east side of Dey funneled into a large entryway. Madi and Brandt had left them in that area, called the Gateway. The buildings were modest there, flat for the most part, and with just the hint of what was to come.

As Orrin and Daniel traveled farther into Dey, the buildings soared higher. Orrin peeked into a clothing shop. The floor was a clear stone, not glass, but still easy to see through. Underneath the feet of shopping patrons, twenty bodies hunched over dresses, suits, robes, and what looked like a big floppy hat. *Entertainment while you shop*, Orrin thought. *And management can make sure the workers aren't slacking.*

"Move along," a voice demanded. Orrin moved quickly and wasn't hit this time. The guard at the first shop had simply kicked him earlier.

Daniel had left him behind and was standing in front of one of the taller buildings in this middle district. They had decided to go straight to the Guild building at Madi's recommendation but were getting sidetracked easily.

Orrin came up beside his friend. "What's this one?" They had found clothing shops, armor shops, food shops, and even a shop for just gloves . . . hundreds of different styles of gloves.

"It's beautiful," Daniel muttered and nodded his head toward the open doors.

The two metal doors stood open to the street, with no guards at the front. Inside was a square marble floor with workstations at each corner. Furnaces larger than the men working them spewed flames into the air. Orrin could feel the heat from across the street.

Along the walls hung weapons—spears, swords, pikes, maces, daggers, and more.

"Oh, it's a weapons shop. We saw a few of those already, but I guess none that were making them as the customer waited, huh." Orrin really didn't get Daniel's new fascination with weapons.

"The sword in the left corner." Daniel started walking. "I need that one."

"D, we've been over this like five times. You can't buy a sword right now. You HAVE one already," Orrin started.

Daniel kept walking. Orrin hurried after his friend.

The heat from the forges kept most people from entering the shop, but as they entered, Orrin saw the beauty of the inside being missed by everyone outside.

A small stairwell to the side led up to another floor above, but the center of the store was vented with a large, open space flowing up to the ceiling. The ceiling was a puzzle of interlocking metal blocks. Orrin watched as the smoke and grime of the workstations flowed up and settled on the slanted metal slats. The shiny metal darkened with soot.

Clink.

The smallest noise preceded the slats' movement. If he had blinked, Orrin would have missed the turning motion as the metal turned in a cascade motion up. Suddenly, the darkened metal shone bright again.

"What the hell?"

Daniel was already standing on the other side of the shop. He was pointing at a sword five feet long and six inches thick. The blacksmith chuckled at Daniel and waved him off. Daniel raised his voice, but over the hammering of metal on metal all around, Orrin missed whatever he said.

He walked closer just as the man in the long, stained, and burned apron turned in anger and snapped at Daniel, "And I'm telling you, boy, you can't handle that sword. It's not made for the likes of you, I don't care how strong you think you are."

"How much is it?" Orrin asked as he came to a stop next to his friend.

"It's two hundred gold, but I'm not selling it to anyone I don't approve of. And I don't approve." The man turned his back again and went back to hammering a long spearhead.

Daniel and Orrin had spent some money as they'd been walking and figured out a rough estimate of how much the coins were worth. A single copper was something like four to five dollars, which made a single silver about fifty dollars. A single meal or some snacks had only cost a copper. The few cheap hostels they'd found were charging five coppers a night or a silver for two nights with stew for dinner. Two hundred gold was the most expensive item they'd seen. *That's about $100,000!* Orrin thought.

"D. He's not selling. We can find another sword later. Let's go."

"Can I at least hold it once, sir?" Daniel was using his teacher voice again. The polite golden-boy persona shining off him.

"Boy, I can barely lift that monster," the man sighed, realizing this customer was not going to leave. "I made it for a friend who never returned from beyond the Wall. I charge five silver for even nobility to see it. Do you really want to waste your money?"

Daniel pulled out a gold piece and handed it over.

The man shrugged, hit the spearhead three more times, and put it in a barrel of water. It hissed with steam. Then he grabbed a metal cube with handles and dragged it over the wall.

"It's mostly Mythril and cold iron, but the shaft and grip is the femur of a dragon, sworn and validated by the Guild. Took me three months to grind that smooth and another two to beat the thing into shape here," he said as he stood on the metal cube and put a sheet of chain mail in his left hand. He balanced it under the sharp edge of the blade and grabbed the handle with his right. "Arden, come spot an old man."

A lanky boy their own age came up and hovered nearby. The blacksmith hefted the sword into the air and stepped off the box at the same time. Orrin heard it creak and moan for the second all the weight had rested on it.

Daniel kicked Orrin's foot. Orrin looked to his friend and said, "What?"

"Buff, please," Daniel muttered. Orrin smiled evilly.

"I'm sorry, D. What was that?"

Daniel took his eyes off the sword for the first time since he'd entered the store to quickly lay them on his friend. "Now, O."

Orrin grinned but acquiesced, sending five quick strengths to his friend. With Daniel's bonus, it was an extra ten strength.

"If you drop this sword, I will not pay any Hospital cost or penalty fee."

"Give it here." Daniel stood tall with his legs apart as if he were about to hit the weights. He put his hands on the hilt and tried to lift the sword up.

Nothing happened. The tip of the sword did not leave the blacksmith's hand.

"I tried to tell you, son. It is not weighted for a human."

Daniel continued pulling his arms up, trying to get leverage. It made no difference.

Orrin took a look at his store list and made an impulsive decision.

> **Would you like to Upgrade [Increase Strength] (1000/1000) for 2 AP?**
> **Yes or No?**

Yes.

> **[Increase Strength] Level 2 (0/5,000): increase target Strength by +2 for 10 minutes. 10 MP**

Double strength and double time but double cost, Orrin thought as he cast the spell on his friend, hoping it would override the weaker level-one spell.

On the fifth cast, the sword's tip raised a few inches from the blacksmith's hand. Daniel's face was covered in sweat.

"Well, I'll be damned," the man muttered before deftly catching the sword again as Daniel let it drop back down.

"S-sorry, sir," Daniel groaned as he sat back on his heels. "I should have listened to the expert there. It's just so pretty." He let out a smirk.

The blacksmith grunted as he stood on the box, depositing the sword back on its horizontal stand.

"No 'sir,' boy. I'm Jovi. This is my corner of the Blast Furnace and you got farther than anyone in a long time. Keep the money—that was worth the workout." He cracked his knuckles and handed the gold piece back. "If you get that mighty strength of yours higher, you might even swing old Gertrude someday."

"Gertrude?" Orrin cut in.

"Named after the one who should have wielded her," Jovi whispered reverently. Orrin wisely dropped it.

"Thank you, Jovi. I'll be back for her," Daniel said, still panting.

Just how heavy was that hunk of metal? Could he even swing it? Orrin thought as he dragged Daniel out.

The dirt road had turned to cobblestone inside the city, but as they got near the western part of the Wall, the cobblestone gave way to finer, inlaid stone. The houses and shops lay farther away from each other, with more height and small gardens. Fences and walls were more frequent. Orrin and Daniel received more looks as they followed Madi's directions to the Guild.

"I don't get it," Daniel whispered. "We've got on basic clothes and armor. We don't look too different from everyone here. Why are we getting all the looks?"

Orrin was also starting to get worried. Humans of every shade were prevalent. Madi had dark skin, but Brandt had been as white as he was. Daniel's light brown features were mirrored by a dozen different people they'd passed as well. Orrin had grabbed Daniel and stared as a group of dwarves had carried large boxes across the street. But nothing that he could see allowed for the constant glances at them.

"Let's just hurry and get to the Guild. Brandt said we'd be able to rent a room there cheap, and we need to discuss our future here." Orrin hitched his backpack up on his shoulder and sped up.

The Guild was housed in one of the largest buildings they'd seen. As they rounded the last corner, it took an entire block, one street off the main road.

Daniel gestured. "It looks like an old Spanish fortress."

"What fortress had six stories and . . . a dozen different towers? I lose count every time. How many do you see?" Orrin asked.

"There's only six . . . no, wait, ten? Magical fuckery." Daniel gave up and started walking again.

It was nearing the end of the day, and people were starting to leave their jobs. As they climbed the steps to the Guild building, about a dozen others were entering as well.

Through the doors, the boys were jostled along with the small sea of people. They were deposited to one side, as most of the group traveled through another door to the right. As the doors swung open, laughter and banter echoed through the hall. *Food.* Orrin nearly floated to the smells coming from the dining hall.

In front of them was a small window in the wall, with a bored man sitting behind the metal bars. A sign above read Reception.

"Excuse me. We were looking to join Dey's Guild?" Daniel inquired politely.

"Not Dey's Guild. Just da Guild," the man drawled. "More kids from the warfront trying to strike it rich, huh?"

Orrin and Daniel glanced at each other. Madi hadn't mentioned a war.

"Uh . . . yeah," Orrin muttered.

"Well, it don't matter much to me." The man pulled out a piece of paper and a fountain pen. "Sign this. It says you won't break the laws of the country you're in. You WILL defend any city you are in from a horde. You WILL take on one quest a month. Break the rules and you get booted. Depending on the local guildmaster, that could be a week before you repay your join-up fee or forever. So don't push your luck. Can you both read and write?"

"Yes," they chimed together.

"Better than most. Sign here and here. If you want to rent a room, it'll be this form. Here for a single, that'll be five silver a month. A double is four silver. A quad is two silver."

"Why so cheap?" Daniel asked. The hostels for a week had been just a few silver.

"Most who pay don't return much, if ever." The receptionist shrugged. "Meals ain't included. Your room is only yours for the night—they get switched up regular. Cuts down on the murders, you see."

With [Dimension Hole] it wouldn't be a problem, not having a solid home base where they could store things. "We'll take a double." Orrin signed the papers, with Daniel adding a scrawl after.

"It's five silver each for registration, plus your four silver for the room. One gold four." He held out his hand, and Daniel paid him.

They got a room key with so many nicks, Orrin was sure he'd cut his fingers. They also got a beaten copper ring to wear on their pinkie—or "smallest finger you got left"—to show they were in the Guild now.

"D. Let's grab some food to go and talk in our room. We haven't really had a chance to decompress, and I'm starting to feel my lack of sleep," Orrin suggested.

Daniel nodded, and the two made their way through the door to the right of the reception area into the dining hall. A man sitting on a stool reading a book glanced up as they entered and put a finger on the page he was on.

"One silver."

"A silver for food? What are you serving?" Daniel asked.

The man grunted and folded the book on his finger. "Newbies, huh? It's five copper a person for as much food as you can eat here or carry off in one trip. It's really more just five copper to come through the doors, as we've also got the quest board over yonder." He nodded his shaved head to the back of the long dining room with twenty large wooden tables lined up, four long and five deep.

"We have to pay to get a quest?" Orrin said in shock.

"And to eat." The man opened his book again. "As I said, one silver."

Daniel grumbled and paid the man. They filled the largest bowls they could find with the night's menu: beef stew. They also each took a large loaf of a hard brown bread. Beer was being served for another charge, but they had their waterskins.

Returning to the reception area, they entered the second door to the left of the entrance. Inside was a hall lined with doors and a large staircase at the end. As they trudged to climb the stairs, one set of doors swung up with a bang, just missing Orrin's bowl of soup.

Adventurers clambered out of the doorway. Orrin glanced in and saw a large green field with dummies for archery practice and some people fighting in practice. *A training area? I though the whole thing was a solid building.*

They trudged up three flights of stairs to find their room. It was small, with two single beds, a table, and two chairs.

Once inside, neither spoke for ten minutes as they scarfed the food. The beef stew was chunky, with carrots and potatoes swimming in the broth with generous slabs of beef. *I hope it's beef*, Orrin thought.

The real star was the bread. When Daniel broke his in half, the smell had stopped both for a second. Warm honey and cinnamon drifted in the air, with a hint of something flowery that Orrin couldn't place. It paired so well with the stew that Orrin used bread pieces as a spoon, mopping the last up with a sigh as he sat back, content.

"So, Orrin. What's the plan here?" Daniel took a long drink of water.

Orrin had spent much of the previous night planning everything he could . . . before everything went sideways. But he still had some thoughts.

"I think we start with three simple rules. One, survive. That means everything. We figure out what we need to get by here. We need to find a library or bookstore and learn about this world. We are screwed if they find out we were . . ." Orrin lowered his voice. ". . . summoned, or that you're a . . ." He mouthed, "hero."

"Two, really goes without saying, but we're a team. We each get a veto on anything party related. We need to see what kind of quests we can do to make money, especially if you plan on blowing it all on some hunk of metal."

"Gertrude is not a hu—"

"Three," Orrin interrupted Daniel, "we find a way home. As much as I love reading stories, I do not want to end up monster food."

Daniel nodded along. "Survive. Teamwork. Get home. Simple plan, but I like it."

"So tomorrow, we'll go out for breakfast, get the lay of the land, and figure it all out. No pressure." Orrin lay on the bed. It was surprisingly soft.

He pulled up his status and went to the store. He'd already bought the upgrade for [Increase Strength] and still had eight AP left.

"D. I have eight AP left after upgrading [Increase Strength] and was thinking of upgrading dex, buying will and intelligence buffs, and maybe upgrading my heal. Think I should go for that or start buying other things?"

Daniel was also lying down looking at the ceiling, likely reading his own status. "I knew you upgraded strength. When you cast it the second time, I think I could almost feel it."

"You don't get a notification or something?"

"Nope." Daniel moved his hand like he was scrolling down pages. "I think you should focus on your buffs and healing. I'll tank. I'm going over some options now, but I shouldn't have bought all this gear. I got a lot of AP to start, but it looks like I only get the normal ten per level now."

"Save your points, then. I want to try and find out more about [Heroes]. I'm sure some of them found overpowered builds, and we can make you the very best."

"Like no one ever was," Daniel singsonged.

"Nerd," Orrin threw at him.

"Geek." Daniel smiled.

Orrin hit Yes.

> [Increase Dexterity] Level 2 (0/5,000): increased
> target Dexterity by +2 for 10 minutes. 10 MP
> [Increase Will] (0/1,000): increased target Will
> by +1 for 5 minutes. 5 MP
> [Increase Intelligence] (0/1,000): increased target
> Intelligence by +1 for 5 minutes. 5 MP
> [Heal Small Wounds] Level 2 (0/5,000) heal up
> to 20 HP. 10 MP

Orrin looked at his list of spells. It had really grown:

> Spells:
> [Heal Small Wounds] Level 1 (max)
> [Heal Small Wounds] Level 2 (0/5,000)
> [Increase Strength] Level 1 (max)
> [Increase Strength] Level 2 (0/5,000)
> [Increase Dexterity] Level 1 (max)
> [Increase Dexterity] Level 2 (0/5,000)
> [Increase Will] Level 1 (0/1,000)
> [Increase Intelligence] Level 1 (0/1,000)
> [Camouflage] (1,490/10,000)
> [Calm Mind]

"Oh, cool. I guess upgrading leaves the last level available, too. That's good to conserve some MP if I need, I guess," Orrin noted.

Orrin suddenly stood up from his bed. "Damn it."

Daniel also stood up, hand already going to his sword. "What? Are we under attack?"

"I've got to shit." Orrin looked at his friend. "God, I hope they've invented toilet paper."

Chapter 6

The next morning, Orrin and Daniel turned in their room key and bought buttery cinnamon pastries on the walk to the Catanzano keep. Each family had a small castle located near the Western Wall, and Madi's directions proved easy to follow.

The architecture of each keep was near identical, and if not for her instruction to approach only the keep flying her father's colors and crest, they would have had to ask for help. However, the green and yellow stripes and the eagle banner gave an easy path to follow.

The guards professionally relayed the message that the lady's guests had arrived, but they did not let Orrin and Daniel leave their sight. As they stood with the two men wearing half plate and holding pikes taller than Daniel, the two glanced around the small courtyard. Despite the height of the keep, with its twin spiral towers, crenellation, and murderholes spaced evenly, the entire keep looked big enough to house only twenty to thirty people. For a keep of a ruling family, Orrin was surprised at the small size.

"I would have thought her father's keep would be bigger," Daniel whispered, giving voice to Orrin's thoughts.

"Maybe they have another one outside the city," Orrin offered.

"Actually, they do not." Sir Bennett appeared at the door. He waved the two guards off and beckoned for Daniel and Orrin to follow. "The four families live modestly—or are supposed to. Most men at arms are stationed with a particular section of the guard, like at the Wall or in dungeon parties. It wouldn't do for us to get used to defending against Hordes just to switch to guard duty for the next two years."

"Hi, Brandt," Daniel said cheerfully. "Good to see you."

Brandt smiled and led them through a small welcoming hall to a sitting room. The furnishings were old but comfortable-looking, with a set of paintings over the fireplace. One was a woman holding a mace in one hand and a dagger in the other. The second painting was a short man, sitting over a board game and holding a book off to the side with one hand. Two large sofas separated by a short wooden table completed the room.

"The Lady Catanzano will be with you shortly. Would you care for refreshment?" Brandt played host.

"Is it normal for a knight to get tea?" Orrin asked.

Brandt flushed. "My lord has seen fit to assign me some small tasks to remind me of my duties."

"So, you got punished for getting shot in the street? That's a bit harsh." Daniel leaped to Brandt's aid.

"No." Brandt pushed a small cart with drinks and small cookies to Daniel's side. "Being attacked by bandits is not what I'm being punished for. I should have stopped her from going in the first place." His voice dropped toward the end.

Just as Orrin was about to ask more, Lady Madeleine Catanzano entered the room. Orrin could not call her Madi as she was.

Wearing a green dress with golden thread that hung off her shoulders and brushed her ankles, Madeleine shone. Expertly applied makeup highlighted her cheekbones and accentuated her eyes. Her short hair from the day before was gone. In its place was a tightly curled, dense coif of hair that covered her head and ran down to her shoulders. She wore a thin golden necklace with a single ruby stud touching her throat and three rings, all on one hand. Orrin noticed the copper ring of the Guild on her pinky.

"Wow." Daniel stood and gave a mock bow. "Madi, you look amazing."

As she smiled, Orrin rolled his eyes at his friend. *Can't go anywhere without flirting.*

"Thank you, Daniel." Madi nodded at Orrin, too. "I was able to have my father collect the balance owed, but if I had known what he'd demand in return . . ." She trailed off.

Brandt smirked behind her. "The lord has demanded Lady Madeleine refrain from any adventuring for one month's time. She'll be attending balls and greeting dignitaries in his place."

"The harshest punishment he could think of," Madi muttered. "Just his way of getting back at me for collecting his late taxes."

Orrin's eyebrows touched. "He punished you for doing his job?"

Madi sighed as another knight brought a small box into the room and dropped it on the table. "Yes . . . well, no. There have been some politics that kept him from forcing the local barons to pay the yearly harvest taxes. I thought that if I showed up and . . . appealed to their better nature . . . I could help."

"She beat up a lot of old men." Brandt chuckled and took a cookie from the tray. "And one old lady."

"Sir Bennett, you are excused." Madi stomped her foot. With a grin and a nod, Brandt left. Orrin heard him laughing down the hall.

"Anyways, I might have stirred up some trouble for him. And I then spent a lot of that money on those two Quests." She shot Daniel a peeved look. "Even if it was a good deal."

"We should have charged more, huh?" Orrin grinned.

"Much more." Madi returned the smile.

Daniel poured himself some of the tea and nibbled a cookie. "So, he was mad you bought the Quests?"

"Oh, not at all. He was excited beyond measure." She held an empty cup out, which Daniel filled for her. She took a sip and sighed contently. "The stat bonus from the Wall Quest will help set me apart for a few years at least. I don't have to push myself as hard, and that means more time for him to make me wear this." She gestured at her dress.

"It really does look good," Daniel murmured.

Madi smiled softy at him. "It's not that I don't enjoy it. I just would rather be leveling and defeating dungeons with Sir Bennett. He's been rather lucky and earned a few extra stats from defeating dungeons, or else Father would never have let me take on any dungeon."

So defeating dungeons can give extra stats. Orrin filed that away for later.

"Of course, he also was livid that I robbed you both of two Quests for only a little gold." Madi looked at her feet. "I thought it best not to mention the other condition." She peeked up at Orrin.

A little gold? Orrin crunched the numbers on the estimates he'd put together. *One thousand gold would be half a million dollars!*

"Well appreciated," Orrin said. "We set the terms, though. I don't think we were cheated."

Madi gave Orrin a thoughtful look. "He wanted to meet with the two of you but was called away early this morning over some crime or another. Perhaps we can treat you two to dinner later this week?"

Daniel glanced at Orrin, who nodded. They agreed to meet in three days for dinner.

After collecting the box full of gold, Orrin had a thought.

"Madi, is there a library or bookstore you'd recommend? We really need to catch up on a few things and don't want to accidently break some law from around here we don't know about."

Madi paused. "There are a few bookstores in the main shopping center I could recommend. Bartholomew's has class theory books and some spell guidebooks. Heidi's Corner is good for fiction but also has the best legal selection outside the courts. Books, Books, Books! has a good selection of other assorted stuff. That's where I go when I'm looking for something on a specific monster."

"Thanks, that will be a big help to us," Daniel said. "We should go check those out, O."

Madi hesitated for a minute. "I know you two are not from Dey . . . I don't mean to be rude, but were you run out of your home during the war?"

Orrin glanced at Daniel this time. He shrugged.

"Yes. We barely made it out alive," he said quietly. *I feel bad for lying, but better keep it simple.*

"Is that when you earned a class?" she pressed.

Orrin's mind was racing. They really should have done research before speaking with Madi again. She was too clever. *Keep it vague and untraceable.*

"Yeah. Daniel defended us, and I somehow was able to heal him when he got hurt. Our village was really small, and I don't think anyone else made it out."

"It is amazing that you unlocked a healing class," Madi continued as she walked them to the front door. "I did not know it was possible to gain healing outside the Hospital training."

"His mom is—was a healer," Daniel offered.

"That could explain it." Madi tapped her chin in thought. "Still, your other skill—"

"Best not to think on that one too much," Orrin said hurriedly. "Thank you for the hospitality. We'll see you in a few days."

They hurried away as Madi frowned after them.

Once they were around the corner, Orrin had tried dropping the chest into his [Dimension Hole]. The small chest was only little bigger than a shoebox and contained seven hundred gold pieces. But when he tried to put it in, nothing happened.

"Shit. I must have reached the storage limit," Orrin griped.

Currently, he had both of their backpacks and bedrolls, the extra clothes, his 150 gold from Madi's first installment payment, and Daniel's crossbow and extra sword from the bandits in his storage space. All that had sat on only half his bed as they'd taken inventory this morning. *I must have about three feet by three feet of storage.*

He was tempted to just try dumping the gold coins in, but Daniel convinced him to just wear their backpacks, minus the bedrolls. The box fit this time.

"So, Bartholomew's, Heidi's, or Books?" Daniel asked.

They had returned to the main street for shopping. Daniel was eyeballing Jovi's weapon store down the road. Orrin kicked him in the shin.

They spent the next three hours browsing all three bookstores. Orrin found a class primer book at Bartholomew's, which was supposed to help parents explain the most common selections to their children. *I guess parents are responsible for guiding the choice.* The store's clerk had even let him peek into the back room where they kept the spell books for a silver coin. He'd boasted that many of Dey's most prominent adventurers relied on them to help supply viable options for their wants.

When Daniel had questioned what a spell book could do, the man peered at him strangely.

"You learn a spell without spending the ability points. What backwater village did you crawl out of?"

Orrin had worked to assuage the man's concerns, and they'd left with the primer and one spell book. Daniel had over one hundred AP left, but Orrin was back to none. He spent one hundred gold on [Side Steps]. It was the cheapest book he'd seen in the back room that he wanted. Actually, it was the only book he'd seen that he'd wanted. The options were pretty slim. The primer had only cost two silver.

That's still nearly a hundred bucks for a book, Orrin thought. *Maybe we can invent the printing press or something.*

The only problem was, he had no idea how to make something like that.

Heidi at Heidi's Corner let them know that browsing the legal section was free with the purchase of any book in the store, but the legal books were not for sale and could not leave the store. Orrin quickly pieced together the little library of law books were a social service that Heidi had assembled to help those who couldn't afford a lawyer. They decided to come back the next day.

Books, Books, Books! ended up being the biggest score. They spent ten gold on fifteen books—four different bestiaries, one dungeon theory guide, two how-to-defeat-dungeon guides, three history books written about different countries, four children's books about various topics that Orrin thought might be helpful, and something called the *Leveler's Guide*, which the shop owner recommended.

All in all, they spent 110 gold and two silver. Daniel complained they had enough to buy the sword he wanted, but Orrin reminded him that Jovi likely wouldn't sell it until he could lift it alone.

They carried their haul back to the Guild, got a key for their new room, and started studying.

The Leveler's Guide *does not purport to give information that helps the adventurer to gain levels but instead gives best practices for the adventurer to survive long enough to gain levels on his own. While most adventurers will gain experience through monster hunts or dungeon subjugation, a Leveler's adventurer will seek to find ways to level his skills outside these dangerous activities.*

Orrin put the dry and repetitive guide down and rubbed his eyes. While the *Leveler's Guide*, or the *LG* as Daniel called it, had a lot of good information, the author had seemingly gone out of his way to make it difficult to find. Luckily, Daniel had read it first and circled particularly good portions with the one pen they'd purchased.

While Daniel was reading the guide, Orrin had worked through the primer book and the four children's books. All five combined were smaller than the *LG*. They'd compared notes and then swapped the books to see if the other had missed anything.

This is just like how we used to study for classes, Orrin thought.

The books had been full of information, and Orrin was replaying their conversations with Madi, as he worried they'd outed themselves as not from this world.

Luckily, his years of reading isekai comics seemed to have paid off.

The primer had noted that most children would not gain a class until seventeen or eighteen years of age. Even then, some didn't until their early twenties. Traumatic events could trigger classes early. A footnote had mentioned that trying to trigger a class early through traumatic means always backfired and created a block to gaining a class until the victim was well out of their teens. *What kind of asshole tried to traumatize kids for a class?* Orrin shivered.

Once someone was classed, they could gain levels in that class. The primer had gone over a lot of civilian classes and how the best way to level was to do a good job. It might have been propaganda to keep a hardworking lower class down, but the *LG* had noted that the only way farmers could level was by rotating crops correctly, getting a good harvest, and running off rabbits from eating their crops. Orrin had a thought of a farmer chasing bunnies, and gaining XP, and laughed.

Adventurer classes, like Orrin and Daniel, could gain XP from Quests, dungeon subjugation, and monster kills. A quick peek into one of the bestiaries showed that each monster had a set amount of XP given based on historic records. Some of the rarer monsters had an asterisk near the XP. Supposedly, if you brought proof of killing one of these to the publisher with the XP blue box, they'd pay you for the information.

Classes could gain XP to level one hundred. The XP costs were exponential. While the first ten levels were only an increased one hundred XP per level (Orrin was currently at level three with 0/300 XP), the next twenty levels were a multiplier of one thousand XP per level. The number jumped again by two thousand XP at every level in the level thirty-one to fifty range. At levels fifty-one to seventy it increased to five thousand XP per level. The book noted that above that the numbers increased, but all high-level adventurers had declined interviews.

The *LG* turned out to be more a lifestyle guide than practical information. It advocated using your spells and skills outside of combat to level your attacks as much as possible before engaging in dangerous activities. The author hammered on about the use of the party function and the problems with an unbalanced team.

Create a Party with Daniel?
Yes or No?

When that box had popped up in Orrin's vision, he'd sighed in relief at the thought of lost XP if they'd encountered any monsters.

Yes.

Strangely, other people did not give XP if killed.

I guess that explains the bandits not giving us XP. We only got it from the Quest, Orrin thought.

A party would split the XP evenly across all who participated in the fight. The paragraph under this worried Orrin. Daniel had even written a note: *How will Orrin get XP?*

Participation in a monster fight is based on damage done to the creature. The use of a healer in a standard five-man party is therefore a detriment. The Leveler recommends hiring a healer to wait his proper place behind the five-man team of damage dealers. Many parties fail to survive the attempt of corralling a monster in an attempt to let a healer strike a beast. Let the healer find his own experience elsewhere.

"D. Do you think my buffs count as participation?" Orrin questioned.

". . . I don't." Daniel put his book of children's fairy tales down. It was the least helpful book Orrin had read so far. "I think you're going to need to get in and do some damage to get the XP from monster fights. Dungeons also give a set amount from crushing the core, according to that book."

Shit!

Orrin shifted on his bed. "That was how I read it, too. I'm going to have to get something offensive, I guess."

Daniel shrugged. "Or we can just subjugate all dungeons together." He smiled at his friend.

Orrin put the *LG* down for now. He flipped through the bestiaries and dungeon books but was feeling off. Had he made a mistake in picking his class? Was this the reason healer classes were rare here? Were there even any other buffing classes? The primer hadn't mentioned one.

He picked up the history book labeled *A Complete and Accurate Account of the Creation of Dey* and started to leaf through. He stopped after a few pages and turned back to the beginning. After reading in silence for five minutes, he paled and stopped.

"Daniel. You need to see this."

Chapter 7

The creation of Dey is unlike the formation of most countries, as Dey is the direct result of a [Hero] turned evil. In the year 1427, a [Hero] was summoned to defeat the newly risen Demon Lord. In only two years, the [Hero] fought back the forces of darkness on the continent of Oshal. With his party slaughtered during the battle, the [Hero] returned a different man.

There exist no concrete records; however, oral history from notable historian, Jaxes of Minocyia, purports the [Hero] cast spells never seen before. Oceans fell and rose the world over. Millions died as storms threw lightning in uncountable numbers. Fires raged and mountains grew. Mass teleportation, the likes of which had never been seen, split families asunder. When the magical cacophony stopped, all the lands of the world were combined into one landmass, which we now call Asmea, or "Mercy."

The people of the world stood together as one, with no fighting between the elves or humans and no tension between dwarf and orc. For across the new mountain range was a land of monstrous horrors. The [Hero] had taken every untamed island and unknown land's monsters and placed them on the other side of the divide.

And thus, four stepped forward to cast the spells of what would become the first Wall of Dey. Those walls did not stand for long, but others filled the breaches. The elves retreated to the forests. The orcs and dwarves battled for a time before founding their own homes. Humans drifted away to start tribes that would become the great countries of Odrana and Veskar. However, Dey was the first.

Daniel put down the book and looked at the cover.

"I guess you can remake the world at a high enough level." Orrin broke the silence.

Daniel threw the book on the table as he stood up. "You think I want to remake the world? O, millions died the last time a [Hero] killed a Demon Lord!"

"That might not be true," Orrin threw back. "Madi said a thousand years ago, a [Hero] killed a Demon Lord and created a lake of fire. That couldn't be this guy—I read more than you, and that took place two thousand years ago at least. Plus, there's no mention of a lake of fire. And not every [Hero] fights Demon Lords. Maybe you can just ignore that Quest."

"It was a Sea of Fire." Daniel calmed a bit and sat back down on the bed.

"Huh?"

"Madi's story. The [Hero] a thousand years ago created a Sea of Fire. Why do these [Heroes] create and destroy after completing the Demon Lord Quest?"

Orrin could see his friend was scared. "Maybe he was trying to make fireworks to celebrate and set a sea on fire instead?"

Daniel chuckled.

Orrin put his hand on his friend's shoulder. "You are not going to destroy the world. I won't allow it. Remember when you wanted to egg Kyle's car and I hardboiled the eggs so you couldn't?"

Daniel lifted his head from his hands and looked at Orrin. "You ass. I knew it was you who did that. Kyle nearly broke Justin's arm when he pushed him down the bleachers. He deserved that egging."

"You're right." Orrin smiled. "But if I let you wreak havoc over every stupid person who hurt a friend, you'd have been kicked off all your teams and clubs and who would have had to listen to your parents yelling at you? Me! Because we both know you just tune them out. But I can't do that, D. So believe me when I say, I will not let you end the world."

He punched his friend in the shoulder. "It's almost lunch, and we've been in this dreary room too much. Let's go find something to eat and then try leveling our skills like that book said."

Daniel cracked his neck as he stood. "What could you possibly level? You have nothing offensive."

Orrin held up the [Side Steps] book. "Want to try and hit me?"

After they got lunch (from the street, not the overpriced Guild dining hall), Orrin and Daniel stood in one of the small side rooms the Guild set aside for its members to use.

Orrin looked around the room. It was only about fifty feet by fifty feet, but the size of the "small" training room didn't add up to the exterior size of the Guild.

"More magic fuckery," Orrin muttered.

"What?" Daniel was strapping his armor on.

"I think the Guild is bigger on the inside?"

"Like the TARDIS?" Daniel started stretching.

"You never watched *Doctor Who*." Orrin frowned.

Daniel did some jumping jacks as he said, "But I heard you mention it enough to know the reference."

Orrin shook his head and looked at the [Side Steps] book. The bookstore clerk had told him to open it only when he was ready to read it. The book would turn to ash after the skill was learned.

Orrin untied the small ribbon around the book and opened it slowly. The book was tiny, about the size of a pocket notebook, and so thin he'd originally balked at spending $50,000—or one hundred gold—on it.

A flash of light hit his eyes, along with a prompt.

> **Would you like to learn [Side Steps] 1% chance to evade any attack (0/100)?**
> **Yes or No?**

Yes.

A warmth spread from his fingers to his shoulders. Then a rush of cold fell over his body. Orrin shivered.

[Side Steps] Obtained.

"That was too easy," Orrin muttered. He looked up at his friend. The training room had wooden swords, little more than long sticks, placed on racks. Daniel was practicing swinging one through the air.

"So should I hit you now?" Daniel asked, too eagerly.

Orrin kicked himself for suggesting this. "Yes, but stop when I say, so I can heal. And don't use anything overpowered, okay? I don't want to die."

Daniel grinned and advanced on his friend.

Three hours later, Daniel and Orrin sat on the floor breathing hard and covered in sweat. Orrin had used his buff spells judiciously on himself and Daniel, testing both the effects and the speed with which he could cast.

Daniel had hit him with the stick sword, doing between one to five HP in damage each hit. By cycling and healing, Orrin hadn't needed to stop except to breathe every twenty minutes or so. Daniel had also hit him with [Power Strike], which did up to ten HP of damage. The training was for both of them, after all.

[Side Steps] didn't trigger as often as Orrin had hoped. It was not a one in a hundred hits evasion, but a 1 percent chance to evade every hit, which left Orrin beaten. It had taken twenty minutes before it triggered the first time.

Daniel's sword was coming at him from the side. It moved just as quickly as every other strike Orrin had tried to dodge manually. Meaning: way, way too quickly. But at the last second, Orrin felt the way he should move. A twist of his foot and turning his hips, Orrin pirouetted around Daniel.

Daniel let out a whistle. "Niceeee."

After three hours, Orrin had only triggered the skill five more times. However, he'd cast enough spells and cycled so much he was starting to feel woozy again.

"Let's stop here for the day," Daniel suggested. "I just got [Power Strike] to level two."

"You leveled it?"

"Yeah. I have 106 points left, too."

Orrin glanced at his progress.

[Side Steps] 6/100
[Heal Small Wounds] Level 2 (430/5,000)
[Increase Dexterity] Level 2 (1,800/5,000)
[Increase Strength] Level 2 (1,850/5,000)
[Increase Will] (1,000/1,000) !
[Increase Intelligence] (1,000/1,000) !

He'd increased his own will and intelligence before starting the training session, getting his will up to eighteen and his intelligence up to sixteen. The increase to will had also boosted his mana pool. Orrin was positive he'd found the formula for what will did now.

[Heal Small Wounds] level one cost five MP for ten HP healing, while level two cost ten MP for twenty HP. With a base of ten will and ten intelligence, those numbers wouldn't change.

Once will went up, the spell would heal more than the base HP. A spell costs X and did Y.

Y was the base HP healed (in this case ten or twenty HP) times (B/10), where B equaled will.

For [Heal Small Wounds] level one, $10*(18/10)$ meant eighteen HP per heal. Level two or $20*(18/10)$ meant thirty-six HP per heal.

As Daniel had slapped him around, Orrin had been focusing on using level two healing for the XP. For some reason, the spell cost nine MP.

Maybe intelligence decreases cost?

He'd need more data points before he could figure out that math.

In any case, casting five will and intelligence boosts on himself and Daniel every five minutes for three hours had quickly maxed out his levels. Taking a hit every few seconds from Daniel had also let him heal himself for over seven hundred HP before MP fatigue set in. He'd drained his full MP multiple times.

"Something just isn't right, D," Orrin said. "All the books mentioned not to use more than one mana potion a day to avoid overexertion. But for some reason, I can drain my pool multiple times before I feel anything."

Daniel shrugged. He'd spaced out when Orrin tried to explain his math formula for will, too, simply stating, "Will makes spells hit harder? Cool."

Orrin spent the next two days leveling his spells with Daniel. Daniel also bought more skills as they worked through the books and made a game plan for the future.

The general consensus was a group of five doing damage was better than the "waste" of a single healer. Classes that gave bonuses to others were not even mentioned in the books they had bought.

Orrin had returned to Books, Books, Books! The owner, an older man with a hunched back and one white eye, had answered questions and done his best to point Orrin to what he sought. A single gold piece and he left with *Esoteric and Obscure Classes*. It had been a waste of money.

"It makes no sense," Orrin complained as Daniel tried a new skill, [Double Strike].

Daniel's sword moved once, but Orrin took two hits. He topped off his health. Daniel's damage was increasing at a ridiculous rate, and he was using his extra ability points to level his skills while Orrin was stuck with no extra points to spend.

> [Side Steps] 48/100
> [Heal Small Wounds] Level 2 (1,350/5,000)
> [Increase Dexterity] Level 2 (5,000/5,000) !
> [Increase Strength] Level 2 (5,000/5,000) !
> [Increase Will] (0/1,000) (1,000/1,000) !
> [Increase Intelligence](1,000/1,000) !

Daniel paused in his attacks. "It has to be an evolution thing. Why would people use classes for fighting that can't gain experience?"

"But that makes even less sense," Orrin continued. "Healers exist and are brought all the time as the nonparty sixth man."

"But they have the Hospitals behind them," countered Daniel.

The Hospitals were located throughout the civilized lands. Almost like a cult, healer classes were forcefully recruited to work a length of time for them before being let out into the world. Most stayed on in some capacity. They provided good health care. Payment was figured out after healing, with some sort of work program allowed. It wasn't quite slavery, but some people were required to work for a few months before being allowed to leave.

And thinking of slavery, Orrin frowned. During their lunch break the day before, they'd traveled down a side street they hadn't explored before. Every meal, they'd ask for a recommendation for the next from the stall they chose. They'd been looking for a noodle shop when they found the slave market.

Prisoners of war, debtors, and even criminals were lined up and being auctioned off. The business was brisk and over quickly, yet Daniel and Orrin had stood in a daze after the crowd dispersed. They'd seen their first elf. He'd looked beaten, with the slavery bracelet on his hand before he was sold.

A few questions to the men in charge and Daniel had dragged Orrin back to the training room. Orrin had to heal himself a lot more than usual that afternoon.

Slavery was legal in the world. Depending on the reason, they theoretically could pay off their debt price or serve their sentence, but the slaver had smirked as he insinuated ways to increase the holding time of a slave.

Most slaves were used as fodder to wear down dungeons.

"One more reason to get trained up and crush them all," Daniel had said later. Orrin agreed.

Luckily, it seemed the slave trade in Dey was small. The man they'd talked to complained of increased taxes and strict demands on timely release.

As Daniel swung at him, Orrin triggered [Side Steps] three times in a row.

[Side Steps] 51/100

"Let's stop for the day," Daniel suggested. "That's the most you've ever evaded. Did you level?"

Orrin shook his head. "No. We should definitely hit the baths before we go to dinner."

"You don't think Madi's dad would appreciate our stink?" Daniel took a sniff. "Okay, wow. Yeah, we've been going hard today."

The Guild had a large, steaming pool used as a bath behind another one of the magical doors. They'd discovered it on the second day after a pointed suggestion by the woman at reception.

After a lazy lounge in the warm water and a quick scrub in one of the side "shower" rooms, they pulled out some clothes they'd gotten at Madi's suggestion. A courier had arrived with a letter for them. It had pointed out that using point-summoned clothing was good for a forest excursion, but not meeting the head of a house of Dey.

They'd gone shopping.

Looking back, it should have been obvious why they'd been getting so many looks. People knew what the basic summoned clothes looked like, and who would spend precious ability points on backpacks and clothing?

Orrin felt wasteful, as they spent four gold each on clothes, backpacks, and even newer (and supposedly higher-quality) leather armor for the both of them. They'd also each spent a single gold piece on one outfit. Dress clothes. It was almost like a tuxedo, but in muted colors instead of black and easier to move around in. Orrin had his made in charcoal gray, while Daniel picked a dark red.

Finally, it was time for dinner with the Catanzanos.

Lord Catanzano entered the dining hall in front of his daughter. His back was straight and his eyes pierced Orrin and Daniel as Madi pushed his wheelchair to the head of the table and kissed his cheek.

"Welcome, guests." His voice was quiet but firm as he tossed a napkin in the air before putting it on his lap. "My daughter has told me much of your heroics. We are in your debt."

She never mentioned the wheelchair, Orrin thought as he copied the action, putting his own napkin on his lap. Daniel did the same.

"No debt at all, Lord Catanzano," Daniel replied. "We helped a little, but I'm sure Sir Bennett and Lady Madeleine would have gotten out just fine."

Cooks entered and put trays down around the small family table where they'd been seated. *Just the four of us.* Orrin looked around. *It's too cozy for just meeting guests. Something is up here.*

Lord Catanzano waved his hand as Daniel spoke. "No, no, no. Here in our family home, please call me Silas. And Brandt has told me the unadapted truth, unlike my own daughter." He threw a look at Madi. "I know that my happiness is alive because of you."

Daniel did not contradict him this time.

"I also know that she swindled you out of a Quest," Silas continued. "I cannot allow my family to be in debt."

Silas poured a glass of wine for himself and offered some to Daniel, who shook his head. Orrin also declined. They both tucked into the food, though.

Steamed carrots and potatoes, slabs of something like pork with tiny onions sprinkled on top, hearty gravy to drown everything in, and more of that honey bread. Orrin had almost hoped for some high-class cuisine, but it seemed everybody in Dey ate pretty normal fare.

"Will you negotiate a reward for the Quest?" Silas questioned.

"The Quests were paid for, my lord," Daniel said. "Sorry—Silas."

Orrin cringed.

". . . Quests?"

Madi had been nearly flawless. Her fork had paused for only a moment as it traveled to her lips. Orrin had barely caught the hesitation.

Her father turned to her. "Dearest. Would you be so kind as to humor your aging father? I distinctly remember only one Quest."

Orrin and Daniel did not move as the room grew dark with displeasure.

"I told you I paid them for their given Quest, Father."

"HA!" Silas let out a bark of a laugh, louder than any noise he'd made since entering the room. "Word games with me! I am so proud I could almost forgive the lie."

Madi looked at her plate, hiding a smile.

"So, she paid for this Horde Quest with a little gold. What was the other Quest? No use lying now, boys." He turned his dark eyes back on Daniel and Orrin, cutting a piece of meat.

"A timed Quest to reach the Gate of Dey." Orrin stepped in. *Maybe I can sidestep someone else finding out about [Blood Mana].*

"And payment for that?"

"She agreed to keep a secret of mine," Orrin stated clearly. *Maybe he'll honor the agreement.*

"What secret?"

Damn!

Daniel chimed in finally, "One that cost a Quest, sir. What would you offer to know it?"

This is why I love you, you dumb jock. Daniel and Orrin had always been an odd friendship. What nobody could understand was they filled in each other's blind spots. While Orrin couldn't play a sport like Daniel, he could help him understand nuances in strategy. While Daniel couldn't write a paper as convincingly as Orrin, he could spot holes in his logic or convince someone through conversation loops that Orrin would never see.

"Hmm. I could just demand my daughter tell me." Silas smirked. "But I won't. I see this means a lot to you. I will let the matter rest."

Madi, Orrin, and Daniel sighed with relief.

"However, now that we have established your Quest has the worth of a secret not to be afforded a lord of Dey"—Orrin felt the walls closing in as Silas's smirk turned predatory—"we can discuss the discrepancy in price of only one thousand gold for the other."

Madi gulped.

"I value two things in my life—my family and the knowledge I obtain and use to defend my family and people. Two Quests given to my daughter, with one's price being knowledge I cannot obtain . . ." He trailed off.

"Yes, I think I know the price Madeleine should have offered for your Quest, Daniel."

Daniel and Orrin did not know the man and had not followed his rambling thoughts. But Madi had. Orrin saw her eyes widen.

"No. Father, you can't—"

"Daniel, you shall marry my daughter."

Chapter 8

The table was silent. Madi was holding back tears and seemed ready to rush from the table.

Silas let out another short "Ha!"

"I apologize, I apologize." Silas chuckled into his glass. "My Madeleine tries so hard to take on the duties of her future station, I sometimes go too far with my teasing."

Madi looked panicky as he spoke but then calmed.

"So . . . that was a family joke," Daniel guessed.

"Father does like to tease me about my future husband," Madi murmured as she resumed eating.

"I'm sure you are a wonderful man, but Madeleine's future husband must meet high requirements," Silas said between bites.

Orrin and Daniel exchanged glances and relaxed. *So he likes to play games.* Orrin filed that away.

"But to the matter at hand. I would have offered much more, but if you are adamant that the price was fair, I will not push further," Silas continued. "However, once you leave this table, no further succor or favor can be given for these deeds."

"We are satisfied," Daniel said immediately. Madi smiled softly at him.

"Good, then. On to the matter of you saving my daughter's life."

Will this never end? Orrin threw a look to Daniel.

Kill me, please? Daniel eye rolled back.

Silas offered more gold, but Orrin had another idea.

"Actually, sir, we are new to Dey and wanted to try our hand at helping defeat a dungeon."

82

Dungeon subjugation in Dey was regulated by the houses. Knights were sent with select teams to destroy new ones. The only way to defeat a dungeon was going with one of these groups or finding one in the wild by chance.

"What level are you, son?"

Not immediately shut down! There's a chance, Orrin thought as he said, "Level three, sir."

Madi choked on a piece of carrot. "Three? That's not possible! You . . . He . . ."

Silas frowned. "And you, Daniel?"

Daniel glanced up from his bread slathered in gravy. "Um . . . two?"

Madi sat still.

"Nobody under level ten goes into a dungeon, boys," Silas started. "But beyond that, how did two freshly classed kids, no offense intended, defeat a band of bandits that took out one of my knights?"

"Shock and awe?" Orrin mustered.

Silas stared at Orrin for a minute and then laughed. This was more than the single guffaw he'd displayed earlier. He pushed back from the table and bent in his chair.

"Ha-ha-ha. Sorry. That— Oh," he tried. "Sometimes I forget that for all the bluster of classes and levels, even a [Farmer] can take down a [Hero]."

Weird idiom, Orrin thought.

"I suppose luck was a great part of it as well," Silas continued. "I mean, you haven't even reached your first stat increase yet. However did you do it? The full story now."

Daniel and Orrin told them of spotting the bandits from a distance and sneaking up, Orrin's distraction, the crossbow discharge into Sir Bennett, and Daniel's judicious use of [Power Strike]. They glossed over Orrin's healing of Brandt.

"So while he was hacking away, what were you doing, Orrin? What kind of attacks do you have?"

Orrin tensed. "I had cast my spells already. I do have some small healing, but mostly I focus on buff spells."

Silas looked lost for the first time at dinner. "What is a buff spell?"

"I increased Daniel's strength and dexterity."

"That's not possible." Silas frowned. "That is not a spell I've ever heard of."

In for a penny, Orrin thought.

"I have them for all four main stats—dex, strength, will, and intelligence." Orrin pulled his level-one spells slots out of his status and held them up for Silas. "See?"

Silas read the spells, and his eyes widened. "This . . . this would be expensive, mana-wise, for one person. But you could charge good gold . . . very good gold to—what was the word?—buff a team before they went into a dungeon."

He looked back at Orrin. "But do have you any attack spells? You must! Every parent teaches their child to get one first. These must have cost you . . . more ability points than you gain when you class."

"I bought will and intelligence recently, yes. But I have no actual attack spells," Orrin explained. "Daniel and I classed together, so I haven't really had the need for an attack spell."

"But you can't gain experience without an attack spell unless you are in melee, and no offense, young man, but you do not have the build of somebody who risks life and limb."

"I'll figure something out." Orrin had spent most of the last three days reading more of the options in the store. He had a general idea of what he needed to do. The problem was going to be gaining another level first.

"Dad, maybe Brandt and I could take them into the Pass," Madi suggested. "Not too far, just the first quarter, where stragglers might be."

Silas did not look excited at the prospect of his daughter going out into danger again. Before he could deny her, Orrin added, "Or if they weren't available to come with us, maybe just access for me and Daniel?"

Access through the Western Wall required approval from a house or the Guild. The Guild only approved access for quests or silver rings, the next rank above Orrin and Daniel. Houses would send their own to train or those who paid enough.

Carrying around more gold sounds good in theory, but I'd rather have favors, Orrin thought. *Less risk of being mugged that way.*

The room fell silent except the clink of silverware on plates as Silas considered.

"You understand that going beyond the Wall has a one-in-ten death rate no matter the distance traveled?" Silas asked.

The little research they'd been able to do had turned up some statistics like that. The *Leveler's Guide* had actually said one in three died.

"We plan on staying within sight of the Wall." Daniel offered their plan. "I will do most of the fighting and let Orrin get a solid blow in if we can. The more we can both level, the better chance we have of helping defeat some of those dungeons around Dey."

Silas grinned at Daniel's ploy to appear noble. Helping defeat dungeons that the houses had kept under control for generations was presumptuous.

But he doesn't know Daniel's a [Hero]. Orrin reached for more meat.

"I can't let Sir Bennett or Madeleine off the hook for their behavior," Silas announced. "I also cannot afford to let their rescuers die in an attempt to gain experience."

He clicked his tongue in thought. "I suppose I can spare a man to take you past the Wall. I'll instruct him personally to stay back and only interfere if things look fatal. There are no guarantees, though, and you must be back before dusk. There have been rumors of darkness creatures roaming the Pass recently."

Madi pursued her lips and shook her head as the chance to escape her punishment slipped away. Daniel grinned at Orrin. They'd gotten access and could gain levels.

"We would be fine going on our own, sir," Orrin tried. "There's no need for you to waste your manpower on—"

"Nonsense. I can't have you both dying so soon after arriving in Dey. The Guild would be at my neck for restitution if I let a new crop of adventurers go off alone."

Orrin had seen the jaws of the trap set and tried to evade it. *His man will no doubt report back every skill we use. He's trying to spy on* us. *We would be fine going alone, and that he knows we're already at the Guild means the spying has already started.*

"Now, enough talk. Which of you two know how to play Kala?"

Orrin silently thanked the shopkeep at Books, Books, Books! for recommending one of the children's books. It had a small section of the popular pastimes and games of the world, including one section on Kala.

Seen usually as a game of chance, nobility and officers use Kala to improve resourcefulness and strategy in the face of unforeseen circumstances. Teaching your child to play Kala with the marbles only will be a great pastime, motor function activity, and counting game. Introduction of the strategy cards should be held until they are older. See my next book, Raising Teenagers to Excel in Class, *for more.*

The game looked at first glance like checkers, but with marbles resting in small depressions on each of the sixty-four squares. Either side started with eight marbles chosen from a black bag. They could be set up on any of the three lines closest to the player.

Different marble types were possible on the draw. White marbles moved forward or back one square and attacked diagonally like a pawn in chess. Black marbles moved diagonally one square but could only attack right in front. Green marbles could be placed once and never moved but had to be taken out before any opposing piece could move past it. The book had called it the forest line. The last type was red. It also could be placed only once but could attack one time before being used and taken off the board.

The game ended when someone touched their own marble to the back line of the opponent or all an opponent's marbles were taken.

Already more advanced than basic checkers. Silas tried explaining the strategy cards as well.

"It's surprising you don't even know the basics," he'd muttered while servants cleared the food and put an elaborate box with tiny drawers in front of him. He started unfolding lids and pulling drawers as the box expanded into a beautifully inlaid Kala set.

"There are ten different cards," he explained as he shuffled them out. "Each allows an extra action on the player's turn. We each receive an agreed number, up to two before the game starts. Of course, you can also sacrifice a marble for another card."

He began to lay the cards down face-up on the table. "There are two of each type of card. Lightning strikes take out a green marble or forest line. Rains will negate the use of a red marble. There are also four change color cards, two red and two green. You can use a color change on a white marble only."

He pulled out the last two cards. "These are special, though."

One card had a man standing on a hill surrounded by a bright light and with a sword raised above his head. The other was a creature of darkness slouched on a throne.

"The Demon Lord and the Hero," Madi said as she watched over her father's shoulder.

"The Demon Lord allows you to bring two extra black marbles to the table for three turns. You place them only on your back line. The Hero lets you bring one white marble to any spot on the first five lines."

"But if both are played, both players lose all the summoned forces and half their remaining forces."

"That sounds too complex for me," Daniel whispered to Orrin.

Orrin cracked his knuckles and smiled.

After Orrin's dad left, his mom worked more night shifts in order to keep the house running. Before Daniel's family found out and began having him over, Orrin had had to learn to heat up whatever dinner was in the fridge and put himself to bed.

He was nine years old.

Of course, instead of following the schedule laid out by his mom, Orrin had stayed up watching TV, playing video games, and eating candy and cereal.

He fell asleep in school, and his grades suffered. But every video game was completed to 100 percent. He searched every hidden room, found all the bugs that let a character off the regular map, and slowly learned how to complete all the puzzles.

His dad's video game selection spanned decades. He played old text RPG games on the computer and more recent ones across a few different systems, more modern shooter games, and even some re-source-building strategy games.

In short, Orrin had spent years perfecting multiple approaches and tactics for different situations. Kala should have been no harder than a side game. Something he'd perfected.

He lost three games in a row.

"That last attempt was clever," Silas praised. "What you attempted with your demon card was called the Hero's Lament, but you placed one of the summoned forces on a different line. If you had put them together like this"—Silas arranged the marbles back on the board—"you would have blocked my attacks for several rounds."

Orrin sighed and shook his head.

"Don't be discouraged. That was quite good for your age." Silas smiled. "But it is getting late, and I should not keep you much later."

Daniel and Madi had sat on a couch chatting as they played round after round. They approached when Silas beckoned.

"Dear, would you escort these gentlemen out? And see about Sir DeGuis taking them out tomorrow or the day after?" Silas put the pieces back in bags and closed up the board box.

"Of course, Father." Madi bowed her head. Silas nodded again at the boys and left.

Madi made introductions to Sir DeGuis on the way out. A constant smile stretched his sparse beard, and his eyes glittered with mischief. He shook their hands while asking what time they could meet. The following day he was busy with other assignments, so they decided to meet the day after at first bell, around eight in the morning.

As they walked back to the Guild, Daniel talked about the food and how polite Silas was. "It's like he wanted to pay us and stay out of debt."

"Mmm-hmm."

"And Madi was telling me about the other houses. Before the last duty change, another house gave a year of tax exemption to all their barons, which isn't actually legal. That's why she was out collecting, but now her father is mad she did it."

"Mmm." Orrin put his hand on the small knife he'd taken to wearing on his hip.

"—when we go out with Sir DeGuis. Madi said his name is Jude and he's a devil with his warhammer. What are you doing?"

Orrin had drawn his knife.

"Two little lambs come out to play?" Three men strode from the dark alley in front of them.

Orrin began pumping boosts on himself and Daniel. Daniel had left his sword at home but had a knife in one hand. Orrin hadn't even noticed him wearing one.

"We're Guild members on our way back for the night," Daniel explained. "You don't want to get in our way."

"But somebody told us you have lots of gold to share." The man on the left snickered. He held his sword to the side of his dark green pants that had helped hide him in the darkness of the nearby alley.

All three had swords naked in the night. They were dressed in ratty leather armor and stank of stale beer. The one on the right squinted, holding his sword to the side as he ran his hands over his greasy hair.

The leader stepped forward, both hands on his two-handed sword.

"There's another behind us, maybe two," Orrin whispered to Daniel. He nodded.

I really need to get an attack spell. Orrin kicked himself. *Tomorrow I'll check for a spell book.*

"If you just want gold, maybe we can all go get some food?" Daniel tried.

"We'll be eating well enough later," the leader said, hefting his sword in the air.

Orrin used [Identify]. The men were all under level ten, but not by much. The leader sat at level nine. All had basic fighter classes. He peered behind him but couldn't catch a glimpse of the following men he'd been concentrating on as Daniel talked earlier.

"Have it your way, then." Daniel squatted and held his knife point out toward the muggers. The three men spread and advanced.

Daniel didn't wait. With a step, he appeared in front of the leader. Shock hit the man's face as Daniel pushed the knife into his neck and withdrew it in a spray of blood. The bandit's sword dropped as he put his hands on his neck and fell to his knees.

The man on the left yelled and swung at Daniel. The man's sword swept across Daniel's back and opened a cut across his shoulder, but Orrin had already cast a heal on him.

Daniel swept up the leader's sword and with a turn of his heel slashed through the other man's leg, leaving a deep cut and darkening his green pants. They exchanged blows as the third man circled and approached Orrin.

Shit, shit, shit. Orrin could try to use [Blood Mana], but he'd promised not to use that. *It's life or death, though. Sorry, Madi.*

He cast [Blood Mana] and tried to target the man with the greasy hair.

Nothing happened.

It must be touch-only . . . Fuck! he thought as the man swung his sword.

The blood on the cobblestones saved him from the first strike. The third man had overextended and slipped a little. Orrin scrambled back and threw his knife.

It missed.

"D. A little help!"

Daniel was still fighting green pants. They both had cuts, but Orrin had been spamming heals as fast as he could. Another minute or two and Daniel would outlast the man.

Orrin didn't have a minute, though. He pulled another knife out of his [Dimension Hole].

His foot turned on a loose cobblestone, and he fell on his butt. The knife handle hit the stone and vibrated out of his hand.

The mugger smiled and raised his sword to strike.

As the sword flowed through the moonlight, Orrin realized he was going to die. He had no spells that would help him here. He tried [Camouflage].

The sword struck his chest. His dress clothes were torn apart as the pain hit.

Damage taken!
HP 54/90

Orrin screamed as thirty-six points evaporated. His chest was on fire, and blood filled the cracks of the street.

The man took his sword and pushed it through Orrin's stomach. "Shitty little asshole. Killed Lenard. Now I'm gonna gut your friend, too." He twisted.

Damage taken!
HP 4/90

The greasy man pulled his sword out of Orrin and turned his back, walking toward Daniel. Green pants had used some ability and was still standing despite the multiple bleeding wounds.

HP 3/90

Orrin was bleeding out, but his mind stayed calm and continued processing. *This must be [Mind Bastion] at work. I think it just turned off my pain processers. Most people would be taken out by the pain alone!*

Orrin quietly cast three heals. His wounds closed, but he could still feel the pain beyond the wall of Bastion. His movements felt sluggish even at full health.

Camo was still active, and his knife was a few feet away. Daniel was being backed into a corner, defending himself and screaming, "Orrin! You killed him!"

I guess [Camouflage] works on the [Hero], too. Orrin picked up his knife and crawled through the bloody street. He pushed himself up to one knee and vomited.

Daniel took two hits as his back hit a wall. He swung wildly.

"Just put the sword down and give us your gold. We won't kill you, will we, Jay?" The man chuckled as his friend circled.

Orrin got behind the man who'd stabbed him and put his blade to the man's throat. "That's enough."

Orrin had meant to scare the man and make them leave. But as the man felt the cold blade touch his neck, he jerked hard to the side, letting the knife cut into his carotid artery. Blood sprayed as he tried to stanch the flow.

Daniel used the distraction and pressed the attack. As green pants watched his friend fountain his life from an unseen attacker, Daniel slipped under his sword and buried the blade in his chest. A turn of the wrist and the man coughed hard before falling forward. His weight pulled the big sword from Daniel's grip.

"Orrin! You're alive? I saw him put a sword in you!" Daniel let the body fall and ran to his friend, pulling his torn jacket open to check. Faint scars were still fading on his stomach and chest.

"He didn't finish me." Orrin was staring at the unmoving body of the man he'd just killed.

During the bandit attack, Daniel had done the hard work. Daniel had not been shaken at the killing. Orrin turned and threw up again.

"I killed him, D." Orrin wiped his mouth and resheathed his knife. "I didn't mean to. He should have stopped and just left. Why . . ." He trailed off.

Daniel had Orrin take their gear out of his [Dimension Hole] and pulled his leathers on over his blood-soaked dress clothes. Strapping his sword on his back, Daniel half carried Orrin back to the Guild.

The other two muggers never showed, Orrin thought in a daze as Daniel explained the blood to the receptionist. Guards were sent to retrieve bodies and look for any witnesses. *Why would they watch their friends be cut down and not take us out?*

Daniel got a dazed Orrin cleaned up with a wet rag and into some new clothes. As he dropped Orrin into his bed, Orrin noticed a few cuts still seeping on his friend.

[Heal Small Wounds]

"Ahh. That feels better. Thanks, O. I guess that means you're coherent again?" Daniel sat on the side of the bed.

"Was I really that out of it?"

"You didn't respond even when I slapped you." Daniel's face was etched in worry.

"Sorry," Orrin whispered.

Daniel sat looking down at his friend. He stood up and went to the window of their new room, peering out from behind the curtain. "After I killed those men . . . after the bandit attack, I didn't sleep for two days."

Orrin shifted and sat with his back to the wall. "I didn't know that."

"I tried thinking why I had been so okay with killing those men and realized I was acting like this was all a dream or a video game and not real life," Daniel continued.

"But it is real now." Daniel turned and waited until Orrin looked at him. "This is our life now, Orrin. You saved my life tonight. Again. I'm sorry I couldn't save you."

Orrin watched as tears appeared on Daniel's face. He turned and angrily wiped them away.

"Why do you think the others never attacked?" Daniel asked.

Orrin pondered. He'd heard someone approaching from behind, but the footsteps had never joined in the attack. Maybe not a mugger then, but not a friend.

"I don't know, but I don't think they were part of that gang," Orrin offered.

"Yeah, that was my thought, too. Maybe one of Lord Catanzano's men? Sent to watch over us?"

Orrin sat for a long moment before lying back down and pulling the sheet over his shoulders. "If it was and they didn't try to help, that's just one more reason not to trust the houses. We need to level. *I* need to level and get something more offensive. I can't believe I didn't drop the knife."

"Yeah, me, too." Daniel forced a laugh. "Good night, Orrin."

"Night."

Orrin dreamed of blood flowing in the street.

Chapter 9

After a quick breakfast from the food stall nearest the Guild, Orrin and Daniel met Sir DeGuis by the first gate.

The Western Wall was separated into three actual walls with a few hundred yards of space between each. Supposedly, if the westernmost gate fell, the defenders would have two more walls to defend before a massacre ensued.

Sir DeGuis stood to the side as guards traveled through the gate. His armor was similar to Sir Bennett's garb, with half plate and the Catanzano colors of green and golden yellow underneath. He kept his head clear of a helmet, though. He had a sword strapped to his side but also carried an oversize warhammer. The shaft sat on the ground, and the hammerhead rested above his head. It was the size of a large watermelon and completely squared.

"Sir DeGuis." Daniel waved as they approached.

The man smiled from beneath his beard and rested the hammer on his shoulder as he strode forward. "None of that *sir* shit while we're out of the house. I'm Jude."

Daniel smiled and began to ask questions about the man's hammer as they walked through the gate. Jude nodded at guards, and they passed without trouble.

Orrin stopped listening to the two men talking about different attacks and scouted the large plains inside the first gate. The dirt road led about three hundred yards to the next Wall and gate. Scattered across the greenery were small, spiked fences, meant to slow any monsters that made it this far.

I can't even make out the mountains on the sides. Orrin squinted, trying to see the growing hazy blur in the distance.

"You won't be able to make out the mountains from here." Jude knocked Orrin from his scanning. "This is the northernmost gate, and the mountains are still about five miles away that way. From the top of the wall, you can see them a bit."

"How large is the Pass?" Orrin queried.

"It varies, but it's about fifty miles wide at the widest." Jude hiked his hammer farther back on his shoulder. "Here at the gates, it's only about fifteen miles wide."

"And how far to get out of the Pass?" Daniel asked.

"Probably about eighty miles." Jude shrugged. "It takes most adventurers a week or more to get through. But we'll be staying within the first few miles today. There are reports of some Sproits by the tree line, which should be enough for you two to level a bit. As long as they stay low level and haven't evolved."

"Is that common?" Orrin asked as they made their way through the second gate.

Jude waved at a guard who saluted. "Nah. Sproits are an annoyance. Actually, the Guild usually has a standing quest to eradicate a few dozen, but most people who can get through the gates don't waste their time . . . not that you'll be wasting your time."

Orrin reached into his pocket and pulled out one of the bestiaries. The index didn't include Sproits. He replaced it and pulled the next. Bingo.

Sproits, or grass goblins, are the lowest form of the goblin evolution scale. These monsters attack with their fingernails, which they have honed to razor sharpness. Sproits attack only in numbers, but a single adventurer can handle a dozen, as they are the size of toddlers. With bad eyesight and slow movement, Sproits are only a one-star danger (*).

However, if Sproits are gathered in numbers exceeding fifty, a goblin is likely present. See Goblin (***) for more.

Orrin marked the page and handed it to Daniel. Daniel looked at the proffered book and raised an eyebrow. "What's the highlights?"

"Goblin toddlers who scratch. Bad eyesight and slow movement," Orrin rattled off.

Jude peered over his shoulder. "Bringing books to a battle? Can't say whether that's the smartest thing I've seen or—"

"Being prepared never hurts," Daniel cut in.

Jude shrugged and walked toward the third gate. Orrin's quick glance confirmed the second field was just like the first.

Unlike the first two gates, the third gate was closed. While Jude walked ahead to announce their little party and get the gate open, Orrin pulled Daniel aside.

"He's definitely working at identifying our abilities for Silas," Orrin started. "You gave him three different skills of yours during his friendly questioning."

Daniel raised an eyebrow. "O. I volunteered the information about what I can do so he could help us get more experience. I only told him about [Power Strike] and [Double Strike]."

"And [Stone Skin]," Orrin interrupted.

"Yes. And [Stone Skin]." Daniel played with the strap on his leather bracer. "I don't really care if he knows my skills, though, Orrin."

Orrin gritted his teeth. "Daniel. The more information they have, the more likely someone figures out your class. According to all the books, [Hide Status] changes your class on an [Identify] to fighter, mage, or healer. That doesn't mean they can't piece together your class with reverse engineering and checking classes off one at a time based on your skills."

Daniel shrugged.

"Do you want people to find out you're the [Hero] before you have the levels to control your own fate?"

Daniel sighed. "I get it, Orrin. I do. But I think you're being too careful. Madi would help us, I'm sure of it. You should have heard her talk about protecting her people last night while you and Silas played that game. She was so passionate."

Damn it. Orrin was struck dumb. *He's falling for a princess . . . or the equivalent, anyways.*

Orrin tried again. "Promise me you'll be careful and not tell her until we are at least level ten. We need some buffer."

Daniel put his hand on his friend's shoulder. *When did he get taller? He definitely got taller, right?*

"I promise, Orrin."

"Don't make promises before going into the Pass." Jude appeared with his hammer resting in both hands. "Be swift, be smart, and leave everyone behind if it means survival."

"That is not what I want to hear from our guide," Daniel joked as his hand fell from Orrin's shoulder. "Shouldn't you say something like 'I'll protect you to my last breath'?"

"Nah." Jude hefted the hammer a few times, testing the weight. "You level quick in the Pass or you die. I'm just here to make the former more likely than the latter."

Orrin had a bad feeling.

After leaving the gate, Jude led them north, following the Wall. After half an hour, Orrin could just make out a forest beginning to creep into sight at a distance.

"Does the forest go all the way to the Wall?" he asked.

"Nope. We keep it culled back." Jude smirked. "Can't have the beasties getting too close. Lots of [Archers] and [Marksman] up there taking out things before they become a problem. Speaking of which . . ."

Jude veered to the side and picked a few arrows from the tall grass. "Collect any arrows you find that aren't broken. The guard will buy them back, but it's mostly a civil service."

Finding the arrows in the grass was a literal needle-in-a-haystack search. It also slowed them down, which Orrin was thankful for. He was scared out of his mind, especially after nearly dying the night before.

"Orrin, we don't need to find every arrow," Daniel complained. "We should focus on hitting the trees."

Orrin stood from where he had been sweeping the stalks of grass and sighed.

The plan was for Daniel to tank the Sproits while Orrin used [Camouflage] and took out any stragglers. He had the spare short-sword from the bandits that had attacked Madi and Brant on his hip. It was cheap and not worth much. *But then again, my melee skills aren't worth much more than this.*

Jude would be there in case the plan went sideways.

After two hours, they reached the tree line. They could see the Wall behind them rising up against the sky. The sun peeked over the top of the Wall, blinding Orrin when he looked back.

"Sun at our backs will slow the Sproits down even more," Jude commented.

Orrin and Daniel drew their weapons. Jude kept his hammer resting on his shoulder. *He must have a skill that makes it lighter. That thing has to weigh sixty pounds or more.*

As they began to creep into the forest, Orrin boosted Daniel's stats, as well as his own. He also camouflaged himself.

"Hey, where'd Orrin go?" Jude whispered to Daniel.

"He's scouting." Daniel used the agreed-upon excuse. Hopefully, one skill fewer would be picked up by House Catanzano.

Five minutes after entering the forest, Orrin spotted the first Sproit. Three feet tall and a sickly yellow, the small goblinoid was crouched over a rabbit and cutting the skin over and over. From the dried blood all around, it had been doing this for some time.

According to everything they'd read, forming a party would split any resulting experience across everyone who did damage. Otherwise, only the person delivering the final blow would gain experience. Orrin and Daniel were still in a party together. That meant that Orrin had to actually do damage to gain experience.

Daniel had spotted the Sproit, too. He stopped and looked around. His eyes flared with a skill, and he peered in Orrin's general direction.

"Do it," he mouthed.

Orrin crept closer. He avoided dried leaves and sticks when he could and stood still at any rustle he made. The last twenty feet were an agony of waiting, but the Sproit didn't look up once.

So far, so good, Orrin thought. He pulled his sword back like a baseball bat and took two quick steps, swinging with all he had.

His sword whistled through the air and struck the Sproit in the head. Unlike in the books and movies, his sword didn't go right through bone but stuck tight about two inches into the Sproit's skull.

It screamed.

The sound was a mix of a child screaming in pain and a cat being stepped on. Orrin's hair stood up, and as he tried to pull the sword back, the sweat on his hands almost made him lose his grip. He held on as the Sproit tugged his head to the side, trying to escape the pain.

Daniel burst from the trees and swung his sword. His motions flowed like a professional. Orrin saw the telltale ghost swing of [Double Strike] pierce the goblin's body, and it fell.

Experience Gained: 10 XP

"Thanks, Daniel." Orrin yanked his sword from the Sproit's head with a sucking sound. "The sword isn't as tough as—"

Daniel put a finger to his lips and eyed to their right. Orrin set up [Camouflage] again.

Three Sproits jogged into sight. The front Sproit let out a scream that clawed at Orrin's ears and then dropped into a sprint at the sight of Daniel standing over the monster's body. The other two followed closely.

Orrin froze for only a moment before getting in front of Daniel. He stood to the side and let the first Sproit pass him. He went to one knee and swung at the second. This time he aimed lower.

His sword took off the Sproit's leg, and it skidded along the forest floor, adding its own scream to the echoing cacophony now surrounding them.

I did it! Orrin took his sword back to swing again. The third monster changed direction and eyed him. *Damn. [Camouflage] drops after an attack.*

Orrin took another wild swing and clipped the chest of the Sproit. It dropped back and tried to circle. *It's actually pretty slow.*

Orrin tried to swing again, but the Sproit simply ducked and then clawed up. The nails on its hands grated as it struck his sword.

Orrin glanced back and saw Daniel had already dispatched the first one and was running through the second.

Experience Gained: 10 XP

I didn't do any damage to the first one, so no gains there. Orrin kicked himself and then lunged. He pierced the Sproit's arm.

Daniel appeared at his side. "Want me to finish it?"

Orrin nodded, and Daniel struck the goblin down.

Experience Gained: 10 XP

Level 3 (30/300)

Orrin breathed hard and leaned on a tree. "This is going to take a while, isn't it?"

Over the next four hours, they found another twenty Sproits in groups of twos and threes. Orrin and Daniel worked out a system, too—Orrin would strike first and Daniel would finish a monster. Or if Daniel got to one first, he'd nearly finish it but leave it crawling along for Orrin to stab.

Orrin was getting better at stabbing crawling monsters.

Level 3 (230/300)

They stopped for a quick lunch. Jude tried to ask Orrin about his buffs, but Orrin only gave terse responses.

"It's fine, Jude," Daniel cut in. "Orrin just doesn't like bragging about himself."

Orrin opened the bestiary back up and turned to the Sproit section again.

However, if Sproits are gathered in numbers exceeding fifty, a goblin is likely present. See Goblin (***) for more.

He leafed to Goblin.

Goblins evolve when enough Sproit are present. While Sproits attack with natural weapons, Goblins use tools. Some also use low-level rage spells to whip Sproits into a fury. A furied Sproit can overcome fatal injuries to continue fighting. However, the Goblin itself is a three-star danger (***). Its fighting prowess is formidable, and it can cast a plethora of low-level spells, including [Vine Tangle], [Whispers], and [Power Strike].

So run if we see a Goblin, got it.

They went back to it. They traveled a little farther into the forest but hadn't encountered a Sproit for half an hour.

"This might be a good time to turn back," Jude suggested. He had stood to the side during the fights, only killing one Sproit that had tried to approach from a different angle. It had ended up behind Jude. A splatter of red was all that was left behind.

Daniel muttered and seemed about to argue.

"We can take a different route on the way back," Orrin suggested. "Maybe find some more?"

Daniel shrugged, and they headed back at a different angle.

"So, have you guys leveled?" Jude asked.

"I have," Daniel whispered.

"Not yet," Orrin added.

"I know it seems like it's slow, but trust me, you guys got lucky today," Jude said softly. "It took three years of regular scouting for me to get where I am now."

"And what level are you?" Orrin asked.

"I'm a level-fifteen [Bruiser]," he said with pride.

Orrin used [Identify].

> **Jude DeGuis**
> Bruiser
> Level 15
> HP: 130
> MP: 100
>
> Strength: 19
> Constitution: 13
> Dexterity: 14
> Will: 10
> Intelligence: 10
>
> Abilities:
> [Hammer Proficiency] Level 3
> [Sword Proficiency] Level 1
> [Identify]
> [Power Strike]
> [Fallen Star]
> [Offensive Fighting]
> [Light Weapon]

Orrin pulled up his own store and checked [Fallen Star].

> [Fallen Star] Requires [Hammer Proficiency] Level 2 and [Offensive Fighting]. Raise your hammer on high. Let it fall with the weight of a star on your enemies. Deals variable damage based on Strength. 10 AP

They found another group of four Sproits, which Orrin and Daniel quickly took down.

Level 3 (270/300)

I guess I won't be hitting level four today, Orrin thought as he glimpsed the Wall through the trees.

The screams of dozens of Sproits rang through the air. Echoing under the high-pitched shrieks, another deeper voice pierced the forest.

"That's a fucking Goblin." Jude paled. "Run for the Wall."

Chapter 10

Orrin topped off his four buffs and did the same for Daniel. He made sure [Camouflage] was active and sheathed his sword. All three of them started jogging, dodging trees, and sticking close.

"I thought you said Goblins were rare," Daniel yelled as the screeches of the Sproits continued.

"They are rare." Jude leaped over a fallen branch, holding his hammer in both hands. "There hasn't been a report of a Goblin this close to the Wall for years."

Orrin struggled to keep up with Jude and Daniel. The extra stats helped, but Daniel was just in generally better shape than he was.

"I—can't—keep—going," Orrin huffed. They had made it halfway back, but running three miles in the forest was wearing on him.

Daniel slowed. "We are almost back, O. I can see Sproits getting closer. We can't stop."

"They're supposed to be slow," Orrin complained as he dry heaved against a tree.

"The Goblin's fury skill." Jude set his hammer down on the ground. "It allows them to move faster. If it was just a few Sproits, I'd wade in there and we could take them out easy."

He took a long swig of water from his waterskin and continued, "But you have to take the Goblin out first in closed spaces like this forest, or those little guys will carve you up quick."

Daniel's eyes never left the path back. "I can make out about fifteen or so Sproits but can't see a Goblin."

"[Eagle Eyes]?" Jude asked.

Still spying even when we're being chased by toddlers with knife fingers. Orrin groaned.

Daniel nodded slowly. "I think we need to head off soon. Orrin, are you okay to go again? I can carry you."

Orrin pushed off his knees and straightened. "I'm good. I just had to catch my breath."

They started running again. But after ten minutes, Orrin was holding his side where a stitch was burning.

Orrin tried casting [Heal Small Wounds] and even [Calm Mind] on himself, but neither worked at reducing the pain or helping him run any longer.

"Sorry, guys," Orrin groaned as he slowed to a stop. "Go ahead, I'll catch up. They can't see me anyways."

Jude's eyes narrowed. "How?"

"I've got a spell that makes it harder for them to see me." Orrin purposefully kept his answer vague.

"We need to get to the gate and get reinforcements." Jude shrugged. "Sproits rarely look up, so just climb a tree and wait. We'll be back with a few guards and take out the Goblin."

"I'm not leaving you." Daniel stood still as he scanned the forest. "They haven't gotten any closer, but we're still a mile or two from the tree line."

"We can signal the Wall," Jude suggested. "They'll send horses and be here within the hour."

"Not good enough." Daniel glared at Jude before turning his eyes back to the clamoring Sproits.

"Daniel, I'm holding you both back." Orrin surreptitiously cast [Calm Mind] on Daniel. *It's supposed to calm stress and make him think logically.*

"I can carry you," Daniel responded. "And don't try casting spells on me," he whispered.

In the end, Orrin climbed on Daniel's back, and they set off again at a slower pace.

"You could buff Jude," Daniel suggested quietly. "He could run ahead and we could maybe get a straggler or two."

"I really don't want Silas getting more information about my spells and skills."

"It's life and death, O." Daniel hitched Orrin higher and kept running. Jude stayed slightly ahead of them.

Orrin struggled inside. His need to keep all his cards close waged war with their safety.

"Jude. I'm going to cast a spell on you. [Increase Dexterity]."

"Huh?" Jude had time to get out before he stepped faster and nearly tripped. "What the hell?"

"Your dex should be up a bit," Orrin explained. "Run ahead and signal the Wall. We'll head right for it and try to creep along toward the gate."

"My job is to protect you," Jude started.

"Your job is to get us back safely," Daniel interjected. "If you don't signal the wall, it'll be all our asses on the line. So hurry."

Jude's face tore for a second, and then he saluted. He turned and looped along, leaving them behind.

"You could be running that fast, too," Orrin tried.

"Not leaving you behind, little man."

Orrin slapped the side of Daniel's head. "I'm almost as tall as you. Don't start that shit again."

Daniel chuckled, and fifteen minutes later they spotted the edge of the forest.

"We made it," Daniel sighed.

From the north, Orrin heard screams of Sproits.

"More coming from the left," he began. But another noise cut through the howls, low and grating.

"Is that another one?" Daniel groaned. "I'm starting to think we're really unlucky, Orrin."

Orrin silently agreed.

Daniel and Orrin made it to the Wall and began traveling south toward the gate. Loud thrashing followed in the forest across the tall grass.

"I can't get a perfect count, but I think maybe forty Sproits," Daniel said. "I saw one Goblin. It was lime green and ten feet tall, O."

"Jude should have signaled and waited for us . . ." Orrin looked around. "I think he left us and went back to the gate."

"He did say, 'leave people behind to survive,'" Daniel muttered.

After twenty minutes of creeping along the Wall, Daniel pointed. Traveling from the south was a cloud of dust being kicked up. Horses.

"Jude is at the front. He brought about ten guards."

"Will that be enough? They don't know about the second Goblin." Orrin made sure his sword was loose and ready to draw.

"I don't like it," Daniel said under his breath. "I—I think I'm going to buy a skill I've been looking at. [Long Cuts]. I'll be able to hit all my attacks from farther away, but it costs ten AP."

"If you think it's worth it." Orrin shrugged.

Daniel stopped and turned back. "I've been saving as much as I can because I have this feeling . . . I'm going to need a lot."

Orrin put his hand on Daniel's arm. "We'll get more if we level. I'm going to keep on you, healing and buffing you as much as possible." Orrin sighed. "I can't convince you to let them do this alone, can I?"

Daniel smirked. "This is why you're my best friend. You know me so well."

Drawing his sword in one hand and his small dagger in the other, Orrin waited next to Daniel.

The guards and Jude were three hundred yards away and waving when the Sproits burst from the forest.

Closer to fifty. Orrin counted as they ran toward the fighting.

The guard nearest the forest went down under a mountain of yellow flesh, and blood sprayed into the air as his screams were cut short.

"Ride and pass formation!" Jude yelled. The men turned their horses and rode toward the Wall. Another guard went down when a Sproit launched itself at the horse's flank. The Sproit was crushed, but as the mount fell, the man's leg caught under the horse.

"He's going to die." Daniel ran and pointed at the pinned guard. The eight remaining guards, including Jude, passed them, running away.

Daniel charged ahead. His sword swung out with phantom double strikes and reached out twice as far to strike with his new skill. Orrin had already increased his stats and kept his own [Camouflage] up. Three Sproits went down in rapid succession.

Orrin picked up the spear the downed man had dropped and used it as a wedge to lift the horse. The armored fighter used his arms to drag himself from under the horse. His leg was crushed.

"Shit, shit, shit." Orrin let the horse drop and healed the man rapidly, throwing a [Calm Mind] on him for good measure.

Daniel yelled at the Sproits around him, trying to gain their attention. *Some new skill?* Orrin guessed.

Every Sproit turned to charge his friend. Daniel locked eyes with Orrin.

No. "NO!" Orrin stood up and started to run just as over forty Sproits dashed as one at Daniel.

Orrin was knocked to the side from behind. He rolled twice and tried to stand. He wobbled and found himself in the dirt again. A quick heal and he stood.

The eight guards hadn't run away. They'd retreated to use cavalry tactics, he realized. Broken bodies of Sproits littered the ground: stabbed, slashed, and crushed beneath the horses' hooves. Some guards had fallen. Orrin counted five down. Jude was standing near Daniel, waving his hammer around like a twig.

Daniel was on his knee, breathing hard.

Orrin picked up the spear he'd left behind and started jogging toward them. He found two Sproits crawling away, wounded but not dead. He stabbed each in the back.

Experience Gained: 40 XP (20 XP x 2)

Nobody in his party of two had damaged these. He got full experience credit. Orrin momentarily felt bad for stealing experience.

Level 4 Obtained!

+10 AP

He stopped to heal one of the fallen guards, pulling the man to his feet. Three guard bodies were too far away and unmoving. The last was in two pieces.

Just as they reached Daniel and Jude, the remaining two guards brought their horses to a stop.

One pointed a long polearm at the forest. "Sir DeGuis, the Goblin is coming out."

"There's two," Daniel gasped out. He had furrows of blood across his chest. Orrin started cycling and healing.

"Orrin, boost them all. Everything. The other one is hanging back up there." Daniel pointed.

Orrin didn't hesitate. He poured three full mana pools through to give all six of them a full set of his best spells.

"What the hell?" The guard he'd healed was holding a mace and looking down at his hands. "Boss, I just—"

"I know," Jude cut in. "Guess you were holding back earlier, huh?"

Orrin grimaced.

"Stay back, Orrin." Daniel pushed himself to his feet. "If anyone falls, try to drag them back. Orrin can heal."

"He just spent how much mana and he can still heal?" the only remaining woman asked incredulously. She had no weapon and wore the robes of a mage. She dismounted and started walking forward with the fighters. The horses ran back to the Wall as soon as their reins were released.

Orrin looked at the list of spells and skills he'd been coveting.

> [Ward] (Class Unique)—Create a ward around yourself or a target to protect against attacks. Protects for MP maximum. 20 MP. -5 AP
> [Lightstrike] casts an unerring beam of light that hits a target for 1 HP damage. 10 MP. -1 AP
> [Inverse] (Spell Modifier) modify a spell to do its opposite. 5 MP. -4 AP

Would you like to buy these spells for 10 AP?
Yes or No?

Yes!

He had explained his plans earlier with Daniel, but Daniel didn't know he'd leveled. *I wonder if he gained some levels from all those Sproits he took out?* The thought ran through his head, and he jogged to catch up with his friend. He cast [Ward] on himself.

"What are you doin—" Daniel stopped talking as a shimmer of air coalesced around him. "You did it!"

"Should give you an extra 130 HP if it works like it says." Orrin was about to cast it again on the rest of the group when the Goblin stepped out of the forest.

Standing over ten feet tall, with skin the color of faded grass, the Goblin held a long sapling in one hand with a large rock tied to the end. A homemade mace. It roared a deep growl that pushed back the long reeds around the six of them.

"Stand ready, men," Jude commanded.

"And women." The mage put her hands over her head and started summoning a tiny globe of water.

"And women." Jude smiled and swung his hammer through the air.

The Goblin looked out at the dead Sproits and pushed a tree out of his way. The two-story-tall oak bent and snapped with a loud crack. It stepped out and ran at them.

"Let Lethe trip it, then bring the pain." Jude stood still.

Lethe, the mage, grew the small ball of water larger. The Goblin was running hard across the football field that separated them. Three steps and it already had closed the distance.

"Anytime, Lethe." Jude sounded worried.

With a grunt, the spell exploded. From the small globe over her head, water and cold air gusted. In an instant, the ground in front of them turned into a large ice rink. She had covered the ground in a few inches of slick ice.

Badass spell. Orrin watched as the Goblin stepped and went down hard. It slid forty yards and let out another roar.

The second Goblin stepped out from the forest. Nearly identical to the first, it held a gnarled staff in its hand.

"Mage Goblin!" Lethe shouted as it pointed its staff at the group. The grass around them twisted into the air, growing thick. It waved against the wind for a long second and then shot out at the guards.

Orrin felt dozens of sharp roots grab at his legs. They pierced his boots, and he felt . . . nothing.

[Ward—60/130]

It worked just like he thought it would. *I've got mage armor.*

Orrin tried his other spell, [Lightstrike].

A light beam flashed from his pointed hand and hit the Goblin mage in the face. It blinked hard and roared.

"Free the guards." Daniel stepped around the guards who were clawing at their feet. Blood seeped through all of their boots. He dashed around the icy ground and charged the Goblin.

Orrin stuck the spear he still held in the ground and started hacking away at the vines with his dagger, healing as he went. Two of the guards took off with Daniel. Lethe and Jude cautiously walked on the ice.

The fallen Goblin's leg had snapped when it went down. It was trying to crawl toward them.

Jude tried to hit it with his hammer, but it dodged and rolled.

"Let me try something," Orrin said as they backed up, keeping out of its reach.

He tried casting [Inverse] through [Increase Dexterity] and targeted the Goblin.

It slowed noticeably.

He did it four more times. "Now hit it hard."

"I've always wondered what this would be like at a higher level," Jude muttered.

He held his hammer above his head. A blue-white light filled the air behind the hammer, and Jude spun the metal around twice before jumping and swinging it straight down on the Goblin's back.

The Goblin exploded.

Jude's hammer had splattered its back, but the shock waves had continued to throw damage down all its extremities. All that was left was a head and bloody meat in the shape of a ten-foot-tall body.

"Bloody hell, sir." Lethe paled.

Jude was stunned, too. "That wa—I . . ."

"Later." Orrin grabbed and pulled the knight. "There's another."

They were too late. Daniel and the two guards had worn the Goblin down. The polearm guard had circled and poked, keeping its attention, while Daniel and the other guard struck over and over. Daniel used a final [Power Strike], and it went down.

Experience Gained: 200 XP

Yes! [Lightstrike] works for experience damage! He had a ranged attack spell.

The group pulled back to the Wall to recoup. Orrin was generous with his healing.

"Seriously." Lethe approached him. "How? I cast two spells and I'm wiped."

"My class," Orrin lied. "Special skill resets my MP, but I'll pay for it later."

He'd made up the falsehood a few days ago. It would let him keep some sort of buffer from people finding out about [Blood Mana], even if asking about class specifics was taboo.

Lethe frowned. "Lucky. Wish I had something like that, but I love my [Freeze Zone], so . . ."

Orrin asked questions about the spell and let Lethe brag.

"That's enough, Lethe." Jude interrupted her explanation of the range and depth she could pull off. "I think it's time we cleaned up and got these men back home."

Lethe mumbled something as she and the other guards went back to retrieve the fallen.

"I'll let you two take horses back," Jude offered. "Just give them to the guards at the gate." He looked at the carnage. "You both did good today."

As he walked away, Daniel clapped Orrin's shoulder.

"Do you know how to ride a horse?"

"Nope." Orrin looked at the huge warhorses behind them. "Do you?"

"Of course not."

Chapter 11

After returning the horses and selling the three dozen arrows they'd collected, Orrin and Daniel headed back to the Guild.

Daniel tossed a silver coin to the doorman, and they entered the dining hall.

Together, they stood in line to get dinner. Slabs of a dark-red meat, a leafy vegetable cooked to a crispy exterior, and more honeyed bread. Orrin took two pieces.

"Should we try and find a Quest for those Sproits?" Daniel looked at the Quest board longingly. He really wanted to start taking on Quests.

"I'm pretty sure we would have needed to cut off their ears or something." Orrin shrugged as he dipped a ladle into a tub of gravy for his meat. "How else would they know how many we took out?"

Daniel sighed and piled his plate with three slices of the bone-in meat.

Dinner was good. People around sat in clusters of five or fewer and rarely even looked at them. The atmosphere was loud, and they ate quickly. They took a quick bath and returned to their room for the night.

Orrin pulled up his status.

Orrin
Utility Warder
Level 4 (200/400)
AP: 0

HP: 90
MP: 130

Strength: 9
Constitution: 9
Dexterity: 9
Will: 13
Intelligence: 11

Abilities:
[Mind Bastion]
[Dimension Hole]
[Identify]
[Blood Mana]
[Meditate]
[Side Steps] (82/100)

Spells:
[Increase Dexterity] (5,000/5,000)
[Increase Strength] (5,000/5,000)
[Increase Will] (1,000/1,000)
[Increase Intelligence] (1,000/1,000)
[Camouflage] (6,320/10,000)
[Heal Small Wounds] (5,000/5,000)
[Lightstrike]
[Ward]
[Inverse]
[Calm Mind]

Orrin pulled up the store, with his growing list of potential future purchases:

Spells:
[Teleport] teleport to any known point within 10

miles. 50 MP per person (0/5,000) (5 AP)

Abilities
[Map]: See the world around you (4 AP)
[Mana Pool]: increase MP by 100 MP (onetime purchase) (10 AP)

Skills:
[Merge] combine spells/abilities for new effects.
Caution: may lose original Spell/Ability (20 AP)

A blinking icon caught his attention.

Unlocked: New Wards

After finding [Ward] with its (Class Unique) mark, Orrin had tried every search he could think of for additional unique spells or abilities. He'd found nothing.

Did buying [Ward] unlock these? Orrin's eyes widened as he read.

"Daniel, you've got to see this." Orrin shook Daniel awake and threw a blue box at him.

Wards—(Class Unique)
[Camouflage Ward] create a ward around yourself and your party within 50 feet that mimics [Camouflage] 50 MP. -5 AP
[Mind Ward] create a ward around yourself and your party within 50 feet that mimics [Calm Mind] 20 MP. -2 AP
[Light Ward] create a ward around yourself and your party within 50 feet that protects against Light magic for MP maximum. 20 MP. -1 AP
[Heal Ward] create a ward around a target that negates all healing for MP Maximum. 10 MP. -1 AP

> **[Utility Ward] maximum possible Level 1 Strength, Dexterity, Will, and Intelligence Increase to yourself and your party within 50 feet. 100 MP. -5 AP**

"Holy . . ." Daniel trailed off as he read. "These are all linked with your—"

"With my spells," Orrin finished. "Every time I buy a spell, I think I get a new [Ward]."

"Do you think [Utility Ward] casts just one time or all five stacked?"

"I'm guessing stacked, which should be plus five for each stat at level one." Orrin ran his hand through his hair. "Once I unlock all four at level two, I'm guessing it'll be up to plus twenty."

"Yeah, I've been meaning to ask," Daniel started. "You told me that level two was only a plus two, but I've been getting plus twenty for strength and dexterity."

"I noticed that, too," Orrin explained. "It's the increase to my will."

Daniel's eyes glazed over. "You're going to explain more math to me, aren't you?"

"I don't have level two will or intelligence increase yet, so I can only increase my will to eighteen and my intelligence to sixteen," Orrin started. "I told you the math already, but in short, that plus-two strength increase gets multiplied by 1.8. So, at 3.6 for each strength increase—and I'm assuming it's just rounding up to four, so let's call it four—I'm increasing strength and dexterity by twenty."

"That's going to get more insane when you get level two will, huh?" Daniel asked.

Orrin smiled evilly. "You'll probably be able to pick up that sword you like so much but probably not swing it yet. A plus ten to will gives me a 2.3 modifier, so I can buff your strength up twenty-five points."

They sat in silence, thinking.

"You know," Daniel started. "Almost none of your spells show up in my store list."

Orrin shrugged.

"It's just weird, don't you think?" Daniel continued. "I'm supposed to be a [Hero], and I don't have anything that will turn my entire party invisible."

"Not invisible. At least not yet." Orrin smiled. "I'm hoping that's what I unlock at the next level, though. And of course you have something that turns your entire party invisible—I'm in your party."

It was Daniel's turn to shrug. "So, if will is increasing all of your spells so much, are you going to focus your level-ten stat points on will?"

They had finally finished reading through the books they'd gotten. Only the *Leveler's Guide* had mentioned stat points, and even that was only a few sentences.

Every ten levels, an adventurer gains a number SP, or stat points, to allocate at their whim. While magic users usually focus on their Will or Intelligence and warriors focus on Strength or Dexterity, Constitution is also a worthwhile choice.

Completely unhelpful, Orrin had thought when he read it. But no other book even talked about SP.

"I think so." Orrin drew out his words. "I haven't nailed down the intelligence math yet, but I know it decreased my MP costs. Either way, I am leaning toward will."

"Good. I'm putting mine into strength." Daniel squeezed his hand shut. "I want my sword."

Orrin shook his head. "How many levels did you get today, anyways? I know you took out a few Sproits on your own."

Daniel puffed up. "I'm at level five. That Goblin took me right over the line."

Orrin smiled and congratulated him but felt a bit down that Daniel had overtaken him in just one outing.

"Should we try a Quest tomorrow?" Daniel turned on his bed to face Orrin fully.

"I think so." Orrin cast [Camouflage] on himself. *Might as well keep trying for the next level.*

"I hate it when you do that." Daniel turned on his back and stared at the ceiling. "You get all fuzzy, and it hurts my eyes to look at you."

"Don't you have anything you can passively level?"

"Not like you," Daniel muttered. "You realize it's going to take me months to level up my few mana-using skills. Whenever I get too low, I feel like I'm getting a migraine."

"I know," Orrin said, slapping his forearm and breaking the spell. "I wish I could help, but I still haven't even figured out why I passed out that one time."

He recast [Camouflage] again.

"Maybe because you didn't sleep?" Daniel suggested.

"I think it has to be more than that." Orrin slapped himself again and recast. "I do sometimes feel groggy after a bunch of spell casting, but I haven't fainted again."

"Maybe you're just getting better at controlling the side effects?"

Silence drifted between them.

"Tomorrow we get some quests, maybe some extermination quests around the outside of Dey," Orrin decided.

Daniel was already snoring.

The next morning, after a quick breakfast, they stood in front of the quest board.

The board was really just the back wall. Although some sort of order was attempted, others were ripping quest sheets off, looking at them, and tacking them back on haphazardly.

The left side was supposed to be for extermination quests, with lower-level quests near the bottom and higher-level ones reaching up to nine feet from the floor. About a quarter of the way down, the quests started changing to collection quests—"find this herb" or "bring me the skin of this beast."

From the halfway point to the end, the quests were more random. "Find my lost son." "Guard my caravan." Daniel chuckled and pointed at one that sought "companionship for aged widow."

Orrin was squatting near the floor and trying to link extermination and collection quests. "I think these look okay. This one is from a farmer who needs help with the large rats attacking his crops." He held one sheet and then waved a second. "This one is from an apothecary looking for bags of large rat teeth."

"I'm not hunting ROUSes for silver," Daniel said as he crossed his arms over his chest.

"Damn it, Daniel. What else would you like to do? We aren't high enough level to try most of these."

"Here." Daniel jabbed a finger at a page at chest height. "Some old cave needs clearing out, pays ten gold."

Orrin squinted at the cramped writing of the advert. "It doesn't say what's infesting the cave. And it's marked four stars."

Daniel shrugged. "It's on the way to your rats. We could check it out, at least."

Daniel brought the three quest sheets to the front receptionist. A different man than last time took the sheets and scribbled their names down in a book before tossing the quests on a big pile of papers.

"What happens if we decide we can't finish a quest?" Daniel asked.

The man sighed and pushed his long hair back. "Newbies. The quests you just handed me will be back on the wall in twenty minutes. If you come back with a letter from the quest giver saying you did it, we'll pull the quest and you get paid. If you give up and don't tell me or another to mark it out, nothing happens. You do it too much and maybe you get reported, but you'd have to be an asshole yanking down multiple quests a day to get that. You die, someone else will finish the quest. Taking on a four star with just the two of you?"

Daniel nodded.

He went back to scribbling notes in his ledger. "Hope you have a bigger party than just you two."

The farmer, Toby, was located about four miles outside the northernmost eastern gate. The cave was in some foothills about two miles north of that. The quest sheet had mentioned bringing ears of the beasts.

With Orrin's buffs, they made the four-mile hike in only an hour. *I love magic.* Orrin looked back at all the forced outdoor running from high school with dread, but with his increased dexterity, they both jogged faster than he could have ever run before.

Toby was a midforties man wearing a wide-brimmed hat. His farm grew cabbage and was easy enough to find. Toby himself was trying to get a yoke back over a mule in the middle of a field.

"Are you Toby?" Daniel yelled over the fence.

"You two here for the rats?" The man waved them over and tossed the curved harness on the ground.

They climbed over the wood logs and tried to not step on any of the green heads growing.

"I'm Daniel, and this is Orrin." Daniel held out his hand. Toby shook it and then gestured to the yoke.

Daniel smiled and picked it up. Although he had no idea what he was doing, Toby held the mule and directed his motions. Soon enough, the mule was strapped in.

"Thanks, boys." Toby slapped the mule's backside, and it started off, dragging some contraption behind it. "She's a good one but hates working days."

"What is that thing?" Daniel pointed at the spade-like device with a basket over it.

"Well, I got to get the ground tilled, but I don't like wasting my time going back over to fertilize and seed. So I set it all up in one." Toby looked proud of his invention.

"That works?" Orrin asked.

"With a few skills I've picked up, it does." Toby smirked. "All right, this way. She knows the lines and can do the rest herself."

"The mule?"

Toby smiled and nodded, walking off toward the farmhouse in the distance. When Orrin looked back, the mule was plowing straight lines down a well-beaten path. *Magic fuckery,* he decided.

"So, they've been coming out at night mostly to get the stores, but I caught one in a trap. Usually, I get a group of five come out. Just you two? That's fine, I guess—just be careful." Toby did not stop talking as they walked.

"So, with the last group I hired, I just let one loose and they followed it back to the nest. That was about a year ago, but they always come back. Nothing you can really do about it, I guess, but, well, you know that, being adventurers. Ahh, there it is."

Around the side of the house was a giant mousetrap—a sheet of hammered-together two-by-fours with a spring and a bent piece of metal. Stakes had been driven into the ground to hold it tight, but they looked as if they could give way at any moment.

Half crushed under the thick pipe was a Labrador-size rat, thrashing.

"It's been here a day or so—it'll be hungry. Good luck." Toby turned and left without further directions.

"What the hell! That's huge," Daniel muttered as he drew his sword. The rat started shrieking and digging its feet into the wood. Long scratches marred the entire trap.

Orrin tried [Identify].

[Rat, dire] HP 12/40 status: restrained/starved

Damn, he'd been hoping for more information from [Identify]. *I need to start using it more on enemies, too.*

Orrin pulled out the bestiaries and found the relevant section.

Dire Rats are vermin grown large. A bite should be treated quickly with healing magic or disinfectant, as their saliva is a mild poison. They travel in large groups with a single Brood Mother hidden nearby. Quick opportunistic attackers, Dire Rats are fearful and will run when attacked themselves. One Star (*) See Brood Mother (**)

Orrin flipped back to read the Brood Mother section, which was mostly the same but with a detailed drawing.

"Daniel, these things build trapdoors in the ground to hide the Brood Mother in," Orrin recited. "It'll look just like the grass around it, but a small piece of wood or other latch should be visible. See?"

Daniel was looking at the rat. "Should we just kill it? I don't really want to go running after it."

"Concentrate." Orrin snapped his fingers. Daniel glared at him. "We need to be prepared."

"Fine." Daniel looked at the book and nodded. "Let's find the entire brood."

He grabbed a piece of wood and leveraged it on the metal trap.

"Get ready to run." Daniel smiled and pulled.

Chapter 12

Even with his increased dexterity, Orrin was having a hard time keeping up with Daniel and the released rat. It darted away from the boys and headed farther east.

I guess increasing my dex doesn't help if I'm not in good shape to begin with, Orrin thought as he ran with all his might.

"You need to start doing more cardio," Daniel said without a hitch in his voice. He was running just as hard as Orrin, but he'd been playing soccer, football, and basketball for years.

"I—don't plan—on—needing to run—that often," Orrin got out between deep breaths.

To Orrin, they sprinted for five days. In reality, it was only ten minutes. They reached the top of a small hill and saw the rat in the distance slowing. Small holes dotted the countryside.

"That's a lot of dens." Daniel smiled. "How do you want to do this?"

"I was thinking of hitting each one with [Lightstrike], then keep [Camouflage] up while healing you," Orrin suggested. "If they are too quick, I can try inversing their dexterity to slow them down, too."

Daniel cracked his knuckles and pulled his sword out. "I'm going to wait for them to get all around me then try out [Whirlwind]."

Orrin nodded. Daniel had finally started spending all those saved-up ability points.

Daniel waited while Orrin cast [Ward] and all the increase spells. Orrin cycled back to full health and nodded. "Let's do it."

As they came down the hill, a black nose wiggled out of a nearby hole. A rat crawled out with a scramble of dirt falling back. It hissed and ran at them.

Orrin hit it right in the face with a [Lightstrike]. The rat fell over its own feet but was back up and running in seconds.

Daniel took two steps and surged forward. His sword swung with multiple afterimages.

The rat shrieked as dozens of cuts appeared. Another few attacks, and Daniel took it down. No healing needed.

Experience Gained: 30 XP

"That wasn't too bad." Daniel took a hard swing at the rat's head, decapitating it, before wiping the blood off on the rat's fur.

"I think a few at a time shouldn't be too hard," Orrin agreed. "Let's try to lure five or six at a time."

Orrin took out his trusty knife and tried digging the teeth out of the head.

"We should have gotten some pliers," he complained.

"Just toss the heads in a pile and we'll get to it later." Daniel was eyeing the nearest dens.

Fighting more than one rat at a time turned out to be harder than they'd thought. Daniel used his yelling skill [Pull Attention] to grab aggro, and four rats left two of the holes to attack.

Orrin hit each one once, then had to slow two of them down with an [Inverse] and [Increase Dexterity] spell. Daniel fought up the hill as the two quicker rats nipped at his heels. After one fell, Daniel charged back down the hill at the two still crawling toward him.

Experience Gained: 120 XP

"I think four at a time is our max right now." Orrin cycled his mana back up as he tossed more rat heads in the growing pile. He rubbed his temples.

"You all right?" Daniel dropped the last head.

"Just a headache." Orrin pointed. "I think if we approach from there, we can pull two or three. Both of the dens these came from were bigger. Bigger holes means more rats inside."

Over the next few hours, Daniel and Orrin perfected their strategy. Orrin would slow the rats as Daniel cut up the rats one at a time.

Experience Gained: 90 XP

Level 5 Obtained!
+10 AP

Experience Gained: 120 XP

Experience Gained: 120 XP

Experience Gained: 90 XP

They only pulled more than four one time, when Daniel stepped too close to a third den. Six rats harried Daniel and surrounded him before Orrin could slow more than two of them.

"Hit them with [Lightstrike] quick," Daniel yelled. He counted off the hits and then activated his skill.

Orrin stood twenty yards away and was still thrown to the ground by the blast of wind that centered from Daniel.

All six rats were shredded meat and gore.

"Daniel, are you all right?" Orrin ran through the matted fur spread around a squatting Daniel.

"Yeah," Daniel whispered. "That tanked my mana. Headache." He spoke in halting words.

Orrin cast [Heal Small Wounds] and [Calm Mind] on Daniel, who shivered and rolled his shoulders.

"That helps, but I'm going to need a break."

"I'll collect the heads. Go sit down." Orrin pulled a waterskin out of his [Dimension Hole] and handed it to Daniel.

Experience Gained: 180 XP

Level 6 Obtained!
+10 AP

Orrin pulled a sword out of storage and started hacking. When he pulled the last head over, Daniel was lying in the grass with his eyes closed.

"This is easier experience than going outside the Wall. I already hit level six."

Daniel grunted.

"Still feeling it?"

Daniel turned over and put his hand over his eyes.

"You should buy [Meditate]."

"Can't," Daniel mumbled. "Not on my list."

Orrin shrugged and then realized Daniel couldn't see him. He did a search for "mana" in the store.

[Mana Pool] increase MP by 100 MP (onetime purchase) (10 AP)

He tried "healing mana," "increase MP," and "cure," but nothing new appeared.

I could level up [Increase Will] but since he used up all his MP, would it give him anything?

Would you like to Upgrade [Increase Will] (1,000/1,000) for 2 AP?
Yes or No?

Yes.

[Increase Will] Level 2 (0/5,000): increase target
Will by +2 for 10 minutes. 10 MP

Orrin paused for a second and then upgraded intelligence as well.

He cast both on Daniel and watched his shoulders slump in relief.

"Thanks," Daniel whispered as he rubbed his eyes. "Zeroing out my MP was a mistake."

Orrin cycled his mana and then cast intelligence and will level two on himself. *My will increase should be the plus two times 1.3, giving me plus three for each cast.*

His will went up to twenty-eight, increasing his mana pool as well. He'd used one hundred MP casting the spells. He went from 30/130 to 180/280.

His intelligence was up to twenty-six. He cycled his mana and cast a ten-MP heal on himself. It cost eight MP.

So, my intelligence decreases the costs of my spells. Base cost of spell times ((100-(intelligence-10))/100) equals actual spell cost.

My will increases the efficacy of my spells. Base damage times (will/10) equals actual output.

He recast the rest of his buff spells on Daniel and himself. *But I get full base cost credit for leveling a spell,* he thought as he watched the counter roll over. *Too bad I can't get the increases to use the increased number as the base when I recast. That would just let me recast up to infinity, though.*

Daniel was still sipping water and blinking against the sunlight.

I've still got sixteen AP points. I'll save them for now and strategize with Daniel tonight.

"Do you want to keep going?" he asked. "We can always come back tomorrow."

Daniel wobbled to his feet and nodded.

Toby looked on in shock as they dumped twenty-five rat heads at his feet.

"You two were gone so long, I thought you'd died." He kicked a head to the side as he counted. "This would be amazing for a full party. How'd you do it?"

"Hit them with a sword until they stopped moving," Daniel grumbled. He was angry that they'd left so early. The sun was still sitting high.

"We strategized," Orrin offered.

Toby tallied out the money and gave them twenty silver. "Sorry, that's all I'd set aside for this. But I can give you some cabbage for your trouble, too?"

Orrin declined politely, and they left for Dey.

"We can always come back tomorrow after you've rested." Orrin tried to comfort Daniel.

"First thing in the morning." Daniel's eyes burned as he stared ahead.

Daniel sulked when they got back to the Guild and went to their room without a word.

Orrin went out and turned in the apothecary quest. The woman behind the counter had actually thanked him for not trying to pull the teeth out himself.

"The best part of the tooth is in the skull, and most of you adventurers just snap the sharp part off."

He'd collected the money and returned to their room. Daniel was fast asleep. Orrin had wanted to talk AP purchases but knew when his friend was sulking.

We'll get more AP tomorrow anyways, he justified as he started buying.

Would you like to buy [Utility Ward Level 1] for 5 AP?
Yes or No?

Yes.

Would you like to buy [Map] for 4 AP?
Yes or No?

I'm tired of not knowing where we are going and relying on Daniel, so YES.

As he reached to buy more, another ! icon appeared.

Unlocked: Map Upgrades
[Party View] see your party on your map. Allows you to cast line of sight spells from a distance. 1 AP
[Monster View] see monsters within a distance on your map. Can be negated by certain spells. 1 AP
[Trap View] see traps and hidden items within a distance on your map. 1 AP
[Zoom] see more of the world around you. 1 AP

Unlocked: New Ward
[Utility Ward Level 2] maximum possible Level 2 Strength, Dexterity, Will, and Intelligence Increase on yourself and your party within 100 feet. 200 MP. -10 AP

Orrin had planned on buying [Teleport]. Walking all day was definitely not his thing. But the map upgrades would make scouting the rat nests easier. Not to mention [Trap View]. *I wonder if it picks up treasure, too.*

He bought all four, leaving him with three AP. *I'll save those for now.*

He pulled up his [Map]. A dot next to him showed Daniel. No monsters showed up around him. He did see a few tiny dots under the bar next door. *Probably dropped money.* He tried playing with the zoom feature and was able to get about a mile around him in view.

He smirked and played with the map until he fell asleep.

~~~~~~~~~~~~~~~~~~~~~~~~

"AHH," Daniel screamed as he hacked at the rat in front of him.

"D! It's dead." Orrin stood off to the side.

After Daniel had woken him before the sun rose, they'd headed right back for the rat dens. Orrin was barely able to keep up. When he'd told Daniel about the [Map] upgrades, Daniel had stopped talking with him.

Experience Gained: 600 XP (20 x 30 XP).

Level 7 Obtained!
+10 AP

Daniel lowered his sword and stood breathing hard.

"I need to get more AP," he muttered.

"Daniel, what is the deal, man?" Orrin took a step toward him.

Daniel's sword rose up again, pointing to Orrin.

"You don't get it, do you?" Daniel roared. "You can just go and go and go, but I'm so tired and have to keep up. I have to get more AP. I have to protect us. Do you realize how many people must already want us dead? I mean, we were almost murdered the other night, for god's sake."

Daniel crossed the distance in an instant, pushing into Orrin's face.

"We've been here a week, and every day is just more killing," he was crying. "I killed people. Human beings."

He wiped his tears angrily. "And on top of it all, I'm expected to kill a Demon Lord. Do you know why I save my AP, Orrin? Look."

He pulled up his status screen and shared a blue box.

[Demon Seal] (Hero Specific)—Seal the Demon
Lord. Only usable one time. The Demon Lord
must be at low health when used. 300 AP

"That's thirty levels of ability points, and it didn't unlock until I hit level five," he was screaming now.

"How many points are you at?" Orrin breathed.

"NOT ENOUGH." Daniel turned and threw his sword like a javelin. It struck a rat and buried into the ground.

Orrin stepped forward. "Daniel, we'll figure it out. We'll find more good farming areas like this and—"

"You don't get it." Daniel spun back around. "You are not the [Hero]. I am. You don't have to deal with the pressure. You never have."

"What does that mean?" Orrin shook in rage. "I'm here with you. I've had to kill people, too. I'm keeping you healed and buffed."

"Because you still think it's all a game. Just like back home. You follow me around and I do all the work while you sit back and relax. And still everyone rewards you for just trying, while I'm expected to be better, to be perfect."

"I'm sorry my friendship stresses you out so much," Orrin shot back. "I'm sorry you feel that pressure, but that's not my fault."

"Nothing is your fault. Nothing is ever your fault," Daniel yelled. "You are the reason I'm here! You got in my way and that truck hit me. You are the reason I have to do so much, get such good grades, and play soccer and football. Otherwise, my parents would pay no attention to me because they have to take care of the abandoned kid next door!"

Orrin stood quietly as Daniel continued.

"You eat my food, you creep on my sister, you follow me around like a puppy. Then you land me in another world and somehow, you continue to try and butt into my life! Why do you always think you know what is going on or what to do? We are seventeen years old! We aren't some heroes from one of your stories. You aren't some mastermind. We should have gone to Silas and gotten his support right away."

"I'm not the hero here." Orrin kept his voice tight. "You're right. If you think I'm holding you back, go ahead. But don't come begging for my help when they use you in political games or just try to kill you. We've learned enough that I thought you wouldn't be this STUPID." Orrin's voice broke as he screamed back.

"I'm sorry I thought you were my friend. I didn't realize I was such a hassle to deal with. But don't blame me for your choices. Don't blame me for trying to save you."

"TRYING AND FAILING," Daniel shot back. "That's all you do. You just get lucky, and people say *good job*. You got lucky with your class and expect me to say *thank you* every time you heal me? Do you not see how slow we are going? You are slowing me down. I should be in a full party, running dungeons and getting more experience. Instead, we have to hide out here because you have a weird and illegal class."

"Just one skill and I don't—"

"You can justify all you want, but you still aren't listening," Daniel cut in. "You don't get tired or run out of MP. That's weird. But worse—" Daniel picked his sword up out of the rat and wiped it clean. "You don't even seem to care that we've been killing people, Orrin. I've been crying myself to sleep each night. I've barely been sleeping at all."

He looked up, and Orrin finally saw Daniel's haunted eyes. The sallow look of his skin and how dirty his hair had become. "You've been sleeping fine. You move to the next thing and don't care at all. You scare me."

Orrin didn't respond.

"Nothing to say?"

"I've heard you break up with your girlfriends," Orrin retorted. "I know how this ends. You are kicking me out of your party, huh?"

"You don't see what I'm talk—"

"See you around, *friend*." Orrin spat the last word. He pulled up his store, purchased [Teleport], and disappeared.

Chapter 13

Orrin stumbled as he appeared on the road outside Dey. A few people glanced his way, but he'd learned that teleportation magic wasn't too rare.

Your Party Has Been Disbanded.

He stormed up to the line of people waiting to get through the gate.

That idiot.

The guard was checking a cart full of goats, moving them side to side as he hunted for something.

He doesn't think about consequences. He just wants to play hero.

The guard said something to the cart driver and went back to moving the goats around.

He thinks I'm not affected by killing that guy? I've— The line moved up as Orrin realized he hadn't really thought about it. *I had a nightmare that night, right?*

The guard was now making an adventurer take every item out of his bag. Orrin shook his head.

Still. He was out of line. I don't butt into his life. I tried to save him from that truck; he just wasn't paying enough attention. And if he wants to go play hero, I can figure it out myself.

Orrin stood in front of the guard.

"Business?"

"I live here," Orrin grunted.

"Reason for leaving?"

"I was hunting Dire Rats for a quest."

The guard looked Orrin over and chuckled, "All on your own?"

Orrin felt himself draw [Blood Mana] in a new way. The sun was still out in force, yet his vision felt dark. A smile crept across his face as the guard stepped back.

"All on my own." He reached out toward the guard.

"Hurry up." The man behind Orrin jostled him. His vision cleared.

The guard was staring wide-eyed at Orrin. Orrin blinked hard and dashed through the gate. Nobody stopped him.

Orrin ran all the way to the Guild, tossed his coins for a single room on the counter, and slammed the door shut behind him

What was that?

He stared at himself in the small mirror over a sink. His eyes looked normal, and the shadows he had felt earlier were gone.

I just need some sleep.

Orrin left his room the next morning and went back to Books, Books, Books! He'd spent so much time in and out of the different book-stores around Dey, the clerk recognized him instantly.

"Orrin! Welcome back. How did Daniel like that book on sword classes?"

"Hey, Rick." Orrin ignored the question. "I need to see all the books you have on [Vampires]."

Rick kept a professional face at the request, but Orrin noted the eye twitch. "You've already bought our bestiaries."

"I need more. I need to know about the weirder skills."

Rick's eye twitched again. "I'm not sure—"

Orrin took out twenty gold and put it on the counter. He'd learned quickly that Rick got a commission on every book sold.

"That's for the first book." Orrin pulled a handful out. "I'm going to leave with my arms full today."

Rick left the counter and closed the door. He flipped the Open sign to Closed.

"Follow me."

Books, Books, Books! was two stories, but Orrin had only been in the lower level. Rick took the rope off the stairs and beckoned Orrin up.

"What you're looking for isn't strictly illegal, but people can try to piece together requirements for those skills," Rick explained. "So we keep the rare ones up here."

"I also want anything you have on mind skills."

Rick stopped. "We have nothing like that, sir."

"Rick, I can pay—"

"Orrin, most mind skills are illegal. We don't keep books like that."

Orrin kept his mouth shut. Getting in trouble was the last thing he wanted.

Rick pulled down two books from the shelves, *Vampiric Data* and *Stake the Heart*.

"These normally cost about fifteen gold apiece . . ." Rick trailed off.

Orrin handed him another fifteen gold. "The extra five is for you. As a tip."

He turned to leave.

"Wait. Um. Listen." Rick got in front of Orrin. "I don't know what's going on, but you look serious. Well, more serious than usual. And I don't see Daniel, so . . ."

Orrin let the pause linger, giving him nothing.

"So—anyways. I know a guy. Well, I know of him. He's an expert on mind magics and keeps to himself, mostly, but we deliver a few books to him on occasion if we come across them.

"I'll get you his address." Rick turned back to his desk and scribbled something on a scrap of paper. "He might be able to help with whatever happened."

"I didn't say anything happened," Orrin muttered.

Rick smiled. "You didn't have to."

Orrin holed himself up in his room and read the books he'd spent thousands of dollars on. *Stake the Heart* was useful if only in confirming that the [Vampire] class was killable. It dealt with the ways to identify a person who had taken the class or evolved another class into [Vampire]. It didn't give specifics, but Orrin could see why the book had been restricted.

Vampiric Data was dull. It was at least a hundred years old and listed every known killed [Vampire] the author had been able to confirm. It listed different skills witnessed and read like an insane person's diary. However, one passage perked Orrin's interest.

Of all the skills used by the Vampyre fallen, the blood feast is the most universal. Each Vampyre has some ability to turn blood to mana. Survivors mention darkness creeping in from every corner, as they lose themselves in the dark eyes of the Vampyre.

That sounded suspiciously like [Blood Mana]. Had he tried to use it on that guard?

Orrin tossed the book in his [Dimension Hole] and left the Guild. He walked the streets of Dey, buying snacks when he got hungry. He weighed the pros and cons of being a [Vampire]. It seemed every person who took the class gained slightly different abilities. Increased strength and dexterity were common, as was some shadow magic. One rumored bloodsucker could turn into a giant bat.

Imagine Daniel's face if I could shape-shift. Orrin slowed to a stop.

He had walked with no direction in mind, but his feet had brought him to the address on Rick's slip of paper. A small row of townhomes lined a treed street. The buildings seemed barely twice as wide as the doors, giving the entire road a haphazard look.

Why am I even here? He turned to leave, taking one last look at the mind mage's home.

"Don't stand out there all day." The door opened a crack. "Come in and kill me. Let's get this over with."

Orrin looked around. Nobody else was nearby.

"Yes, I'm talking to you," the voice continued. "Hurry up—I'm too old to wait."

Orrin cautiously stepped up the three steps to the door and pushed in.

"Hello?"

"Don't yell." The voice came from farther back, and Orrin saw a small man move quickly from a door frame. "I'm making some tea. Two drops of honey, right?"

Orrin felt frazzled. For the first time since landing in this world, he hesitated, unsure.

"Come in or leave, but don't come back next week, because you'll be dead by then."

Orrin stepped through the door and closed it. He walked down the long hallway filled with small paintings until he entered a cluttered kitchen. A shock of white hair stood up from the hunched bathrobe pouring tea into two cups.

"Sit." The voice came again, and Orrin realized it was in his head. "Of course it's in your head. How else would I talk to you?"

The old man turned and stuck out his tongue, or at least a severed stump that had once been a tongue. He smiled merrily and put the cup of tea in front of Orrin.

"So, bad mind skill? Who sent you? Jonathan? No. Rick? That's a first. I wonder if he could feel it. It is pressing hard against you, isn't it? Headaches? Blackout spells? Murderous rage? Yes. Once. Sort of. Hmm."

"What the fuck is going on." Orrin picked up his tea and sipped. Chamomile with honey, just like his mom made him when he was sick.

"Sorry, I could feel the aura coming off you three streets away. Thought you might be coming to kill little old me. You're tucked into a skill of mine right now. Totally harmless unless I want it to be harmful, but you seem okay, so you'll be fine."

"You've hijacked my body?" *But damn, that tea is good.*

"Thank you. I grow it myself. And yes." It was a bit creepy watching the man smile into his tea as his voice appeared straight in Orrin's mind. "*Hijacked.* Interesting word. I like it. So, headaches. And what else? Depression? Anxiety? Apathy? Apathy! Strange."

Orrin sat in silence as the man rambled. He couldn't have been out of his fifties, but the wrinkles on his face attested a hard life.

"Who are you?"

The old man's eyebrows shot up. "Doesn't even know who I am? What kind of mind mage is he? Not a mind mage. Utility Warder? Never heard of it."

"Get out of my head," Orrin growled.

The man fell back out of his chair like he'd been slapped. He stood slowly with blood running down both nostrils. The merry smile was gone, and his eyes sparkled as he stood tall.

"That's some power, kid." The voice continued in the same timbre as before. "Be careful with that. I apologize for getting nosy, but you did walk through my street."

"Don't worry, I'll avoid it from now on." Orrin tried to stand and made it halfway up before he slumped back again.

"Yes. Probably for the best. Don't want the muckety-mucks to see us together or they'll cry about conspiracies, and I don't have time for that. My name is Anthony Ferandus, Tony to my friends. You can call me Anthony for now. Can I poke around a bit, or do you really want to die?"

"Why do you keep saying that?" Orrin said through gritted teeth.

"What?"

"That I'm going to die."

"Because you are. I need to look closer, but I think two or more of your skills are tearing your brain apart."

"What?"

Anthony's voice sighed in his mind. "Look, I'm the resident mind mage expert because I can use a little telepathy and root around in a sentient mind a little better than most. People with mind skill problems seem to be drawn to me. Either they try to kill me or I try to heal them."

Orrin stuttered out, "Th-that's insane."

Anthony shrugged and grabbed a tin from his cupboard. "Cookie?"

Orrin ran through his options. There was no way he could let this guy go through his mind. He'd find out where he was from and—

"Oh, it's active right now."

"What?"

"Seriously, most people with some mind magic can say more than 'what'?" Anthony complained. "You are using one of the skills right now. Or is it a spell? I can't really tell."

"I'm just thinking."

"Show me your skills." Anthony filled his cup up with more tea.

"No."

"Okay. There's the door. 'Bye."

Orrin felt the pressure release, and he stood. He started for the door and stopped.

"You're just going to let me go?"

"I told you. You'll be dead in a week. Two, tops. And if you actually aren't going to try and kill me, not my problem."

Orrin sat back down slowly.

"I've got some ground rules," he began.

"Me, too," Anthony shot back.

"No rooting around and reading my mind again. I've got secrets I'd like to keep."

"Don't do that force slap thing again and I'll stay only in the guided lanes."

"I—I don't know what I did."

Anthony sighed audibly, no mind projection. "Skills?" the voice asked.

Orrin pulled up his abilities and spells. He pulled [Blood Mana] out, as well as [Ward] and [Utility Ward]. Then he turned the box over to Anthony.

Anthony's white eyebrows climbed back into his hair. Orrin was spared the ongoing commentary. He suddenly missed it.

"Where did you get [Mind Bastion]? I've never ever heard of this."

Orrin thought of the walk-through for his favorite game. *You don't have to use the underwater materia but it makes the fight easier.* "Outside the lanes."

Anthony harrumphed. "That seems to be the problem skill. I can see it lighting up right now as you try to distract yourself. It does more than just let you control your mind. You actually are numbing yourself. Great for small use, but you're just running it nonstop, aren't you?"

"I am?" Orrin stopped thinking about different nuts and greens.

"Yes, but that alone shouldn't be enough to twist your aura up that much." Anthony tapped his finger on his chin. He looked up. "You hid something, didn't you?"

"Just class-unique spells."

"Lie. I won't pry, but if I don't have all the data, you'll be on your own."

Orrin had just met this man, and already he'd given him more information than even Daniel probably had guessed. He couldn't trust him with the knowledge of [Blood Mana].

"Shame and fear," the voice said. "No. Not reading your thoughts, just emotions. I keep my word. Unless you have a skill that you will use to harm others unprovoked, I swear by my name to keep it a secret."

"[Blood Mana]." Orrin offered the skill box.

"Oh, you sweet fool." Anthony's face fell. "No. Not a [Vampire], but . . . You've been converting your own life energy to mana, haven't you? How much mana conversion have you been doing?"

Orrin started trying to do the math and stopped. "Multiple pools a day. Training nonstop. Eleven days of that."

Anthony grimaced. "I'm going to talk. Listen carefully. I've never heard of [Blood Mana] outside of a [Vampire], and they use somebody else's blood. I'm not getting that reading off you, so your secret is safe with me. Don't reveal that to anyone else. Later, if you survive, I'll teach you how to rename your skill. It costs only one AP, and you will need that. If some guard used [Identify] on you . . . Well, you're still alive, that's all that matters.

"You should be able to only use two or three mana pools a day, with mana potions. The NORMAL way to level. Anything after that, you'll get a mana headache, maybe pass out. Idiots who keep pushing bleed from everywhere, and I do mean everywhere. At least one fool kills themselves of mana exhaustion each year.

"Your [Mind Bastion] has let you ignore the exhaustion and keep going. It also seems to make you a little dick, but that could just be your regular personality. Everything has a cost, though. [Mind Bastion] and [Blood Mana] would let you get around needing to rest after two or three pools. A good night's rest and you'd be fine. If you turned off [Mind Bastion]. This is all guesswork, but my skills make my guesses an art form."

"So what, just turn off [Mind Bastion] and stop using too much mana?"

"NO!" Anthony yelled in his mind and tried to verbalize with his missing tongue as well. "No. I mean, yes, but not yet. You've been going too hard for too long. If you don't turn it off, you'll die when your body just can't keep up with your mind. But when you turn it off, all that exhaustion is coming due."

"So, I'll sleep all night and be fine, right?"

"You'll probably be hit with migraines, rolling blackouts, and more pain than you've ever felt. You could bleed from your eyes. You'll vomit for sure. You'll sleep for a few hours and then it'll start again. If you're really lucky, you'll sleep longer. A few days, maybe? I don't know—I'm not a healer."

"I am. I could heal myself and—"

"No. Listen. Any magic during your recovery could start it all over again."

"So I need to just ride it out?"

Anthony gave a rueful smile. "Do you have someone to help? You'll need lots of fresh water and broth. Cold, wet clothes. That sort of thing."

"Yeah, Da—" Orrin stopped. "No. No one."

"Then may I welcome you to Anthony's House for the Wayward Mind Mage? Specializing in recovery and subversion of errant mind skills. Initial evaluation is on the house, but room and board is one gold a day."

"I don't have a choice, do I?"

Anthony's smile left his face. "We always have a choice." He put the cups in his small sink. "But I will see you through, if only to find out what else you are hiding from me." He smirked over his shoulder.

"Okay. How do I turn off [Mind Bastion]?"

Chapter 14

Anthony took Orrin upstairs. The thin staircase creaked, and more pictures filled the walls from floor to ceiling.

"Once you deactivate your skill, you'll probably either be in so much pain that you pass out immediately or your exhaustion will knock you out." Anthony chuckled in his mind. "Either way, you'll be dead to the world for a few hours until you wake up screaming."

"That's not reassuring," Orrin complained.

"I'll be here with some home remedies I've cooked up. You're not the first fledgling to fall into my nest, and you won't be the last."

Anthony stopped in front of a large metal door and took a key out from under his shirt. Opening the door, he stood to the side and tried to usher Orrin inside.

"This looks like a prison cell." Orrin peeked inside at the bare mattress, bucket, and barred window. "Why do you have a room like this?"

Anthony tilted his head. "You do realize I cure mind mages—or people dumb enough to get conflicting skills? That's not a safe occupation. I wasn't kidding when I asked if you were here to try and kill me."

He waved his hand at the room. "Layers of different metals keep most spells in and interested third parties out. You've got a pot to piss in and a mattress to sleep on. You don't need anything else, because it's gonna be real unpleasant for a few days."

Orrin started weighing pros and cons and felt the headache spike again.

"Fine."

Orrin entered the room, and Anthony slapped the door shut. Orrin heard the key turn. *I can always teleport out—*

"Now sit down on the mattress and pull up your status. Pull out [Mind Bastion] in a box and squeeze it. Right now, it's in charge. But you can always take control of your own skills. Show it who the boss is."

Orrin sat on the floor, avoiding the sweat-stained mattress. He pulled up his skill.

[Mind Bastion] Individual is able to control his own mind and therefore part of his body.

He gripped the box in his hand and felt something give in his mind. Orrin put more pressure on the blue cube and screamed as shards of ice pushed into his eyes from behind.

"Sounds about right." Anthony's voice in his mind sounded like a hundred rusty nails scratching the world's longest chalkboard. "Do you feel it yet?"

"Feel . . . what?" Orrin was sweating as he held on.

"Some find a switch or a lever. I've always seen skills as a dial. One poor kid had an entire door he'd open. Something that you control. Find it."

Orrin had no idea what Anthony meant, but he kept squeezing. The pain increased more with every passing second. Sweat poured down his neck.

Then the pain stopped, and Orrin felt something new. Instead of a box around his fingers, he held a game controller. An old Atari style with a single button. The stick didn't move. But somehow he knew the button was the trigger.

"Found it."

"Flip it, twist it, whatever. Try not to scream too much."

Orrin hesitated for only a second before pressing the button.

Pain.

The truck running him over had been a light feather falling on him. The attacks he'd suffered so far gentle tickles from a child.

Pain.

The stabbing in his eyes turned to hot fires. His neck hairs prickled as he flushed hot and cold. Scratches ran up and down the inside of his throat. Every beat of his heart pushed molten lead through his veins.

Pain.

Orrin screamed. He cried. Mercifully, he fainted.

Orrin woke with a scream. Anthony sat beside him, water dripping from a rag. He'd been pressing the cold water against Orrin's forehead.

"Hush. It's early morning. Don't wake my neighbors again." Anthony's voice in his head felt quieter. Not as harsh.

"Water," Orrin croaked. Anthony handed him a pitcher, and Orrin drank deeply.

"Want to try some food again?"

Orrin pulled the pitcher away from his mouth. "Again?"

"Hmm. Some block it out. That's not good. You'll try and do it again. Remember the pain, son."

Orrin frowned and then gasped as images flooded his mind. Days and nights of vomit, crying, and pain. He'd begged and screamed. Anthony had to come in to stop him punching the wall, his fists a bloody mess. Orrin cursing Anthony for using his magic to stop Orrin from healing himself. Orrin lying in Anthony's lap as he sang a soft song. The images flashed by, and Orrin felt his bile rise again.

"Enough. Please. No more."

Anthony took a bowl of broth and a slice of buttered bread from under a small sheet. "Try. You're improving. I suspect it's almost over."

"What . . . how many days . . . ?" The smell overwhelmed him, and Orrin tore the bread with his teeth. A little stale from being out for so long, it tasted better than anything he'd ever had.

"Four days. Well, five now—it's almost morning. Eat and clean up. There's a bucket of clean water and a towel. Come downstairs when you can." Anthony took his own bucket and left, leaving Orrin to devour the broth.

It took him an hour to wash his body. He felt weak, and the small towel dropped from his shaking hands a few times. He couldn't remember ever being so sweaty and smelling quite so bad. *This is Daniel after soccer practice–level stink.* He chuckled to himself.

Daniel.

Oh shit. Orrin felt tears start again. *Oh shit, oh shit, oh shit. I really fucked things up.*

With [Mind Bastion] off, all the feelings and emotions of the last ten days poured over him like a wave. Anger, fear, depression, guilt.

I killed a man.

Orrin almost threw up but swallowed hard.

[Mind Bastion] didn't let him control his mind. It blocked emotions. He'd stopped caring about his friend. He'd only acted robotically, focusing on leveling and completing tasks. No wonder Daniel had lost it on him.

I need to find him and apologize. Orrin dried quickly and noticed his clothes had been cleaned and folded in a pile.

After he dressed, he made his way downstairs. Anthony was making another pot of tea.

"Good, you made it down the stairs."

"Thank you." Orrin had stopped at the bottom step. "I think you saved my life here."

"Of course I did. Now, sit. We ain't done yet."

Orrin frowned but sat. "I feel much better. What else—"

"Don't go using that skill." Anthony's voice cut him off. He slammed a cup down in front of Orrin. "You feel better now, but you could build up again from overuse. Skills are a muscle you have to exercise. You tried lifting a wagon with a baby's left toe."

Orrin looked down at the cup of tea in shame. "Yeah, I know now."

"You don't." Anthony sipped his tea while yelling in his head. "I've never seen a skill detox that bad. I was worried you were gonna die, kid. Promise me—don't use it for another week at least, a month if you can do it. When you do, don't you dare push more than one or two extra mana pools a day. You have to build your tolerance up slow."

"And I'll keep my word. Not a word about your other skill. But if I hear so much as a whisper that you use it on a person . . ." The room seemed to darken, and Anthony's face filled Orrin's vision. "I will find you and make the past five days seem like child's play."

"I swear, Anthony." Orrin was shaking in his seat. "I just want to find my friend and go home. Thank you for everything."

Anthony huffed and stared at Orrin for a long moment. "Call me Tony."

"Thanks, Tony." Orrin pulled a smile.

Tony smiled back. "Your bill is five gold."

After Orrin had paid him, Tony started up his nonstop talk again. Orrin got the impression Tony didn't get out much.

"So you save people's lives often?"

"Nah. Every few months, I'll get some idiot in here trying to skirt the laws and finding out the hard way why mind mages don't last long. Other than you, I've only had three or four cases over the years of just crazy skill combos going wrong."

"But like, is it a job?"

"Something like that." Tony went quiet. Orrin had stuck around to help clean the detox room. It still stunk, so Orrin had volunteered to mop the floors.

Tony stood at the door not talking for so long, Orrin thought the conversation was over. He startled when Tony's voice appeared in his mind again.

"When I was young, about your age, I picked up a few skills too many along the path to being an illegal mind mage. Most nobles and people in power don't want others taking a glance at their thoughts, so most countries outlaw some skills. But unless you get dumb, a lot of people still have one or two and it's overlooked.

"I overheard some things and talked about it to a friend. He started a riot when he shared the information. He lost his head, and I lost my tongue. Really, I shouldn't have gotten off so easy, but someone thought up a new plan—let a mind mage hunt for illegal use around town.

"So for years, I was a chained dog. I'd catch people using [Thought Manipulation] or [Mind Read] on judges, nobility, or whoever I was tasked to watch."

Orrin had stopped mopping and was listening with wide eyes.

"After a while, they stopped thinking of me as a danger. I overheard more and more that made me rethink what I'd gotten myself into. It took a lot of deals and the promise to stay in my house, but I got out of it all. But people still already knew. I was the boogeyman. The one who'd cleaned up others like me.

"At first, people stayed away. But one girl showed up crying, begging me to help her get rid of [Mind Read]. She'd wanted to know if her boyfriend really loved her and got the skill when drunk. More came after her. Now, I'm sort of a therapist-slash-doctor. It's not what I wanted or thought my life would become, but life rarely is what we expect."

Orrin chuckled. "Thanks for telling me. I appreciate it."

Tony smiled his crooked smile and pointed to the floor. "You missed a spot."

Orrin spent the morning helping the old man do chores. His body felt weak, but he felt clearheaded. He also knew he was avoiding the one thing he really needed to do—find Daniel.

With a wave and promise to check back in a few days, Orrin left Tony's and headed back to the Guild. He bought some meat on a stick on the way. After one bite, he got back in line for two more sticks. *I need to remember this place.*

At the reception desk, Orrin tried asking after Daniel, but the receptionist just shrugged and refused to give out any information on fellow Guild members.

"He's my friend. I just need to make sure he's okay," Orrin tried.

"If he's your friend, he'll show up."

Orrin tried to sleep that night, but nightmares now plagued his dreams. He was tempted more than once to just put [Mind Bastion] back on, but the smells and images Tony had shown him were still fresh. He spent two days waking early and staying in the front hallway. Every receptionist rejected his efforts to find Daniel. Finally, one offered a new solution: "Put up a quest and leave me alone."

"How?"

The woman hadn't given any response the day before when she'd been on shift. She took her feet off her desk and pushed a scrap of paper forward.

"Write your quest down. It's one silver. You also better pay your reward, or we'll come after you for it."

Orrin scribbled down, "Locate Daniel. Fighter. Dark hair. Five silver for information. Contact Orrin, Guild."

"Hmm. Add credible information or you'll have everyone telling you they saw him," the woman suggested.

Orrin did it and paid.

"Now get out of here." He was shooed away.

Orrin sat on the steps outside the Guild thinking of other locations where he could look. The sword. Jovi's.

He ran down the street to the blacksmith's store. A guard yelled at him to slow down. Orrin did a fast walk until the guard turned, and then he darted around a building.

He arrived sweating.

"Hi, sir, can I interest you in—"

"I'm looking for Jovi." Orrin spoke over the salesclerk. The man rolled with the rude interruption and guided Orrin to the back, where Jovi was happily hammering.

Orrin's eyes scanned the walls, and he sighed when he saw the sword, Gertrude, was still there.

"Mr. Jovi, this young man—" Orrin waved his hand at the man.

"Sorry, I—uh. I forgot my money, I'll be back." He ducked out before Jovi even turned around, leaving the clerk sputtering.

He walked slowly back to the Guild. There was no way that Daniel had tried to do that cave mission without him, right?

He had just reached the Guild steps when someone tapped his shoulder. He turned and found a woman in her midtwenties, holding a spear and small arm shield. Her hair was short and shaved at the sides.

"You Orrin?"

He nodded.

"Daniel's the guy you're always with, right?"

He nodded again.

"Five silver if I tell you where he is? That simple?"

Orrin guessed his Quest had been put up already. "Yeah. I haven't seen him in a few days. Just trying to find him."

She shrugged. "He's been staying at the Catanzano house." She held out her hand.

Orrin's mind raced as he processed her words. *He's okay. At the Catanzanos'?* He felt cold run down his spine. *He told her. He went right against our promise. No, he wouldn't do that, would he?*

"Excuse me, payment time." A frown line appeared between the spear holder's eyes.

"Sorry, yeah." Orrin pulled silver out of his pocket and gave it to her. "Here you go."

"Listen, if you were hoping to party up with him, I'd give up. Word around the street is Lady Catanzano is putting together a team for a dungeon dive. Don't know what she sees in a little sword wielder but then again, I'm no lady." She forced a laugh and left without another word.

Orrin's heart sank. Daniel had already found another party.

Chapter 15

Orrin felt a punch to his gut as he realized Daniel had found another party so quickly.

It has been over a week, I guess. He had been stuck in Anthony's house unconscious for most of that time. *If only I could have apologized before . . .*

The woman with the spear turned back and watched him with pity on her face.

"Sorry, kid." She really did look apologetic. "Um. If you don't mind me asking. What is it about him? Nobody has ever heard of him, and suddenly all the houses are clamoring."

Orrin looked away from her face with tears in his eyes. "He's my friend. We had a fight, and he kicked me out of his party."

Orrin knuckled the tears away. "Thanks for the information."

"Yeah, no problem." She hesitated. "Listen, if you're looking for a group to run with, I've only got two others, but we are a solid team. We could use some fresh blood. What's your level?"

"Seven," Orrin muttered.

"A bit low, but not too bad. I'm eighteen myself. [Waterspear]. Probably a bit obvious, though." She nodded at her spear. "My name is Tin."

"I'm Orrin. Nice to meet you. Sorry, but I don't think I'm—"

"Don't say no right away." Tin smirked and playfully pushed his shoulder. "Meet the others. At the very least, grab some food with us. You look like shit."

Orrin smiled back. Tin was bubbly, but he felt a steadfast personality underneath. The kind of person who would worry after giving bad news to a stranger.

"I've been a bit under the weather, but I could eat."

Tin pumped her fist in the air. "Great. Emily, our spellslinger, is holding a table outside at Fredric's for the three of us, but I'm sure we can pull an extra chair up.

"I couldn't believe such a simple recon Quest was still up. I don't know why nobody found you earlier. Like I said, everybody's trying to figure out what Catanzano is up to. Do you know that—"

Tin kept up the one-sided conversation as they walked down the street toward the fancier section of town. Restaurants and theaters for the rich lined the road. Orrin hadn't spent any time here, and without [Mind Bastion] running, he felt like a tourist. He turned to watch a sign with stenciled people dueling, showing the name of a play underneath. One building's windows were blacked out, and the doorman was handing blindfolds to people in line.

"—ing, huh? Orrin?"

Orrin blushed and apologized for not listening. Tin just laughed and pulled him along. She began pointing out different places to him and telling him all the rumors and secrets of each chef or theater troupe.

"—and when they found him, Peitro had already sewn him into the outfit with his skills. It took burning the cloth to get it off, so the guy was extra crispy when it was all done." Tin let out a loud laugh. Several outdoor diners looked up in disgust at the adventurer. She ignored them.

"Here we are. Fredric's. Best food in town, but don't tell him that. He'll just raise his prices again."

Tucked between two massive buildings with lines around the corner to get in, Fredric's was a small window. Two tables sat chained to metal posts, and a stack of beaten-up old chairs toppled precariously to the side. Orrin could just make out a shock of red hair moving behind the window.

"Emily! You already ordered?" Tin slumped into a chair next to the only occupied table. While Tin was tall, buff, and carried herself with grace, Emily slunk into the chair as if to escape from her friend. Her dark skin contrasted with the red robes marking her as a fire user. Most mages wore colors announcing their spells.

"You were late," Emily muttered. She bent over the bowl on the table and slurped loudly. "Garret's late. I'm hungry."

"Garret's our third," Tin explained. "[Earth Archer]. Emily, this is Orrin. Orrin, Emily, our spellslinger."

Emily shook her head. "I'm a [Fireflower Mage], not a 'spellslinger.' But nice to meet you."

"[Fireflower Mage]. That sounds cool. What's your build?" Orrin found himself interested. Learning all the different types of classes was a lifetime's work, but it all fit in with his perfectionist, min-max mentality from gaming.

Emily's withdrawn attitude disappeared as her smile bloomed. "Well, I started off [Fire Mage] for the first ten levels, as you do, but then the group I was in found this crevice in the cavern we were clearing out. Inside was a slow-moving lava river with about a hundred Fire Geckos—"

"The number goes up every time she tells the story." Tin slapped his back and walked to the window to order.

Emily continued, unfazed, "After we took them out—which is no easy feat, as I'm sure you know—I used [Fire Friend] to run across the lava. I could feel it calling me, you know? And then I found a mana construct of fire against the far wall, from where the lava flowed. A tiny flower of fire."

Emily looked pleased and looked at Orrin expectantly.

"So what happened next?"

Emily frowned. *Shit, something I didn't find in the books. Mana construct?* Orrin kicked himself.

"How do you not know—"

"And here's dinner." Tin saved him as she slapped two bowls down. Orrin dug right in.

Heaven. He'd found heaven. The bowl wasn't soup but noodles. Noodles in a creamy sauce with peas and mushrooms. The flavors exploded with each bite, and Orrin ignored everything as he worked on the bowl.

"Damn," Tin laughed. "When is the last time you ate?"

Orrin stopped devouring the food and sat back contently. "Wow. Just wow. That is amazing."

Emily was still giving him a funny look.

"Sorry, Emily, you were explaining the flower? I'm from a small village with almost nobody going beyond farmer, so I'm still learning." He started eating slower.

Emily shrugged at that and continued, "Anyways, after I absorbed it, I worked my way up to level twenty and changed classes when I got the prompt. [Fireflower] gives me fire-growth abilities. Sort of a mix of fire and plant magic."

"She's being modest. Emily is level twenty-four. She can grow a field of fire in a few seconds. She took down a Dryopl with a big flower thing that just ate it up. By herself." Tin complimented her teammate between bites.

"I had to." Emily smirked. "Otherwise, Tin would have spent hours attacking it and laughing as it tried to hit her with all its legs."

The banter between friends was a balm that Orrin didn't realize he'd needed. Emily warmed up quickly, and Tin's naturally exuberant personality left an imprint that had Orrin laughing along to their stories in no time.

When Garret, their third party member, arrived, Orrin had already finished his dinner. The man stood a full head taller than Orrin but smiled and shook his hand gently.

"I see the ladies found some eye candy for us." He gave Orrin an appraising look before heading to the window to order food.

Orrin blushed, not used to being called eye candy. Especially as he spent most of his time with Daniel.

"Oh. Did Garret get to you? You're red!" Tin laughed and clapped her hands.

"Just tell him you're not interested and he'll leave off." Emily finished her drink. "He's good people."

Garret returned and ruffled Tin's hair. She slapped his wrist.

"So, Tin finally found us a new man to drag around?"

Orrin had just returned to normal as his skin flushed again.

"Leave him alone, Gar." Emily closed her eyes and leaned her chair back.

"He hasn't agreed to join," Tin chimed in. "Just dinner and meeting us."

"So, you must want to know all about me, then." Garret pushed his food around as he looked at Orrin.

"I heard you are an [Earth Archer]?" Orrin asked.

"Yep. Level nineteen."

Orrin waited.

"Oh, I don't just put out like these two. I want something in return." Garret winked.

Orrin blushed. He stammered, "I'm a [Utility Warder]."

Garret, Tin, and Emily looked puzzled. "That's not one I've heard of," Emily started. "Mage or fighter class?"

"Neither, really," Orrin hedged.

"Now I'm actually interested." Garret's eyes pierced into Orrin. "I'll play. [Earth Archer] lets me create arrows from damn near anything. I can make the arrows heavier or lighter and ignore gravity to an extent. With these two lovelies, I usually just clean up the edges or create nice little rows of big rock arrows to pen monsters up for slaughter."

Garret paused and looked expectantly at Orrin.

"I'm only level seven. But I can heal and buff. I can increase your strength or will. I can also put a ward—um—a magic barrier of sorts around you that soaks up damage."

Garret's eyebrows went up in disbelief. Then he laughed.

"Oh. Oh, Tin. That's a good one. Where did you find this guy? He's hilarious."

Orrin frowned a bit. "I'm telling the truth."

Emily was frowning again, too. "Orrin, if you don't want to share, that's fine."

Only Tin was smiling like she had won the lottery.

"Is that what Daniel can do, too?"

Orrin's heart sank as he realized Tin had set him up. She just wanted information on Daniel. This was not a real interview to bring him into a new party. He was only level seven.

What an idiot.

Orrin just shook his head. "Thanks for the meal. Sorry to have wasted your time."

As he stood up, Tin put her hand out.

"If what you say is true, it's obvious why the Catanzanos snatched your friend up. What kind of buffs are we talking here?"

Garret was surprised. "You don't actually believe—"

"I believe every word he said." Tin didn't take her eyes off Orrin's. "I want him on the team. Any complaints?"

Emily shook her head. Garret opened his mouth, and then closed it again. He shrugged.

"We'd have to get him up a few levels. Grinding can be fun with the right partner." He smiled a wicked grin.

Orrin's skin turned red again.

Garret turned to Emily. "Oh, I'm so in trouble with this one."

"So, what do you say, Orrin? Want to join our little party?"

Tin Has Invited You to a Party
Yes or No?

I've lost my mind, Orrin thought for the hundredth time. *How else am I going to level?*

After he declined as nicely as he could to join their group, the three friends had taken it in stride. They invited Orrin to hang out anytime or even come on a Quest as a temporary add-on "just to see what we can do." None of them were more than a few years older than him, but they'd all been leveling for years. They'd chatted for a few hours about different builds and skills. Orrin shared a little of what he could do. Garret had still questioned his abilities until he wasted one spell and buffed Garret's dexterity. He'd shut up after that.

They'd waved as he left, and for the first time in years, Orrin felt the rush of making new friends.

But joining the first group he found wasn't the smart way to do things. He might have turned off his analytical robot-brain skill, but Orrin was still a smart guy.

Right?

He'd turned around three times to go back and accept the offer.

No. He turned back to the Guild.

As he slid his coins across the counter, the receptionist tilted her head. "You're Orrin, right? Letter for you."

Orrin took the key and a large vellum envelope to his room. A stylized C was on the front.

He rushed to his room and tore it open.

To Orrin,

It has come to our attention that you are attempting to contact Daniel. He has decided to rely on our family as he moves toward the future.

While we do not doubt your friendship, we request you do not interfere with his training in the next several months. His will be a hard regimen of training, with no time left to frolic with others. We know that you will make the correct choice.

In return for your discretion, your name has been added to the entrance list for both of Dey's dungeons. A party of your own may enter as you wish.

Best,
Lord Catanzano, Protector of Dey

Orrin read the letter twice.

"Fuck that."

As he neared the Catanzano house, Orrin tossed [Camouflage] on. He also pulled up [Map] and activated all the different options. Nothing for party or monster appeared, but [Trap View] showed three separate items.

The front door had a long rope near the two guards. *Obviously an alarm of some sort.* The windows also had a small bar across the inside. If the window was pushed up from the outside, they'd probably break. *Another alarm?*

The third was a general haze around the building itself. While the map itself was blue, a light red washed across the Catanzano estate. Trying to zoom in farther only showed the roof.

I guess I have to be inside for more.

Orrin had briefly considered just showing up and knocking. But if Lord Catanzano had tried to buy him off, he would likely just throw him out before Daniel even knew he was there.

Maybe I can try inviting him to a party?

Orrin probed the menu until a prompt appeared.

Create a Party with _____.

As soon as he thought *Daniel*, his name filled the slot. The box disappeared.

Did he get it? Orrin had no idea how party creation worked. He'd never asked Daniel.

After waiting a minute, nothing happened. He went back to his original plan: infiltration.

While [Camouflage] didn't make him invisible, in darkness he was merely a dark blob moving. Even if he was caught, he hoped he could make enough noise that Daniel would hear him.

He made his way to the servants' entrance and waited.

Only two minutes went by before a young maid brought a full trash can out. She hefted the can with one hand and gently placed it down among the other rubbish. Before she turned back, Orrin had already darted inside.

He found himself in the back of the kitchen. It was almost ten at night, so nobody was actively cooking, but a few people were up cleaning. He stood against the wall and shuffled his way to a door, ducking through as fast as he could.

He slammed into someone coming the other way.

"Agh— Sorr—"

"Orrin?"

Daniel stood in the door for only a second before grabbing Orrin and dragging him up the nearby stairs. He threw Orrin through an open door.

Orrin landed on a heavy carpet. He looked up at a four-poster bed, a small balcony, and Daniel's armor gleaming on a chair.

"How did you get in here?" Daniel whispered as he closed the door. "I've been trying to find you for a week! What happened to you?"

The abrupt manhandling and Daniel's concern etched across his face broke the little remaining calm Orrin had. He let out a single sob as he tackle-hugged Daniel.

"I'm so sorry!" Orrin held his friend. "It's no excuse, but my skills were messing with my head. It's fixed now, but I was sick and unconscious for days. Then I couldn't find you anywhere and people were saying you were here. It's fine if you told them; we'll work it out. I'm just so sorry for what I said and how I treated you."

Daniel slapped Orrin's back and pulled him away. He looked him over and smiled. "I'm sorry, too. I felt like an idiot right after you left, but I couldn't catch up to you in time. I found a book that said fighters that use mana skills can have mood swings with overuse of mana. I was wrong, too. Tell me everything."

Orrin laughed and told Daniel what had happened over the last week. Scaring the guard, meeting Tony, the little he remembered of being sick. He even mentioned putting up a Quest to find Daniel and meeting Tin.

"You got invited to another party?" Daniel looked impressed.

"But I said 'No,'" Orrin quickly added.

"Good for you, O." Daniel smiled and punched his shoulder.

Orrin looked around the room. "Doing all right yourself, huh?"

Daniel shrugged. "When I couldn't find you, I decided to see if Madi could help. She had her dad put out some feelers to find you and told me she was interested in doing some questing in the meantime. She agreed to help so fast that I was a little suspicious, but nobody has used the H-word. I just got back an hour ago. We hunted these panther things in the forest. They attack from the trees and weigh a few hundred pounds. But I'm up to level nine now." Daniel puffed up.

"Then I got your party prompt and knew you were outside. I'm in a party with Madi and didn't want to drop it. I was just drying off from my shower. They have showers here. I came to try and find you, but the guards up front said nobody was around. I was just coming to check the side door when I found you."

Orrin frowned. "What did you ask the guards?"

"Just if anyone had been asking for me. They just shook their heads."

"You didn't use my name?"

"No." Daniel caught Orrin's anxiety. "Orrin, what's up?"

Orrin sighed and handed over the letter he'd gotten.

Daniel read, and Orrin watched his normally affable friend get angry.

"D. There could be a perfectly reasonable explanation," Orrin started.

The door to the room suddenly opened. Madi and Lord Catanzano entered the room.

"Of course there is," the man said as his wheelchair came to a stop. Guards flooded in behind him. "Why don't we have a nice little chat?"

Chapter 16

Daniel moved quickly, his sword springing to his hand. He moved in front of Orrin and held his weapon pointed at the man in the wheelchair.

"Bursting into my 'private' room with guards, trying to separate me from my friend, and lying to me." Daniel's skin glowed. "You better explain, and fast."

Madi bent over and whispered to her father. He made a few quick hand gestures, and the guards funneled out as quickly as they'd appeared.

"You are a [Hero]," Silas stated.

Silas and Madi stood in the room waiting for Daniel to respond. Daniel's body shielded Orrin from seeing his facial expressions, but Orrin knew Daniel couldn't play poker to save his life.

"I—I'm not a . . . What's a her— Why would you think that?" Daniel stammered.

Shit. Orrin slapped his face.

Madi stepped around from behind her father. "We've known for a while. You took out those bandits too easily. You even took out Lenard and his gang. You take on low-level quests but destroy every quota and record."

Lenard . . . they did set us up. Orrin got ready to start casting all his boosts on Daniel.

"You did set us up," Daniel just blurted it out. "We had to kill those guys."

Madi gaped for a second and turned back to look her father. Silas sat silently as his daughter stuck her foot in her mouth.

163

"We had people watching. It was a test. You were in no real dang—"

"Orrin took a sword to the chest." Daniel's voice went cold.

"We had healers. And besides, he's just some local freak with a weird class. You're the [Hero]. You're the one we need to help. Don't you get it? [Heroes] appear when the world will need them!"

"Enough."

Silas's single word cut the tension of the room. Madi stepped back, eyes on her feet. Daniel swayed and let his sword dip.

Orrin activated [Mind Bastion] automatically. He felt the magic hit him and rebound. Silas grunted and turned his eyes directly on him.

"Sit."

Daniel's sword dropped to his side as he slumped on a nearby couch. Madi sat on the floor next to her father's chair.

Orrin put his hand in his pocket and pulled a dagger from his storage. "Stop now."

"It's been a long time since someone resisted me." Silas put his hands together. "Maybe you are not a waste of our time."

Orrin used [Identify] on Silas.

Silas Catanzano
Allure Sorcerer
Level 48
HP: —
MP: —

For the first time, Orrin's skill failed to give him much information. *[Allure Sorcerer] and obvious mind magic skills. He must use a high will.*

"I said, SIT."

Orrin felt the magic roll around him. It felt like oil dripping down his back. "I said, STOP. Now." Orrin cast [Inverse] through [Increase Will] five times. At ten MP per increase and another five MP per inverse, his mana pool dropped to 55/130 MP.

Silas physically slumped. Orrin had just dropped his overall will by fifteen points. Probably not a lot for such a high level, but it was likely something Silas had never dealt with before.

"How?" Silas gagged but held it down. "You are just some kid from nowhere. You just have a unique buffing skill. This is not possible."

While Orrin held Silas's attention, Daniel sprang across the room and held the sword to Madi's neck.

"That's just a small taste," Orrin bluffed. "Want to feel what negative will feels like?"

Silas blanched.

"I think I requested an explanation." Daniel took charge. "I can't believe I trusted the two of you."

Madi looked up the sharp edge of Daniel's sword with fear in her eyes. "You must understand. We were not lying. I told you we scouted you for your martial prowess, and that's the truth. We didn't tell you we knew you were a [Hero], but we planned to. Actually, I had just been telling Father that you were nearing level ten. We were going to tell you tomorrow before we went out."

"And I'm just supposed to believe this? What about 'searching' for Orrin? And trying to buy him off?"

"We found him only two days ago," Silas interrupted his daughter as she opened her mouth. "That was my choice. I meant for you to have only my daughter and retainers as your friends. It would be easier for you not to make connections outside the household."

"You mean, easier for you to control him," Orrin chimed in. Daniel nodded in agreement.

"Yes and no. Daniel, when [Heroes] come to this world, most are found immediately. They have no limit to their power, like all of us." He gestured around the room. "Most are actually summoned, although that practice has been mostly outlawed. Asmea itself actually brews up enough magic to pierce time and space when some great catastrophe is close."

He pushed his chair closer to Daniel, who immediately grabbed Madi's hair to steady his blade against her throat.

"That you are here means something is coming or someone is making a move," Silas continued. "While I won't deny the benefits to my family from being connected to a [Hero], I swear that we do not want to control you. Far from it. [Heroes] who are put on a leash always end in disaster."

Orrin's mind absorbed the nuggets of information Silas dropped and turned them over. They thought he was a local, befriended by Daniel before getting to Dey. Silas either truly wanted the best for Daniel or was an amazing liar.

"I thought a bribe the easiest way to get rid of a potential problem," Silas explained. "I never dreamed a true friendship had been created so suddenly. Or with such a powerful mage."

Silas's eyes glittered with excitement as he looked at Orrin. "Truly, I apologize. I can't wait to explore your skills in detail. My library is open to you both."

"Give me one reason I shouldn't leave right now," Daniel growled.

Silas smiled like a man with the winning cards. "You never left my daughter's party, did you, Daniel?"

Daniel glowered.

Come to think of it, Daniel could have dropped the party and joined Orrin's when he first sent the request. *Why didn't he?*

"I still could," Daniel spat.

Silas shook his head. "But you won't. You know that I have the resources to help you. You are a smart boy, if a bit headstrong. That's not an insult. You'll learn to turn it to your advantage. But few else have the connections, money, and power you'll need to reach your goals."

"I don't need your help." Daniel's grip on Madi weakened as he talked, though.

"What goals do you have, then?" Orrin interjected. "What do you get out of it?"

Silas gave Orrin that smile again. The smile of a cat interested in the slow-moving wounded bird within reach.

"Besides the prestige of being known to help raise a [Hero]? Tell me Orrin, did your village have many stories of what [Heroes] do?"

Just play along—better he think I'm some local than another sum-moned [Hero], Orrin thought.

"Just a few. Mostly those who defeated Demon Lords and destroyed the world."

"[Heroes] bring change. There have been a few that were actually here to save the world from a Demon Lord, but Darius stopped that about a thousand years ago when he created the Sea of Fire right on top of the demons' homeland. [Heroes] now are sent to uproot despots, create new magics, or end wars. So if my family helps, we gain political power. I would have been up front with you about all this, Daniel. I just did not think it time yet."

Orrin shared a look with Daniel. *Fuck, they think Demon Lords are not even an option.*

We should tell them, right?

No way—they'll freak out and kill the messenger.

"It was apparent to me as soon as I knew you had multiple Quests. My guess is Asmea brought you here to stop the war in Odrana. They are our closest neighbor, and coupled with the placement of your arrival here, it makes the most sense."

Orrin didn't actually think quicker with [Mind Bastion] on, but it definitely increased his analytical side. *Robot brain makes it easier to be logical. Maybe I should call it Spock brain.*

If they lied and said Daniel was here to stop the war, Silas would want the Quest shared. He probably wanted the boost for his daughter, as well as the prestige and benefits of bringing up a [Hero].

If only he could create Quests. It would help protect us until we could figure out the whole Demon Lord thing . . . and who to trust.

As soon as Orrin had the thought, a new blue box filled his vision.

New Quest:
Stop the war in Odrana
Reward: 200,000 XP and Variable
Failure: Loss of 10 levels.

What the fuck?

Orrin stood mute, staring at the box. He had thought it, and a Quest appeared. Exactly what he needed.

Daniel was waiting for Orrin to take the lead again. Silas was watching them both, searching for any minute detail or look they shared for a deeper meaning.

"I think we need a minute to discuss. But it goes without saying, Orrin is part of my party." Daniel pushed Madi against her father's legs. Orrin saw a bead of blood pearling on her neck.

"Of course." Silas knocked on the wood of his armrest, and two guards reappeared. One handed a small cloth to Madi, who dabbed her neck as they left.

Madi turned back at the door. "Orrin. Daniel. I do hope you can forgive us. We really were only doing what we thought best." She ducked out.

Orrin stood still reading the Quest over and over.

I'm not the hero. How did I get a Quest?

It wasn't the first time, he remembered. He'd gotten the Save the Hero Quest right after they'd first arrived. It was how he'd gotten his oft-forgotten [Identify] skill. But he'd figured that a fluke because he was near the [Hero].

"Orrin?"

Daniel was standing close to him, both hands on his shoulders as he slowly shook him.

"Dude, are you there? What happened?"

"I—I got a Quest," Orrin got out.

"That's great." Daniel smiled softly, like he thought Orrin would bolt at any minute. "Is it to get the fuck out of here? Because I don't know if I can trust someone who—"

"I got a Quest . . ." Orrin lowered his voice and leaned in close. ". . . to stop the war in Odrana."

Orrin almost shared it with Daniel, but he paused. He didn't know how parties worked. "Drop out of their party and make one for us."

Create a Party with Daniel?
Yes or No?

Yes.

After mashing the accept button, Orrin shared his new Quest with Daniel.

"Maybe you really are a—"

"Don't even say it," Orrin interrupted. "This is your Quest. Silas is right about one thing—they have much better resources. That group I was talking to complained about how hard it is to get a dungeon. Madi and Silas can get us in. Plus he mentioned something about hitting level ten for you. They already know you're a [Hero]. You didn't even try to deny it. What we should do is—"

Daniel slapped Orrin's cheek. Not softly, but not enough to knock him over.

"What the hell?"

"You're using that skill again. I can tell. I want to talk with Orrin, not this logical and unfeeling thing."

Orrin hesitated. If he dropped [Mind Bastion] then Silas could . . . no. Orrin pushed against the skill. He was in charge and could make his own decisions.

He deactivated [Mind Bastion].

"Hey, there you are." Daniel smiled as Orrin's eyes filled with the anxiety he had been holding back.

"I just attacked a leader of the community . . ." Orrin put his hands in his hair. "Silas is going to have me killed. He already has tried once. Damn it, Daniel. How do we keep getting into shit like this?"

Daniel chuckled and patted Orrin's back. "Listen, as long as we stick together, I'm fine using them a bit. Maybe they can help you find a way to use your skills without becoming an asshole."

Orrin shrugged Daniel's hand off his shoulder. "Too bad that's just a permanent fixture of your personality."

Daniel laughed out loud. "There he is."

"You really think we should go along with this? What if they . . ." Orrin whispered the rest. ". . . find out about the other Quests?"

"We already shared the Wall Quests with her." Daniel shrugged. "She's level twelve, so the level-ten Quest is out of her reach. They'll probably want us to share this one, too."

"We could tell them that's all of them?"

"What if the variable reward for the Defeat the Dungeon Quest is like a full suit of armor? How do we explain that we didn't share that?"

Orrin pulled up his Quests.

> Defeat the Demon Lord—In the southern lands, the Demon Lord has risen. The dark armies have been assembled. Seek out and defeat the Demon Lord before the Dark Horde attacks.
> Reward: 1,000,000 XP and Dark Essence Unlocked
> Defend the Wall—Help push back a Horde
> Reward: Variable on participation percentage/ Horde Type
> Defeat a Dungeon.
> Reward: Variable
> Obtain Level 10
> Reward: [Hero Kit Level 2] Unavailable reward
> Stop the war in Odrana
> Reward: 200,000 XP and Variable.
> Failure: Loss of 10 levels.

"Yeah, I agree with you. That's too risky. These vague rewards suck. I still don't know if I'll even get anything for hitting level ten. Maybe we just show them the war Quest but make them earn our trust before we share it? Defeat a Dungeon we can give to Madi, as I'm guessing Silas is killing two birds by using the [Hero] to power level his little girl."

Daniel nodded. "She's been with me the whole time. She's no slouch, though. She uses light magic but totally different than you."

"So, is that our choice? Are we really going to stick around with them?" Orrin hated the idea, but Daniel appeared to be warming up to it.

"For now," Daniel decided. "There's nothing to say we can't just leave when we want to. I know someone who's pretty good at disappearing when he wants to."

Orrin blushed and stammered out another apology. "I said I was sorry."

Daniel punched his shoulder as he walked to the door. "So, to recap, stick with them, war is my hero reason, and you'll be my trusty sidekick from Asmea."

Orrin nodded.

"Come on in," he yelled through the crack as he opened it.

Silas and Madi reappeared. Madi still held a cloth at her neck.

"First, I'm sorry for that, Madi." Daniel pointed at her throat. "I've been here for only a few weeks and really wanted to get my bearings before announcing I was a [Hero]."

For all of Silas's blustering earlier, his eyes went wide. "So it's true. Daniel, my boy, I was mostly sure, but my [Identify] only told me you were a fighter class. You have no idea what—"

"Hold on," Daniel cut in. "I don't appreciate being used. By anyone. I'm a team player and will give respect, as long as I receive it in turn. But you are not in charge, Silas. I am. Orrin was my first friend on this world, and I intend to keep him nearby. You will not interfere with that again."

Silas nodded eagerly.

"If I find someone else, I'll replace you. If you try to attack me or control me . . . well, you saw what Orrin can do. However, I have never let loose around Madi yet. So whatever reports she's been feeding you don't cover the half of it."

Orrin grinned to himself. Daniel's ability to show enough respect to the lord while also vaguely threatening him reminded him of all the times he'd talked the two of them out of trouble. Daniel's understanding of authority figures was really coming into play.

"I would never—" Silas began.

"Next, I will allow Lady Madeleine to continue to participate in MY party. If you would like to sponsor us in any way, that would be appreciated, of course. I don't have many other options right now, so the other two members can be retainers of yours. But if I find a better option, I will have final say."

"Of course, of course. I would ask only that Madeleine remain as a full-time member," Silas quickly agreed.

Daniel nodded and squinted at something.

Madeleine Catanzano has joined your Party.

Interesting. Orrin had never seen that prompt before. Daniel must have sent her an invite.

"In exchange for your discretion, I'll share another Quest with her. I'll decide if I share it with someone else before we complete it."

Orrin just watched as Daniel threw another prompt at Madi. She suddenly leaped at Daniel and hugged him.

"Thank you. Thank you." She was nearly crying. "I won't let you down, Daniel."

"May I ask?" Silas began. Madi looked up at Daniel, who nodded. She turned around and handed an invisible blue box to Silas.

"Variable? From the texts I have, that's rare. To have two Quests with variable rewards . . ." He trailed off.

"Daniel, Orrin, I do apologize for my earlier behavior. I agree to your terms, of course." Silas wheeled himself to a long nightstand and poured some water for himself. "Defeating a dungeon is no easy feat. You must get through every layer of defense, fight floors of monsters, destroy the final guardian, and then figure out how to break the dungeon core."

He sipped from the cup. "A variable reward also means if you wait for a simple dungeon to spawn and defeat it, the reward won't be as good as if you tried to take on one of the more established dungeons. But those have not been defeated for decades or centuries. I'll begin gathering information on all of it, regardless."

Silas turned from Daniel to Orrin. "And you, sir. Although I must admit I'm quite peeved that you broke into my home, I hope you become friends enough with my daughter to put yourself at risk for her, as you have for Daniel."

Orrin didn't hear an outright threat, but a chill ran down his spine as Silas turned away.

Chapter 17

Daniel decided that Orrin would spend the rest of the night with him. The room he'd been given was big enough, and Orrin didn't mind sleeping on the plush carpet.

Madi wheeled Silas out of the room, excitedly chattering about different options for a dungeon run and possible rewards.

Orrin closed the door and put his hand in the air.

"D. That was a masterpiece." Orrin slapped Daniel's hand. Daniel smirked a bit.

"You tired?" Daniel asked.

It was late, but Orrin felt buzzed. Maybe the flipping on and off [Mind Bastion] had some lingering side effects, but he was still wide-awake.

"Want to talk strategy a bit?"

Daniel leaned in close, staring into Orrin's eyes.

"What the heck, man?" Orrin pulled away.

"Just making sure you are not using it." Daniel shrugged. "What do you want to talk about?"

Orrin explained his purchase and use of [Teleport]. "I think it's too expensive to use right now, especially if I'm going to be cutting back on cycling. Tony told me I can probably get away with two or three full mana pools a day. That's about average for people using mana potions, too. He also told me that if I try to cycle and use a mana potion, I'll be able to do six full mana pools a day but will most likely have a headache the next day. But what I really want to know"— Orrin paused—"is what is it like fighting in a full party?"

Daniel scowled. "It sucks."

Orrin was taken aback. From how Tin had talked, he'd assumed the group thing would be awesome. "Why?"

"Maybe I'm being too harsh," Daniel backpedaled. "I'll explain. Madi uses light magic. It does some damage, but it also disorients monsters. She can do minor illusions, too, so they'll get misdirected, but everything we fought had a good smell sense, so that didn't help."

Daniel started picking pillows off the twin bed. There were way too many pillows. He dumped them on the ground and tossed a blanket on them as he continued.

"Brandt is actually pretty capable on his own, but he hovers at Madi's shoulder. I had to physically drag him into the melee a few times. We had another knight there, too, Jon. He fights like a berserker. Super strong but just goes off on his own. Silas also hired a [Fire Mage] from Veskar to join us. He's a much higher level for sure but only cast a few spells. Honestly, I did like 99 percent of the work."

Daniel finished making a pillow nest just as he stopped talking.

"So, lots of moving parts and no teamwork." Orrin knew that would drive Daniel crazy. Having grown up playing every sport, Daniel was used to being team captain and being listened to.

"Exactly!" Daniel threw up his hands. "And when I tried to give pointers, the only one who listened was Madi. But she actually does her job fine. The Veskar mage just ignored me and said he was hired by Lord Catanzano to protect his daughter, not listen to a lowly fighter."

Daniel and Orrin spent a few hours talking about potential plans. As Orrin couldn't go all out anymore and had to be more judicial in his spell use, they agreed it would be best for him to buff the team once before a fight, tag monsters with his [Lightstrike], and then save as much as possible for emergency healing.

"I know it will really bring down the total damage output having me there," Orrin admitted. "Thanks for fighting for me."

"You are wrong," Daniel argued. "The extra damage the other four party members do from having their stats increased is better than having another sword swinging about. I didn't even realize that dexterity let me hit more accurately and quicker until I didn't have your boosts. Jon's entire build was dexterity based. Just hundreds of small cuts to bleed a monster dry."

Orrin nodded as he realized Daniel's argument was sound. "I could increase dexterity to level three? Just cast that as needed?"

"Maybe wait until you have all the increase skills ready to level, then [Utility Ward] is what you should use. It's cheaper and hits us all at once. How many ability points do you have? I've been saving mine still."

Orrin winced as he remembered that conversation. "I've got eight."

Daniel ignored his wince and asked, "What else are you looking at still?"

"Increase [Heal Small Wounds] to level three. [Mana Pool], but that costs ten. Get [Utility Ward] to level two, but again that's ten and two hundred MP to cast. And [Merge], but that costs way too much."

"I think you should hold off and try to get that [Mana Pool]. From what little the [Fire Mage] said, most mages run out of MP too quick to be really useful. That's why so many people go with a fighter class instead. Or do something mixed."

Orrin agreed, especially now that he couldn't just cycle back to full.

They sat in comfortable silence for a few minutes.

"So, are you planning to mix in any magic?" Orrin questioned.

"Maybe something with wind magic," Daniel responded. "I'm planning on building out lots of strength, and wind magic will allow me to make sure I actually hit. For all Silas's faults, they have an incredible library here. I learned things that were most definitely not in anything we bought. Like, you know that every ten levels, you get extra stat points . . . But did you know it's completely dependent on what class you have? Like, a farmer might get one or two points that they can put into strength or constitution, while a fighter class usually gets four to six they can put into strength, dexterity, or constitution."

"Wait, so I might be able to increase my will or intelligence even more? That would massively benefit every spell I have!"

Orrin exclaimed. "That must be why level ten is a cutoff for going into a dungeon."

"Yeah, Silas wouldn't even let us talk about a dungeon until after I hit level ten. But he kept saying we need to talk before that."

"Maybe he knows a way to change your class? That Emily girl I was telling you about, she said she found a flower that let her class change. Maybe that's why she was so excited about it and why she acted weird when I didn't catch the significance. Maybe class changes are really rare."

"Why would I want to change my class, though?" Daniel shook his head. "What could be better than [Hero]?"

They chatted a bit more about inconsequential things and drifted off.

Moonlight crept into the dark alley as the hooded figure strolled along the street. He stepped out of the lamplight and into the blackness hiding beyond the eyes of those still up this late.

"You have news?" The hooded figure couldn't see the figure that spoke but knew who it was from the timbre of the voice.

"The boy has revealed himself. You were right. The other is not planar."

"Of course not—he almost died from a mere sword strike."

"I still worry about him, though. Something about him . . ." The hooded figure stopped talking as two silhouettes passed by the dark back street. A drunken question and a tittering laugh pierced the night before they continued along to whatever destination was open at such an hour.

"He is insignificant." The voice picked up as the two people narrowly avoided an untimely death. "Will he side with us?"

"It remains to be seen."

"You know that I despise evasive answers."

Silence permeated the air as both figures felt violence settle in the tiny walkway. With the field only two yards wide, any fight would be fervent, fast, and fierce.

"I will do my best." The hooded figure readied for flight. This was not a fight one wanted.

"See that you do." A swift wind flitted down the alley, and one presence disappeared completely. A minute later, the other left and the street was vacant again.

Silas had been telling the truth about setting them up for success. Orrin woke up and discovered a tray heaped with eggs, bacon, something like pancakes but crunchy like cookies, and coffee.

Blessed coffee!

"I take back everything I said about him," Orrin mumbled around crumbs as he sipped his second cup. The first he'd shotgunned, burning his tongue.

"Traitor," Daniel spoke with his mouth full, too. "It's just coffee."

"How are we even friends?"

They bantered until a knock at the door startled Daniel.

"Who is it?"

"Sires, I am here to outfit the young adventurer," a voice called out.

"Oh, good, come in." Daniel's smile turned evil. "This is going to be so much fun."

"Huh?" Orrin was confused. Daniel just shook his head.

"Consider it payback for ditching me."

A lady wearing smooth, dark leather from neck to ankle walked in. Orrin saw no buttons or zippers, just strategically placed seams that highlighted her natural curves.

Two girls followed her. One wore a frilly dress that started as yellow and morphed through the colors of a sunset as it went down. The other wore long strips of gray and black cloth that hid her frame like a ghillie suit. Both carried bundles of leather and bags spilling over with different thread and plates of metals.

"What are you talking about— What the hell are you doing?" The lady in leather had grabbed Orrin's shirt and pulled. It fell apart in her hands. Orrin barely felt the whisper of cloth as he was stripped to his boxers.

"Esme has been sent by Lord Catanzano to outfit you properly in acceptable armor," the girl in bright colors explained as she held different pieces of cloth and leather against his bare skin. "Please behave better than Mr. Daniel and stand still."

"Daniel?" Orrin waved for help, but his friend was snickering as he walked out the door.

Orrin was handled like a doll. They prodded him and moved his arms. Shirts and robes were pulled over his head. Leather armor with sleeves and without appeared out of nowhere and then disappeared. Esme used some combination of skills and magic to create and destroy different clothes and armor. The two girls— Monochrome and Polly—were her daughters, just a bit younger than Orrin and learning her trade. They were monsters and tried to stab him with needles every chance they got.

"Melee or distance caster?" Esme asked one question the entire time.

"Um. Distance caster, I thin— OW." Monochrome stabbed his thigh with a needle.

She didn't talk to him again. Instead, she gave small nods and one-word instructions to her daughters. After an hour, Orrin was cold and miserable.

"Acceptable. Finish it." Esme nodded and left. Orrin was still in his boxers.

"What the hell is happening?"

Her daughters let out a malicious, simultaneous chuckle and moved in.

Orrin checked himself out in the mirror. The two girls had behaved much better once their mother was gone. Orrin wore a half-sleeve dark leather cuirass with a layer of metal underneath. It moved better than his old leather armor. He also had a matching set of leggings, a silk shirt to wear under the armor, and a solid set of lightly armored shoes.

The best part was the knee-length cloak with pockets inside and out. It had tightly woven metal links sewn in between the layers and would supposedly turn anything but a direct strike from an arrow or sword. Claws and teeth stood no chance.

"Damn, better than mine. Esme must have liked you." Daniel stood at the door.

"I didn't throw things at her." Orrin laughed and twirled his cloak dramatically.

"Which twin told you?" Daniel entered, and Orrin saw he was dressed for the day, too.

Daniel spread his arms. "Take it in."

His old leather armor had been traded in for chain mail. Except instead of a clunky, one-size-fits-all dress of interlocking rings, his armor fit his form exactly. Different-colored metal covered his armpits, spinal column, and stomach. A swirling design drew Orrin's eyes to Daniel's sides. He blinked and noticed his eyes had slid off to the side.

"Some kind of magic on that?" Orrin blinked his eyes.

"Yeah, Esme complained enough that Silas brought in some enchanter to help give me an edge in melee combat."

Daniel also wore greaves and studded metal boots. He still had the same sword and scabbard. Orrin quirked an eye at that.

"I know, I know." Daniel shook his head. "Esme wanted to do a whole thing with straps and my sword, but I couldn't justify it. I'm getting Gerty as soon as I can. This sword is fine for now, but . . ." He trailed off.

They spent a few more minutes striking poses and laughing at each other.

"So, what's the plan today? Go kill some things and level? Hit their library?" Orrin questioned.

"Silas wanted to talk but then probably go hit the forest. There are always some quests to beat back roaming monsters. Brandt keeps on top of it for us."

Orrin's mood soured. It made sense to work with Silas. They'd talked about just setting off on their own, but Daniel's few days working with him had already shown how much better a full party and support was.

When Daniel and Orrin had looked over the quest board, they had not known that what made it to the board was the leftovers. Most people contracted directly with the Guild, who gave the best quests to higher-ranking adventurers . . . or those that paid best.

That meant that while Daniel and Orrin had fought rats for scraps and low experience, Madi and Daniel took on Cloudsabers, the panther things that Daniel had mentioned before. Although Cloudsabers were only a few stars stronger than rats, they had a better return on investment. In fact, the experience was so much better that Daniel had barely exerted himself and had to split the XP with a group of five, yet he'd still leveled twice in the few days they had gone hunting.

Connections in this world meant everything to getting the first chance at sightings for high-experience monsters.

They gathered the few things they'd need, Orrin putting a few extra pancake cookies into his [Dimension Hole] for later.

Daniel walked down the upstairs hallway. He obviously already felt comfortable in the Catanzanos' house. Orrin kept close.

A few guards and maids nodded at Daniel as they walked, but nobody stopped them from going farther into the house. At the end of the hall, they found Sir DeGuis sitting on a stool with his hammer leaning on the wall.

"Jude, how are you?" Orrin smiled at seeing a familiar face.

Jude grinned. "Young Orrin, why am I not surprised you weaseled your way back in? Good for you." Jude stood and stretched in front of the door. "If you are here to see Lord Catanzano, you'll have to wait. He's in a meeting."

"Oh, that's fine, we can just talk with him later," Daniel began, but Jude shook his head.

"Orders are you don't leave until talking with him, sorry."

"We are not prisoners." Daniel put his hand on his sword.

"Whoa, whoa." Jude waved his hands in front of him. "That came out wrong. He wants to speak before you go out, so Madi is under strict orders not to fight anything with you until after. You're always free to leave; we don't mess with slavery in this house. If you say you're going to go out and look to level anyways, I've been instructed to interrupt his meetings. But, really, it should be over in about ten minutes."

Orrin put his hand on Daniel's shoulder. "We can wait in the library maybe?"

Jude started nodding. "It's just across the hall there. Have at it. I'll tell him you are waiting for him."

Daniel and Orrin crossed the hall and opened the door to the library. Orrin had expected a room with books stacked around the edges, a desk, and maybe a sofa. Instead, the large room had rows and rows of bookshelves that reached to the ceiling. A small mechanical lift sat at the end of an aisle, perfectly sized for Silas's wheelchair.

Orrin cracked his knuckles. "Now this is what I'm talking about."

Chapter 18

Daniel had already been in the library with Madi, so he showed Orrin around.

"He's got it all separated into different sections. The first two rows here are mostly history and record books, stuff that he used in Madi's education," Daniel pointed out as they walked through the aisles.

"Here, he's collected a bunch of different class books, split into fighter, magic, and other. Some of the melee books are pretty cool, but unless you have the qualifications for them, the classes are basically useless . . . or that's what I thought before you mentioned class changes might be possible. Don't ask me what that means—I didn't spend too much time looking at 'other' yet."

Orrin's eyes ran over the different classes printed on the sides of the books. Although his menu store gave him so many options, he had to manually select one to read the description. Maybe some of these would help him pick out something helpful.

"Over there are the fiction books his late wife loved. Madi told me nobody actually reads those books, but Silas won't get rid of them. The aisles in between are everything else he can get his hands on. Lots of different skill builds, theory books, strategy guides, and stuff like that. That's where I found my idea to combine wind magic with my class. There's a book on past [Heroes]." Daniel ran his finger along the books until he found what he was looking for.

He pulled a battered-looking book out and handed it to Orrin.

"A few hundred years ago, some guy Steven was summoned to fight a war for one country or another. He used wind magic to partially become the wind, attacking with some custom weapon he had made. 'Handheld triple-punching knives' is what it says. I swear if it wasn't for the fact that he lived about four hundred years ago, I'd say he was cosplaying Wolverine."

Orrin held the book close and started reading over the other book spines. He pulled out a few that looked interesting. *Spatial Magics. Alchemy and You. How to Avoid Getting Stabbed or Crushed.*

"I see you two are already preparing." A voice came from behind them. "I respect that."

Orrin turned to find Silas wheeling himself into the room.

"Someone told us we couldn't go out and level until I talked with you." Daniel crossed his arms.

Silas waved away his comment and rolled past them. "Come on. This is what I want to talk about."

Orrin stuck close as Daniel followed Silas to the far side of the library.

"These were my wife's." Silas ran his hand along the shelves, wiping dust off. He rubbed the dirt between his fingers and looked off into the past.

He turned and smiled at the boys. "The best place to hide something is in the open."

He took four books out from the middle of the stack and reached behind the resulting hole. Shorter than the fiction books he held, he pulled a thin and shabby book out. "Nobody would search a sentimental keepsake of a widower. As far as I know, this is the only copy of this book still in existence."

He handed the book to Daniel.

"Secrets to Being a [Hero]?"

Silas's eyes lit up. "So it's real?"

"What?" Daniel looked up as he opened the book.

"I was sold this book when I was a young man. It gives off a distinct magic flavor, but no intelligence or scouting magic could pierce the hidden text. The crazy old man who sold it to me swore on everything important to him that it was a book for [Heroes], by [Heroes]. It's nice to have it confirmed."

Orrin peeked over his shoulder. "It's blank."

Silas's sneer was quickly controlled, but Orrin saw the judgment. "Of course it is. Only [Heroes] can read it."

Thank god, Orrin thought. With all the weird things happening lately, he was glad for this little confirmation that he was not in charge of saving the world.

"Other books I've read have mentioned things like this," Silas continued as Daniel flipped through the pages. "Help sent through the ages from one [Hero] to another. One of them." He wheeled back to the section Orrin had been browsing. "It is in here somewhere; I read it just a few years ago."

A minute later, he found what he was looking for. *A Tale of Wind and Earth.* "Scholars ignore this, as it's a romance novel written by the only surviving party member of a failed [Hero]."

"What exactly is a failed [Hero]?" Orrin interrupted.

Silas sighed. "What does it sound like? He died before completing his mission. His lover wrote a book; it wasn't a success and she died in obscurity."

He leafed through the pages. "One passage stuck out to my wife. She was a [Hero] expert, or maybe I should say fanatic. Her dream was to meet one, but as far as I know, Daniel is the first one in sixty-five years.

"Here it is."

Silas read aloud.

"'Liam would rarely talk of his home or even his time before creating our party. I had met him when he was already nearing level forty, and he spoke little of the trials before. After completing our mission for the elves, we were plied with elven wine and food. Elven food is mostly plants, and elven wine is created for elves. To put it simply, we all were drunk after one glass.

"'We told drunken stories and secrets. Most of what the party talked about that night was forgotten by morning. Except when Liam talked. His struggles in the desert where he was summoned, the days without water as he tried to find civilization, and his first few monster kills wove a story so compelling and terrifying, I will never forget his words.

"'Liam's magical abilities were already unique, but he told us that upon hitting level ten, he'd made a mistake. He had been given multiple choices for changing his class. He'd taken one interesting in name but that plateaued quicker than the rest would have. Abandoned in the middle of the desert, with no knowledge of our world, he'd had to spend the next thirty levels trying to undo his blunder. But not all was gloom; he told us of his homeland and . . .'" Silas stopped. "That's why I wanted to talk before you hit level ten. You must select the proper class upgrade at level ten."

"I haven't heard of anything like that," Orrin said.

"Of course not—it is only [Heroes] who naturally upgrade. And from every source I've been able to find, level ten starts you on the path. I have found almost no information on what parameters are needed for further upgrades, but I'm sure it is just as onerous as it is for the rest of us."

Orrin thought of Emily's flower story.

"This book has some information on that." Daniel had finished flipping through and had returned to the beginning to read in depth. "But the first page specifically says I should never share this information with anyone but another [Hero]."

"Respectable, but I am here to help at your pleasure." Silas smiled, but Orrin saw the gritted teeth.

This guy is totally out for himself, Orrin thought. *We need to get all we can from him and bail. I should see what the other countries are like.* He made a mental note to check out the history section.

Silas excused himself, as he had more meetings. Running Dey was a full-time job.

Daniel went back to his room to read his book, and Orrin wandered aimlessly through the stacks of books. He'd put together about seven books total to read when the door opened again.

"You finish already, Daniel?" Orrin asked over the bookshelf.

"It's not Daniel," a voice said as Orrin heard the door lock.

Chapter 19

Orrin fell into a squat, cast [Camouflage], and pulled up his [Map]. If Daniel was near enough, maybe he could scream. If he couldn't hear, Orrin could toss enough buffs on him, using the [Party View] option to cast spells from a distance.

Instead, he saw a second dot approaching him on the map.

"Madi?"

Lady Catanzano was dressed in her leather armor and holding a spearhead. No, it was a tiny spear. The shaft of wood was only about a foot long.

"Hi, Orrin." Madi rounded the corner and looked confused as her eyes slid off him. She squinted and tried to focus on him.

"What are you doing here?" Orrin stayed low. He primed an inverted debuff in case this was an assassination attempt.

Her eyes still looked above him, but his voice gave her a direction to look at. "It is my house. That spell of yours is amazing. I didn't realize you were stealth, too."

"You locked the door." Orrin spoke and then tried moving to the side. Better to be somewhere else if she threw her short spear at him.

"I wanted to talk." Madi kept looking at where he had been. "I—I didn't want my father to overhear. Is that all right?"

Madi and Orrin had not had the best relationship. Sure, he'd saved her life with Daniel. But then she had wanted to kill him. She'd paid them off for the Quests they'd given her. But Orrin believed both Silas and Madi thought of him a waste of space. So when Madi said she wanted to talk with him, he had only one response.

"No. I'm good. 'Bye."

Madi's obvious privilege shone through. She pouted prettily but must have felt silly with no obvious response coming from a nearly invisible Orrin. She tried demanding instead.

"You can't leave until I dismiss you." She actually stamped her foot on the ground. "I'm in charge here."

"Sorry, princess, Daniel is in charge, not you." Orrin tried to move quietly by her but had spoken too loudly and too near.

Madi held her spear out in his direction and twisted her wrist. The short spear burst in length, growing into a full spear in an instant. The metal sank into the wood a handbreadth in front of Orrin's nose.

Orrin dropped his [Camouflage] and backed up with his palms facing Madi. "Okay. No need to get stabby."

Madi had blanched. "I'm so sorry, I thought you were so much farther back. I would—I shouldn't have—" She started to cry.

Orrin had never had a girlfriend. Sure, he'd had a few crushes, but standing next to Daniel did him no favors. So he had no idea how to react to a girl his age crying in front of him. After she had nearly impaled him.

"Maybe try again?" he questioned. "What are you doing in the library?"

Madi retracted her spear so it was small again and wiped tears from her eyes. Orrin noticed they shimmered in the morning light. "I really just came to talk. We are in a party now and should get to know each other better. I know you probably hate us, but you should know, we only did what we thought best."

"If all you are going to do is give excuses, I will make my way back to my room, thanks." Orrin did not move, though. Best not to chance it with her magical weapon.

"No. That's not what I want to do. I am sorry. I did see how close you and Daniel seem, but I think part of me was too excited to meet a true [Hero] to consider your feelings." She took a step toward him. "But since we are going to be fighting together, I do not want bad blood between us. I mean, we are going to be protecting each other's backs out there.

"So, truce?" She put her hand out.

Part of him wanted to push by her and leave. He couldn't teleport, as he had found out last night. The third hazy trap around the house was an antiteleport rune set up to keep away thieves and killers. The other part of Orrin craved another friend. *Maybe she really means it. She seems friendly enough with Daniel—why couldn't I have a friend who is a girl, too?*

Madi noticed his pause and let her hand droop a little. "I mean, I get it. I'd hate anyone who tried to keep me from being on a [Hero]'s team, too. Just know, we are a team now. I will fight for you now that Daniel has decided that."

Orrin grabbed her hand just as she turned to leave. "Just don't be so commanding. Our party should be equals." He smiled.

Madi beamed. "Thank you. I won't let either of you down. Father said he wanted to talk with Daniel more before he goes out again, but I heard you are still a few levels down from us. Maybe I can get Sir DeGuis and Sir Bennett to take us out for the day? Some more Cloudsabers were spotted near the southern forest line a few hours out."

"I'd rather wait for Daniel," Orrin responded. "But I have been slacking on my training. Maybe a few rounds?"

Madi nodded.

Orrin landed on his back again. Madi's spear skills were only level one, according to her, but Orrin's dodging skill had yet to level.

[Side Steps] 93/100

While Orrin could hit her with a [Lightstrike], Madi's own magic could reflect half the damage back on him. Daniel had not been kidding when he said her light magic was on another level.

In their first practice fight, Madi had cast [Shimmersight] on Orrin. Ten minutes later, when he could see again, she'd laughed and said she'd thought he could dodge it. While [Lightstrike] was low damage but unerring in hitting a target, Madi had to manually aim her spells. She said [Shimmersight] was best used against stationary targets. A first-strike type of spell.

Orrin had pulled it up:

[Shimmersight] send a ball of light floating toward a target. Brilliant lights explode across the target's vision for 10 minutes upon hitting. 20 MP. -15 AP

"That's quite the spell," Orrin commented. Madi smiled at the compliment.

They'd taken turns casting a few spells, Orrin showing her both the [Increase Will] and inversed version. Unlike her father, Madi did not hold down her breakfast when she lost three points of will.

"That was . . . enlightening." Madi wiped her mouth and pulled her spear to full length. "Weapons?"

And that was how Orrin learned the hard way that even one level in a weapon meant all the difference.

Brandt had shown up and stood smirking as the lady of the house beat the intruder soundly. Every once in a while, Orrin slipped past her with his [Side Steps], but more often than not, Madi just left him on his ass.

Her laughter filled the small courtyard–turned–battleground. Every time [Meditate] filled up enough of his MP, Orrin topped off his [Increase Dexterity], but he simply could not get through Madi's guard.

"So, what else you got?" Orrin huffed as he put the bo staff back on the small weapons rack. He'd failed with the staff, sword, spear, and even tried a mace before realizing how terrible that matchup was.

"A few different light attack spells." Madi glowed in victory.

"Anything worth showing off?" Orrin's entire reason for sparring with Madi was to try and help Daniel create a better fighting strategy.

"I've got something like your [Lightstrike], just a beam a little bit tighter in diameter than yours. It can cut through a target. Then I have a few party-trick spells—floating light butterflies and things like that. Not useful in battle." Madi waved her hand at the last.

Orrin shook his head. "If they distract for even a second, anything could be useful. Do they cost a lot of MP?"

"One mana per butterfly, or two for each light stream."

"Light stream?"

Instead of answering, Madi pointed and let out a flash of blue light from one finger. It shot into the air and splashed as if hitting a roof.

"Like a firework! Nice!" Orrin complimented. "Wait, can you do different colors?"

"Yes. Why?"

Orrin smirked. "I think I've got an idea."

Chapter 20

"How many different colors can you make?" Orrin asked excitedly.

"I have no idea," Madi responded as Orrin grabbed the staff and sword. He walked to one end of the courtyard and stabbed the sword into the ground.

"Does it do any damage?" Orrin asked, walking to the other side and wedging the staff so it stood up. He tried to straighten it but gave up quickly. It did not matter for his experiment.

"Not much more than your [Lightstrike]." Madi was intrigued and caught up in Orrin's fervor.

"But you have to aim it, so you can hit a specific area instead of a monster if you want to, right?"

"Yes, but Orrin, why would I want to do that? This spell was something I should never have wasted a point on. It's weak and pointless."

Orrin smiled as he stood next to Madi. "You know, something I keep reading is that everybody is so focused on overall damage output. Why?"

"The party wants to take down the monster quickly. If you don't, it is more likely that someone gets hurt," Madi explained as if by rote.

"I don't think that is the reason." Orrin took the spear and drew faint lines in the sand of the small, enclosed space. He split the rectangle into thirds. "I think everyone wants bragging rights for doing the *most* damage."

"I think—" Madi began.

"Hold on, listen. You get the same amount of experience whether you do 1 or 99 percent of the damage to a monster, right? So, why don't groups have more healers? Every healer has at least one offensive spell, but party structure is based on single battles. What if, instead, we played to our strengths and did just enough to hit each creature, distract them, and herd them into the meat cleaver that is Daniel or Brandt? You are good with that spear, but honestly, Daniel could probably wipe the floor with you."

Madi stuttered and tried to come up with a retort.

"No offense—you still kick my ass easy enough. But that's the point. Here, look."

Orrin had finished setting up his grid. The courtyard had been split into different sections, with the sword and spear at the left and right portions. Orrin and Madi stood in the middle.

"Let's say both of the weapons are monsters. We have the whole party here. Me, you, Daniel, Brandt, and another fighter. What would happen?"

Madi looked around for a second and played along. "Daniel would take one, while the other fighters took the other monster. We would support whoever needed help the most. After one fell, the other would be the main target."

"Classic strategy. But what if we did this instead . . ." Orrin pointed as he talked. "If both monsters are rushing us, could you hit one with [Shimmersight]?"

"If they were coming right at us, yes. It's hard for most monsters to dodge a charge. But then whoever took it on would have to deal with it flailing about. Monsters are still dangerous when they can't see."

"What if we ignored it, though?"

Madi looked stumped. "Why would we do that? We need to kill it before it attacks."

"Would it attack if it couldn't see?"

Madi paused. "I don't know."

"So, if you see two or even more targets rushing us, you hit one with a red firework. We know that's the target you are going to hit with [Shimmersight], and we focus on the others. You can also come up with other signals. Toss out a yellow if someone needs help reinforcing. Throw a green on something we should all target faster. You be the eyes telling the pieces where to move. You'll be playing Kala, while the rest of us are the pieces."

"That seems like a lot to keep track of during a fight." Madi shook her head as she realized the pressure Orrin was hoisting onto her.

"Oh, don't think you'll be in it alone." Orrin smirked. "I'm a backline fighter, like you. I think if we stay close, we can have the melee fighters take out most anything while we orchestrate the battlefield.

"Brandt, come over here," Orrin called to the knight. "Let's try it like this. The weapons are monsters. Direct us. I'll be Daniel."

Madi pursed her lips.

"Yeah, yeah, give me a break." Orrin explained what he wanted Brandt to do.

"Attack a staff in the ground?" Brandt had obviously not been listing to their conversation.

"It's a big monster coming to kill Madi," Orrin explained. Brandt stood up tall and drew his sword.

"Madi, it's your show." Orrin handed control over.

Madi had been raised to take over her house someday, but bucking the tried and true method of an every-man-for-himself fighting style threw her. She hesitated.

After a few seconds, Orrin tapped the spear butt on Brandt's turned back.

"Dead."

"What?" Brandt turned around at the gentle ting.

"We're dead," Orrin explained. "She hesitated. The staff monster barreled into us, and she didn't stop the sword monster. We got pincered. Dead."

Madi scowled. "Okay, again."

Orrin smiled. "On your mark."

Madi drew herself up and tossed a red firework light out at the sword and a green one at the staff. "Brandt and Orrin, take out the green. I'm casting [Shimmersight] on the red."

Brandt blurred, and the staff was in two pieces. Orrin hadn't meant for him to actually attack the weapon but forgot Brandt was pretty literal.

"Great, now on to the sword monster." Madi pointed.

"Okay. We don't need to destroy more stuff," Orrin quickly cut in. "You see what I'm getting at, though, right?"

"You want to use battlefield tactics against monsters," Brandt stated.

"Basically, yeah."

Brandt scratched the side of his head. "Won't that put more pressure on us? I mean, I'll do as the lady demands, but it'll just tire me and Daniel out if the party doesn't do any damage."

"Who said we won't be doing damage? Madi will just be directing our focus instead of everyone fighting whatever they want. We'll have to learn to trust each other. If she says run, you need to run, because she signaled Daniel to blast the whole area. If she says charge, you better expect me to buff your strength up to maximum. Stuff like that."

Brandt looked at his sword for a long moment, then nodded. "I trust her already. I like this plan. But who will keep her safe if something slips by? You?"

Orrin smiled. "I promise you, Brandt, if something gets close to us, I'll teleport us both out."

"You have [Teleport]?" Brandt and Madi yelled at the same time.

Fuck, not again.

After calming Brandt and Madi down enough, Orrin went back to his room. Well, Daniel's room.

Daniel was waiting.

"This damn book," he spat when Orrin closed the door. "This damn book is the worst."

"Hello to you, too." Orrin tried to lighten the mood.

"You seriously couldn't read it?" Daniel asked hopefully as he handed the book over to Orrin.

Orrin looked down and saw only blank pages. "Sorry, D."

Daniel sighed. "Okay. Here are the highlights. This isn't just a guide for [Heroes]; it's a history book. It describes all the ways past [Heroes] tried to stop Demon Lords from coming back. Because they always do, Orrin. They spawn from places of Dark Essence. It's like hell magic, from the description. So what do these idiots do? They try to reshape the world and end up destroying it instead. Or creating seas of fire. And those are the ones who succeeded!

"Some of the information is helpful. Like, I-wish-I-had-found-it-before helpful. I've been stressing so much about points, but at level ten, I get some choices. I can basically add a moniker to my [Hero] class. The dude who killed a Demon Lord a thousand years ago and then made the Sea of Fire? His name was Darius. He decided on fire—the Fire Hero. How original. But whatever I pick has consequences, and there are only a few known paths. I think Darius might have started this leave-a-note-for-future-Heroes thing. But I'm spiraling a bit here now."

"Calm down." Orrin put his hand on Daniel's shoulder. "Should I cast [Calm Mind]?"

Daniel nodded, and Orrin dosed up his friend with some sweet mind magic. Daniel sighed.

"That's better. The book has a lot of great information, but none of it is organized. There will be a long paragraph about the best skill choice progression, then someone else writes at the end, 'This will make you easy to kill by X magic type' and 'do this instead.' It is so frustrating."

"We'll figure it out. We can lay out the options and pick one that works best with what you want," Orrin said. "How do other [Heroes] end up finding the book? Or is it just luck?"

"There's a skill that one of them created that makes people want to give it to us. I think it's the same one that lets only [Heroes] read it. [Through the Ages] or something."

Orrin froze. He recognized the name of that skill from when he had been looking at time and space magic and skills, trying to piece something together to get back home.

Daniel noticed. "No fucking way."

Orrin pulled up his store. He found it easily.

> [Through the Ages] A unique skill created to pass
> knowledge through the ages. Only those with the
> skill or those deemed as the chosen target can read
> and write information using this skill. -2 AP

Daniel shook his head in disbelief. "You are a fucking cheat code."

"Did you already buy it?"

"I don't have to—I think [Hero] is the 'chosen target,' so I can already read and write in the book."

"Should I?" Orrin whispered. "I don't want to impose on your [Hero] gig."

"Please." Daniel dramatically wrung his hands together. "Save me, Obi-Wan Kenobi, you're my only hope!"

Orrin grimaced as he used two of his remaining points. *Down to six. We really need to level more.*

The book wiggled in Daniel's hand. Then lines of ink crawled across the paper. It looked like a madman's manifesto. Different handwriting, different color ink. Drawings typically found in high school textbooks. *Seriously, who draws genitals on the holy hero book?*

"I can see why you've been having trouble." Orrin nodded.

"YES." Daniel threw the book to Orrin. "Have fun decoding. I can't stand this shit. Did I see Brandt down in the training yard? I need to hit something."

"Sure, just leave me here to figure out the musings of crazy people," Orrin yelled at his friend's back.

"Thanks, buddy. I owe you one."

Daniel had come back after two hours, bruised but happy. They spent the rest of the day locked in the room. At some point, a maid brought lunch, and another magicked an actual bed for Orrin. The suite had more than enough spare room for it.

By dinner, Madi had shown up to ask for them to join her and Silas for dinner. They'd declined, electing to receive dinner in their room. Once the moonlight shone through the window, Daniel and Orrin had decided to stop until morning.

The following day saw them decipher enough of the book to break it down into parts. It had only taken another solid ten hours of locking the door and taking copious notes.

The first half was generally about Demon Lords. Spotting signs for increased activity, best tactics, and levels for when Daniel should take certain skills or spells. At level fifty, his class gave him the [Demon Seal] skill that had stressed him out for so long.

"Level fifty is far away, though," Orrin had countered. Daniel had waved away his concerns.

"By the time we get to level fifty, I should have a much clearer idea of my strengths, anyways. Maybe I won't even need the seal."

The remainder of the book described different paths the [Hero] could take at level ten. Fundamental nature monikers, like Fire, Wind, Water, Earth, Metal, and Ice, were common and safe. Other [Heroes] had tried stat paths, like Dexterous Hero or Strong Hero. At some point, those had plateaued. Of the nearly twenty [Heroes] they could differentiate, only one had gone another route—Magic Hero. His notes were the most sporadic, crossing out lots of what the nature [Heroes] had written and describing them as short-sighted fools who did not understand what they were talking about. He theorized that the moniker gave insight into a particular skill field. That was why every [Hero] should choose magic, as it covered the largest spread and allowed knowledge that touched almost everything.

"So, the broader the moniker, the better?" Daniel scratched his head as Orrin put their findings together. They'd already decided to burn all their notes as soon as they finished. Some of the secrets they'd found were too valuable to share right away.

"I don't know if he's right," Orrin argued. "Remember, he couldn't explain why the Metal Hero could take on people with his axe that had a higher level in weapon proficiency so easily. And the Magic Hero really focused on long-range spell casting. I mean, he ended the war at level forty by just wiping out an entire city."

"Sounds like he nuked it." Daniel shivered. Orrin agreed. That section had been particularly brutal to read.

"So, I think you should really go with your gut," Orrin suggested. "But all the other tips and level-up tricks are nice to have."

"How soon are you running down to buy those plants?" Daniel grinned.

"Tomorrow," Orrin confided. "It's not like I could do it today." He looked out at the setting sun. Another day of potential leveling gone.

One of the [Heroes] had listed different ways to increase skills and upgrade spells. One she'd mentioned had stood out to Orrin immediately—[Meditate].

[Meditate] currently allowed him to regain one MP per minute or sixty MP an hour. It was passive, and he forgot about it most of the time. Other spell casters had to drink MP potions or sleep to regain their mana. It was already a cheat for Orrin to have it. Plus, any regained mana wouldn't count against his daily mana use before being overexerted.

The Ice Hero had written about a few plants used to calm nerves or increase clarity during regular meditation rituals. She'd played with them and found a certain combination allowed for a temporary increase in the regeneration. For one hour, the regen went from one MP per minute to one MP per second. The downside was it was only usable once a day. She'd tried it twice and burned out her [Meditate] skill for a week. No mana regeneration except through sleep like all the other normies.

Orrin was going to get some of those plants and make a few of the regen potions, as it was not an actual alchemy skill but rather mushrooms floating in water. He also planned to finally pick up some MP potions. Although such potions were supposedly expensive, they'd decided the price worth it. With the extra MP, Orrin could heal someone in an emergency. As HP potions cost almost twice what an MP potion did, it was another loophole to be exploited.

"I'll keep reading our notes for now," Daniel said. "Maybe something will click for me. Thanks for the help—I never would have gotten through this without you."

"You would have managed." Orrin rubbed his eyes. All the reading had worn him out.

"I'll burn these when I'm done." Daniel waved his hand over the paper they'd commandeered. "Get some sleep."

Orrin passed out before his head touched the pillow.

Chapter 21

Daniel woke Orrin up a few hours later. The night was heavy, and moonlight streamed through the open window.

"Wake up."

"Mahh, what?" Orrin sat up and rubbed the sleep from his eyes. "Daniel, it's gotta be midnight."

"Sorry, but this could not wait." Daniel practically bounced as he sat on the bed. "I figured it out."

Orrin struggled to get a hold of the conversation. He had really been out.

"Orrin, do you hear me? I figured out what the entire book actually means. I know what my moniker should be!" Daniel looked more alive than he had in days.

"You look hyped. Did you drink more coffee?" Orrin finally pulled his head off the pillow and sat up.

"Two cups. You are missing the point." Daniel paused for effect. "I can get us home."

Orrin paused and then focused on coming fully awake. "What? How? What do you mean by 'what the book actually means'? How long until we can go?"

Daniel pulled out the different sheets of paper they had written their notes on and separated a few into a stack.

He handed the stack to Orrin and asked, "What do these have in common?"

Orrin pulled the papers close and started flipping through them. They were the notes on the different [Heroes] that had written the book. Orrin had started a list of their names, then of the skills and spells they used, before finally just giving each one a page with all the information they could gather pertaining not to the advice but the status and abilities of each [Hero].

"These are some of the [Hero] profiles I tried putting together," Orrin started, but Daniel shook his head.

"No. Well. Yes, but no. What do these particular profiles have in common?"

Orrin looked through them again. Both male and female [Heroes]. The Magic Hero was here, but so was the Metal Hero. A Fire Hero and an Ice Hero. No stat [Heroes], just a handful of elemental monikers.

"I don't get it." Orrin gave up.

Daniel frowned but explained, "These are the best ones. The ones who didn't plateau. The other [Heroes] would choose the same name, based on the success of one of these guys. But it did not always help. Like, the other Ice Hero. He tried to replicate the earlier Ice Hero, but his notes complained that he could not get the same spells as her. He ended up just giving up toward the last of his notes in the book and went back to using his bow and arrow, remember?"

"And?" Orrin asked.

"That was the problem. That is THE problem. I can't choose something based on what others have done. Your class shows that there should be other options out there." Daniel stood and began to pace. "So, I started thinking about why each one of these [Heroes] had chosen their particular moniker. Look."

Daniel turned back around and pulled the notes from Orrin's hands. He riffled through until he found the Metal Hero notes.

"This guy. I went back and looked at some of his sections. He complained early on that he just hated using anything but his axe, remember? There was an entire section before he hit level ten on discussing whether it was worth it to take fire or wind?"

Orrin nodded. The Metal Hero's early notes had been rambling and fell into logic loops as the guy had tried convincing himself to take one name after the other.

"He decided to take 'Metal' as his name because he just was so over thinking about it. But it worked perfectly for him. Because that was what he was actually focused on. Do you get it?"

"You woke me up for a lecture? Get to the point, Daniel."

Daniel frowned. "Yeah. Sorry. I'm going to be the Dimensional Hero and get us home."

Orrin tried to process what he'd just heard.

"Huh?"

"I'm picking 'Dimensional' as my moniker at level ten."

"I still don't get it."

"I'll be able to create a wormhole or something and get us back home." Daniel was smiling ear to ear.

Orrin chose his words carefully. "You are an idiot."

Daniel's smiled slipped.

"You woke me up to tell me you want to pick wormhole hero so that you might get a skill to get us home?"

Daniel was full-on scowling now.

"Dimensional Hero. And yes, basically. What the Magic Hero got wrong is intent. The reason behind the moniker makes it more powerful. It has to line up with what you want."

"How do you think the system is going to react to you essentially saying, 'fuck off with that hero shit'?" Orrin asked.

"No. That's the genius of it," Daniel began. "It will also help with how I want to fight. Blipping around the battlefield, swatting down monsters left and right."

Orrin pulled up his store and searched for "blink," "dimension," and a half dozen other words he could think of.

Nothing.

"I don't think something like 'blink' exists. Or, at least, I can't find anything in the store for that."

"That doesn't mean it doesn't exist," Daniel argued.

"That's true," Orrin conceded. "I agree with your theory that the name probably goes further if it jibes with you as a person. I just don't see you as . . . dimensional."

"That almost sounds like an insult." Daniel folded his hands over his chest.

"Whoa, no." Orrin shook his head. "I'm still waking up. Let me pick a better sentence." He paused and spoke. "I really do like your theory. I actually think it's totally on the money. But I'm not sure the word you picked describes you. Sure, it describes what you want to do, but . . . how do I say this? It just feels off."

Daniel went into full pout mode. "Well, that's what I'm choosing."

"Then great," Orrin said. "It's your choice. I'm just trying to be a sounding board for you. I support you 100 percent."

"Now you are just being an asshole," Daniel complained. "You come up with something better, then."

Orrin shrugged. "No, really. If that is what you choose, I support you. I don't know how this all works. I'm flying blind, just like you. But maybe we can brainstorm some other things, just in case Dimensional isn't allowed?"

Daniel paused at that. "That would be okay. I actually had already considered Time Hero, too. Because you know . . . time travel, and maybe I could pause time."

Orrin doubted that would work any better than "dimensional" but did not want to piss off his friend further. "There you go. Having options is fine. The book said you have ten minutes to choose a good moniker, anyways. One of those could work."

Daniel nodded along as Orrin agreed with him finally.

"Daniel, you really should get some sleep," Orrin suggested. "I think you're going a little manic."

"Just a few more hours, I want to double-chec—" Daniel stopped talking when Orrin threw a pillow at him.

"That was not a suggestion. Shut up and sleep," Orrin demanded. "You are not at level ten yet. We can discuss this tomorrow. You look like shit, and I know how crabby you are when you don't sleep."

"I am not crab—" Daniel dodged another pillow. "Okay, fine."

Daniel crawled into his bed and gave Orrin the cold shoulder for being the responsible one.

Dimensional or Time Hero? Orrin thought as he tried to get comfortable again. *I do like the idea that it should be tied to his abilities or fighting style. Or even just who he is as a person. But what would work?*

Orrin thought about it as he closed his eyes. Daniel was his friend, but he was also popular. People liked him and were naturally drawn to him. He excelled in most everything he put his mind to, like a force of nature hurtling toward his target.

The last thought he had before sleep took him again was *What would I choose if I were the hero?*

Orrin woke before Daniel the next morning. Daniel grumbled and pulled the covers over his head.

"This is why I made you go to sleep," Orrin said loudly and very close to Daniel's head. "Come get some breakfast when you wake up."

Orrin walked to the door and felt his body move to the side. Daniel had thrown a pillow at his back.

[Side Steps] -94/100

I COULD HAVE BEEN DODGING PILLOWS!

Orrin took a few of the books he'd squirrelled away and found Brandt and Madi finishing some pastries and coffee in the smaller dining room. The larger dining room was only used for political dinners and such.

"Morning, you two," Orrin greeted them as he piled a few different cinnamon buns and a side of bacon on his plate. He took the entire pitcher of coffee. It might be enough for him.

"Good morning, sir," Brandt responded.

"Good morning, Orrin." Madi smiled his way. "Is Daniel still sleeping?"

"Brandt, I've told you already. I'm not a sir. Just call me Orrin." He poured the first of many cups of coffee to come. A small dash of cream, and he sipped. "And yes, Madi. The Sleepy Hero is not up yet."

Madi snickered at the joke.

"What are you reading, si—Orrin?" Brandt asked.

Orrin pushed the two books he'd brought down across the table. "Just an alchemy book and a spatial magic book."

Spatial Magics and *Alchemy and You* were two of many books he'd picked up at the library. He had gotten the alchemy book to look up more on potions, health, and mana. *Spatial Magics* was in case there was some hidden path to getting [Teleport] powered up to interplanar travel. He and Daniel still needed to get home somehow.

"Are you interested in alchemy?" Brandt asked eagerly.

"A bit." Orrin talked around mouthfuls of almond croissant. "I'm not sure I would ever pick it up, but I was interested in how potions work. Mostly mana potions, to be honest. There are benefits to knowing how things work, especially when those things go into your body."

Brandt nodded along.

"You know, Sir Bennett here is an amateur alchemist himself," Madi teased the knight. He blushed and ducked his head.

"Really? I didn't see that on—know that about you," Orrin corrected his mistake. [Identify]ing people wasn't something you just admitted to.

"No, Lady Catanzano jests," Brandt mumbled. "It is just a hobby. I have no skills, nor would I waste them for such an endeavor. [Alchemists] take few apprentices, and books such as these"—he pointed to the book—"are for beginners only. The true knowledge is hidden behind years of training."

"So, save me some time," Orrin segued to keep the conversation going. He hadn't ever heard Brandt speak this much. "What's in a mana potion? Why can we only use a few of them a day? Can I make one if I have the ingredients?"

"Hmm. Well, the ingredients for low-tier mana potions are easy enough, but each [Alchemist] adds their own something. For instance, I could mix up a mana potion myself, but it would restore only about ten mana points if I were lucky. To take a side trip, you can only use two or three potions a day. And that is inclusive, so two or three mana or health potions combined. The reason being, your body is taking on somebody else's mana or health."

"Wait, what?" Orrin had not gotten past the introductory paragraphs yet. This was all new to him.

"When you make a potion, you infuse a bit of your own mana or health into it. It's how you get the ingredients to merge and store even more residual mana or health, the natural mana and health that permeate the air and earth."

"Is that how we gain our mana and health back with rest?" Orrin was learning more from Brandt than he had in multiple books.

"Yes. [Alchemists] tap into that potential residual mana and use their own mana along with the ingredients, to capture more. Depending on where you bought the potion, you might have more residual mana than personal mana, which results in being able to use an extra potion or two. You'll feel it when you drink the third potion in one day. It's like a small animal is inside your stomach, trying to claw its way out. You will not want to drink a fourth."

"What happens if you do?"

"If you are lucky, you die," Madi said seriously. "Some people lose the ability to do magic or activate a skill. Others go blind or have lifetime ailments that no healing can cure."

Brandt continued, "One squire I knew drank an extra health potion during an expedition. He had taken point to prove himself and kept getting hurt. He had hidden a reserve and started screaming. He hallucinated dark figures coming from the trees. He never recovered and lives in an asylum now."

"Damn." Orrin felt shaken. He'd been lucky his cycling hadn't ended the same way. "But wouldn't making your own potions mean you could take more? With less foreign mana in your body, it would make sense, right?"

Brandt smiled. "Exactly. That is why I considered taking a few skills at first. But even with the best efficiency, an [Alchemist] can only take an extra two potions a day."

Orrin took the carafe and filled his cup with coffee again. "Why? Wouldn't that just be like drinking your own mana?"

"Are you sure you haven't read this book?" Brandt laughed. "You're asking questions that took me years to think of."

Orrin shook his head.

"The way it was explained to me was like this . . ." Brandt leaned across the table. "Do you know what dust is?"

"Dead skin mostly, right?" Orrin responded as he took another pastry off the plate.

"Um . . . yes, actually," Brandt stumbled. "How did— Never mind. So our bodies are constantly shedding. You are not the same person today that you are tomorrow. So your mana is actually different from day to day. Of course, the longer the time between making and using a potion with your own mana, the more it essentially becomes the same as a regular store-bought potion."

"I guess that makes sense." Orrin scarfed the last pastry and sat back with his third cup of coffee. "Thanks for the primer."

Brandt had really come out of his shell talking with Orrin.

"Morning, all." The door opened, and Daniel shuffled in. "Any food left for me?"

"Of course, sir." Brandt stood and hurried around to pull a chair out for Daniel. "Would you like a pastry? Or I could have the kitchen make you something?"

"No, Brandt, a pastry is fine." Daniel sat. "I can get it."

Brandt looked around and half bowed. "I better get to work. If you both would like, we can go out today. I have pinned down another litter of Cloudsabers."

Daniel looked at Madi and Orrin for confirmation. Both nodded.

"Sure, do we have someone else for our fifth?" Daniel asked as he dug in.

"Sir DeGuis has volunteered his time, if that is acceptable?" Brandt answered.

Daniel responded, "I think that would be great."

While Orrin sipped his third cup of coffee, savoring the taste, Madi explained the strategy they had created. Daniel listened and nodded along.

"That sounds perfect," he commented after she finished. "It leaves me free to focus on kiting and killing without needing to worry about everyone else. I trust you and Orrin to direct us."

Madi's pride at the compliment was evident in her smile. "I already explained everything to Brandt, too. He was hesitant to leave me unguarded, but I put my foot down. But—what is kiting?"

Daniel had just stuffed the last bit of breakfast in his mouth and tried to talk but choked. Orrin answered for him as he poured water down his throat.

"Basically, kiting is getting a monster to follow him without actually being able to attack him. Kind of playing keepaway while someone else does damage. If D can keep a few monsters targeting him, then that is even less we need to worry about."

Madi smirked. "You two really do make a good team. I'm glad this worked out."

Daniel finally choked down the rest of the food. "Yeah, I guess we can keep him around."

After breakfast, Orrin got dressed in his armor and cleared out his [Dimension Hole]. Now that they had a place to stay, he put the extra clothes in a drawer and condensed what he was bringing.

"Hey, Daniel, do you think I have time to grab a few mana potions? And maybe try and find those mushrooms for the regen potion?"

"Yes, you have time." Daniel was strapping his leg armor on. "I won't let them start without you. Do you want me to come with?"

"No, I need to stretch my legs anyways." Orrin punched his friend as he passed him. "You would just slow me down."

Daniel rolled his eyes. "Just meet us by the southern gate in about two hours?"

Orrin gave a thumbs-up as he left. He departed the Catanzano house and made his way back toward the merchant street.

He asked a random person who had the best mana potions and was pointed to one store. However, somebody else heard him ask and offered another suggestion. Within a minute, four people were arguing about the benefits of lower cost versus higher mana payout. Orrin sneaked off with [Camouflage].

He ended up at the Alchemist's Friend. The old lady behind the counter pointed out the different costs of mana potions, with different amounts of MP restoration for each. For five silver, a mana potion could restore fifty MP. One gold would restore one hundred MP. Every additional fifty MP cost another gold piece.

Orrin didn't feel the need to shop around too much. It was a weird feeling, having so much wealth. He had not grown up poor, but with his mom working long hours to keep up after his dad left, he'd learned to budget pretty quickly.

He bought ten 100-MP potions. The vials were small test tubes, and the lady explained that they could be kept on a thin belt with clasps for easy drinking. The glass was magically tempered so it would not break, and he could get a small discount if he used them over and over. The belt was only two silver, so he bought one.

Ten gold and two silver poorer, Orrin asked, "Do you stock penidrop mushrooms?"

The lady peered over her glasses. "Are you an [Alchemist]?"

"No, ma'am." Orrin gave his best innocent smile. "I just dabble a bit on the side for fun."

"Penidrops aren't used in too many things, but I think I have a few in the back. Would you want a certain amount of clippings or a mothershroom?"

"Um. I don't know," Orrin answered truthfully.

"A mothershroom will let you grow more penidrops, but it'll take a few weeks before you can start clipping for use. I'm pretty sure I have an extra one that I could sell for three gold. If you just want some clippings, I can sell you about four ounces for three silver."

Orrin was tempted to just buy both, but he had a full day of fighting ahead of him.

"Just the clippings for now," he decided. "And if you have a mortar, pestle, and some spare vials, I'll take them, too."

Orrin ended up spending a gold piece total for the penidrops, ten vials, and a nice mortar and pestle set. He would try and make the regen potion later. Orrin hurried toward the southernmost gate.

He didn't notice he was being followed.

Chapter 22

Daniel and Madi were waiting for Orrin inside the gate. Brandt and Jude were talking with the guards, probably getting permission to bypass customs completely. A slow-moving line of people entered and exited after answering a bored guard's questions.

"You get what you need?" Daniel asked as Orrin waved to Madi.

"Yes, I did." Orrin moved his cloak to the side and showed off his new belt with vials of murky potion sloshing about.

"That looks disgusting." Daniel recoiled. "Shouldn't they be blue?"

Madi chimed in, "Why would they be blue?"

"Mana potions are always blue in video games," Daniel muttered so only Orrin could hear. "Do health potions look the same? Like sewer water?"

"They look basically the same," Orrin responded. "But health potions have a green stopper. These are white."

Orrin unclipped a white-topped mana potion from his belt and handed it to Daniel, who held it up against the sun and tried to peer through it.

"I'm glad I don't have to drink these too much." Daniel shivered.

"They really do not taste like much," Madi said. "But I do know a person or two who always plug their nose when drinking a potion."

"I did that one time," Brandt interjected as he joined the group. "When I was still a squire. Are we ready to go? We are going to take horses down the road a ways, then leave them picketed. We'll have to hike for the last few miles. Reports coming in say at least one litter of Cloudsabers, but we've also been getting word of people hearing screams from deeper in the forest. A Treelurker shows up and we all run, understand?"

"What's a Treelurker?" Daniel asked.

"Nasty monster that sits in trees and grabs you with its vine arms as you walk by. They don't kill you right away, though. They pin you, cut you up, then when you open your mouth to scream, they shov—"

"That's enough." Madi stomped her foot. "We do not need to tell horror stories before going into the woods. It is bad luck, anyways."

Madi strode away quickly, joining Jude on the other side of the gate.

"What do they do?" Orrin asked quietly.

"They grow more lurkers inside you. Keep you alive with some sort of milk for a few weeks. Then the offspring rip you apart as they hatch. Nobody survives meeting one. They're too damn smart and impossible to evade. Huge rewards for killing one, though. They were bumped up to five-star monsters a few years back."

Orrin pulled his trusty bestiary book out and looked up Treelurkers as they joined the rest.

He nudged Daniel and showed him the rough sketch next to the small paragraph describing its tactics.

"Fuck," Daniel drawled. "That's what almost got me, huh?"

"It seems like it. Look at how much they will pay for a body of one of these." Orrin pointed.

"I would be happy never to see one of those things again." Daniel shivered at the memory. "To think I could have been used as a live breeding factory."

They got closer to the group.

"You do realize we are going to have to ride horses again?" Orrin asked.

Daniel smirked. "I've been getting better. Not everybody spent a week lazing about."

Orrin groaned when he realized he would be the slow member in the group today.

Despite a few accidental gallops and only two falls off the horse, the party set a good pace and kept Orrin in the middle. He got pushed back on his saddle as many times as he almost fell, but his horse simply kept pace with the other surrounding equines.

Daniel had added Jude and Brandt to the party, rounding out their five-person group. Jude had agreed to try Madi and Orrin's strategy and even gave a few extra tips, including one important topic they'd forgotten to consider.

"What will you do if we need to run?"

Retreat was such an obvious thing to plan for, and Orrin had completely missed it. Madi had looked a little ashamed, too.

"Don't beat yourselves up," Jude said as he stood tall in his saddle, looking around the long grass. "Every plan can be improved, every strategy made better. But you will always forget something. That is the thing the enemy will spot first."

"What about just a few black bursts around everyone? You see darkness around you—run," Daniel suggested.

"Would work until we found something that uses darkness to attack," Brandt responded. Jude nodded in agreement.

As the group continued to discuss the merits of different colors for different actions, Orrin found a good purchase on his horse and finally felt comfortable enough to look up Cloudsabers in his book.

[Cloudsabers] Lithe felines the size of a small horse, these monsters use magic to "walk" on air. They cannot fly but can turn on the spot by creating small puffs of clouds that allow quick turns, swift ascents, and brutal attacks from above. While their claws are sharp and deadly, the bite of a Cloudsaber can mean death (****).

"So, how do you kill a Cloudsaber?" Orrin asked.

Brandt had ridden ahead to check out a wagon that was sitting on the side of the road. Jude answered.

"You need to get it on the ground and then crush or take off a foot or two. It is harder for them to be as agile when they can't create their little air cushions."

"Air cushions?" Orrin watched as Brandt waved from a distance and a small man waved back from the side of the wagon. A broken wheel sat on the ground next to him.

"Yeah, they use a small air spell on each paw that gives them a movable wall to run on. It only supports their weight for a moment, but they are already naturally quick." Jude was watching Brandt, too.

Please don't let this be a bandit attack, Orrin thought. *I just want to get some normal levels.*

Orrin suddenly thought back to the man he'd killed. Tears threatened to spill over.

"You okay?" Madi asked.

Orrin grunted and nodded. She looked at him with pity.

Brandt was heading back and signaled all clear.

"Folks hit a rut and snapped a wagon spoke right off," he explained as he drew near. "Nothing to worry about."

Orrin very much worried as they passed by, but to his surprise, nothing happened. They continued down the road for almost two hours before heading off into the tall grass to the south. The forest Orrin and Daniel had appeared in could be seen in the distance.

"We'll bring the horses off the road a bit, just to be safe," Brandt explained. "The forest is only a mile or two over there, but we might have to cut in for a bit to get where the runners have reported the saber sightings."

"Runners?" Orrin could not wait to get off the horse. His inner legs were feeling chafed, and it was taking all he had to not cast [Heal Small Wounds] on himself.

"[Pathfinders], [Trackers], or even the occasional [Druid]," Brandt continued. "They get paid by the Guild to keep an eye out for dangerous monsters. Anything that the lords would pay to exterminate for the safety of the people."

They found a clump of large bushes and tied the horses together and then to the brush. Jude got down and hobbled the horses' legs as well.

"They'll be able to make it to the road if they smell anything approaching but won't wander unless there is danger this way," he explained as he finished tying everything off.

"So, I think we should all stay close," Orrin suggested. "I have a skill that lets me boost all four main stats as long as you stay within fifty feet of me, but it doesn't say how long it lasts."

"Is it like your other increase spells? How long do those last?" Madi asked.

"At level one, those last five minutes," he answered.

"It's probably better to use that before battle, then," Brandt suggested. "If it only lasts five minutes, better to not waste the mana now. Does it cost a lot?"

"Nearly my entire mana pool." Orrin checked the spell.

[Utility Ward] maximum possible Level 1 Strength, Dexterity, Will, and Intelligence increase to yourself and your party within 50 feet. 100 MP.

"Definitely save it, then," Brandt said. "And then get a potion down your throat as soon as possible. If shit goes sideways, take Lady Madeleine and teleport to this location. Priority one is everyone's safety. Priority two is getting Daniel to level ten. Priority three is clearing any monsters we can from the surrounding area. There are a few small towns out this way that will appreciate the help."

Jude stayed in the back as Brandt and Daniel took point. Madi and Orrin stayed in the middle as they crossed the grasslands to enter the forest.

Oh, I should use [Map], Orrin thought. He pulled up the small interface and saw the other four party members appear as blue dots. The horses behind him were white and still clumped up together but were nearing the edge of his one-mile-radius map.

The forest was empty.

"Um, guys. I have [Map], and the forest seems clear."

Brandt quirked his head as he looked back. "You are a multitool, aren't you?"

Madi stepped closer to Orrin and asked, "How far have you progressed your [Map]?"

"I have party, monster, and trap view." Orrin saw no reason to hide the skill. They would all figure it out once he started being a radar machine in the forest. "Do you know a lot about [Map]? I haven't had time to research it too much yet."

"You are the strangest person I have ever met," Madi admitted. "Most adventurers do not purchase a spell or skill unless they have their entire path plotted out. Not to mention you can pick up abilities from completely different builds."

She shook her head as the trees started growing closer together. "As far as I know, [Map] will let you see anything you want to search for. Mining communities use a [Mapper] to target different veins of precious metals, or parents might hire a [Tracker] to search for the smallest traces of a lost child. I don't know all the particular subskills, but [Map] is one of the largest skill sets available."

"That's enough talking, you two," Jude whispered from behind them. "We're in it now."

Orrin focused back on his [Map]. Despite it only giving him sight to within a mile, being able to see through the trees gave him a view better than the rest of the party.

I wonder if I can share the view. He tried to toss the blue box to Madi, but nothing happened. She raised an eyebrow at his hand motion.

"I was trying to share my [Map] with you," he whispered and shrugged.

They moved slowly through the forest. Orrin saw red dots appear at times on the periphery of his sphere of vision, but whatever monster had crept out of the darkness quickly turned and ran at picking up the scents of all five of them.

An hour into their slow crawl through the forest, Brandt held up a hand. They all gathered to him.

"Cat scratches," he mouthed and pointed at the tree nearest him. Large furrows had been dug out of the tree. Orrin noticed several trees in the area were also scratched bare of their bark.

Orrin saw a red dot appear and then move fast toward the party.

"Incoming," he whispered and pointed in the direction of the moving monster.

A light-blue cat appeared between the trees ahead of them. It looked more like a panther but had the bulk of a tiger. Muscles rippled beneath its short hair as it charged along the forest floor.

Orrin used [Identify].

[Cloudsaber] HP 95/95

Brandt and Daniel drew their swords, while Jude twirled his hammer once. The three of them stepped in front of Madi and Orrin.

Madi splashed a green firework in the saber's face. The spell didn't do much damage, only a point or two. The cat's eyes flashed as it lunged toward her. Daniel let out a yell to catch the cat's attention. It turned with all its momentum, not slowing a bit. Orrin caught the smallest puff of air where the big cat's paws hit an invisible wall a few feet up.

It creates air walls to jump in different directions. Orrin cast [Utility Ward] at level one. An extra five points to each stat ticked up, and his mana pool increased by fifty MP.

He popped a vial off his hip, flicked the wax top off with his thumb, and drained the liquid down his throat.

The potion tasted like a day-old green juice—grassy but not disgusting like he had feared. Orrin felt his mana fill back up rapidly.

The cat got close enough for Daniel to swing at it. He held his stance until the last second and swung from the right.

The cat barrel-rolled, and the sword tickled the monster's whiskers. Daniel had missed.

Brandt did not.

As Daniel's sword whiffed, Brandt struck with a piercing attack. His sword dug into the cat's shoulder and dug a long furrow along its left side. The blue feline sprang off another burst of air and landed in a tree above, hissing down as drops of blood fell.

Orrin tapped it with a [Lightstrike] so he would get the experience and tried to see if he could do anything else.

[Cloudsaber] HP 73/95

"It's at seventy-three of ninety-five health," he yelled.

The Cloudsaber eyed him and then dove. A two-hundred-pound cat falling from two stories above him should not be that quick.

Jude appeared from the side and smashed his hammer into the saber's side. It was close enough that Orrin and Madi heard the cracking of ribs. The cat twirled in the air, hitting a tree with its back hip. A snarl and yelp of pain echoed as it hit the ground.

Daniel used a burst of speed to glide across the forest floor and stuck his sword into the cat's head. The back legs twitched once, and the fight was over.

Experience Gained: 160 XP

Orrin looked at his status.

Level 7: 450/700 XP

The fight had been harder than fighting a Dire Rat, but for that much experience split across five of them . . . Orrin did the math. Eight hundred XP for one monster? That would level him if he were able to kill one alone.

"Orrin, check your map." Daniel wiped the blood off his sword using the saber's fur.

Orrin looked back at the map. He'd never closed it.

Six red dots were traveling fast, with a seventh appearing as he watched. Three from the same direction as the one they had killed and four from a bit more south.

"Seven more, three from there and four from over there."

Brandt and Jude shared a look and moved a bit closer to Madi.

"No, stick to the plan," she ordered.

"But—" Brandt began.

"We will do this right," she demanded. "Do not embarrass me in front of the [Hero]."

Brandt and Jude set back up next to Orrin.

"You'll need to try and hit a few with [Shimmersight]," Orrin suggested. "I'm going to boost up your intelligence and will with my level-two spells. It will only help a little, but . . ." He trailed off. He felt useless without more than [Lightstrike] to do damage.

"Sounds good." Madi breathed heavily as she prepared, obviously nervous.

Orrin cast [Increase Will] and [Increase Intelligence] five times each on Madi at level two. With his boosted stats, the cost wasn't quite at one hundred, but he went ahead and downed a second potion.

This is going to be expensive, he thought as he felt his mana filling up again. His stomach fluttered as the potion worked. Then it settled back down. Orrin felt he should be able to take one more potion today. *I really don't want to turn to cycling. I might have to call it after this fight.*

The first two sabers appeared from the secondary direction, with another two close behind them. Moments later, the other three toppled over each other as they ran along the footprints of their fallen brother. They used air puffs on their feet to run upside down and balance back out.

Madi tossed a red firework at the three on the right and a green toward the four on the left.

Orrin waited. The sabers were getting closer and closer.

"Madi?"

Nothing happened.

"MADI?" Orrin prepared to jump forward and teleport the two of them out of danger.

Madi cast three [Shimmersight] back to back to back. Three perfect casts. Orrin watched as one hit the lead Cloudsaber between the eyes, the second splashed across another's nose, and the third tried to bite the glimmering ball of light, only for it to encompass its face.

Three sabers were blinded and fell into each other, scratching and biting. Orrin threw out three [Lightstrikes].

The three melee fighters had stood against the four remaining racing Cloudsabers. Daniel yelled something Orrin could not hear and dashed into the middle of the four monsters.

Daniel activated his [Wind Blades] skill.

Orrin realized how much Daniel had grown in the past week. While that first time he'd used this skill against a few rats, the monsters had been shredded, but Orrin had also taken a small hit from the blast wave. Daniel had been working on control.

The four sabers were thrown hard, hitting trees and rolling across the ground. Large slices of fur and meat had been sheared off and lay in bloody chunks around a heavily breathing Daniel. The sabers were slow to get back up.

Jude and Brandt took the initiative and finished off two of the sabers before Orrin remembered he had not hit these four yet. He cast two more [Lightstrike] spells on the struggling Cloudsabers. A small burst of light that looked like a laser hit each one a second later, burning a small hole into their brains. Orrin looked over at Madi and gave her a thumbs-up.

She was pulling a potion from a bracelet on her wrist. She drank it and sighed. "We still have three left over here, guys."

Finishing the three remaining sabers was quick work without their sight. Although they could smell the party easily enough, they were more likely to hit a tree or each other when they tried to strike. Madi and Orrin let the other guys take turns whittling them down. Daniel and Brandt cut off limbs, while Jude used his hammer to make bloody pancakes out of feet.

Experience Gained: 800 XP (160 XP x 5)
Level 8 obtained!
+10 AP

Orrin looked at his status again

Level 8: 550/800 XP

I'm almost to level nine, too! These things are totally worth the extra headache, Orrin thought.

"Orrin?" Daniel called out as he sat back on his knees. He waved frantically.

"Daniel, that was amazing," Orrin gushed. "I'm level eight now. Did you get to level ten? Did you choose your moniker?"

"I hit level ten, but shut up. I got a prompt that said I had ten minutes to select my moniker. That's all it says. It has a list of suggested shit below, but it is all fire and wind and stuff like that. I tried to enter Dimensional in this prompt and it said, 'Not Accepted,' and my time went down to five minutes."

"That's fine. You still have time to—" Orrin started.

"I put in Time next. The system declined that option, too, and now I have two minutes left." Daniel looked panicked. "Orrin, what do I do?"

Chapter 23

Orrin wasted no time. "Try Space. If that does not work, go with Wind. If the timer hits zero, we don't know what will happen."

Daniel did waste some of his precious remaining time by asking, "Why Space? I don't want to summon comets or something. Wouldn't it be better to try—"

Orrin interrupted him. "Space is more than comets. Think black holes, gravity, and interstellar travel. You already have a magnetic personality and draw people to you. Look around. You have Madi, the daughter of a lord of Dey fighting beside you. You have Brandt and Jude here. I'm here. Space might allow you to find a way home, but more than that, it fits you, I think. I kept thinking about what word was most like those past heroes' monikers, but that still fit you. Space. You fill up a room when you enter. People gravitate toward you. You are a sun burning brightly that keeps us alive and thriving."

Daniel's eyes widened as his friend gave him compliments deeper than the love letters his past girlfriends had written. Orrin watched him process his words, and then steel determination flitted across his face.

"I won't need to choose Wind. Space is going to work," Daniel said confidently.

The party held their collective breath as Daniel looked at a blue box in front of him.

He let out a sigh. "Space Hero accepted."

Madi had suggested continuing a bit more, but Daniel had wanted to get out of the forest before he read any more of his level prompts. He noted he had a lot.

They made their way back to the horses and put together a late lunch. It was midafternoon, and the sun was high in the sky. The bushes gave a small amount of shade as they all sat down.

Orrin pulled up his status, too.

Name: Orrin
Class: Utility Warder
Level 8: (550/800)

Ability Points: 16

HP: 90
MP: 92/130 (+50)

Strength: 9 (+5)
Constitution: 9
Dexterity: 9 (+5)
Will: 13 (+5)
Intelligence: 11 (+5)

Abilities:
[Mind Bastion]
[Dimension Hole]
[Identify]
[Blood Mana]
[Meditate]
[Map]: [Party View]; [Monster View]; [Trap View]; [Zoom]
[Side Steps]

Spells:
[Calm Mind]
[Heal Small Wounds]
[Increase Strength]
[Increase Dexterity]
[Increase Will]
[Increase Intelligence]
[Camouflage]
[Lightstrike]
[Inverse]
[Teleport]
[Ward]
[Utility Ward]

Orrin pulled up the store icon and noticed blinking exclamation points next to all his level-two stat-increase spells. After how quickly he had gone through his mana pools during the fight, Orrin knew exactly what weakness he wanted to shore up.

[Mana Pool] increase MP by 100 MP (onetime purchase) 10 AP
Would you like to purchase for 10 AP?
Yes or No?

Yes.

Orrin felt something inside him bubble up. He felt like he had chugged a soda without breathing. He burped loudly, and everyone looked at him.

"Sorry, purchased something."

Madi shook her head and went back to tying the pelts from the Cloudsabers into a bundle. Brandt had skinned them quickly before they left.

MP 193/280

Yes, Orrin cheered internally. *Now I can cast a lot more before needing a potion.*

He looked at the potions on his hip. All would restore only one hundred MP. *I should have thought ahead. These are wasted now, I guess. Maybe Daniel can use them.*

Daniel was still sitting a few feet from them, smiling as he read blue box after blue box. Nobody had interrupted him since they had returned.

"Yo, D." Orrin did not hold his friend in the same regard the rest of the party did. Jude shot him a glance. "When are you going to come out and play?"

"Shut up," Daniel retorted. "There's so much and so many choices now. I'll fill you in later."

Orrin considered pushing an increase spell to level three, or even bringing [Heal Small Wounds] up but held off.

Once Orrin, Madi, Brandt, and Jude had eaten their fill of cheese and bread, Jude brought a small tray over to the [Hero], who was still ignoring them.

"Eat something, sir," Jude prodded. Daniel just nodded and ate mechanically.

"You think everything went okay?" Madi asked nervously. If anything had been messed up, her father would probably blame her.

"Yeah, he gets like this," Orrin responded. "He'll probably pop out of his trance and then not shut up until we get back to town."

True to his nature, Daniel finished up and turned around with a wide grin a few minutes later.

"Orrin, you are a genius." Daniel clapped his friend on the back.

"I know." Orrin sat up and stretched his arms over his head. "But why don't you tell me why?"

Daniel smirked as he sat down with the group.

"First thing, Space Hero gives me ten points every ten levels to spend. Of course, I dropped them all into strength." Daniel reached out and picked up a saddle. They had removed them while the horses waited and put them across a log to remain somewhat clean. Daniel picked up the heavy leather like it was a dinner plate. He gently placed it back down.

"Ten points!" Jude exclaimed. "That's the highest I've ever heard of. I only get six and the rest of the guards hate me for it, you lucky bastard."

Daniel just smiled and continued, "I also get access to space magic, which actually merged with some of my current skills. [Pull Attention] changed to [Gravity Well]. Instead of just grabbing a target's attention, it physically pulls them toward me as well. [Eagle Eyes] became [Telescope]. It doubles what [Eagle Eyes] gave me in terms of sight. But the best thing is it allowed me to upgrade [Dash]."

"What did [Dash] do?" Orrin asked. "Stupid question. That was how you would get a burst of speed, huh?"

Daniel nodded. "But now it is called [Shooting Star]." He shared a blue box with everyone.

[Shooting Star] upon activation, you can move in straight lines at incredible speeds for two minutes. Speed increased by Dexterity. 10 MP.

"Is that better than [Dash]?" Orrin asked.

"[Dash] costs more and was a onetime move," Daniel explained. "But the best thing is all the new abilities I'll be able to unlock. I want to keep reading more before I upgrade. It's just pages and pages of stuff."

"We can head out now, then," Brandt suggested as he stood and started to clean up the mess they'd made. "We can make it back in time for dinner."

"Sounds good to me," Orrin agreed. "When we get back, is there a way to get a lot of pillows?"

"Pillows?" Madi asked, confused.

"Yep." Orrin nodded. "I'm also going to need someone to throw them at me."

Brandt and Jude exchanged a glance and laughed.

"What?" Jude tried. "What nonsense is this?"

"Daniel threw a pillow at me, and it activated my [Side Steps]," Orrin explained.

Brandt and Jude shut up immediately.

"That doesn't work," Brandt countered. "If it did, everybody would know."

Orrin shrugged. "It did for me. Maybe the [Hero] has to throw it, or maybe people just think it has to be a weapon dodged. It wouldn't be the first time people did something only because 'this is the way it has always been done.'"

Brandt and Jude started debating if this was a viable option to pursue as Orrin tried to keep up in the conversation.

"Is this why you wanted to keep him around?" Madi asked Daniel. "Because he always comes up with the strangest ideas?"

"It is part of it." Daniel smiled, watching his friend arguing with the two knights. "He's perceptive. While he has a hard time seeing the forest through the trees, he picks up on things faster than I ever could. And he's thoughtful. I bet he suggests Brandt and Jude get a book on [Side Steps] just to help the party. He might even try to pay for it."

"That would be too expensive for a theory." Madi picked herself up and tried to lift a saddle. Daniel helped her.

"That wouldn't matter to him." Daniel set the saddle on the first horse and then grabbed two more, letting Madi finish the straps. "He wouldn't even see it as a cost, just an investment in the people around him. Focusing on the big picture, I would worry if Brandt or Jude would stick with us long term. Sure, I'll help them both as much as I can. But Orrin will get lost in helping them maximize their classes."

"So the two of you complement each other's skills and weaknesses." Madi pulled the last clasp tight. "I get why you wanted him in the party so bad now."

Daniel settled the last saddle down. "No. It's really none of that. He's just my friend."

Daniel sighed and yelled, "Orrin, do not make Jude throw mud at you."

They made good time back to Dey. Jude and Brandt offered to take the horses back, and Madi followed them back to the Catanzano house.

"So, what else do you guys want to do today?" Madi queried.

"I'm going to just play around with my new store options," Daniel replied. "See if I can chart a good path forward."

Orrin laughed. "You aren't going to go buy Gerty?"

Daniel stopped in the middle of the street. "Holy shit, I can probably get it now, right?"

"What's a Gerty?" Madi looked confused.

"Yeah, I'm going to go get it." Daniel's eyes glittered crazily.

"It's a sword that he's been drooling over since we got to town." Orrin chuckled as he explained to Madi. They had to take a few quick jogging steps to catch up to Daniel.

Orrin did some quick math in his head. Last time, Daniel's fourteen strength, with the addition of Orrin's five [Increase Strength] at level two that came out to an extra fifteen strength, had barely moved the sword. Daniel was now at twenty-four strength as his base, with the extra five from Orrin's [Utility Ward] still running, equaling the same as the boosted twenty-nine from his first attempt.

Orrin went ahead and tossed five level-two [Increase Strength] spells on his friend as they neared the blacksmith's shop. If his math was correct, each cast would increase his strength by four points, or an extra twenty strength. That would put him near fifty total. If a fighter started at ten strength and spent ten points on strength at level ten, twenty, and so on, they'd have to be level fifty to have the same strength that Daniel did right now.

As they entered, Orrin admired the ceiling again. The way the interlocking metal flowed and moved to clean the soot was fascinating.

Daniel wasted no time and went right up to Jovi.

He gave no preamble and just laid it on the line. "I'm here to buy Gertrude, sir."

Jovi laughed and gave a few more instructions to the apprentice hammering a shortsword into shape.

"It hasn't even been a month, and here he comes to try again." Jovi pulled the stool over and reached for the massive sword. "No charge up front, but if you can't give me a clean swing, I'll not take her back down for a year."

As he put his hands on either side of the hunk of metal, Jovi turned and yelled, "Oi, Franklin. Bring out the armor dummy."

A boy of eleven darted into a side room. He returned pulling a canvas doll larger than himself across the ground.

Franklin set the wood and canvas man up in the middle of Jovi's corner, far away from any working forge. Jovi nodded at him and hefted the sword into the air. He took two quick steps down the stool and held the handle near Daniel.

"Even a down slash would be enough, but don't hurt yourself, boy," Jovi began. "You can always come back next year an—"

Orrin watched his friend take the hilt in both hands and lift it straight up like Arthur and Excalibur—if Excalibur had eaten a car, grown a few extra feet, and weighed a few hundred pounds.

Jovi's face lit up as Daniel took a few steps and then swung, not from above, but a diagonal angle. He miscalculated the weight at the end and had to twirl with the sword, but Daniel had cleaved the armor dummy in two.

Daniel stood breathing heavily as he put the flat of the sword back up on his shoulder, the blade pointed away from his neck.

"Two hundred gold, right?" Daniel asked, smiling broadly.

Chapter 24

Daniel was all grins as he left with his new sword over his shoulder. Madi was aghast at how much he had spent.

"It'll be worth it," Daniel repeated for the third time. "Just imagine how hard I can whack a monster with this thing."

"You still need my buffs to actually wield that thing," Orrin joked. Well, half joked.

"I have a few ideas on how to fix that," Daniel muttered. He turned back to Madi and Orrin. "Did you guys want to do any shopping?"

Madi shook her head. Orrin considered getting a few new potions but decided it was not worth it right now. He could always grab a few tomorrow.

"Let's just head home," Orrin suggested. "I'm getting hungry anyways."

They made their way back to Madi's house. Orrin waited while Daniel took the first shower. Orrin looked around at the marble bathroom with old-timey plumbing. Thick pipes would pump water over his head. Daniel had explained the pricey contraption used his own mana to get the water hot.

Orrin spent half an hour just soaking.

When they finally dressed and went down to eat, Lord Catanzano welcomed them in the dining room, along with Madi, who was all dressed up.

"I hear you had success today," Silas began. "But that you spent nearly all your money on a sword. I hope you don't intend to ask for loans."

Daniel waved off his concern. "You have nothing to worry about. I have more than enough to pay for things. The blacksmith told me the sword was made for a high-level orc woman, so it should last me quite some time."

Silas raised an eye. Orrin also looked at Daniel in askance.

He blushed. "I might have spent some time there just chatting him up."

Madi let out a laugh. "More like every day. For hours."

Silas looked at his daughter laughing with the [Hero] and re- laxed a bit. He raised a hand, and the staff brought dinner in. As they ate, Madi told him of the strategy that Orrin had come up with and their success with the fighting tactics against the Cloudsabers.

"—raced right into the middle of the pack of four, and they just exploded, Father," Madi regaled as Silas sipped his wine. "Cleaning up the three that I had blinded took only a few moments after that."

"And you received experience on all seven?" Silas queried.

"Yes, sir," she responded. "I think everybody got fully split expe- rience on five. Somebody missed two of them, as I got a bit more experience than I should have."

"That was me," Orrin admitted. "I wasn't quick enough on the draw."

"You'll need to do better," Silas said simply and held his glass up for more wine. An attendant rushed forward with a bottle to refill it.

"I think Orrin proved himself well enough," Daniel defended his friend.

"No, he's actually right," Orrin said, surprising Daniel and Silas. "I let my guard down for a second and missed some easy XP."

The table was silent except for the sounds of forks hitting plates.

"But Orrin helped Daniel when he leveled to ten, too," Madi con- tinued after a minute. "Daniel was having some sort of trouble, and Orrin helped him fix it."

"Trouble?" Silas asked a lot with his one word.

"I tried to bite off more than I could chew," Daniel answered vaguely. "Orrin helped remind me of who I really am."

Orrin was sure Jude and Brandt would have given Silas a full rundown by now of everything said, but he still appreciated his friend talking him up.

"Would you be willing to share your upgrade?" Silas asked pointedly.

Daniel looked at Madi then Orrin. He could tell Daniel had the same thoughts. Silas already knew and was asking for politeness.

Daniel gave in. "Space Hero."

"I will admit, not what I would have thought," Silas continued, like Daniel had told him the price of an item he was selling. "Space magic always ends up . . . messy."

"How so?" Daniel asked, intrigued.

"Those who look to the stars rarely understand the forces they are playing with," Silas said. Orrin was sure Silas's eyes had touched on him for a moment.

"I'm no astrologist," Daniel said as he finished the last of his vegetable medley. "But I paid attention in school."

Orrin almost corrected Daniel's mistake out loud. *He meant to say "astronomer." Astrology is what your girlfriend used to explain why she was being a bitch.* He caught himself as he opened his mouth, though. No reason to tip off the Catanzanos.

"I don't know this word," Silas admitted. "I've heard that other [Heroes] come from worlds with different levels of scientific backgrounds. One historian even says some [Heroes] never believed in magic or it did not exist in their worlds."

"Magic was just fiction in our—my world." Daniel pushed himself back from the table and leaned in his chair. "No such thing as dragons, unicorns, or monsters there, either."

"Most fascinating." Silas leaned forward over his empty plate. "Tell me more about your world."

Daniel shrugged and told Silas about cars that people used to travel faster than horses, planes that let humans fly, and cell phones, the tiny boxes that let you talk to anybody, anywhere in the world.

"Surely there were some distance restrictions?" Silas's eyes were wide, like a kid on Christmas morning.

"Not that I know of," Daniel replied. "I'm pretty sure it has something to do with satellites. They could beam the data around or something. I honestly don't know."

The word *satellite* sent Silas into another round of questioning, and soon even Madi had had enough.

"Father, it's late. We should all get some sleep."

Silas blinked and looked at the window. The sun had fully set.

"I apologize." He brushed the front of his shirt and pushed his wheelchair from the table. "I have work to do. Thank you, Daniel. And you, too, Orrin."

With a nod, he left the room. Madi followed close behind.

Orrin and Daniel made their way back to their room, full and tired from a long day. Orrin fell on his bed facedown.

"Mh mh mh mh mh mhmh mhmhmh," he mumbled into his pillow.

"Orrin, you just made sounds but no actual words."

Orrin lifted his head. "Do you think I should level anything?"

"How many points do you have left?"

"Six."

"Anything totally necessary?"

"I think more strength increase for you might be worth it." Orrin flipped on his back. "Especially if you plan on taking that thing out with us."

Daniel had leaned his sword against the wall. The table had started to creak when he'd rested it on top.

Orrin looked over what he wanted to do and what he had. With only six current points, he could get two of his increase stat spells up to level three based on what he'd read. He wanted to try upgrading [Dimension Hole], too, but did not see the point in that currently. [Heal Small Wounds] costs six ability points to level a third time. He could level [Utility Ward] once for only five ability points, but that would cost nearly his entire mana pool to use. He'd thought about the

[Camouflage Ward] as well for only five points but wasn't sure Jude or Brandt could ever be the quiet type, even with magical camo.

"I'll be fine." Daniel smiled. "While you were in the shower, I went through a few more of my boxes. Do you remember what else happens at level ten?"

Orrin pursed his lips then shook his head slowly. "No, I do not, oh great [Hero]. Enlighten me."

Daniel threw his pillow. [Side Steps] did not trigger, and Orrin took it on the face.

"I obtained level ten," Daniel said mysteriously.

"Yes, you did." Orrin copied his weird voice. "And?"

Daniel smiled. "I completed the Quest."

Orrin had forgotten about the Quest. More likely, since the reward was unavailable to him, he'd just not thought about it at all.

Obtain Level 10
Reward: [Hero Kit Level 2] Unavailable Reward

"What did you get?"

"First, all my level-one weapon skills went to level two."

"All of them? That's like ten skills, right?" Orrin pulled up [Sword Proficiency].

[Sword Proficiency] Level 1—You are adept at using swords. -10 AP.

"How much does it cost to go from level one to two in a weapon skill?" Orrin asked.

"I have nine weapon skills that went to level two." Daniel smiled. "And level two would have cost twenty ability points per skill. Now I can see it'll cost thirty to go to the next level, but I probably won't spend that."

"That's insane," Orrin muttered as he did quick math. "One hundred and eighty points' worth of skills for a reward? That's eighteen levels. Wait. Why not upgrade to level three for swords now? I don't get it."

Daniel flicked his hand toward Orrin. "The second thing I got."

Daniel, Hero Level 10, is sharing a Quest.
Quest: Obtain Level 20
Reward: [Hero Kit Level 3] Unavailable Reward
Would you like to accept it?
Yes or No?

Orrin whistled low. "The reward is still unavailable to me."

"Accept it anyway," Daniel suggested. "You can share it for gold, if nothing else."

"Damn. We could do that, huh?"

"I don't know." Daniel shrugged. "But I'll probably share it with Madi, Jude, and Brandt. Brandt hit nineteen the other day. I'm not sure about Jude, but Madi is also under twenty."

"Jude was around fifteen, if I remember correctly," Orrin offered as he accepted the Quest.

"So we can see if Brandt gets a reward," Daniel noted. "That way we will at least know one way or the other."

"Sounds good to me." Orrin felt sleep starting to creep up on him. Riding a horse was the worst. "Good night, D. I'm about to pass out here."

"Same." Daniel checked the position of Gertrude one last time. "See ya in the morning."

After an early breakfast, Daniel and Orrin tried to recreate the [Side Steps] pillow debacle.

Daniel gathered about twenty pillows and threw them at Orrin. It only took a few minutes before Orrin triggered an evasion.

[Side Steps] 95/100

"YES!" Orrin yelled.

"Shut up." Daniel covered his ears. "Some people might still be asleep—it's only around eight a.m."

"Do you not see what this means?" Orrin asked. "Team-building exercise."

"Huh?"

"We are going to get [Side Steps] for everyone and then have a pillow fight."

"You cannot be serious," Daniel groaned. "There is no way anyone is going to take this seriously."

Daniel was wrong. Brandt and Jude were completely open to having a massive pillow fight in the courtyard. Madi also chimed in, and the four party members besides the [Hero] were talking loudly when Silas rolled in.

"What is going on?"

Madi ran to his side. "Father, Orrin found that thrown pillows can trigger growth on a skill, [Side Steps]."

Orrin had to share his skill and then stand there as everyone threw more pillows at him.

His luck was holding on, and [Side Steps] triggered twice.

[Side Steps] 97/100

"Brandt, go find the book on this skill. Jude, go talk to Kevin about available funds. I might have every knight in my household participate in this."

Daniel moaned at the image of a house-wide pillow fight.

Brandt returned quickly with a book entitled *Dodging Death: A Fighter's Collection of Useful Skills*.

"Sire, the skill caps at the tenth level with a 10 percent chance to evade an attack," Brandt read. "There are better options for evasion, but there is nothing in the book that talks about using a nonlethal attack to trigger the skill growth."

Silas read the passage himself and looked around at the four faces watching. Five faces, as Jude approached from talking to the Catanzanos' treasurer. "Let's buy one and make sure it is not a fluke of Orrin's class."

Silas and Jude talked money, while Madi approached Orrin. "Do you realize what this means?"

"Yeah." He smirked. "Do you want to be on my team?"

Madi looked confused. "What? No. Not a pillow fight for triggering the skill. Do you realize what this means for Dey? You just upset an entire industry. Anybody who can create a skill book for [Side Steps] is going be rich overnight. Of course, Father will figure out who can make the books and employ them before the information is released. But beyond that." She put her hand on his shoulder. "More people will live because of you. Even a 10 percent chance of evading an attack can mean life or death. You made everyone's life a little better today."

She smiled and walked away. Jude left to hit up a local bookstore that sold skill books. Daniel straddled up alongside Orrin. "I should be getting credit. I'm the one who threw the pillow."

Orrin raised an eyebrow. "But I'm the one who pissed the [Hero] off enough to throw it in the first place."

They bickered back and forth, laughing at each other.

Jude returned within the hour with a single book. Silas handed it to Madi.

"Me? Shouldn't Sir Bennett or—" She tried to push the book back into her father's hands.

"If this works, I'll outfit the entire party. Eventually the entire house." Silas smiled at his daughter. Orrin saw a softness in his face for the first time.

Madi gulped and opened the book. A second later, she nodded.

Brandt and Daniel were already waiting behind her and chucked pillows at her. They slapped against her head, and she fell forward a step, laughing.

"Nothing yet," she chuckled.

Silas watched as the four young men continued to throw pillows. After a few minutes, he called for a stop.

"It looks like it might have just been another oddity for Orrin's class," he sighed. "Oh, well."

He turned his chair around and began to wheel himself back to his office.

"We can still all beat up on Orrin." Daniel smirked.

Madi threw a pillow at Orrin, who caught it and threw it back. Madi was facing him, holding the pillow, when Brandt threw another one.

Madi dodged to the side.

"Holy shit." She looked at her status screen. "It worked."

Chapter 25

After Silas confirmed Madi's status, the man moved quickly. He sent Jude back out, brought in his secretary, and put together the beginnings of a new business venture in the space of a few hours.

"Why is he on such a warpath?" Orrin asked Madi. "He's got everyone running around like the world is about to end."

Madi looked around and then pulled Orrin around the corner. "Spies."

"Here?" Orrin turned on his [Map] but saw only the normal household members and his own party, minus Jude and Brandt.

"Everywhere," Madi confided. "It's part of being one of the houses of Dey. On the surface, we all help each other and work for the common good. Behind closed doors, they all try to bankrupt each other and take more power."

"So, your dad thinks the other houses will catch on and try to get a piece of the [Side Steps] pie?" Orrin caught on quick.

"Yes. So, he'll move to take over as many skill book creators as possible, possibly throw out a few false leads, or even have Sir DeGuis plant them." Madi kept her voice low.

"What's my cut?" Orrin asked jokingly.

"He'll give you a fair percentage," Madi answered disinterestedly. "But we should really be worrying about the best way to level our skill."

"I'm sorry, what?" Orrin was sure he had misheard her. He was actually going to get paid for this entire debacle?

"I'm sure Kevin has come up with a fair share to put aside for you as the discoverer of this, to be fair, loophole in the system. It is rare but not unique. There was a skill called [Detect] a few hundred years back that everyone used until [Identify] was discovered. Somebody figured out that people with the skill got a boost for using the skill on something new. Like, if they had never used [Detect] on a fork before, the skill would level a bit faster. He created a zoo, but of just hundreds of normal, unique items. He made lots of money, and people leveled their skills."

Skills can be discovered? Orrin learned more every day. When would he stop being surprised?

"I'm not sure how I feel about this," Orrin muttered.

"Oh, he wouldn't try to undersell you." Madi turned her full attention to Orrin. "If he did, one of the other lords could use it against him. If you are unhappy with the price he offers, just let him know."

"No." Orrin waved his hands. "I meant, I don't know how I feel about cornering a market. Wouldn't it be easier for everyone to just take the skill normally? Why the need to make this about money?"

"But not everybody can take the skill." Madi hit her head. "I keep forgetting your class is all over the place. Most people can't just buy the skill. They have to find a skill book."

Madi saw a maid heading down the hall and pulled Orrin into a side room. It looked like a storage room for extra chairs and a large chandelier that was half-covered by a sheet.

"Orrin, who do you think is going to buy the most skill books once this becomes common knowledge?"

"The Guild? Maybe just random adventurers?" Orrin wiped a cobweb off his shoulder.

"The other lords," Madi whispered. "They'll want to outfit all their knights and maybe more with a one-in-ten chance of dodging an attack. Do you have any idea of how expensive it is to train up a knight? Or the loss to a house when one dies?"

Orrin realized the implications. This would make the houses more powerful. He was at fault for making the rich and powerful more rich and powerful.

"So, your dad is going to keep all the power for himself," Orrin spat. "Or charge a pretty penny and allow just enough to the other lords to keep them happy."

"What? No! What kind of person do you think he is?" Madi asked angrily. "He's going to get as many of those who can make the skill books and get contracts with them. That way they will be protected. He'll work with them to create a fair market value, so the other lords can't force them to work at outfitting their entire house with the newest skill. He's working so hard right now because it is very likely someone in our house has already reported everything to another lord. Those few people in Dey who can make this particular skill book? They're in danger right now. I know my father hasn't made the best impression for you, but know that he is working hard to protect the people of Dey."

Orrin felt slightly moved by her speech but still remembered the way Silas had demanded obedience with his skills just a few days before. Madi could stick up for her dad all she wanted, but Orrin would keep his eye on him all the same.

"Let's head back." Madi peeked out the door. "Nobody's around."

Orrin could tell she was still upset about him insulting her father. "Madi, I'm sorry I didn't realize what he was doing. I hope he finds them all. Next time I come up with some way to break the system, I'll be sure to tell him in private."

Madi let out a chuckle. "Yeah, Orrin, if you come up with another system-breaking loophole, please do it only behind closed doors."

They made their way back to the entryway, where Silas was signing papers. Jude and Brandt had returned and already given their reports, as they were both chatting away excitedly with Daniel.

"Orrin!" Daniel waved. "I had a great idea. Come over here."

As Orrin and Madi got closer, Orrin felt a sense of dread. Daniel was holding a ball. It looked a little bigger than a soccer ball and was a little beaten up.

"What's that?" Orrin pointed. "I really don't think that's a good idea, Daniel."

Daniel tossed the ball up in the air and caught it. "While everybody was running around thinking about the skill, I was about to start gathering up more pillows. One of the maids yelled at me for trying to dirty them up. I guess the Catanzanos have good taste and these are filled with some monster feathers that cost their weight in gold."

Madi ducked her head but didn't rebut what Daniel said.

"So naturally . . ." Daniel paused for effect. "I thought of dodgeball."

Hours later, and more bruises than Orrin could count, he crawled into bed.

Despite all his best efforts, the two knights and Daniel had decided that waving pillows around was not manly enough. They had to pelt each other with hard leather balls.

At least my skill leveled, he thought.

[Side Steps] Level 2—2% chance to evade any attack (43/200)

Orrin would admit to himself that playing dodgeball was still better than playing sword dummy for Daniel. He'd never admit it to Daniel, though.

That asshole knows how much I hate dodgeball.

After Silas had worked out his contracts with the four known skill book writers in Dey, he'd allowed Jude and Brandt to also get the skill. He'd also gotten the skill for the [Hero] as a gift. A few hours of play had resulted in the same results as a few months of dangerous, life-threatening adventuring.

Silas had also confirmed Madi's story. The four writers were under his protection and had agreed to exclusively write [Side Steps] skill books at a reduced price. Each book would sell for between seventy and seventy-five gold, depending on other contracts with various bookstores around town.

Orrin would get two gold pieces for every book sold. The information had already hit the streets and every skill book had already been sold. It took an entire week for a writer to create a book, so Orrin wasn't going to be rolling in immediate gold. But Silas said Kevin could invest the steady income and keep him well-off.

Orrin had a question, though.

"With the price being so high, won't that just mean all the houses are buying the skills?"

Silas, who had just finished explaining the great deal he'd cut, looked a bit miffed. "I believe that for the foreseeable future, yes. The houses of Dey will likely purchase the books for their own use."

"What about the adventurers and normal people this could help?"

"If an adventurer truly desires the skill, there are other ways to get it," Silas said. "Or they could try to cut a deal with a house. I cannot control the third-party market."

Orrin thought and asked, "Instead of me getting, what would it be, eight gold a week, could we earmark one book every other month to go to the Guild? They could sell it to an adventurer only. It would make Dey stronger, too, right? Because we'd have stronger people to defend the Wall?"

"You want to give up sixty-four gold every two months so a random person the Guild picks is able to get a skill book?"

Orrin had never really played poker, but Silas's face was unreadable.

"I know I wouldn't be paying full price for one of the books, but I think it would help spread the skill a bit more, right?" Orrin asked hopefully. If Silas turned him down, he could always save the money and do it on his own anyway. If he could find someone to sell him the book.

"You continue to surprise me." Silas smiled at Orrin for the first time with warmth. "I'm beginning to see what the [Hero] likes about you. I'll work it out with the Guild. I can't promise they won't do something untoward with the skill, but giving the adventurers of Dey a chance will be enough."

Silas turned his chair around but stopped and turned back. He'd put his hand out to shake Orrin's.

Orrin sighed in his bed. He considered casting [Heal Small Wounds], but as it was sitting on the maximum and waiting to be leveled, it wasn't worth the extra mana. Instead he used his last mana pool of the night trying to get [Camouflage] higher.

When Daniel came to bed a little later, he didn't even see Orrin there, hiding in plain sight.

There had been no additional sightings of Cloudsabers or other high-experience, low-star monsters in the area for several days. The party played dodgeball whenever Jude and Brandt weren't on duty. Madi worked on controlling her spells better, and Orrin tried to max out all his spells. He was still waffling on what to work on leveling next.

Daniel's growth after hitting level ten was enormous. He'd stopped worrying about saving his skill points and gone a little overboard with his skills and spells. He'd shared them with Orrin the morning after their first dodgeball game.

> [Control Motion] Individual is able to control his body with minute control. (25 AP)

The spell was similar to his own [Mind Bastion] but in the physical sense. The description also didn't give the additional text of controlling his mind, so Orrin wasn't too worried about him turning into a bigger ass than he already was.

Daniel had also bought [Gravity Strike], which looked like an upgraded version of [Power Strike].

> [Gravity Strike] 4x damage on your next hit (20 AP) Error. Similar skill. Replace [Power Strike] for 10 AP.

"I got an error when I bought that," Daniel had explained. "I only had to pay ten points for it, but I had to give up [Power Strike]. I had one hundred points left and might have wasted it, but this looks upgradable and it doesn't cost any mana, which I definitely need to focus on at level twenty. I told you that my ten stat points could go in any stat block, right? I just chose strength because—"

"You're rambling, Daniel," Orrin interrupted. "What did you do?"

Daniel blushed and threw another box.

> **[Home Base] teleport yourself and your party to a destination of your choice. Once set, the destination cannot be changed for one week. Uses per month: 1. -100 AP (Upgradable: 200 AP) (Space Hero Specific)**

For the first time since landing on this world, Orrin couldn't find the skill in his store.

"I tried to set the destination to Earth, and I felt resistance," Daniel reported. "But Orrin, I think this is our ticket home."

The days began to run together, and before Orrin knew it, he'd maxed out [Camouflage] and all his increase spells, and he'd gotten [Side Steps] to level three.

> **[Side Steps] Level 3—3% chance to evade any attack (4/300)**

Orrin felt more comfortable with a shortsword now. Daniel showed him how to stand and swing, using the knowledge that [Sword Proficiency] gave him. Not for the first time, Orrin considered getting a level in a weapon skill. First, he would need more levels.

They hadn't gone on any more leveling excursions. Not because they didn't want to, but because the monsters were unusually quiet.

"I believe a Horde might be attacking the Walls soon," Silas mentioned over dinner. "I was hoping that a new dungeon would be found, but it seems our luck might run out. I don't believe your party is ready to defeat a dungeon. Neither are you ready to defend the Wall to the extent a variable reward warrants."

"No offense," Daniel started. "But I am not sitting on my ass when monsters attack the Wall."

Silas smirked. "I know, Daniel. That's why I'm going to be sending you all to the Aqua Chambers. I've arranged with the Tarris house to allow you all access."

The two dungeons in the area were the Silver Vaults and the Aqua Chambers. The Silver Vaults had been active for over 150 years, but the Aqua Chambers were only a decade old.

Orrin asked, "What about me? I'm not level ten."

Silas waved a hand. "It will be fine. I took care of it. But I do suggest you try to get to ten before going farther than the first or second floor. Sir Bennett and Sir DeGuis have taken turns going through the Chambers, so they will be useful. Maybe you can take a few monsters down on your own before the harder monsters attack."

Orrin did not feel at ease, but Daniel and Madi were ecstatic to be getting a chance to go dungeon delving.

"Please do not get the wrong idea," Silas cut across their chatter. "You will be only going to perhaps the first nine levels. This dungeon has turned back parties at levels in the thirties and forties. Sir Bennett and Sir DeGuis will be under strict orders to return you safely and not go past the ninth level."

Daniel nodded along like a good soldier, but Orrin saw that glint in his eye. The one that always spoke of one thing: trouble.

Chapter 26

Orrin spent the morning after Silas's announcement considering his skills and spell.

He had assumed they would be able to get in another fight or two, possible giving him more ability points and more options. But with Silas's plan to send them away to avoid a Wall horde, the lack of actionable monster sightings, and Brandt's near constant patrols to get fresh information, Orrin decided he was better off spending the points to level an existing ability.

> **Would you like to Upgrade [Increase Strength] (5,000/5,000) for 3 AP?**
> **Yes or No?**

Yes.

> **Would you like to Upgrade [Increase Intelligence] (5,000/5,000) for 3 AP?**
> **Yes or No?**

Yes.

Orrin decided intelligence would be better to increase, as he could cast it on himself and reduce his MP costs. He'd spend more on himself so that the entire party would benefit.

[Increase Strength] Level 3 (0/10,000): increase target Strength by +4 for 20 minutes. (15 MP)
[Increase Intelligence] Level 3 (0/10,000): increase target Intelligence by +4 for 20 minutes. (15 MP)

Wow. Orrin was surprised. *The bonus doubled, the time doubled, and the cost only went up by five mana.*

Orrin used some scrap paper left over from deciphering the [Hero] book to do math. His will was at thirteen and his intelligence was at eleven. [Increase Intelligence] should normally give plus four, but with his will at thirteen, the number would actually bump up to five, and 1.3 times four should mean 5.2 increased intelligence. *Twenty-five extra intelligence on top of my eleven!*

At thirty-six intelligence total, any spell would be cast at three-quarters of the normal cost. Orrin checked his math again. Base cost of spell times (100 minus (36-10))/100 equaled base cost times 74 percent.

So, I could cast [Ward] on everyone before we go into the dungeon for only seventy-five MP and cast [Utility Ward] at level one on everyone as well. I could even give Daniel twenty minutes of plus-twenty-five strength for only a bit over fifty-five-ish MP. I need to figure out the math on that.

Orrin sat with numbers running through his head and sighed. "This is too much math without [Mind Bastion] running."

Daniel, who was rereading the [Hero] book on the bed, looked up. "What is too much math?"

"I bought level-three strength and intelligence, but I don't want to do more math to figure out exactly what I could cast. I think I can boost myself to make spells cheaper, get a [Ward] on everyone to give more breathing room in the dungeon, and get a [Utility Ward] on us as well, but that about uses my entire pool and only lasts a little bit."

"Wouldn't it make more sense to cast [Utility Ward] on everybody before [Ward]? That way, you would get the will bonus and your MP would be higher?" Daniel asked distractedly.

"That . . . would be genius, actually." Orrin threw down the pencil. "I hate just waiting around. I want to fight something and try this."

"Why don't you do something with those gross mushrooms?" Daniel waved in the direction of Orrin's backpack. "They are starting to stink up the room anyways."

Orrin slapped his head. He'd completely forgotten about the regen potions.

"You totally forgot about the potions, didn't you?" Daniel looked up from his book, grinning.

"No," Orrin responded unconvincingly. He yanked the book out of Daniel's hands. "I'll be needing this."

Daniel sighed and stood with a stretch. "That's fine. I'm so done trying to figure out all the rest of the nonsense they talk about. It's like reading the comments section on a superhero movie review. Everyone is arguing that only they have the best interpretation of what is best. I still can't figure out if I'm supposed to get more upgrades every ten levels or if it is just a fluke from a few different [Hero] builds."

"I guess we'll just have to wait and see," Orrin said as he flipped through the pages. "Oh, that reminds me. Are you going to share the level-twenty Quest with Brandt?"

"You want to test out if you'll get something at level ten?"

Orrin nodded.

"If you think it's a good idea, I don't see why not." Daniel shrugged. "Should I try to extort our evil overlord? Maybe give it to Madi and Jude, too?"

Orrin paused in his reading and looked up. "Maybe just share it with all three of them at once. Do it as a good-faith gesture. It's likely they won't get anything at level twenty, but it might keep Silas from asking after the reason you are here."

"You mean the Demon Lord or the war?"

"Both." Orrin shrugged. "Eventually, he is going to get pushy. You can show him the War in Odrana Quest when you have to, but, to be honest, I have no idea what we could do to stop a war."

Daniel picked up a book from his own stack from the library. Orrin had forced him to do more research—on anything—but Daniel had not shared any actual useful information yet.

"I tried reading through this." Daniel crossed the room and left it on Orrin's nightstand. "It goes into the politics of the different countries and the race relations between the elves, orcs, dwarves, and humans. I'll be honest, it's dry and totally stilted."

"How do you mean?" Orrin asked as he picked the book up and read the cover. *Beyond Borders: Relationships Between the Races.*

"The author blames a lot of stuff on the other races. He basically said that anyone can make it in this world with hard work and implies they just don't try as hard."

"That sounds a bit fucked up." Orrin flipped through the pages. It did look a little dense.

"He gives a good overview of relations between each country and the 'preserves' that the main populations of the orcs, dwarves, and elves live on. But when he starts talking about the races individually . . . big oof."

"Racist?"

"Yeah. Real privileged energy."

"Great," Orrin said sarcastically and rubbed his eyes. "I'm guessing you found out more about Odrana and this war?"

"Not directly." Daniel was clasping his armor on. "I asked Jude about it. He told me. It fits with a little bit of what's in there, but something is missing."

Orrin tossed the book back on the nightstand. "Can you give me the highlights before you go meet Brandt for your daily beatdowns?"

"Ha," Daniel chuckled. "I'm taking him out about half the time now."

"Odrana?" Orrin prompted.

"Odrana is a neighbor of Dey. They are actually the only real border country, as the bottom third of Dey's lands run up against the forest we arrived in. It's technically the Untamed Forest, but everyone just calls it the Forest. Odrana covers most of the lands east and north, all the way to the sea. It's pretty massive. I got a peek at Silas's map, and Dey is about one-twentieth the size."

"So who are they fighting? The other country, what was it called again?"

"Veskar? No. They are the other superpower country, but that border is actually pretty secure, according to Jude. Odrana is fighting the elves. The elven nations live in a big forest north of Dey and in the top corner of Odrana's lands. Everybody has always considered it a small sovereign nation, but Odrana has been pushing the forests back, I guess. Or the elves attacked first to create more forest. The rumors fly both ways."

"So, a human-and-elf war. That sounds super original," Orrin muttered as he picked up the ingredients for the regen potion.

"You going to come by and work on your sword skills more later? I still think you should take [Sword Proficiency]."

Orrin dropped a handful of the mushrooms he bought into his mortar. "I'll stop by once I make a few of these potions. I want to see how far I can push myself. Regenerated mana doesn't count as a new pool, so I might be able to increase how many spells I can cast a day."

Daniel paused. "As long as you don't go and—"

"Yes, Dad, I'll be keeping [Mind Bastion] off."

Daniel just rolled his eyes and went to find Brandt.

A few hours later, Orrin finished his first batch of regen potion. He had ground the mushrooms into powder, boiled water, and then, using a small sieve he'd borrowed from Silas, run the hot water over the powder.

According to the book, this first cleanse would take out all the poison from the mushrooms.

For a minute, Orrin considered finding a real [Alchemist] and having them make this instead. Ingesting poison mushrooms at the behest of an ancient dead [Hero] was terrifying.

The book was clear, though—this step, if done correctly, would remove any toxicity from the mushrooms and leave behind the first step to creating regen potions. He had to wait for the powder to dry again over the small candle he had just for this.

He kept an eye on the candle to make sure none of the powder burned and was wasted. He moved it in small circles, following the book's recommendation of every five minutes for an hour.

Finally, the powder turned white again from the wet gray damp it had been. Orrin removed the candle.

Next, take the white residue and mix with the 10 grams of leaves of a blueberry bush.

Crush in the 5 grams of hips from redthorn flowers.

Add 5 grams of purified water and mash into a paste.

Orrin had picked up the different ingredients from four different shops, just as the book suggested. This [Hero] might have been more paranoid than he was. Orrin appreciated the thought process as he mixed and crushed the different bits.

Spread the paste evenly into eight 10 milliliter bottles. Add an additional 5 grams of purified water to each bottle. Shake.

Orrin used a tiny spoon no longer than his finger to scoop the paste into each bottle, stopping once each was half-filled. He topped each bottle off with the large beaker of purified water he had and shook each little glass vial separately.

Now for the dangerous part. Orrin groaned at having to be his own guinea pig.

Daniel and Brandt were still going at it when Orrin arrived. Brandt noticed him first and signaled for Daniel to stop.

"Good afternoon, Orrin." Brandt was breathing a little heavier than he would have been even a few days ago. "What brings you out today? Want to go a few rounds?"

Daniel chuckled and sat heavily on the ground.

"Actually, I was hoping to cast a few spells and try out a potion I made." Orrin waved the goopy-looking vial.

"Sure?" Brandt answered, confused. "Do you need us?"

Orrin cracked the fingers on one hand and then the other. "Just get me to a healer if I start shaking."

"Wait, what?"

Orrin chugged the potion and started casting all his most expensive spells.

He started with [Increase Intelligence] level three, five times on himself. Normal cost fifteen MP per cast. Total cost seventy-five MP. But now his intelligence was sitting at thirty-six.

MP 155/230

Orrin watched as his MP started ticking up, one every second.
It works!

He cast [Increase Strength] level three on Daniel five times. Normal cost fifteen MP. With his intelligence at thirty-six, he only spent fifty-five MP. He slapped another five [Increase Strength] spells on Brandt, too.

Only ten seconds had passed, and his MP was down to under one hundred but swiftly climbing back up.

"You're smiling like you found a secret cheat or something." Daniel smirked.

Orrin smiled and pulled up his status. Time to max out everything he could.

Since the potion only lasted one hour, Orrin planned to use every second. He would keep his own intelligence maxed out the entire time to reduce the actual cost. He should be able to regenerate thirty-six hundred MP. Since casting a spell gave the entire cost as experience for leveling that spell, even when the cost was reduced, he could probably increase the total experience output by 24 percent.

Almost forty-five hundred points to his spells.

Except Orrin had forgotten one thing: he could level [Increase Strength] and [Increase Intelligence] using only the three of them. And the spell lasted twenty minutes. So he could only cast a full set three times each. He had nothing else to level . . . except [Teleport].

"You guys want to go on a trip?"

Chapter 27

Brandt shook his head. "No way. We can stay here and—"

"Yes," Daniel interrupted. "I want to take a look at the Pass. How far can you teleport?"

Brandt looked between the two boys with panic.

"Ten miles per jump," Orrin answered. "But with all three of us, I would need a minute or three between jumps."

Brandt stood up and started to walk out. "If you really mean to do this, I must report before we go. Lord Catanzano will want to talk before—"

"Brandt, if you leave, we will just go alone," Daniel teased the knight.

Brandt stopped and turned back. His duties conflicted, so he decided to do his best to keep the young [Hero] alive.

"Jude said the Pass is about eighty miles long." Daniel chatted as he retightened his armor. "Do you think we can make it all the way?"

Orrin pulled his armor out of his [Dimension Hole] and started pulling it on. "We have about fiftyish minutes. If I can get three or four teleports off every ten minutes, that's about fifteen to twenty jumps. We might be able to make it to the end, especially if I keep my intelligence up."

Brandt was still floundering.

"We could always just camp out in the woods overnight if we don't make the full distance," Daniel joked, giving Orrin a wink at Brandt's unease.

"Yeah, if we brought Madi along, we could—"

"No." Brandt put his foot down. "Lady Madeleine will not be coming on this trip."

Orrin chuckled. It was rare to get Brandt so worked up.

"All right, then, let's go do some scouting. Maybe we can find this Horde that's supposed to be coming," Daniel said as he strapped his old sword to his back. Gertrude was still too big to carry around for daily use yet.

Brandt, Daniel, and Orrin left the house through the side door. Brandt's neck swiveled as they walked through the house, trying to find Silas. He had no luck.

Once they were outside, Orrin cast [Teleport] on all three of them and directed his thoughts past the Western Wall.

With no sound, the three disappeared.

There was also no sound as they appeared in the tall grass outside the city. Orrin could see the Wall in the distance.

"This isn't ten miles, O," Daniel complained.

"Shit," Orrin sputtered as he realized his mistake. "I can only teleport to a known point. I think this is as far out as we went last time."

Brandt had drawn his sword and was watching the nearby forest. Orrin reacted quickly and pulled up his [Map].

"There's nothing there, Brandt," Orrin comforted the man. "I took a look with [Map]."

"There are monsters that can hide from scrying spells," Brandt said. He didn't lower his sword, but his posture relaxed a little.

"If we can't teleport to the edge of the Pass, want to try and find some monsters to fight?" Daniel asked, eager to gain some experience.

"That is well outside what I agreed to," Brandt replied. "We should head back now. Or go to the Untamed Forest."

"That's not a bad idea," Orrin admitted.

Daniel had other ideas, though. "Brandt. Hey, Brandt, look at me."

Brandt turned his eyes off the forest line and looked at Daniel questioningly.

"If I share a Quest with you, will you be cool?"

Brandt's eyes widened in excitement, then narrowed suspiciously. "I won't betray my house."

Daniel laughed. "I'm not asking you to do that. I just want you to cut loose a bit. Let's kill some monsters and have some fun. If there is anything too crazy, Orrin can teleport us away."

Brandt thought only a moment before giving a curt nod.

Daniel flicked his hand and threw his level-twenty Quest to Brandt.

"This says the reward is unavailable," Brandt read aloud.

"Yeah, I'm hoping the system gives you something anyways," Daniel said and shrugged.

Orrin kept his eyes on his [Map] and set a [Utility Ward] on them all. He followed up with a personal [Ward] on all three of them. As they neared the woods, his MP was almost full again.

I've probably got forty-five minutes left, he thought. *This regen potion is the best.*

Ever since finding out the downside to cycling with [Blood Mana] and [Mind Bastion], Orrin had been bummed. Not being able to use a cheat really grated.

A red dot passed by the edge of his [Map].

"We got something at the northwest," Orrin said and pointed in the direction. Then, he cast [Camouflage] on himself.

"I hate that spell," Daniel muttered. "It gives me a headache trying to keep track of you."

Orrin whispered directions and stayed between the two fighters as they moved in the direction of the red dot. Orrin watched his [Map] until he spotted something different.

"Five red dots surrounding a white dot," Orrin whispered. "About three or four hundred yards ahead."

Daniel and Brandt nodded. Orrin recast all his highest-level buff spells on each of them, trying to keep his own mana pool at least halfway full.

As they crept closer, Orrin gagged at the sight in front of them.

A body was being pulled apart by large dogs. One arm had already been snapped at the forearm, and two of the dogs were tearing into it with their teeth. One dog shook a leg in its mouth, while the fourth kept a tight grip on the neck.

The dog that had led them here was circling the pack.

Orrin used [Identify].

[Fetid Canine] HP 80/80

That poor adventurer, Orrin thought. He wondered if he could get a name to report the death back at the Guild. He cast [Identify] again.

Elliot Hart
Pathfinder
Level 35
HP: 3/130
MP: 0/150

Strength: 14
Constitution: 13
Dexterity: 19
Will: 15
Intelligence: 14

"He's alive!" Orrin yelled as he cut off [Identify] before the skills and spells started rolling in. He ran past Daniel and Brandt and cast his highest [Heal Small Wounds], which dropped his [Camouflage].

"Orrin. No!" he heard Daniel yelling behind him. But Orrin hadn't been using [Mind Bastion] for over a week. He hadn't been able to drown out the dead bodies or stop the dreams of the man in the street bleeding out.

I have to save him, Orrin thought, his emotions overriding every bit of logic.

The dogs gnawing on his extremities let go and sniffed the air, then turned toward Orrin. The latest to join the circle was already running his way.

Using [Inverse] through [Increase Dexterity] five times dropped the charging dog's dexterity. With his will and intelligence boosted, the cost was only thirty-five MP for the actual spells and an extra seventeen MP for inverse. The dog tripped over its own feet.

Orrin hit it with [Lightstrike] and kept moving. The dog stayed frozen on the ground.

Some small logical part of his brain yelled at him, while another realized his boosted spells had taken away twenty points of dexterity from that dog.

I don't have to fight them if they can't move. Orrin's grin was feral.

In moments, another three of the dogs were lying on their sides, whining. Orrin's MP was nearing single digit but quickly ticking back up.

The final dog was too close. Orrin didn't have time to cast the full five inversed dexterity debuffs. He got one off before the Canine jumped.

[Side Steps] activated, and the dog sailed past him.

"What the . . ." Brandt trailed off as he approached. He swung his sword and took the Canine across the face. Another few quick swings and it was dead.

"Are those dead?"

"I zeroed out their dexterity," Orrin explained.

Daniel was only a few seconds behind Brandt. He squatted by the first frozen dog. "How long does this last?"

"Should be ten minutes," Orrin said as he plunged his sword into the head of a Fetid Canine. It died without a sound.

Experience Gained: 100 XP

"Kill them all," Orrin demanded.

Daniel shook his head. "This is all your experience. We'll check out the body."

"He's alive." Orrin didn't argue and stabbed another frozen Canine. "I tossed a heal on him."

Experience Gained: 100 XP

Daniel and Brandt knelt near the fallen man while Orrin killed another two Canines.

Experience Gained: 200 XP (100 XP x 2)
Level 9 Obtained!
+10 AP

Level 9: 50/900 XP

"Hey, Brandt," Orrin called out. "How close are you to level twenty?"

Brandt looked up from the unconscious man. Despite Orrin's healing, the man's arm was still shattered, and his legs were cut up something fierce.

"A few hundred, why?" the knight asked.

"Just wondering if you completed the Quest," Orrin answered. He started walking toward the man they'd saved. "I need to heal him up."

"Do you have enough mana left?" Daniel asked. "You . . . you kind of went a little wild there. Are you—are you okay?"

"I'm not using [Mind Bastion], if that's what you're asking."

Daniel put his hand on Orrin's shoulder. "No. I'm asking if my friend is okay. You scared me, running in like that."

Orrin shook himself and took a deep breath. "Sorry. I saw him laid out there and just . . . I lost it."

"More like found another cheat. I didn't know you could just take down an army of monsters," Daniel said as he nudged Orrin and tried to lighten the mood.

"If it weren't for the potion, I couldn't have done it. The buffs really start stacking the higher in level I get them." Orrin put another two heals on the man and then realized his zeroed-out mana was probably the reason he was unconscious now.

[**Increase Will**]

The man's eyes fluttered, and he let out a long groan.

"You're safe." Orrin remembered some of his mom's first aid training. "We took care of your wounds, but you shouldn't move yet. Stay still while we—"

Hart's eyes snapped open, and he tried to sit up.

"Let me up," the man yelled as Daniel held him down. "I have to get back to Dey. There's a Horde coming. A Fogbinder is leading a small army of Kniferunners and Fetid Canines."

"What?" Brandt pushed in closer. "Did you say a Fogbinder?"

The man nodded and tried to push Daniel with his broken arm. He let out a pained gasp.

"You're still not fully healed." Orrin tried again. "These wounds are closing up slow, and I can't get your bones to set."

"Daniel. Orrin. We need to get back to the Wall, now." Brandt talked over Orrin.

"We just took out those Canines," Daniel argued. "We've got some time. Just let Orrin heal him u—"

"You don't get it," Brandt interrupted him again. "You just fought Fetid Canines. They aren't much on their own, but their bites are slow to heal and can spread necrosis if not healed. A Kniferunner is just a big spider, about the size of a horse. Its legs are sharper than swords and they generally just dash over adventurers, stabbing them multiple times."

Brandt paused and made sure both were looking at him. "Fogbinder is a type of demon class. It means we need a full Wall response army set up now. One of those could kill every person in Dey."

Chapter 28

"Elliot, how far behind is the Horde?" Orrin turned and asked the man. He was still trying to make it to his feet. The Canine bites festered and took off a few HP at a time.

That must be how he went down, Orrin thought. *A few bites from a Canine and anyone who can't heal would have to use everything they had to try and make it back for healing before they passed out.*

"How di—" Elliot started but grimaced in pain as his leg slipped out from underneath him. "Never mind. I've been running a full two days. They had just made it into the Pass. I'd guess we have another day or two before they get here."

Daniel put Elliot's arm over his neck and hefted the man upright. "Orrin, we need to teleport back."

Orrin watched his mana ticking back up. "I need another minute, max."

Elliot looked between the three of them as Brandt started cutting the tails off the five Canines.

"Proof of kills," Brandt said to Orrin's questioning look. "Plus, some ingredient shops will pay a lot for the tails. They can be used to make necrosis-resistance potions."

As soon as his MP was full, Orrin teleported all four of them to the Catanzano house.

"Why back here?" Daniel complained. "We need to get to the Wall and warn them."

"And tell them that we just popped over for a quick jaunt?" Orrin asked. "I think just telling Silas would be better, don't you?"

Daniel grunted but didn't argue. The guards at the front door let them in, and one went running for a healer at Brandt's order.

"Why does he need a healer?" Orrin asked. "Is my healing not enough?"

"I don't know the exact skills," Brandt answered as he helped Daniel lower the man onto a couch inside the front door. "But something else is needed here. See? The bite and claw marks open back up after a few minutes to weep."

Orrin saw what he meant. The bite marks that had closed over with his initial healing spell were breaking open like a popped suture. The couch was already covered in blood and pus.

The sound of wheels on the tiled floor alerted Orrin to Silas entering the room behind him.

"What happened?" Orrin could see Silas take in the scene as he put his hand on the man's head and turned to Brandt.

"Found a runner being attacked by Fetid Canines. He reported more Fetids, Kniferunners, and a Fogbinder, sir. Twenty-four to forty-eight hours," Brandt reported.

Orrin would have added a lot more to the story but quickly realized Brandt was a soldier reporting to his superior officer. Details could come later.

"Sir Bennett, I want you to go straight to Lord Wendeln and alert him of the Fogbinder. The only reports we have so far are of the dogs and spiders." Silas closed his eyes as he touched his other hand to Elliot's head. A long second passed, and Silas's eyes opened.

"Tell him I've confirmed a Fogbinder. Then go to the Timpe House. She'll try to resist, but have her evacuate the nearest residents from the western side or this could be a bloodbath. Dismissed."

Brandt saluted and ran.

"You two can tell me more later," Silas said. "I'm guessing Brandt sent for a healer?"

"Yes, he did," Daniel answered.

"My healing doesn't do more than put a bandage on the wound for a few minutes," Orrin complained. "I can top his health off if he needs it, though."

"Best to wait," Silas said as he put his hand over Elliot's eyes. The man fell back fast asleep.

"What?" Orrin started to ask but just rolled his eyes. "Was that necessary?"

"He's in pain," Silas explained. "I simply let him sleep. Now, what were you doing on the wrong side of the Wall with my knight?"

Orrin explained what had happened, telling Silas that Daniel had told him about the potion and not giving the full extent of the potion's strength.

"So, this was just luck?" Silas asked doubtingly. "You just happen upon a man about to die. A man who has information that will give us enough time to turn back a Horde that most likely would have killed hundreds. And you say it was due to testing a potion?"

Daniel stepped forward a bit. "You can believe us or not, but what Orrin said is the truth. If it weren't for his [Map], we wouldn't have even found Elliot."

Silas sighed and rubbed his eyes. "I believe you. But that's the problem. You two seem to have a knack for finding your way into things you should avoid at such a low level. Do you even know what a Fogbinder is?"

Orrin had already searched the F section of his bestiary and come up empty while he waited for his mana to regenerate in the woods. He shook his head. Daniel did the same.

"The demon race lives on to the west. The lands dip south to where the Demon Lords usually lived but also far to the north as well. Demons roam in droves. Some build cities, but most wander alone. They wander with the monsters." Silas paused.

"They wander with the monsters and become monsters themselves. A Fogbinder uses water or wind magic—we don't know for sure, as the class is demon-only. They use this magic to control monsters. They can direct them remotely and don't have to even attack themselves. That one is leading a Horde down the Pass. . ." Silas trailed off.

"You two and my daughter will take Sir Bennett and Sir DeGuis and get out of town tonight. I've already made arrangements with the Tarris family. You will have access to the Aqua Chambers. Brandt knows the way."

A woman in her forties entered through the door. She bowed to Silas and then began moving her hands over the passed-out runner. Silas chatted with her quietly as the man's wounds closed slowly after every pass.

This was the first healer that Orrin had seen up close. He wondered what other spells she was using.

He used [Identify].

Silas's head swiveled to Orrin, and his eyes flashed. Orrin's skill failed, and Silas gently shook his head.

"Orrin, we should probably get ready," Daniel said, oblivious to what had just happened.

Orrin didn't know [Identify] could be completely rebuffed like that. Silas hadn't shown that ability when Orrin had used it on him. Of course, Silas had also just been hit with a debuff for the first time, so maybe he hadn't reacted quickly enough.

"Yeah." Orrin nodded slightly to Silas and left the room with Daniel.

"What's wrong?" Daniel asked as soon as they were out of sight.

"I tried to use [Identify] on her, but Silas stopped it somehow," Orrin responded.

Daniel hit him upside the head. "You did no research on the Hospital?"

"Ow!" Orrin rubbed the back of his head. "What the hell? No, I've had more important things to research lately. Why would I care about some healing facility?"

Daniel opened the door to their room and stepped inside. He started throwing all sorts of items on his bed from the drawers nearby. Ropes, a small axe that Orrin recognized from their first days here, and even a rolled-up sleeping bag.

"The Hospital has a monopoly on healing," Daniel explained as he started shoving the items into his old backpack. "You have to work there for a few years before they teach you how to unlock a healing class. Nobody really knows how it works, because healers are sworn to secrecy."

"So if they know I can heal, they'd come after me?" Orrin asked, suddenly worried about yet another thing.

"No." Daniel shoved the sleeping bag into the top of his pack and tried closing it. "There are other people who occasionally figure out how to heal, but as long as they don't go trying to compete with the Hospital, they mostly leave them alone. Madi said—"

"You got all this information from Madi?" Orrin interrupted. The look on Daniel's face shut him up again. "Sorry."

"Like I was saying," Daniel continued as he finally got the top closed. "Madi said that rogue healers work mostly as midwives or triage doctors during wars, but they have other skills they use most of the time. The last time somebody tried creating a competing Hospital, everyone was found dead and the building was burned to the ground."

"Fuckkk." Orrin whistled. "So using [Identify] to figure out their skills would probably be a highly terrible idea."

Daniel nodded. "Silas probably just saved your life. If that healer had [Awareness], she would have known you tried to read her."

"What's [Awareness]?" Orrin began to ask. "Never mind, I can look it up."

Orrin pulled his store up and searched.

> [Awareness] allows you to know when scrying spells and skills are used on you. If used with [Hide Status] allows you to block most scrying spells and skills to a greater extent. -3 AP

"That reminds me," Daniel said as he plopped his bag on the ground and sat on his bed. "You can see skills already, right? With your [Identify]?"

"Yeah." Orrin closed the blue box. "Why?"

"Don't share that with people," Daniel warned. "Madi said that [Identify] has some unknown power-ups. After a time, some people can read more than a general class type for people, with a health amount for monsters. But it is rare, and nobody shares how that gets upgraded."

"I just could see people's stats and skills from the beginning, though," Orrin countered. "Why would I get an upgraded . . ." He trailed off. "I got [Identify] from that first Quest I got to save you. Remember?"

Daniel shivered. "Don't remind me. I guess saving the [Hero] was worth it."

Orrin finished packing, too. He didn't bring a bag, though. He put a sword and a few knives in his [Dimension Hole], along with his original bedroll. He left everything else in his drawers.

"Did you have enough time to look into the dungeon at all?" Orrin asked. Daniel shook his head.

"No, but Brandt has gone in a few times. He said the Aqua Chambers is mostly ice monsters. People turn back because they get too cold. Fire magic barely works in there. He said every time his party had to turn back because they ran out of supplies."

"I have ten points. I could upgrade my [Dimension Hole] and carry food and water," Orrin suggested.

Daniel shrugged. "We can ask Brandt. I know the general idea for a dungeon is just working our way farther down until we find a core, but I'm not sure how long we should plan to be away. Silas doesn't think we can really finish this dungeon off, but it will be good practice for the party."

"So you've already given up?" Orrin chided. "What happened to the guy who ran stadiums until he threw up just to prove a point?"

"I did that because Mr. Johnson said I wasn't in good shape anymore because I played basketball the season before. I had to show him that . . ." Daniel trailed off. "You're just trying to rile me up."

Orrin smiled. "Why would I do that?"

"You want to defeat this dungeon, too, don't you?" Daniel smirked.

"Just imagine the look on Silas's face when we get back and tell him we destroyed the Aqua Chambers," Orrin said, changing the tone of his voice to mock Silas when he named the dungeon.

Daniel's eyes twinkled.

Orrin pulled up his status and selected only his skills and spells with progression.

Utility Warder 9 50/900 XP
AP: 10
Skills:
[Side Steps] Level 3 (5/300)
[Dimension Hole] upgradable

Spells:
[Increase Strength] Level 3 (1,530/10,000)
[Increase Intelligence] Level 3 (1,665/10,000)
[Increase Will] Level 2 (5,000/5,000) !
[Increase Dexterity] Level 2 (5,000/5,000) !
[Teleport] (800/5,000)
[Heal Small Wounds] Level 2 (5,000/5,000) !
[Camouflage] (9,780/10,000)

He also could still buy [Utility Ward] level two for ten AP, but it cost two hundred MP to use. [Merge] was too expensive right now at twenty AP. He also had the [Camouflage Ward] and [Light Ward] options for five AP and one AP, respectively.

"Hey, Daniel," Orrin called out. Daniel was lying down and reading another book. Actually, it was one Orrin had originally grabbed, *Spatial Magics*.

"Hmm?" Daniel didn't put down his book.

"You said the dungeon is all ice magic, right?"

"Yep."

Orrin pulled up the store and searched for "Ice."

Thousands of options scrolled by, the same as normal. Orrin set the filter to show by smallest AP cost.

[Ice Dagger] summon a dagger of hard ice. Does minimal damage but will not melt in the hottest of fires. Each dagger lasts one hour. 1 MP per dagger. -1 AP

[Fists of Ice] coat your hands in hard ice. Counts as unarmed combat. Adds strength modifier damage to all attacks. 10 MP for one hour. -1 AP.

Orrin scrolled through all the different ice weapon options. *Ice Sword, Ice Spear . . . Who would ever want an Ice Lance?* he thought.

[Icebolt] shoots a bolt of ice. Damage scales with Will. 50-foot range. 5 MP per bolt. -1 AP

[Shaved Ice] creates shaved ice by the gallon. 5 MP per gallon of shaved ice. -1 AP.

[Ice Defroster] makes natural ice within 10 feet melt into water. 10 MP. -1 AP.

The options started getting weirder and weirder. Most seemed to be set to specific jobs and not geared toward adventurers at all. The few that he did find were situational at best.

[Ice Shield] create layers of ice in front of you to protect from attacks. 20 MP. -1 AP

[Ice Scream] let out a shout of frozen icicles that pierce your target. 10 MP. -1 AP

Orrin went back and pulled up [Icebolt] and [Ice Dagger].

"Take a look at these," Orrin said and tossed the blue boxes toward Daniel.

Daniel read and frowned. "Why would you want these? Don't you already have your [Lightstrike]?"

"I'm testing something," Orrin responded. "I'm leaning toward Ice Dagger, just because I can throw them as knives for really cheap."

"Throwing knives are not a real thing. First, you have to be amazing at throwing them. Second, you have to be able to compensate and hit a moving target. Third, most knives wouldn't penetrate bone, so the most you'd do is scratch someone . . . or, in your case, yourself."

Orrin threw a pillow across the room. Daniel didn't move, and the pillow landed by his feet.

"See?"

"Fine, but it could be any type of weapon, not just a dagger. Maybe a sword?" Orrin asked.

Daniel put his book down on the nightstand. "What's the play here? Why do you want to waste an ability point so bad?"

"If it doesn't work, I'll feel stupid," Orrin admitted. "But what if I can unlock an ice ward?"

Daniel gave it a thought, making Orrin feel better that his friend hadn't dismissed the idea outright.

"That'll work, I'm sure," Daniel responded after a minute. "You shouldn't take anything that you'll have to aim. No offense, but with me, Brandt, and Jude doing up-close fighting, I don't want us to have to worry about you chucking daggers or throwing spears. Why don't you want to take [Icebolt]?"

"It just seems so . . . lame," Orrin admitted.

"Anything else useful?"

Orrin spent a few minutes reading names off the store list. Although the names appeared, he had to select the name to read a description. Most were pretty easy to guess, though. Daniel chuckled at [Ice Scream] when Orrin read it aloud. Orrin hadn't gotten it the first time around.

"Just take [Ice Sword] or [Icebolt]," Daniel suggested. "It's not like you are planning on actually using this long term, right? Just to unlock a potential ward?"

Orrin nodded.

"It doesn't really matter too much, then, does it?"

Orrin selected [Ice Sword] and spent a point. *Down to nine ability points.*

"You bought the sword one, didn't you?" Daniel smirked.

Orrin stood up and cast the spell. A shortsword appeared in his hand. Although it was made of ice, the handle wasn't slippery or cold. It just felt right in his grip.

"How'd you know?" Orrin asked.

"You really seemed to hate the idea of [Icebolt]," Daniel said and picked his book back up.

A cursor started blinking on his status page. Orrin opened it up.

[Ice Ward] creates a ward around yourself and your party within 50 feet that protects against Ice Magic for MP maximum. 20 MP. -1 AP.

Orrin hit *buy* right away and smiled.

"It worked, huh?" Daniel was grinning. "You really think we are going to take down a dungeon that has stood for decades before you even reach level ten?"

Orrin swung his ice sword around the room. It really was weighted better than his sword that he carried around.

"Of course we're going to defeat the dungeon," Orrin responded smugly. "This is the [Hero]'s party, after all."

Daniel let out a long groan.

Chapter 29

When Brandt returned, he gave an hour time frame before they would leave. Daniel had a problem.

"If we are taking horses, I can't bring Gerty," he complained.

"We can't take a wagon just so you can bring your big sword," Brandt retorted. "Get stronger for next time."

As he walked away, Orrin felt bad seeing the dejected look on Daniel's face.

"I could try to put it in my [Dimension Hole] if you want," Orrin offered.

Daniel looked up with hope. That hope turned to ashes when Orrin failed to make the sword disappear. His magical space pocket was too small.

Orrin looked over his choices and made another one of his spur-of-the-moment decisions. *I'm going to really regret not sticking with the plan.*

Would you like to upgrade [Dimension Hole]? 3
AP
Yes or No?

Yes.

Gertrude disappeared. Orrin was able to put all the rest of his supplies into [Dimension Hole] as well.

"What? It didn't work at first—what gives?" Daniel queried.

"Upgraded it. I can try to bring more food, too."

According to Daniel, who had actually been doing the research this time around, most dungeon delves failed due to one of two main issues: One, a party member or two died. Without a full party, it was pretty much pointless to try defeating a dungeon. Two, the party ran out of food or water. Large packs were hard to carry and slowed an adventurer down. Finding the right balance between bringing enough food to survive, while also not weighing yourself down so much that you were vulnerable, was a fine line.

"Water is probably a better idea," Daniel suggested. "We can carry lots of jerky, but water is crucial."

"Isn't the entire dungeon ice?"

Daniel looked at Orrin like he was an idiot. "You want to melt and drink magical ice from a magical dungeon that is trying to magical kill you?"

They went down to the kitchen and borrowed a barrel. Orrin could fit either the barrel or Gertrude in his storage. In the end, he used another three ability points to increase the size of [Dimension Hole] again. The skill lost the upgradable tag.

With [Dimension Hole] maxed out in size, Orrin had no trouble stuffing in a barrel of water, Gertrude, all his and Daniel's gear, and the four roasted chickens sitting out to cool that he eyed nearby.

Daniel just shook his head. "You're ridiculous." They made their way to the front of the house.

Brandt and Jude had finished saddling the horses. Madi hugged her father and told him in no uncertain terms that he was to behave while she was away.

"You know, for someone who tried to kill us, Silas is a softie when it comes to his daughter," Orrin said, standing next to Daniel.

Daniel readjusted his small sword. "Madi promised that they had it under control. A healer nearby and everything. They hired some local thugs to rough me up, but they took it too far. Jude backed her up—he was there, too."

"And you just believe him?" Orrin asked incredulously. "I'm all for using the guy to get us some levels, but come on . . ."

Daniel fiddled with his Guild ring. "I'm on your side. They went too far." He paused. "But I think they didn't mean to and really regret it. Silas has kept his word so far."

Orrin sighed. "You are the softie."

Daniel pushed Orrin. What a few weeks ago would have sent Orrin swaying knocked him to the ground instead.

"Watch it, asshole," Orrin muttered as he picked himself up.

"Shit," Daniel said as he stooped to help Orrin up. "Sorry, I'm still adjusting to this new strength."

Orrin let Daniel help him up. "You know I could just inverse strength on you. Knock you over like a kitten."

"Knock a lot of kittens over, do you?" Daniel smiled. "Sorry, truly."

Orrin waved his hand. "I'll just summon an ice sword in your sleeping bag tonight."

Daniel chuckled.

"You boys ready to go?" Jude asked. "We can make it about halfway before the sun's down."

Orrin was dreading riding a horse again. He wanted to just teleport them all, but it would require multiple jumps. Not to mention, he couldn't use another regen potion until tomorrow.

"Let's head out, then," Daniel answered.

With a wave to Silas and the few knights standing guard, they made their way down the street and out of Dey.

The Aqua Chambers was located thirty miles due east. The plan was to travel the main highway that led toward the kingdom of Odrana. Dey's lands extended almost two hundred miles from the gates in a semicircle. Odrana covered two-thirds of that border, with the Untamed Forest covering the bottom third. Trees lined the side of the road.

They didn't talk much as they rode. Orrin tried not to complain, but the looks of sympathy turned sour after the first hour.

"If it hurts, just heal yourself," Madi finally said.

"I should save that for if we need it," Orrin snapped back.

Daniel pulled his horse back next to Orrin. Of course, he had already figured out how to control his horse. "O. Just do it. We aren't going to go into the dungeon until tomorrow anyways."

Orrin grumbled but cast the lowest-level healing spell he could. The chafing went away, and he let out a moan of pleasure.

"Somebody really likes horse riding through the countryside," Jude joked.

The trip didn't last much longer, as once the sun started to sink behind the mountains' peaks at their backs, Brandt pulled them off the road.

"We will set up camp here," Brandt began. "Three-shift rotation. Daniel and Jude will take first watch, I will take second, and Madi and Orrin can take third."

"Why not Orrin and me?" Daniel asked.

"Because if we are split up, it's less likely that we kill everybody and try to run away," Orrin answered before Brandt.

Brandt shook his head. "I split it this way because I don't know how you two are on watch. I trust Sir DeGuis to guard the [Hero]. I also trust Lady Madeleine to know how to keep a watch. We will all get to know each other's strengths and weaknesses in the next week, so be patient with each other."

"You really think we can defeat the dungeon in a week?" Daniel asked as he jumped off his horse.

"We won't be going past the tenth floor," Brandt answered as he began taking the saddle off his own horse. "If we are lucky, we can reach that in nine to ten days. Regardless, we will then turn around and come back. Dey will need us to help rebuild after the Horde."

"Rebuild?" Orrin stood bowlegged and tried to squat the kinks out of his thighs. "Will it really be that bad?"

Jude slapped Brandt's back as he passed him. "No, Brandt just likes to be a downer. We have enough notice. They'll put a few hitters out in the woods to take the Fogbinder down quick."

"What if we do defeat the dungeon, though?" Daniel asked.

"My father asked that we not go past the tenth floor," Madi chimed in. "Anything past that would be too dangerous. Not to mention, nobody knows how deep it really goes now."

"That's true," Jude said as he began gathering fallen twigs and brush to start a fire. "Farthest anyone has gotten in the last decade is . . . what . . . floor twenty-seven?"

"That sounds about right," Brandt replied.

"But if we get to level ten before the seven days, we could keep going, right?" Daniel pushed.

Brandt and Jude shared a look. Jude shrugged and gestured to Brandt to answer.

"We cannot order you, but Sir DeGuis, Madi, and I will not be going farther. At least not this time."

"That's bullshit," Daniel argued. "What if we hit a great stride and click as a party? Taking out the dungeon would be a great morale boost for the city, right? They'll need something to cheer at after a Horde attack."

Jude laughed. "Silas warned us you were persuasive. Don't worry. It's very unlikely we get past the tenth floor anyways."

"Why?" Orrin asked. He began pulling their gear out of [Dimension Hole].

"Because of the floor boss. Every ten floors has a boss monster. Something bigger, meaner, and nastier than what you've faced before." Jude smiled as he talked. "In the Chambers, it's a Frost Troll. Ugly thing. Quick, too. Its health regenerates so fast, I've seen it get an arm cut off and just pop it right back on. Truthfully, we probably won't make it in that far on our first run. If we do, Brandt and I would take point and just tease it a bit. Just to show you what you're up against."

Orrin was regretting not going full library mode on this dungeon.

"What's after the tenth floor?" he asked.

"Hell if I know." Jude shrugged. "I've never had a party go farther. Brandt has, but likely he won't talk about it. People who get farther in keep the secrets to themselves. Greedy bastards."

"Why wouldn't you all share the information? Wouldn't that make it easier to break a dungeon?" Daniel asked as he rolled his sleeping roll out.

"Of course it would," Jude continued. "But then somebody else—other than you—might defeat the dungeon and crush the core. Somebody else would get those extra stat points given to the party who kills the dungeon."

Silence surrounded the small party. Jude got a small fire going, and Brandt finished with the horses.

"Enough chatter." Brandt broke the stillness. "Sleep now. Orrin and Lady Catanzano, I'll wake you for your watch."

It took Orrin less time than he thought to fall asleep. It also took less time than he thought before Madi was shaking him awake.

"Orrin," she whispered in his ear. "Our watch."

Brandt was already lying down, his chest rising and falling slowly.

Orrin followed Madi to the edge of the small encampment. They kept their backs to the fire so as not to lose their night vision.

"How far do you think we'll get?" Madi asked quietly.

"In the dungeon? If Daniel gets his way, the whole thing. Honestly, though? Probably only to level ten. I don't think Jude or Brandt will break Silas's orders."

They sat in silence for a few minutes.

"What was it like where you lived?" Madi asked.

Shit, Orrin thought. *How did she figure it out? What should I say?*

"Um . . ." He trailed off.

"It must be hard having to leave everything you know due to somebody else's war," Madi continued. "I'm sorry for everything you lost. But at least you gained a friend in Daniel. And me, I hope."

Fuck, she meant my fake backstory, Orrin realized with relief. He let out a sigh.

"I am grateful," Orrin whispered. "Daniel has been a better friend than I've ever deserved. You and Brandt and Jude aren't too shabby, either." He grinned at her. She smiled back. "I'm not ready to talk about home. I hope you understand."

Madi nodded and put a hand on Orrin's knee.

In the darkness, with the moon above, Orrin kept watch and waited for his friends to wake.

After a quick breakfast, but no coffee, they saddled back up and started down the road.

Seriously, why no coffee? Orrin complained to himself. *What kind of insanity is that?*

Riding at a gentle pace, Brandt said they had made good time. They pulled off the main road.

In the distance, Orrin could see a large tent and some movement around it.

"I will do the talking." Jude rode ahead.

He returned a few minutes later and waved them ahead.

The tent was situated against a small tumble of rocks. It looked almost like a giant hand had pushed out from the ground, dislodging the earth, and then . . . disappeared. Two guards stood by the tent entrance.

"You the party who gets to go for a spin in the Chambers?" one guard wearing yellow and silver livery asked.

"Yes, Pete," Jude answered. "We just went over this."

"Just doing my job, Jude." The man grinned. He took a knife from his hip and started cleaning his teeth. "You know the rules."

The other guard stood forward. "Once you enter the tent, you have entered the Chambers. If you leave, you are done for a month. Multiple entrances might spark an outbreak."

He continued, "Once you enter the tent, be on your guard. The first level begins at the entrance. You'll know it when you see it. Once you enter the tent, no other party may enter for one day's time. In the unlikely event that you run into another party, you are not, I repeat, are not to engage with them in any way. Go in opposite directions. No more than two parties a week can enter the dungeon at a time. If you find evidence of a party's failure, please bring proof of death, if you can. Once you enter the dungeon, all monsters on previously defeated floors will respawn. Please wait until exactly noon to reset the dungeon, and also be aware of the noon cutoff for yourselves. As for current parties, only one party has entered in the last two weeks but has not returned. No other parties are scheduled at this time. The next party is scheduled in one week's time. Good luck."

With no further fanfare, the first guard spat, sheathed his knife, and stood to the side.

Brandt stepped through first, followed closely by Madi. Jude held his arm out. "After you two."

Daniel hitched his sword on his shoulder and stepped through the tent flap. Orrin followed his friend into their first dungeon, and Jude was on his heels.

Inside the tent, the temperature dropped. Madi and Brandt were waiting to the side. In front of them was a set of stairs going down. The first two steps looked like stone, but the third was ice. So were the fourth, fifth, and remaining steps that led down into darkness.

"Can you see down there?" Orrin asked Daniel.

Daniel shook his head. "I can't see past the tenth step."

Brandt spoke up. "I'll go first. Jude will take the back. Daniel, you're behind me. Orrin and Lady Catan—"

"Brandt, I swear to you, if you don't call me Madi while we're in here, I'll kill you myself."

Brandt smirked. "Orrin and Madi, you'll be in the middle. Heads up at all times. First two floors are a gauntlet. Let's go."

He stepped on the first step and began to descend.

Daniel followed close behind.

Orrin stepped up next. As his foot touched the third step, the first one that was iced, a prompt hit his eyes.

Welcome to the Aqua Chambers!

Chapter 30

Brandt put his helmet on and turned back to talk over his shoulder. "At the last step down below, the first floor begins. It will look like darkness, but you can step through it. We are going to run. The first floor is a snow-covered plain with nowhere to hide. You will be disoriented. The sky is not real—it's all a magical construct. It's only five miles across in every direction, and there is a room to rest in at the end. Just follow the sun to find it. Ignore the newts. If they get close, don't let them bite your exposed skin. Everybody ready?"

Madi and Jude tensed up, ready to follow Brandt's orders.

"Why are we running? Can we just kill the monsters?" Daniel asked.

Brandt paused. "There are a few hundred of them. Do you really want to get worn down and hurt on the first floor? The newts do not do much damage, but with the number that are on the first floor . . ."

"We have Orrin to heal us," Daniel said. "Plus, didn't you say we aren't here to actually defeat this place? The goal is just to gain some experience, right?"

"I can't protect you all from that many newts," Brandt complained.

"How about we get to the end, then farm some experience?" Orrin suggested. "We can jump through into the room at the end and defend from there if we need to."

"The monsters don't follow into the safe rooms," Brandt answered. "But I like that idea better than having to leave the dungeon because somebody spooked hundreds of tiny monsters into attacking us."

Daniel just shrugged. "I'm fine with Orrin's idea."

"Wait," Orrin said. "Let me cast a few spells, just in case."

Orrin didn't wait for an answer and cast [Ice Ward] on the party. He cast [Ward] individually on everyone as well. It costs almost an extra hundred MP, but if they were going to be running for an hour anyway, he'd make most of that back. The spell descriptors gave no time limit for [Ward] and [Ice Ward], but Orrin was willing to bet it would reset if they fell asleep. Both wards up would give each party member 460 damage resistance if the spells stacked like he hoped they did.

He explained what he'd done. Brandt and Jude gave him another one of their looks. He was getting used to everyone thinking he was crazy.

"Brandt, if what the kid says is true . . ." Jude partially unstrapped his hammer from his back. "Maybe we should just play smash the ugly newt."

Brandt shook his head. "While I do believe him, we don't know what could go wrong. We run to the end. Best-case scenario, we can spend the rest of the day killing newts with the safe room at our back. Worst case, we don't have to retreat out of the Chambers before a day has passed. We won't be allowed back in. That would defeat Lord Catanzano's entire reason for sending us here."

Orrin agreed with the logic but thought Brandt was being too safe. He also really didn't want to run five miles.

"Get ready to run," Brandt ordered. "We go on three."

"One. Two. Three! Go."

Brandt took the last step into the darkness and disappeared. Orrin followed Daniel.

After going down the dark and icy stairway, Orrin blinked at the bright light. He could hear birds singing in the distance. The sky above was bright, like the start of the day. Snow covered the ground all around. It was only a few inches deep but enough to have to lift his leg to step forward.

Madi and June appeared behind him. Brandt was scanning the frozen plains. The sun sat high and slightly in front of them.

"Everybody here? Good. Move out," Brandt ordered and began to jog. His heavy armor helped kick up snow, moving it to the side a bit. With Daniel on his heels, a path was already forming.

Orrin let out a groan and began running. *Why is there so much running involved in this world?*

Orrin kept his [Map] up in front of him as they moved. "Cluster of ten monsters to your right."

Brandt turned left and kept running. They'd been running in a zigzag for half an hour, and Orrin needed a break soon. Brandt was pushing them hard but being the snowplow for the group had to be taking a toll on him, too.

"I think if you turn a bit more to the left, we can rest. That group is the nearest right now," Orrin got out between ragged breaths.

Orrin assumed Brandt was feeling it, too, because he took his suggestion. They came to a stop after having run probably two to three miles in the snow.

"Five minutes," Brandt said and pulled off his helmet. Sweat had matted his hair to his forehead. He wiped it off and unstrapped one of his many water bottles to take a long drink.

"How are you doing?" Daniel asked, turning back to Orrin.

"I'm dead," Orrin answered. "I'm dead and this is hell."

Madi didn't look much better. She sat on her knees and was taking big breaths of air.

"Stretch and try to drink some water at least," Daniel suggested. He went to talk with Brandt and Jude. Both were looking into the distance.

Orrin took a gulp of water from his own single waterskin and then handed it to Madi. "Daniel says to drink and stretch."

He started doing lunge stretches, feeling his muscles burn. Madi mirrored him after a few seconds.

"It's incredible we've made it this far so quickly," Madi breathed out. She sounded winded still.

"I guess we've made good time," Orrin replied. "I'm sure Daniel could have run a lot quicker, though."

"Not without getting into a few fights," Madi retorted. "From the little Brandt has let slip to me over the years, it usually takes the entire day to get all the way through the first floor. Fights are common, even when they just try to run through."

"That makes no sense." Orrin stood up and reached toward the fake sky. "Why wouldn't they just outrun the newts or bring somebody to use [Map] to avoid them?"

Madi let out a burst of air that could have been a laugh. "Nobody who had [Map] would be in a dungeon. And if you caught the attention of a few newts, it would be better to kill them instead of letting them follow you, making noise and drawing in more."

Orrin touched his toes then stood still. "I still don't get that. Someone who could map out the dangers would make the floor easier. Someone who could heal would make the danger less permanent. Why does it always need to be five people with sharp pointy things defeating a dungeon?"

Madi shrugged. "That's the way it has always been. And we haven't seen what else is in store for us. Maybe we do need five damage dealers to take down a level." She winced and backtracked. "I'm sure we can do it with you, though."

Orrin waved his hand. "Nah. I get it. This is new for me, too. If I'm too much of a burden, you guys could always take someone else for the next dungeon crawl."

Madi hesitated. "If you truly mean that, you are a better person than me. I would never give up my spot on this team."

"I just want to be safe. And for him to be safe, too." Orrin nodded his head at where Daniel was pointing toward something in the distance. Jude was covering his eyes with his hand to try to see. "And you and Jude and Brandt, too, of course."

Madi smiled. "Let's go keep the [Hero] safe, then."

It took another hour to get the final few miles. Most of that was spent with Orrin using [Map] to slowly evade the red dots. They still hadn't actually seen a newt. Brandt explained that they usually jumped right out of the snow when you got close, then ran along the top, barely touching the icy top layer.

"They bite with tiny teeth that can't pierce leather but have an uncommon knack for finding flesh. Even then, the bite only stings a bit—but it causes frostbite."

Orrin unconsciously pulled the collar of his cloak up higher around his neck.

"There," Daniel said and pointed. "There's a door, right there."

Through the haze coming off the snow, Orrin could just make out what looked like a door of ice. If he wasn't looking for it, the door might have faded into the snowy background behind it.

Orrin looked at his [Map]. Nothing was between them and the door. He told them the same.

Jude hit Brandt on his shoulder. "We just made the first-ever no-damage run. You owe me a drink."

Brandt smiled. "Gladly. But let's get through the door first."

"Wait," Daniel said. "Let's get close and then earn some experience."

Brandt's smile faded. "Are you sure? They are quick, and the frostbite takes days to heal on its own. It would be safer to—"

"I'm sure," Daniel interjected. "Besides, we need the practice, right?"

Brandt didn't argue but looked less than thrilled as they made their way to the door.

Orrin's MP was nearly full again, with over ninety minutes passed and [Meditate] giving him the standard one MP back. "Are we going to wait in the safe room before going on to the next floor?"

"We can if anyone is hurt," Jude responded as he took his warhammer off his back.

"I could boost everybody. Or even just the three of you. Get your dexterity up so it's easier to hit the newts?" Orrin suggested.

"Could you boost your own will first to max out how much dexterity we get?" Daniel asked.

Orrin started doing math. *So much running and math.*

For whatever reason, casting [Increase Will] or [Increase Intelligence] didn't stack on their own but would increase the output of dexterity or strength. If he gave himself five boosts of [Increase Will] at level two, he'd get up to twenty-eight. With his original will at thirteen, he'd get 1.3 times the plus-two output for each spell, or 2.6. Rounding up to three, the five boosts would increase his will by fifteen. That would cost him fifty MP, as his intelligence wasn't currently boosted. Casting [Increase Dexterity] at level two would cost another fifty MP per person but would increase each person's dexterity by 2.8 times, plus two output, or 5.6. An extra thirty dexterity would make any fighter insanely fast at their current levels.

He would only have to wait three hours to make most of that back.

"I can increase your dex, Jude's, and Brandt's by thirty, but I'd be nearly useless unless I drank a potion." Orrin finished the math and reported back.

"Thirty?" Jude spat. "Brandt, I want to try this. The kid hasn't been wrong yet."

Brandt still looked hesitant, but the entire group was begging for this. "Okay. We will set up here. We can bring a few back at a time and try it out. We retreat at my first command. Orrin, if you see us running toward you, get"—he paused and visibly forced himself to say—"Madi back through to the safe room."

"Yes, sir." Orrin saluted dramatically. Daniel chuckled.

Orrin zoomed out on his [Map] and pointed. Daniel, Brandt, and Jude readied their weapons and crept away.

"I guess when they get back, just hit the things with any spells you have," Orrin said.

Madi nodded and watched. They could see the three men in the distance, but it was harder with every minute to make out details. It looked like they were moving around, but Orrin couldn't make out any monsters at that distance.

"Can you see anything?"

"I think they're coming back," Madi said after a minute.

Instead of the slow careful pace of before, Brandt and Daniel sprinted the last few hundred yards, racing like schoolchildren. Daniel had a burst of speed at the end and won.

"Hah." Daniel huffed out a laugh. "You guys. That. Was. Amazing."

Jude came in at a more normal but still fast jog.

"What happened?" Madi asked.

"Five Ice Newts jumped us before we were ready," Jude answered her. "Brandt cut two in half before they hit the snow, and Daniel here swept the other three up before I had a chance to swing my hammer."

He looked slightly peeved.

"You'll get one next time." Daniel smiled. "Now do you believe in us?" he asked, turning to Brandt.

Brandt turned to Madi. "I think we should have some fun."

"Don't forget that spell only lasts ten minutes," Orrin warned.

Brandt frowned but then shrugged. "We can just camp out here and wait for you to cast it again, right?"

"Yes, but I want to get some kills, too," Orrin replied.

"I could just let out a [Gravity Well] shout," Daniel suggested. "Everything within a few hundred yards is supposed to target me."

Orrin looked at his map and zoomed all the way out. "There are about twenty-something within that distance."

"We can take on that many." Daniel smirked. "I'm going to do it."

"No, wait—" Brandt tried, but it was too late. Daniel had already let out a yell with a small circle of air that forced the ice to push back around him. The sound echoed over the snow. "What have you done? They can communicate over short distances. You might have only triggered those closest, but they can call for reinforcements. It's why we don't just run through, letting a band be created."

"Sorry," Daniel apologized. "Maybe it'll be okay and only a few will—"

"Guys," Orrin interrupted. "We've got about sixty or so red dots moving in fast."

"Fuck." Daniel grimaced.

Chapter 31

Brandt responded immediately. "Okay, everybody through the door. Quickly, now."

"No," Daniel answered. "There aren't too many of them. I made a mistake, but we can take out a bunch of these monsters. They aren't any bigger than a kitten."

Brandt turned toward the [Hero]. "You want us to take on sixty newts at once? Even with this increased speed, that's a huge risk. What if Orrin's buff wears off midstrike?"

"Then we better get to it." Daniel took off running. Orrin could just make out the snow in the distance moving slightly as something zipped underneath it.

Brandt wasted no time arguing and leaped right into action. "Madi, Orrin. Jump back through the door as soon as you run out of mana. Jude, we rush them. Fall back before you take too much damage. Go."

Brandt ran forward, with Jude on his heels.

"I guess we're doing this," Madi said with a twinge of fear in her voice.

"If you get hit, I can heal you," Orrin responded. "I don't know how much help I am going to be here."

I really need to get some long-range attacks or multi-target attacks that don't cost as much as [Lightstrike].

Orrin looked at his hip and considered his options. *I could take an MP potion, but that would only give me ten or so shots from [Lightstrike]. A regen potion means I can't drink another until we rest for the night, and I'm sure Brandt wants to get farther than the first floor before sleeping . . .*

With a sigh, Orrin took an MP potion out. His damage output wouldn't really be worth much. Wasting his one daily regen wasn't practical when they could all just retreat.

He drank the potion and reattached the empty bottle to his belt.

His MP had been rising slowly, but the extra hundred gave him a quick boost of confidence. At least he wouldn't be useless now. He started forward, waving Madi on with him. "Let's go do some damage, at least."

A minute later, they caught up to the three fighters. Dozens of amphibians the size of small dogs were already in pieces or flattened.

The newts were about two feet long, off-white in color, and moved across the top of the snow like a water strider. Orrin used [Identify] on one as it popped out of the snow a few feet away.

[Ice Newt] HP 20/20

"They only have twenty health?" Orrin drew his sword. *Maybe I can get some experience.*

He swung at the nearest and missed completely. The newt tunneled back into the snow.

"Get back!" Brandt yelled. "Just tell us what direction they're coming from under the snow."

Orrin felt useless as he shouted instructions while watching his [Map]. Madi was able to take down a few newts with her spells and threw colored markers where he pointed out in between getting all that good experience Orrin was missing out on.

After another minute or two, the three fighters slowed noticeably. What once was a flash of metal became a slow-moving sword that Orrin could follow with his eyes.

The newts started pushing harder. More than two-thirds of what had been on Orrin's [Map] had been dealt with, but the remaining twentyish newts struck as one.

Jude let out a yell for help as five of them swarmed over his body and climbed toward his unprotected face.

Orrin froze as he watched. One bit Jude's neck, and another slipped around his arm and tried to gnaw on the fingers holding his hammer. Orrin had nothing but [Lightstrike] to attack with, and it would take twenty shots to take down one of those newts.

Jude started to laugh.

"They can't do any damage to me," he chuckled. He reached up and grabbed on without hesitation and squeezed. The newt popped as Jude crushed its head in his hand. "The kid's wards stop all the damage. It feels like a tickle."

After that, Jude started chuckling as he played whack-a-newt in the snow. Daniel joined him, stabbing the moving furrows that cropped up. Brandt stood near Orrin and Madi. Orrin tossed out a few [Lightstrikes] so he wouldn't feel completely useless.

Experience Gained: 25 XP (5 XP x 5)

He'd shot five of the newts before Daniel and Jude finished them off.

The two trudged back through the snow. They had left the stomped-down section surrounding the original battleground to chase a few remaining newts down.

"See?" Daniel put his shortsword on his shoulder and looked over the carnage. "Piece of cake."

Jude was grinning like an idiot. "Brandt, can we do that again? I took out fifteen of the slimy bastards by myself. That adds up really quick when I'm not worrying about my health."

"I got twenty," Daniel bragged. "Not including the ones somebody else hit first."

"Only eight," Madi chimed in.

Orrin was pissed. "I got five, but only half credit for them."

Brandt looked exasperated. "Sure. That was fun. I even got enough experience to level, but you guys, that was dangerous and—"

"Level twenty?" Daniel cut him off.

"... yes."

"The Quest?" Daniel asked.

"I haven't had time to look at my messages," Brandt said.

"Orrin will tell us if anything approaches." Daniel was bouncing from foot to foot in excitement. "We can talk about how to do this better next time, but check that Quest."

Brandt shook his head, and his eyes unfocused as he read his own blue boxes.

"Well?" Orrin asked.

"The Quest is completed, but it just says, 'Reward Not Available,'" Brandt answered finally.

Orrin's heart sank. He'd been hoping that the Quests would let him get something; even just one level of [Sword Proficiency] would make him worth more in a battle.

"Sorry, Daniel." Brandt put his sword back in its sheath. "I know you were hoping that it would still reward me."

Daniel shrugged. "Can't win them all, I guess. Now, how about we take advantage of this place and farm some more experience?"

Brandt sighed at the looks on their faces. "I can't say no, can I?"

Jude picked up his hammer off the ground and twirled it. "This is going to be fun."

There were exactly two hundred [Ice Newts] on the first floor. Orrin kept track. He was in charge of [Map], leading the group back over the grounds they had covered. With the wards working as well as they did, Brandt eventually began to loosen up and started a wager with Jude and Daniel on who could kill the most.

Obviously, Daniel won.

The final count was: Orrin with fourteen, but he only got half experience for each one. Madi killed twenty-three, and Jude took out thirty. Brandt and Daniel were tied at thirty-two when Daniel took the last three down using his [Wind Blades] skill to take the lead.

Experience Gained: 70 XP (5 XP x 14)

Orrin slumped into the snow.

Utility Warder 145/900 XP
AP: 2

Useless, Orrin thought to himself. *I barely got any experience.*

"Hey, Brandt." Daniel caught the knight's attention as they used snow to clean the blood and gore off their blades. "Are these things edible? Or is there anything we should harvest from them to sell?"

"Eating monsters in a dungeon will kill you," Brandt responded. "While they are still in the dungeon, they are tied to the magic creating the dungeon. Think of them as more . . . mana constructs. Something happens to them when there is a dungeon break. That's what drives them to run from the dungeon in the first place. Outside, you can cook anything you want . . ." Brandt kicked the newt with his toe. ". . . although why anyone would want to try with one of these is beyond me."

"So that's why bringing your own supplies is so important," Jude said as he joined them. He had splattered a newt with a stomp of his boot. The mess had gone up his pant leg, and he'd had to go off a distance to wash the pants off a bit. The left side of his pants still looked wet.

"Good thing we've got Orrin, then." Daniel sat down next to him. "We really loaded up before we left, huh?"

Madi, Brandt, and Jude looked confused.

"Because of his storage," Daniel elaborated.

"He brought nothing but a water bottle," Madi pointed out.

Orrin stuck his hand into his pocket and pulled out one of the roasted chickens he'd swiped from the Catanzano kitchen. Steam was still rising from the meat.

"What . . . how . . . where?" Brandt's eyes were wide.

"I thought you guys knew," Orrin said with a shrug. "I've got dimensional storage."

Jude started laughing again. "I'm never going on another dungeon delve without him."

Madi's eyes narrowed, and she looked at the chicken. "Did you steal a Veskarian game hen from the kitchen?" she asked incredulously. "That is for a state dinner my father is throwing."

Daniel joined in on Jude's laughter. "He took all four." Daniel wiped his eyes. "Anyone hungry?"

After eating two of the chickens, which Madi explained were an imported delicacy, they made their way back to the door.

"Just step through and wait," Jude said. "We can rest up a bit more and then try for floor two before we call it a day."

"What's on floor two?" Orrin asked. They'd spent almost an hour lounging about, but his MP was still lower than he felt comfortable with. He'd taken a look with [Identify], and Daniel, Jude, and Brandt still had over half of their [Ice Ward] running and the full [Ward]. Still, each had suffered almost one hundred points of damage from the newts. *No wonder people usually just run for it.*

"[Frost Apes]," Brandt answered from behind him. "But this one we really do have to run for. We don't have the ranged attacks necessary to take them down. Get inside and I'll explain."

Orrin pushed against the door and stepped through. Inside was a twenty-by-twenty-foot-square room of ice. Ice floors, ice walls, and another ice door on the opposite side of where he entered.

"Don't stand in the doorway, O." Daniel pushed him into the room. Orrin took a step and slowly slid across the ice skating rink–like floor.

"So . . . this is weird," Orrin said as he stopped his momentum against the far wall.

Madi and Jude entered, with Brandt following behind. He dragged a few of the dead newts in with him.

"Set up some blankets against the wall there," Brandt said and pointed. "I'll get a fire going."

"In this small room?" Orrin asked. "Won't that . . . kill us?"

He had paid enough attention in chemistry to understand car-bon dioxide. *Or was it carbon monoxide? Or both?*

"No."

"I'm gonna need more of an answer than that," Orrin retorted as the group started laying their sleeping rolls out on the ice.

In the center of the room, Brandt had knelt down and was run-ning his hand over the ice. He drew a small knife and slammed the butt into the ground.

"Something in the dungeon allows the smoke to escape," he explained as he started crushing a small circle. "I just need . . . to get . . . to the floor. There."

Brandt finished shattering the layers of ice and pulled the chunks out. Only an inch down was a layer of rock or marble, Orrin couldn't tell. Brandt tossed the four newts into the small depression and start-ed using a flint to make small sparks.

"Don't you need wood to—" Orrin's question stopped in his mouth as the fire caught and the newts went up in a blaze.

Brandt grinned. "The upside to all these ice monsters is they all burn rather easily. We should get an hour from these few bodies. The bones take a long time to burn out completely."

Daniel leaned in close to Orrin. "Magic fuckery."

After the fire was flickering brightly, Brandt sat down on the bed-rolls laid out.

"This will be our routine," he explained. "Get to a safe room and rest. Even if it's just for Orrin and Madi to get their mana back. There is no reason to rush. I'll do my best to bring a body or two, but some floors are going to be cold. It's why we brought these." He patted the makeshift bedding they all sat on. "It'll keep the worst of the cold away."

"Orrin, how much food did you actually bring? And water?" Brandt asked.

"I've got another two chickens . . . sorry, game hens," he answered while getting a quiet glare from Madi. "I also have a barrel of water and—"

"A barrel?" Jude asked. "Just how big is your storage? I've only heard of small [Legerdemain] skills."

"Jude, let him finish," Brandt demanded. However, he looked stunned, too.

"What's a [Legerdemain] skill?" Daniel asked. "I've seen that somewhere."

As Jude and Daniel started talking, Orrin barreled on. "I also stocked up on jerky, like you suggested. I put in a few fruits that I saw at the market. I also have Daniel's sword, but honestly, he can't use it unless I've buffed his strength all the way up."

Madi let out a sigh. "You brought that hunk of metal in here?"

Daniel turned from his conversation with Jude. "Gerty is not a hunk—"

"Anyways." Brandt cut off that conversation before it started. "That much preparation could get us well past level ten, but you knew we aren't going farther in than that. Why bring so much?"

"To be prepared," Orrin responded and gave Brandt the Boy Scout salute. Brandt blinked in confusion, and Daniel stifled a laugh. "Seriously, though? I just didn't want to have to turn back because of food or water. Let's push until we have to turn back, you know?"

Brandt nodded a bit. "How much longer do you need before you can cast more spells?"

"I mean, I can cast spells now, but if you are asking how long until I'm topped off . . ." Orrin checked his status. "Two hours."

"Recast [Ice Ward] on us, then," Brandt suggested. "You said that was the only thing that took damage, right?"

"Yeah." Orrin cast it right away. "We'll have to wait an extra twenty minutes, but you all took about eighty to ninety points of damage. Especially Daniel. He took 120."

"Because I was in the thick of the battle," Daniel said and raised his fist in victory.

"Because you were arrogant and didn't trust your party," Brandt retorted. Daniel lowered his head. "In a fight, we should be standing close and covering each other's blind spots. Next fight, we do better."

"Floor two won't know what hit it," Daniel promised.

Jude just shook his head. "You want to tell him or should I?"

Brandt's smile came back. "No fighting on floor two. The apes stay up in the hills. We have to run through a valley to the door on the other end. It's only two miles long, but they throw blocks of ice that hit hard and knock you backward. If you go down, get up quick. If someone else goes down, get them up. A fallen target stirs them up into a frenzy. They'll target that person."

"Can't we just go up the hill to them?" Daniel asked.

"If you want to try and climb up a sheer two-hundred-foot cliff while dozens of large balls of jagged ice shatter on your back."

"You can just say 'No,'" Daniel muttered.

"No." Brandt continued, "We run. Like I said, it's only two miles. There isn't much snow, so it won't be as hard. But watch out for the black ice. Some parts of the trail are slick. Again, remember to get up as fast as you can. We need to try to stick as close to each other as possible."

"Should we go in the same order as before?" Orrin asked. "I'm not too sure Madi or I should be in the back. I can't lift you in all that armor."

"That's a good point," Jude answered. "Send those two up front to pick the path. The three of us can run right behind them."

Brandt pursed his lips together but didn't argue. Wisely, as Madi was glaring at him, as if daring him not to treat her as a normal part of the party.

"Everyone rest up, then." Brandt laid back. "We'll start when Orrin is ready."

Chapter 32

Once Orrin gave the go-ahead, the party lined up in front of the second ice door.

"Why are they called floors?" he asked as Madi got into position next to him.

"Sometimes the doors actually lead down," Brandt answered as he readjusted his helmet. Daniel and Jude both strapped their weapons to their backs. "Ready?"

Orrin held his hand out. "Ladies first."

"Scared of getting hit?" Madi stuck her tongue out and hit the door with her shoulder, bouncing inside at a run.

Orrin took off after her.

At level ten, I should put some points into constitution . . . or would it be dexterity? I need to ask which one makes running easier.

Just as Brandt had described, they ran through a valley. Large cliffs seemed to swallow up the ground, rising into the air on either side. The lightly snow-dusted grass had craters the size of basketballs pockmarking the otherwise serene view ahead.

Madi was already a few dozen yards ahead and running hard. Orrin started jogging and pulled up his [Map]. He saw red dots on the cliffs ahead, but the first was almost a quarter mile away.

They ran for a few minutes before the red dot nearest on the map moved a little.

"Get ready!" Orrin yelled, and not a moment too soon.

A chunk of ice the size of a football fell from the cliff on the right at high speed. At the front, Madi was the first target. She moved to the side and dodged. The spray of dirt from the impact went up into the air. If Orrin had been closer, he would have taken the shrapnel in the face.

More red dots started to move slowly, and Orrin dropped [Map] to concentrate on running.

If Orrin hadn't been forced to play dodgeball so much in the past few weeks, he would have been taken out by the first missile that targeted him. With all that practice, he calculated the distance and where it would hit, naturally avoiding the projectile.

At least, that's what he had hoped would happen. The block of ice clipped his thigh. Luckily, his [Ice Ward] took the brunt of the damage. The attack most definitely did not tickle, as Jude had described the newts' attacks. He stumbled and almost fell.

"The attacks still count as ice magic," he shouted over his shoulder. He didn't look back and prayed the others could hear him.

Orrin ran and dodged. He watched Madi deftly maneuver over the snowy terrain. She occasionally stepped on spots of ice and would skid for a moment before catching herself.

Orrin considered casting a few [Increase Dexterity] buffs on himself or Madi, but with how much the first hit had taken off his [Ice Ward], he wanted to save his mana.

[Ice Ward] 145/230
[Ward] 230/230

His quick check of his status was a mistake. A block of ice hit his right shoulder, and Orrin spun before bouncing on the ground. He scrambled back up and started running.

"What are you doing?" Daniel was in front of him, running at him.

"What are *you* doing?" Orrin yelled. "When did you get ahead of me?"

"You got up after getting hit and are running the wrong way." Daniel was closing in fast. "Turn around."

Orrin could have hit himself. He dug his foot down and pivoted. Madi was a speck in the distance.

I can't be a burden again, he thought.

[Increase Dexterity] Level 2 x 5

The extra fifteen points of dexterity hit his legs, and Orrin almost went down again. He adjusted and began to lope along faster and faster. The apes missed every shot by larger margins. The wind was singing in his ears as, for the first time in his life, Orrin enjoyed running.

He caught up to his previous position behind Madi. He could just make out the ice door at the end. They would make it there in just another minute and nothing could stop hi—

Two apes on opposite sides of the ravine threw perfectly timed shots at Madi. If there was only one, she could have dodged to the side. With two, she hesitated and took a hit to her leg and chest. Orrin watched as she flipped head over heels and landed on her face.

He was only four steps away. He could pick her up and—

As Madi lay stunned, with dirt up her nose, four apes let out a wild howl and let loose.

Orrin was three steps away when four more missiles fell from the sky. He pumped his legs harder than he had ever run before.

Two steps away. One.

The first ape had thrown too fast. The ice block hit Madi in the head. Her face slapped back into the ground, and she let out a cry.

Orrin slid and grabbed her, wrapping his arms around her and casting another [Ward] on Madi and [Ice Ward] on the party. Or anyone within fifty feet.

"Can you—" he started to ask but got hit by the other three blocks of ice.

[Ice Ward] 0/230
[Ward] 20/230

Direct hits do a lot more damage. Orrin put another [Ice Ward] and [Ward] up.

He didn't wait to see if Madi was ready. He yanked on her arm and half dragged her to her feet.

"Run."

They stumbled together for a few feet. Madi mumbled and tried to talk, but Orrin concentrated on the door just fifty to sixty yards ahead of them.

Madi hit a slick of ice, and her feet went out from under her.

"Fuccckkkk . . ." Orrin tried holding her weight but started to go down.

[Increase Strength] Level 2 x 5

He picked her up and tossed her over his shoulder. The half spear strapped on her hip dug into his neck. Ice boulders continued to rain down around them.

Orrin slammed into the door and hit the safe room's ice floor.

Seconds later, Brandt burst into the room.

"Madeleine!" he bellowed and took her weight off Orrin. Daniel and Jude entered behind and stood to the side.

"She took a few hits, but I put new war—"

"Heal her. Now," Brandt shouted. His helmet had been tossed to the floor, and his brown hair stood up from the sweat.

Orrin looked at Madi and choked back vomit.

One of the ice projectiles had scraped her face raw; teeth were missing and an ear was hanging on by a small flap of skin. She looked dazed and uncertain of where she was.

Orrin pulled up his status to check his own mana.

MP 54/230

Then he used [Identify] on Madi, cutting off to only the important bits.

Madeleine Catanzano

Prism Conjurer Level 14
HP 26/110

Orrin started stacking [Heal Small Wounds], level two on Madi, healing over twenty HP for each cast. He got four off before his own MP was too low to push farther. Even with her health at full, the damage to her face was slow to heal.

"Should I keep healing her? She's at full health now, but her face . . ." Orrin watched as the skin of her ear slowly grew back together. Brandt gently held it in place.

"It'll come back slowly," Brandt whispered as Madi moaned. Thankfully, she had passed out. "Overhealing would fix it faster, but you don't have to—"

Orrin chugged another mana potion and threw more magic at the problem. Teeth grew back, and skin scabbed over into fresh flesh. The bruising reduced, and Madi's moans of pain turned into the heavy breathing of a deep sleep.

"Thank you," Brandt said as he looked up at Orrin. "I saw you carry her. You took the brunt of those hits. You picked her up and saved her life."

"How did she get so hurt?" Daniel asked from behind. He'd been quiet and waiting but took his chance. "We all took one or two hits, but . . . nothing like that."

"I didn't see what happened." Brandt looked to Orrin. "Did you?"

"She got clobbered by two at once and ate it hard," Orrin explained. "Four more snowballs came in fast, but I blocked three of them. One hit her head before I—"

"Shit," Jude cut in. "A direct hit to her head? A critical hit?"

"What's a critical hit?" Daniel turned to Jude.

"A natural twenty," Orrin said. Brandt gave Orrin another look.

Jude continued talking as if Orrin hadn't interrupted. "A critical hit is when you target a monster . . . or person's weakest spot. For a magic user like Madi, her head. There is no hard-and-fast rule, but a critical hit can do anything from double damage to instant death. It's why most people don't start fights, even with a much lower-level person. Anyone can get lucky . . . or unlucky," he said as he waved a hand at Madi's form.

"But she'll be okay?" Orrin asked uncertainly. *A blow to the head that hard . . .*

"She'll be back up and being a pain in my ass soon enough." Brandt smiled. "Get some rest—you earned it."

"Anyone else need healing?" Orrin looked around. The three fighters shook their heads. *I guess my wards did a good job.*

Orrin helped Jude put down the blankets. He noticed Brandt hadn't tried to start a fire, so he pulled two torches out of his [Dimension Hole].

"It's not much, but they'll give off some heat, right?"

Brandt gave Orrin a hug and then turned back to keep Madi warm with the small flames.

Jude walked up and put his arm around Orrin's shoulder. "I think you just made a friend for life."

Orrin watched Brandt tenderly tilt Madi's head and splash a small stream of water on her lips, which he dabbed with a corner of the blanket.

"Two torches for a friend," Orrin replied. "Not a bad deal."

Even fully healed, or overhealed, Madi wasn't back to herself for four hours. She thanked Orrin for his help.

"And, of course, I'll reimburse you for the mana potion you had to use," she finished.

"Shut up," Orrin retorted. "We're a team. I'm sure you'll have to save my ass a few times before we leave. And I'm not taking anything from you. I was happy to help."

They chewed jerky and drank water, waiting for Brandt to give the final okay.

"First, this party has made it farther in than a lot of teams, so be proud," Brandt started. "The gauntlet turns back a lot of parties. But the next level requires patience and teamwork."

"And hopefully killing something?" Daniel asked.

"Don't be so experience hungry," Orrin joked.

"Yes, we will encounter monsters," Brandt said. "This next section is actually Jude's favorite, so . . ." He waved the conversation to Jude.

"I'm flattered that you remembered." Jude took off a small knife from his hip and drew two long lines on the ice floor. "The third floor is a frozen river. It's a mile wide at all points . . . or at least it is as far up or downstream as anyone has ever reported. All we have to do is get to the other side, and the door will appear."

"I could teleport us all across," Orrin suggested. "Damn, I could have done that back in the last room, too."

"[Teleport] doesn't work in dungeons," Brandt said.

"Good idea, though," Jude continued. "So, to get across the frozen ice, we just have to test each step in front of us for weakness. If it can hold the weight of my hammer, we can walk on it. Follow the footsteps of the person in front of you, and we can make it all the way across."

"You said monsters," Daniel reminded nobody.

"If my hammer breaks the ice, Frozen Carp will jump out and try to pull you back into the freezing water to either drown or be eaten by their razor-sharp teeth."

"Okay, I vote no getting eaten." Daniel shook his head.

"Same," Orrin said.

"We can pull the fish out of the water and beat them to death on the solid ice," Jude said. "It's all really just a puzzle or maze of where you can stand out there. The fish themselves aren't a problem if you don't get pulled under the water. If you do go under . . . you are on your own, because nobody is jumping in after you."

"Why?" Orrin asked.

"Once you go under, it's impossible to find where you are or know how many enemies are under the ice," Brandt said. "It's suicide."

"But I have [Map]. Couldn't I just point out how many fish are down below and follow where the person who fell in went?"

Brandt and Jude whispered to each other.

"What if it's you that falls in? We still won't know where you are. But if anyone else does, we can use that to our advantage," Jude answered.

"After this floor, we'll hole up for the night in the next safe room." Brandt slapped his hands on his knees and stood straight. "Let's go."

Chapter 33

The party entered the third floor without concern. Brandt and Jude had been in the Aqua Chambers a couple of times each. The river was a few hundred yards from the door. No enemies would attack until they reached the water.

Brandt had returned the torches to Orrin with another round of thanks. Orrin was just glad Madi seemed to be back to normal, though he did see her flinch a bit as the doors opened and light spilled into the safe room.

Orrin pulled up his [Map] and scanned ahead. He stopped walking at what he saw.

The path ahead was covered in randomly placed yellow squares. Red dots, obviously showing the fish monsters underneath, swarmed around each square.

"The ice is all a trap . . ." he realized as he zoomed in and out, double-checking to confirm what his brain was telling him. "[Trap View] lets me see the path across. Hey! My [Map] is a cheat sheet!"

"What do you mean?" Brandt turned back from the water's edge. *Or the ice's edge*, Orrin thought.

"I see yellow squares across the river, with red dots circling each one."

"That sounds like how they usually set up," Jude said. "Where's the closet one?"

Orrin pointed off to the side. The nearest yellow square was only ten feet past the shoreline. "Right there, ten feet in."

Jude walked over and hit the ice with his hammer. Nothing happened.

"A little farther, but that was almost the edge of—"

Jude struck again, and the entire yellow section on Orrin's [Map] blinked out. The ice shattered and fell into the rushing water of the river below. Jude made his way back with a giant grin on his face.

Daniel shook his head. "Damn it, Orrin. I wanted to kill some monsters."

"We still can," Orrin said. "Hell, we can clear the entire floor if we want. There's a pretty rambling path if we do this . . ."

Orrin used his sword to draw a rough maze in the snow. He pointed out where each trap of thin ice would be and counted off the fish.

"There's two to three fish on each square, and I'm not going to sit here counting them all . . . but there's at least a hundred or so."

Brandt threw his hands in the air. "We can't kill every monster in the whole dungeon. That's not the point. We should just push ahead and bypass the entire floor."

Madi crossed her arms over her chest. "Just because you hit level twenty doesn't mean the rest of us are satisfied. I seem to remember the whole point of this dungeon run was to get me safely away from the Wall."

Brandt looked at Madi guiltily. "You did hear us talking then, huh?"

Madi walked through the group to stand right in front of Brandt, her small frame dwarfed by his armored mass. "Yes, I heard him. I heard you agreeing as well. I'm not a child, Sir Bennett. And you and my father better get that through your heads."

Daniel stepped closer to Orrin. "Any idea what's going on?"

"The young lady obviously overheard our marching orders from her father," Jude whispered. "You being the [Hero] and this whole Quest business is just an excuse to keep Madi away from a Horde attack."

"But why?" Orrin asked as Madi continued to poke her finger against Brandt and call him names. "He's a lord of the city. Couldn't he just . . . lock her up or something if he didn't want her fighting?"

Jude shook his head. "She's an adult. She's over level ten, and she's part of the Guild. If he tried something like that . . . well, honestly I have no idea what the fallout would be, but it would be bad."

Madi finished telling Brandt off and rejoined the rest of the party. She was breathing hard.

Brandt looked away for a minute and slowly moved closer to Orrin's crudely drawn map. "We can probably get some fishing done, but only in spaces where we have enough room to move freely. Orrin, are there any large areas near the other side that seem good?"

Orrin took another look and picked a long stretch near the other side of the river that seemed a likely candidate. He nodded and drew it out on his snow map.

"Good." Brandt seemed subdued, like a puppy that had been yelled at. "We will make our way across and then pull a fish or two out to kill."

Crossing the river took twenty minutes. They had to go slowly, as the ice was still slick, but Jude complained the entire time.

"This is usually my favorite floor," he grumbled. "I get to hit the ice with my hammer, and if I can't break it, it's safe to go across."

"You can still hit that section to your right," Orrin said without looking up from his [Map]. "It should be thin, and it doesn't have any red dots around it right now."

"It's not the same," Jude mumbled.

When they got to the other side, Orrin led them to a spot a few hundred yards farther to the right of the original door entrance. The new door to the next safe room had appeared behind them as soon as Brandt's foot had hit the riverbank.

"There are about ten yellow squares that should be only five or six feet wide in diameter from there to there." He pointed.

"We'll need to mark them off somehow." Daniel glanced around. "I don't want to go swimming in this cold."

Orrin put his hand out, and a sword of ice grew in his palm. "Leave that to me. I'll stake it all out."

Orrin's idea would have been perfect, except he couldn't plunge the swords in the ice deep enough to stick. In the end, he had to enlist Jude's help to hammer the ice of his sword handle, turning the entire endeavor into a construction exercise.

Jude, on the other hand, loved using his hammer. "So, right beyond these swords will be the Carp?"

"Yep. Actually, all the hammering seems to be drawing even more over here, too," Orrin answered after checking his [Map] again.

They spent ten minutes slowly and carefully marking a safe area. Then Brandt had the party line up.

"Frozen Carp are about the size of wagon wheel and weigh about two hundred pounds each. They will bite anything that touches the water, so make sure to wait for me or Jude to pull one out."

"How will you do that?" Daniel had his old shortsword out. He'd begged Orrin to increase his strength so he could pull out Gertrude, but Orrin had just ignored him until he went away.

"I'll just put my hammer in the water and drag them out. Brandt can try fishing with a rope. Like he said, they bite down and don't let go, so it's actually really easy to drag them out of the water . . . as long as it's not you they're biting," Jude answered with a twirl of his hammer.

"Could you use Madi's spear?" Orrin asked. "Just retract it to make the magic do the work instead of hauling two hundred pounds of fish?"

Madi smirked. "I can pull a fish out, too, then."

"No," Brandt said sternly. "I'll use your spear to pull them out and then hand it back to you. Jude and I can just pull out a few at a time while you three get your fill of monster kills. Then we can go rest. Safe and sound."

Jude went first. He stepped just beyond Orrin's ice sword and brought his hammer down in a double-handed overhead swing. A perfect replica of the yellow trap on Orrin's map exploded into small pieces of ice, swiftly carried away by the current. A dark-blue fin crested the top of the water.

Jude lowered his hammer into the path of the fish.

Orrin had never been into fishing, but the thing that appeared did not look like what he'd thought a carp would look like. In fact, it looked more like a goldfish. A goldfish that had grown fifty times bigger, was dark blue, and had literal ice all over it. The Carp's mouth opened, and teeth out of a horror movie appeared before it chomped down on Jude's weapon.

"Got one!" Jude yelled in joy and pulled. He dug his heels in and walked backward, dragging the fish out of the water. It stubbornly would not let go.

Once Jude cleared the row of ice swords, Orrin, Daniel, and Madi fell on it. Brandt had already told them the monsters were near immobile out of water, so they hacked and slashed away. Orrin had little trouble sticking the pointy end of his sword into the large, fleshy fish.

After less than a minute, they'd killed the first monster of floor three.

Experience Gained: 30 XP

"Only thirty?" Daniel complained. "I need to hit a thousand to get to the next level. This is going to take forever."

"I need nearly three thousand more," Madi chimed in. "I'm only halfway to the next level right now."

Orrin saw the future slough of experience grinding and sighed internally. "I only need a few hundred to hit level ten."

"How much?" Daniel turned and asked. Madi handed her spear to Brandt as Jude sat on his heels and caught his breath.

"I'm at 175 of nine hundred."

Daniel looked at Madi, who nodded. She turned and yelled to Brandt, "We need to get about ten of these for just Orrin. He's nearing level ten."

Brandt nodded back.

"All yours, buddy." Daniel took a step back.

"Wait, what? I'm not taking all these kills myself." Orrin tried to step back, too. Daniel gently pushed him forward.

"You are the weakest link. Let's see what level ten does for you."

"But we can both do it." Orrin tried again. "You can't be too far off from what I need. We can just—"

Daniel shook his head. "It's time for you to catch up. You aren't technically supposed to be in here, right?"

Orrin looked around. Jude and Madi were smiling at him.

"Traitors. You're all traitors."

It took five minutes for Orrin to do enough damage to kill a Frozen Carp on his own.

Experience Gained: 90 XP

By the time he killed seven more, he was out of breath, his ice swords had disappeared, and his arms felt heavy.

Experience Gained: 630 XP (90 XP x 7)

Orrin pulled up his status.

Orrin
Utility Warder
Level 9 (895/900)

"I only need one more, but I don't need to do all the damage," Orrin shouted to the rest of the party. Brandt was taking a break, and Jude was standing near the edge of the churning water.

Jude nodded and pulled another Carp up. He dragged it back and waited. "Go ahead, hit it once."

Orrin slashed the Carp.

"Now back up," Jude instructed.

Orrin moved back to the group, sitting along the edge of the frozen river.

Jude grunted and picked his hammer up. The fish was still latched to the head. As Jude straightened his arms, the fish came off the ground, rising slowly into the air until it floated vertically above Jude's head.

He let out a yell and brought the hammer down.

The fish exploded on impact.

Experience Gained: 45 XP
Level 10 Obtained!
+10 AP

A second box appeared under the first

Congratulations on Obtaining Level 10!
10 Stat Points have been awarded.
Usable Stats for Utility Warder:
Strength
Constitution
Dexterity
Will
Intelligence

Holy shit, Orrin thought to himself. *That's just as many as Daniel!*
A third box blinked to life under that one.

Quest Complete:
Obtain Level 10
Reward: [Hero Kit Level 2] Unavailable Reward

Just the same as Brandt. I had kind of hoped tha—

Error
Quest Reward Unavailable
Debug
Debug
Error
Administrator Access Override
Error
Reward Runtime Error
Reward List Debug
Rebooting . . .
Select your reward_

What the fuck?

Chapter 34

Orrin watched the blinking cursor.

Select your reward_

"Orrin? You okay?" Daniel spoke from behind him.

"Give me a second," Orrin responded and concentrated.

What kind of reward can I ask for? he thought. *Maybe a way home?*

Nothing changed on the prompt. The system had always seemed to respond to his thoughts before.

How about a skill or spell upgrade for free? More ability or stat points?

A list began to appear.

> **Upgrade one spell or skill**
> **Increase Strength Stat + 5**
> **Increase Constitution Stat + 5**
> **Increase Dexterity Stat + 5**
> **Increase Will Stat + 5**
> **Increase Intelligence Stat + 5**
> **+10 Ability Points**

"Daniel? We need to chat," Orrin called over his shoulder. "Alone, please."

"What's the matter?" Madi stepped forward. "Are you all right?"

"You two don't have to plan every step alone, you know." Jude also walked back, having dunked his hammer in the water to clean the fish guts off. "We are a party, after all."

Orrin considered it. Madi, Jude, and Brandt would have more information about this world and the possible rewards for a Quest than Daniel. But telling them would let them know something was weird with his system.

This is the second time I've seen this "Administrator Access" line. Did I somehow tap into the system when we came through?

Orrin tried thinking about an ability to go home. He thought as hard as he could about magical gateways and even an automobile with a terrible driver. Nothing happened.

"Maybe. Thanks, guys," he finally responded to Madi and Jude. "But I think I really need Daniel."

They grumbled but moved away as Daniel got close.

"Did it ask you for a moniker, too?" Daniel asked gently.

"What?"

The question was so unexpected that Orrin started to laugh.

"You think," he said between laughter, "I'm a [Hero]?"

Daniel frowned a bit. "I was kind of hoping yes."

Orrin stopped laughing at the suddenly haggard look on Daniel's face. "You don't have to shoulder all the pressure, even if I'm not a [Hero]. But we'll talk about that later. Look." He waved the third message with the errors to Daniel. Except it didn't budge.

"What are you trying to show me? Is it the [Map]? That doesn't work, remember?"

"No." Orrin tried again. It still didn't work. "Piece-of-shit system. I unlocked a reward for the tenth-level Quest. Some kind of Administrator Access error popped up, and now it's letting me pick a reward."

Daniel was silent, then asked, "What?"

"Exactly!" Orrin waved his hands around. "This happened when we got here the first time, but I forgot between surviving and the tree-vine-monster thing and saving you. But this time . . ." He trailed off.

"Can you get it to change your class to [Hero], too?"

"What kind of dumb ide—"

> Change class to [Hero].
> NOTICE—Administrator Access is denied
> to [Hero] class. Administrator Access will be
> rescinded.

"What the fuck is going on?" Orrin almost screamed.

Daniel waved back Jude and Brandt, who had started to walk back toward them.

"What happened?" Daniel asked as Orrin started walking in circles.

"You put the idea in my head, and now I can change to a [Hero], but I'll lose Administrator Access, whatever that is."

Daniel's face lit up, but then he frowned again. "I wonder what that Admin Access is. Do you think you could override Brandt's Quest too? Make all of us [Heroes]?"

"I don't know, Daniel." Orrin wanted to pull his hair out. "I don't know what any of this means."

"Should we ask them?" Daniel nodded over his shoulder.

Orrin looked at the rest of the party, waiting patiently by the ice door. Brandt and Jude were trying to act like they were having a conversation, but both were casting surreptitious glances their way. Madi wasn't trying to hide it and was staring them down.

"I don't know. What if they want to kill me because it's something like blood magic again?" Orrin was spiraling.

"Orrin, you're losing it, man. Cast that antianxiety spell on yourself."

Orrin took a deep breath and cast [Calm Mind].

Okay. Okay. I can create a reward. Daniel got about a hundred ability points' worth of skill upgrades as his reward at level ten, and I can get ten. That's fine, but stats outweigh ability points in rarity. So ability points are out. Skill upgrades I can buy with ability points, which I've already ruled out. I'm NOT going to change to another class. I kind of like my class. Maybe I wish I had something that did more damage or targeted more monsters at once, but—

> Upgrade [Lightstrike] to [Lightstrikes] cast un-erring beams of light that hits multiple targets (up to five) for 10 HP damage. 5 MP

Good to know that exists.

"Thanks," Orrin said to a patiently waiting Daniel. "That helped."

"Of course." Daniel punched his friend in the arm. "I was thinking, if you can do this, what else could you do?"

"Like what?" Orrin rubbed his arm.

"I don't know, like hack the system and get us home?" Daniel asked expectantly.

"Nothing comes up for that." Orrin shook his head. "And I've tried before searching everything for a way home. Still nothing. But it did just tell me about a better targeting spell. I can hit multiple targets and deal more damage."

"Not worth it," Daniel said. "You are a buffer and healer. You start slinging spells around and you might as well be any other mage. Better to stick with what you are. You make everyone around you better and keep them going."

Orrin felt himself blush at Daniel's words. "So stat points, then?"

"I was thinking more ability points. You could get more spells to the next level. Imagine if you could cast [Utility Ward] at third level." Daniel's eyes twinkled at the prospect of wielding Gertrude unhindered.

"Don't be selfish. More will means more mana. I can just cast strength on you then."

"Sold!" Daniel almost jumped up and down.

Orrin went back over his options. He tried to think of anything else that he could pick, but the big-ticket item of going home wasn't giving any results.

Increase Will Stat + 5

Orrin felt his mana pool grow, a small warmth growing in his chest before the feeling dissipated.

"Should I put my extra points into will or intelligence?" he wondered aloud.

"Strength all the way," Daniel joked. "But shouldn't you spread it out a bit?"

Orrin thought back to all the fights they'd been in so far. He had the regen and mana potions. He also had blood cycling in an emergency, although that would likely knock him out.

"I think full will for now," he decided. "If I don't run out of mana, then it doesn't matter how much the spells cost . . . right?"

Before he could question himself further, he threw all ten stat points into will.

Name: Orrin
Class: Utility Warder
Level 10 (40/1000)
Ability Points: 12

HP: 90
MP: 380

Strength: 9
Constitution: 9
Dexterity: 9
Will: 28
Intelligence: 11

"That should help a bit," he said with a smirk.

"How many points did you get for level ten?" Daniel asked as they looked over at the rest of the group.

"Ten."

Daniel punched him again. "You fucking cheat."

"What should we tell them?" Orrin worried as he saw Madi standing with her hand on one hip.

Madi was pissed. She'd respected her party members' request for some privacy, but she was furious at being excluded.

As soon as a smiling Daniel and Orrin joined them at the door, she demanded an explanation.

"We shouldn't have secrets in here," she started. "Especially since we have to watch each other's backs. I get level ten is a big deal, but we've been pretty open and—"

Orrin cut her off. "You're right. Sorry. I just freaked out a bit because something happened."

"Are you going to tell us or claim it's another [Hero]-only thing? Because the [Hero]'s party is supposed to be a team."

"My class unlocked other rewards for the level-ten Quest," Orrin said. He'd argued that keeping the reward skill tied to his unknown class would make the most sense. Daniel had been all for telling them all about the Administrator Access part, but Orrin had wanted to wait. He'd research himself first.

"How is that possible?" Jude stepped forward curiously. "I've never heard of anything like that. Although, to be fair, I've never heard of a locked reward before, either."

"It said something about Utility Warder unlocked rewards, and I got to choose," Orrin lied. "But Daniel had the thought that maybe Brandt could share his blue Quest box with me and maybe I could do it again?"

Brandt raised his eyebrows in disbelief. "I'll show it to you to sate your curiosity. But I would like to get into the next safe room before too long. It's been a long day."

"We could kill some more Carp first," Daniel chimed in.

"No. We got Orrin to level ten. There will be more enemies and experience in the next room." Brandt waved his hand around and then held it out to Orrin. "Here's the completed Quest."

Orrin opened Brandt's Quest.

Quest Complete
Obtain Level 20
Reward: [Hero Kit Level 3] Unavailable Reward

Unlock other rewards? he thought uncertainly.

Unlocking Limited Reward Set for Nonadministrator_
Increase Strength Stat + 3
Increase Constitution Stat + 3
Increase Dexterity Stat + 3
+5 Ability Points

Holy fuck, it worked, Orrin thought.

"Fuck, he did it," Brandt echoed. He looked up with near-glistening eyes. "Stat increases? Thank you."

Orrin shrugged. Daniel was already sharing the level-twenty Quest with Jude and Madi.

"I'm guessing it gives you the option of half a normal level of ability points or half a stat increase," Orrin explained. "I got some other weird options but ended up just increasing my will."

"You really should keep that kind of information more private," Jude admonished. "You never know who could use that kind of stuff against you."

Orrin felt touched that Jude was giving him reconnoitering advice.

"Let's get off this floor," Daniel suggested.

Jude grabbed half a fish carcass and dragged it along. They made their way inside the door and began to set up camp. This would be their first night actually sleeping in the Aqua Chambers.

Brandt still demanded a watch rotation. "Although nobody is supposed to be allowed inside, it does happen that people can slip in. Monsters never enter the safe rooms, though, unless it's a dungeon break."

"The guards said nobody was supposed to enter for a week," Daniel argued. "Do they let people in or are we talking about thieves and the like?"

"No sanctioned group will enter for a week. But they also said a group had been in here for two weeks. Likely, they are near level ten. That's the normal time frame. Honestly, the fact that we are at the third safe room on the first day is astounding. The fastest run I've ever been on. The fourth and fifth floors are mostly unavoidable fights, but the sixth floor is a long one. I'll explain more about that later. But to answer your question, Daniel, yes. Guards will let in assassins for a price. It's actually common for a party to go missing in a dungeon and for families to point fingers at each other over old grudges. But actual assassinations in the dungeons are rare."

"Why?" Orrin asked. He was pulling apart one of the chickens and making a stew out of it, much to Madi's dismay.

"Imagine trying to get through the first two or three floors alone." Brandt smirked. Then he frowned. "Well, I guess you wouldn't have a hard time. I'm sure some families would pay a lot of gold for you to lead a killer into a dungeon."

"No, thanks." Orrin chuckled. "I don't need that kind of guilt on my conscience."

Jude gave Orrin a serious nod.

"So, what's on the next floor?" Daniel asked.

"It's a hallway with multiple doors," Brandt explained. "With large rooms beyond every set of doors. If you open a door, you get pulled into a fight. If you win, the door disappears. You win three times, and the safe room door appears at the end of the hall."

"Any traps or ways I can cheat it?" Orrin asked.

"Not that I know of," Brandt replied. "But I'm sure you'll figure out a way to surprise us."

Orrin handed out the stew. He also pulled a loaf of bread out, and Jude moaned.

"I could kiss you." He dug the bread slice into his stew.

"So, Orrin . . ." Daniel started after he finished eating. "I totally didn't listen to you the first time around when you explained all the math for your spells and stuff. But doesn't increasing your will make your spells hit harder?"

Orrin nodded.

"If you don't want to do more math and figure out how high your buffs work now, I'll happily take a few practice swings with Gerty before bed."

Orrin chuckled and obliged his friend. His mana would reset after he slept anyway.

Increase Strength, Level 3 x 5

"Orrin, my strength just went up by fifty-five points!"

Brandt dropped his bowl. "What?"

Chapter 35

Jude immediately demanded a turn with maximum strength in the next fight.

"That's not how this team works," Brandt cut him off. He turned back to Daniel. "Are you sure? It's not just a false notification?"

"We don't get notifications from his buffs—you know that." Daniel gestured at Orrin with a give-me motion. "I checked my status, and my strength is up by fifty-five."

"I know Orrin can increase our stats, but fifty-five is more points than most people will get in their entire lives . . . more than most top adventurers have in any one stat. Only monsters and orcs have that much strength."

Orrin listened to Brandt's disbelief as he put his hand into his cloak pocket and pulled the handle of Gerty to the surface. The weight wouldn't hit him until it was all the way out, but he'd already learned his lesson—Gerty was Heavy with a capital *H*. He just wasn't strong enough to pick up Daniel's sword. He held the cloak out with Gertrude sticking halfway out.

Daniel smiled and pulled the massive sword out the rest of the way. With his last attempt, he'd still struggled with the weight. Now, Daniel hefted his sword like it was a cosplay prop. He twirled it in one hand and changed it to his other. He spun and let the tip drag along the ice wall, creating a shallow scratch. Daniel kept playing with his giant sword as Madi scooted closer to Orrin.

"You realize that spell could change everything. You can use [Inverse] and your strength buff to make the floor-ten boss so weak we don't even have to fight him."

Orrin felt odd being the center of attention. Jude was laughing as Daniel tried to roll the massive sword over his back and dropped it. Brandt was staring at him again.

Brandt turned to Jude. "Can you imagine what he could do against a Fogbinder? They are mostly intelligence based. If he dropped the stat by fifty-fucking-five, even a child could take it out."

"Should we head back to Dey?" Jude approached, leaving Daniel to his swordplay. "We could probably get back before too much fighting starts. Faster if the kid would teleport a few times."

Brandt was lost in thought for only a moment. "No. Lord Catanzano gave us our orders." He looked sheepishly at Madi. "We stay for a week or until the tenth floor and then turn back."

"What if we beat the tenth floor?" Daniel came up from behind and asked. "Couldn't we just keep going? How great would that be for Dey? The whole town is down, and we come back after defeating the entire dungeon."

Jude's eyes lit up, but Brandt was already shaking his head again. "Nice try . . . again. But the Troll is more than capable of taking us all out. Even if Orrin can drop his strength, it's one of those monsters that is just beastly."

"What if I dropped its dexterity and strength?" Orrin asked.

"You could try, but it also has a cartload of health and regenerates. I've only gotten past it twice, and once cost two lives. I'm all for showing you the level of monster you are itching to fight, but then we are going to retreat to the safe room and get out."

"Could we try a few different strategies out before leaving? We can just pop in and out until we find—"

"Once you reenter a safe room you left, you appear outside the dungeon," Brandt injected. "You get one chance, and honestly, you three will wait by the door."

Madi and Daniel grumbled a bit but let the issue drop for now.

Daniel had hacked up the ground enough practicing that Brandt had no problem starting a fire with the fish remains. Something about the magic in the monsters let it burn brightly for them. Daniel and Orrin took first watch—Brandt was trusting them more.

"You're totally going to fight the Troll, aren't you?" Orrin asked. He created an ice sword and turned it over the fire. It didn't melt at all.

"Of course." Daniel chuckled. "With an extra dose of strength from you."

"Yeah. Making you all stronger. The only thing I'm actually good for around here."

Daniel reached over and flicked Orrin between the eyes.

"Ouch. What the hell was that for?"

Daniel put a finger up in front of Orrin's face. "Listen. We wouldn't have survived this long without you. You led us around the entire first floor without one battle. You saved Madi's life. You got us across the river and even killed some monsters. Why are you being so down on yourself?"

When Daniel put it like that, Orrin sounded pretty badass. However . . .

"You all can fight. Madi can cast actual offensive spells. I have to use [Lightstrike] to do one damage point. Sure, I can boost you guys, but is it really helpful in a fight? You didn't really need my boosts against the newts. I was able to take out a Carp once we got them out of water. Brandt has taken down the Troll before with a normal group. What if we get into more fights and you guys realize you don't actually need my spells?"

Daniel laughed. "You idiot." He wiped his eyes. "You haven't used strength or dexterity boosts on yourself in a fight, have you? You make the fights easier. You don't *need* to do damage, except to get the experience."

"But if I don't contribute, then how wil—"

"Do you remember when we were at Finn's house playing that fighter game he liked so much?" Daniel spoke over him.

"Yeah. But what does that—"

"And his little brother wanted a turn?"

Orrin just nodded.

"Do you remember how you felt playing against him?"

"He was, like, four. He didn't even know what buttons to push, and I just jumped around him. It was one-sided."

Daniel bobbed his head as Orrin spoke. "Exactly. That's what it feels like to fight with my dexterity and strength increased by you."

"The Newts wouldn't have been hard to kill. Annoying, yes. But Jude said most parties make it through to the second floor without major problems. But they have to rest to recover health. That's more time wasted, more time that they have to dig into their supplies to survive. We didn't have to do that because of you and your wards."

Daniel leaned back from the fire. "Same with the third floor. It's a slow-going process. Jude thought we'd make it halfway in one day and have to camp out on the far shore."

Orrin was quiet as the fish bones in the fire popped.

"You think you don't contribute, Orrin? We have a chance to defeat this entire dungeon because of you. Now stop moping and hand me some more of that bread. I'm hungry."

Orrin handed over a loaf and stared at the floor. He moved his foot to gather some of the ice bits that Daniel had made when he dug out the fire pit.

The fire didn't melt the broken shards of ice that littered the ground. The dark-blue ice glittered with the reflection of the fire. It reminded him of a night sky, filled with bright stars.

"On a brighter note, what spells are you buying?"

Orrin smiled. "I'm going back and forth. Part of me wants to upgrade dex and will. I was also thinking of just getting the second-level [Utility Ward], but that's ten points."

"Which one makes me stronger?"

Orrin threw another piece of bread at Daniel. He caught it and ate it. "Don't waste food."

"I guess [Utility Ward] would help the group more right now."

Daniel put a fist out for Orrin to bump. "That's right, get me stronger."

Orrin rolled his eyes. He spent the ten AP.

[Utility Ward] Level 2: maximum possible Level 2 Strength, Dexterity, Will, and Intelligence increase

on yourself and your party within 100 feet. 200
MP. -10 AP.

Orrin woke when Madi gently shook him.

"Time to get up," she whispered gently. "Floor four awaits."

Orrin groaned and rolled over. Everybody else was up and getting dressed.

"Thanks," he mumbled and started pulling on his armor. Then he
yelled over to Brandt. "Do we have time for me to get some wards up
on everybody? If we could wait a bit, I could also do a [Utility Ward],
but I don't want to go into a fight without a full mana pool."

Brandt nodded. "We'll take a long breakfast and start when
Orrin gives the okay."

Orrin used [Utility Ward] first to get the boost to his own intelligence. The less everything cost, the better.

His intelligence went up by thirty points. All of his stats went up
by thirty points.

Will is definitely my favorite stat, he thought.

At forty-one intelligence, his spells would cost only 69 percent
the normal cost. He chuckled at his math.

Get it together.

He cast [Ice Ward] on everybody for only fourteen MP. Five
[Wards] cost another seventy MP. The [Utility Ward] had cost
198 MP.

MP: 397/680

*Wait four and a half hours, or pop a mana potion and wait three
hours . . .*

"Hey, Brandt, is four hours too long?"

Brandt and Jude were staring at their status screens, mouths open.

"Kid. Take all the time you need."

Four hours later, Brandt and Jude were sweating slightly. They
had spent the time having an impromptu training lesson with Daniel,

using their boosted stats in an attempt to get used to the increased speed and strength.

Madi had just chatted with Orrin. He'd tried to explain the calculations he'd figured out for his stats and what they did to different spells. She'd eaten it up. Most mage classes didn't share much information unless they were part of a sect or cabal. Orrin's mana was still not full, but it was close enough.

Brandt wiped the sweat off his head and walked over to the door. "Today, we work as a team in monster fights. We already have some experience in that, but remember that Madi and Orrin will call the shots. If they say jump, we jump. Protect each other this time. We need more practice working in tandem."

"We've both been through the next floor," Jude said. "And what we can agree on is that nothing is ever the same. I've never seen the same monster twice, nor has anything I've seen matched up with Brandt's fights. It might be one big guy or a bunch of tiny beasties. Stay on your toes."

Everybody nodded, and with that, the party entered the fourth floor.

Just as advertised, Orrin thought. *A long hallway full of doors. It looks like a Scooby-Doo episode.*

The hall was still covered with ice, but a faint carpet runner went down the middle just under the frozen water. A door was situated every ten feet or so at alternating intervals as far as they could see.

Daniel could see the farthest and reported, "I don't see an end."

"The end appears after three doors are opened and the rooms cleared," Brandt said and unstrapped his sword. "There's no difference between the doors. Might as well pick any one of them."

"Wait, please," Orrin said. "I'm going to check [Map]."

That was a bust. Orrin's [Map] showed nothing—no red dots behind the door and no end to the hallway a mile out.

"Shit. Nothing."

"Can't win them all," Daniel said and slapped his back. He was holding Gerty on his shoulder. The increased strength gave him just enough to carry his sword around freely. He still moved a bit slower than with his shortsword but promised he'd drop the big sword if needed.

"So which door?" Madi asked.

Daniel shrugged. "Just point one out. Jude and I will rush in."

Orrin shook his head and walked forward a bit. "If it doesn't matter, let's just do the first three. Why waste the stamina?"

Everyone agreed, and Brandt put his hand on the handle of the first door.

"Let's do this." Daniel hyped himself up. Jude was holding his hammer over his head, ready to run in.

Brandt opened the door, and the party surged inside.

Chapter 36

As planned, Jude and Daniel went in first. Brandt followed closely behind, with Madi and Orrin taking up the rear. The rooms were supposed to be large on the other side; about two hundred yards back, the same width and vaulted ceilings that you could just make out.

The room they entered was significantly larger. Orrin could barely make out the back wall through all the snow, and he could not see the ceiling. It looked like a sky but had the same tint of dark blue the safe room floors usually had.

Ice? He thought briefly. He couldn't figure out how high up it was.

None of that mattered compared to the monsters they saw up ahead, though. Shambling along slowly toward the party. Two colossal behemoths of ice, the humanoid shapes stepped forward in near sync. A frozen leg broke as it left the ground behind it and regrew before planting itself on the ground in front. Each step leaving a five-foot-tall column of ice. The ground was littered with the ice trees.

Orrin used [Identify].

[Ice Elemental] HP 400/400

"Ice Elemental. Four hundred health. Madi, hit the one on the left and blind it. Everyone else, attack the one on the right," Orrin yelled and proactively hit both with a [Lightstrike].

He stood by the door and pulled out his bestiary.

"What are you doing?" Madi screamed at him as she ran forward to cast her spell. "This is no time for reading."

"Knowledge is power," he replied, already flipping through the pages. *There you are.*

Ice Elementals are formed from cores of wild ice magic. Attacks against the ice body are meaningless, and adventurers should take care to retreat if confronted, as damaging the core is mostly luck. Each Elemental keeps the core in a different part of its icy body, which can be regenerated at will. The height of an Elemental displays its strength, with anything taller than five feet being a five-star (*****) monster.

"Don't waste your time attacking the body—it won't do any good . . ." Orrin trailed off. Nobody was listening to him.

Daniel and Jude were hacking the legs off the right Elemental, while Brandt was trying to flank it. The one on the left was walking in slightly larger circles. Madi had already hit it with [Shimmersight].

Orrin ran forward and slid to a stop next to Madi. "They're doing no damage to it."

"Are you kidding? Look at Jude—he just took off half its thigh with one hit."

Orrin pulled up an [Identify] box on the Elemental being attacked and threw it to Madi. "See?"

She gasped and then started winding up another spell. "I'll blind it. You pull them back and get them to listen."

Orrin moved closer but kept his distance. The Elemental was taking large, unwieldy swings with its arms at the much smaller fighters. It had to be fifteen to twenty feet tall.

"Daniel. Jude. Retreat," he ordered, waving his hands to try and get their attention.

Jude listened and fell back, but Daniel swung twice more at the legs. Gertrude flew through the first leg but got stuck in the second. The mass of ice creaked and began to tilt back, its balance gone.

"Brandt, get out of the way!" Orrin screamed. The knight held his shield up in front of him as small chips of ice began to fall. He ran sideways and barely missed being crushed beneath the Ice Elemental's body.

The monster shivered on the ground, the ice pulling into a vaguely rectangular shape and then pushing back up into its previous form.

"It's like the fucking metal guy from *Terminator*." Daniel appeared next to Orrin.

"Asshole, listen to your overwatch!" Orrin pushed Daniel. He actually teetered for a second. *This extra thirty stat points is no joke!*

The Elemental was back on its feet and took a step forward. Then Madi's spell hit the lumbering beast.

Daniel looked sheepish for only a second. "Sorry, but did you see how much damage I'm doing?"

Orrin gave him a dead face and threw the same box as earlier to the [Hero]. "Absolutely nothing."

Brandt made it back. Madi and Jude ran up as well. With both Elementals blinded by Madi, they had a few minutes. The party crept closer to the door again. One of the monsters was walking away from them, while the recently knocked-down one stood still.

"What gives?" Jude prompted. "We were doing all right. Why pull us out?"

"And please be more careful, Daniel." Brandt used his sword to dislodge some slivers of ice stuck to his shield. "I'd rather not become a smear on the ground."

"You were doing no damage. These things have a core in them somewhere. Only that takes damage—the rest of it is like a big rechargeable armor piece," Orrin explained. "Have either of you en-countered something like that?"

Brandt and Jude shook their heads.

"Could I just crush the entire thing?" Daniel asked.

"You saw how it got right back up, right?" Madi commented. "You took off a leg and a half, and it was walking in seconds."

The party was quiet as they all thought.

"So what do we do?" Daniel looked to Orrin.

Orrin shrugged. "Dude, I don't have the answer every time."

Brandt took his helmet off. "Damn, this thing gets hot. What if we attack together? Everybody take a limb; Jude takes the head or center mass. Orrin can let us know if anyone hits it."

"It has four hundred health," Orrin countered. "That's going to take forever."

Jude smiled. "So, like a normal dungeon delve without our solution kit here." He jostled into Orrin. "Time for us old-timers to show you kids how it's done."

Old-timers? They can't be out of their early twenties. Orrin just shook his head as the fighters started strategizing.

"I could cast a few [Lightbeams]," Madi supplied.

"I'll hit an arm with [Lightstrike]," Orrin said. *Might as well waste the mana.*

The second Elemental was far in the distance now. The first was standing with its side to the party. They moved around into position.

"Attack," Daniel whisper-shouted.

Daniel swung for the upper leg again, intending to cleave the limb off. Brandt stabbed at the ice of the other leg. Madi and Orrin hit the two arms. Nothing changed on his [Identify] box.

Jude wound his hammer over his head and jumped from behind, bringing the metal down on what would have been the neck. The ice groaned and cracked, a fault line appearing down the middle of the chest.

"Still no damage," Orrin yelled.

Daniel shoved Gertrude into the crack and wedged the sword deep. Then he hauled the handle to the side. He let out a roar of a yell, and the Elemental split in two pieces.

The side of the body to Orrin's right melted down into water and then flowed across the ground toward the still-frozen left side.

"There." Brandt yelled and struck something only he could see.

[Ice Elemental] HP 348/400

"You did fifty-two damage," Orrin yelled out. "Again. Quick."

Brandt struck but not quickly enough. The ice reformed around the core and pushed down, creating new legs. In seconds the outer shell body stood tall.

It took a step toward the party.

"Shit." Madi started winding up another spell. "When it re-forms, it must have shaken my shimmer."

She hit the slow-moving target again. "Having this much intelligence is paying off. I can totally see your math adding up, Orrin. My spells cost so much less."

Orrin just nodded. "Same plan?"

This time, Daniel took the center and used [Gravity Strike] to cut the Elemental in two. The top half stayed solid and landed on the slush that had been legs and hips a moment before. Brandt and Jude went wild.

"Over here." Brandt pointed and began to hack.

"Move." Jude held his hammer high and brought it down in a [Fallen Star] attack.

[Ice Elemental] HP 83/400

"It's down to eighty-three," Orrin yelled out.

The rectangle of icy doom formed again. As the Elemental fully formed, Brandt let out his own [Power Strike], carving a swath of ice from the Elemental's side.

The chunk of ice stayed solid. Brandt quickly struck it with his shield as hard as he could.

A small softball of deep-blue ice, with flickering lighter-blue veins, rolled to a stop near Orrin's feet.

Madi hit it with a [Lightbeam] before Orrin moved. He swung his sword, completely forgotten until this point, and hit the core.

It shattered, and the lights inside dimmed. The small ball of ice lay inert at his feet, the cracks letting off a final glimmer before going dark.

Experience Gained: 200 XP

"Nice!" Daniel ran and slid to a stop. "And we have one more."

"I got a level," Madi said, her eyes already flickering over her invisible boxes. "I only need a moment."

"Better make it quick," Jude answered. "I think your original spell wore off."

The other Elemental was heading back.

Orrin's sword fell from his grip, and he sat hard on the ground. *Fucking Elementals.*

The second monster had been slightly bigger than the first. They'd had to cut it down three times before they got the first hit on the core. After that, Brandt and Daniel made sure to keep an eye on where it was. The monster didn't move it around too much during its rebuilding phase.

Experience Gained: 200 XP

All in all, they'd been fighting for only thirty or forty minutes, but it was a lot of spell slinging and even more physical exertion. Fighting the thing in cycles had been the smart play, but it took so long.

Orrin had tried casting an inverse buff on the Elemental but nothing happened.

"Maybe I needed to target the core?" he muttered to himself.

"Stop overthinking." Daniel plopped down beside him. "Enjoy the victory for a minute. Strategize later. You did amazing."

Madi sat down, too. "He's right, you know. We would have wasted who knows how long figuring out that fight. Smart to bring a bestiary."

"I'm just surprised Brandt didn't know what it was." Jude leaned on his hammer haft, digging the head into the dirt under the snow for balance. "Aren't you always yelling at the recruits about being prepared?"

Brandt's helmet was off again, his hair a matted mess. "Oh, shut up, Jude. I can't know every monster backward and forward."

"The kid did," Jude countered.

"I cheated." Orrin held up the bestiary and then slipped it back into his [Dimension Hole]. "Might not have the time if the second door is something too fast."

"We'll deal with that tomorrow," Brandt said. "We can go back into the hallway and start camp."

"No, we can go more," Madi argued.

"You used how much mana?" Brandt asked. "I know I used so many skills that I'm going to feel it in my bones. And there is no rush. Orrin, you'll wake up early tomorrow to cast those spells again. I want to start earlier. But only one door a day. Let's not push too hard."

Madi grumbled as they made their way back to the hallway. Brandt carried the cores of both Elementals in the crook of his arm.

Even though it was still early in the day, Orrin had to admit he felt tired. The fights he'd been in up to this point with monsters had all been relatively quick. The constant repositioning and few spells he'd had to cast hadn't worn him out, but the loss of the adrenaline of the fight left him weary.

"We did better today," Brandt said over more soup. "Working as a team and responding to Orrin and Madi's plan. Let's keep that up tomorrow."

"Most of us, anyways," Orrin said with a look at Daniel.

Daniel tilted his cup of soup back and then sighed. "I said sorry. I was just in the zone."

"You have to be better. Brandt could have gotten hurt."

"All right, all right. I promise to listen better."

Madi laughed. "You two are like an old married couple."

Daniel and Orrin scowled at her.

"Okay. Orrin and Madi, last watch. Wake us up whenever. Your [Utility Ward] stops when we sleep, right?" Brandt asked.

"Yeah. I think that was the trigger for it to reset last time."

"Then I'll take middle watch again and—"

"You took it last time," Daniel interjected. "You and Jude get some uninterrupted sleep tonight. Let me take middle watch. For my fuckup."

Brandt smiled. "I won't turn down the offer. I'll wake you in a few hours."

Orrin crawled into his sleeping mat and fell asleep quickly. It felt like seconds later that Daniel was shaking him awake.

"Orrin, something's wrong with Jude and Brandt. Wake up. You need to heal them, now!"

Chapter 37

"Huh?" Orrin sat up slowly. *How long was I asleep?*

"Get up," Daniel demanded, pulling Orrin's arm and dragging him out of his sleeping mat. "I was just coming to get you for your shift. I passed the guys and heard Jude crying in his sleep. Look."

Orrin stumbled and righted himself. He followed Daniel the few steps away to where Jude and Brandt were tossing in their sleep.

"What's wrong with them?"

"I don't know," Daniel said with agitation. He ran his hands through his hair. "I was hoping you could [Identify] them. I couldn't get Jude to wake when I shook him."

"Is Madi all right?" Orrin squatted down and tried shaking Jude. He just moaned and rolled farther into his blanket.

"I'll check." Daniel moved to the other side of the room.

Orrin cast [Identify] on Jude.

> Jude DeGuis
> Bruiser Level 16
> Status: Fatigued, Dizzy, Brain Fog, Nauseous
> HP: 130
> MP: 100
>
> Strength: 19
> Constitution: 13
> Dexterity: 14
> Will: 10

Intelligence: 10

What the hell? Orrin ignored all of Jude's spells and skills. *Where did all those status effects come from?*

"Orrin! Madi is shaking, too. Are they sick?"

Orrin turned his [Identify] to Brandt, who had the same odd statuses. He ran over to Madi. She was the same.

"They all have status effects—fatigue, brain fog, dizzy, and things like that," Orrin explained. "How do you feel?"

Daniel put his hands up in the air and stretched down. "I don't feel bad at all. A little weak after I woke up. Your [Utility Ward] wore off when I was asleep. But I figured that was just me getting used to my normal stat build."

"Shit. Do you think it's my buffs?" Orrin felt terrible. If he'd hurt the party . . .

"I mean, we all ate the same food," Daniel said. "But then you and I should feel it, too, right?"

"I have no idea." Orrin went back over the Brandt and tried waking him again. "Brandt! Brandt!" Orrin slapped his cheek lightly. Brandt's eyes fluttered open.

"What . . . do you . . . need?" Brandt's voice was low and slurred.

"Everybody's sick. How are you feeling? Can you remember your name?" Orrin asked.

Thank god for all Mom's hospital stories, Orrin thought. He could just remember basic concussion protocols.

"I feel . . . heavy." Brandt tried to sit up, and his eyes rolled back. He fell with a loud thump. "Ow."

"Stay with me." Orrin snapped his fingers over Brandt's face until he opened his eyes again. "What is your name?"

"Brandt Bennett."

"Good. Do you know where you are?"

Brandt paused. A long few seconds passed. ". . . no." Brandt's voice was small and afraid.

"Can you tell me how you feel? What do you remember?" Orrin asked as Daniel brought a waterskin over. "Thanks, Daniel."

Orrin took the water and wet Brandt's lips. Then he pointed to Jude and Madi. Daniel nodded and went to keep them hydrated.

"I . . . feel heavy."

"Yes. Anything else? Does your head hurt? Do you feel any nausea or tingling?" Orrin wished he had listened better to the symptoms of a concussion. It wasn't the problem here but would have given him more to work with.

"Head hurts. Yes. Dizzy when I sit up. Hard to think. Can I sleep now?" Brandt's normal demeanor was shattered. He talked to Orrin like a small child with his first flu.

"Yes. You did great, Brandt. Get some sleep."

Orrin stood and joined Daniel. He was just finishing giving Jude something to drink. Jude hadn't even come fully awake.

"So?" Daniel asked as he stood. "What's going on?"

"I have no idea." Orrin took the water from Daniel and walked to Madi. "Maybe she'll be able to talk better."

Madi roused easier than the men had, but she could barely move her body.

"Ugh. My head is pounding. What happened?" Madi asked as she stayed very still.

"We don't know," Daniel offered. "I think it's Orrin's buff. Side effects, maybe?"

"My body feels like Brandt threw me through his knight workout again." She tried to push herself up and fell to her side. "Oh, that's embarrassing."

"Just let us help," Orrin said. He and Daniel sat her upright in the corner. Madi kept shaking her head sporadically.

"I feel . . . weird. My head isn't doing what I want it to," she said as she shook her head again.

"I'm going to try to heal you, okay?" Orrin said. "Let me know if you feel any different?"

"Sure. You're much kinder than we thought, you know." Madi smiled wide. "I'm really sorry you got hurt." She started to cry.

Orrin cast [Heal Small Wounds] on Madi.

"Anything?"

"Hmm? No. I still feel off." She tilted on the wall, and Daniel reached out to straighten her. "I'm cold. Can you pull that blanket up?"

Orrin looked to Daniel. "Can you pull her closer to the fire? It's dark in here anyways. I want to—"

"I can help with that," Madi interrupted and pointed her finger to the ceiling. "I can make pretty, pretty butterflies."

She cast her spell and immediately threw up on Daniel.

"Come on." Daniel let her fall to the ground and shook his hands. Orrin quickly backed away.

"Shurry," a muffled voice moaned. Madi's face had landed in the blankets, and she didn't have the strength to move.

"At least the lights let us see a bit better." Orrin smirked.

"I'm going to use your sleeping bag to wipe this off," Daniel huffed. Orrin laughed and poured some water out over Daniel's arms. Then he knelt and washed Madi's mouth off.

"Okay. So no more spells," Orrin instructed Madi as they worked together to pull her around. He turned to look at Daniel. "We need to keep them hydrated and feed them small meals so they can keep it down easier. I have no idea what is going on, but concussion protocol shouldn't hurt at least."

"Whatever you say." Daniel helped prop one of the bags on its side, letting Madi sit up a little in front of the fire. The ice cores were still burning away merrily. "How long do these things burn for?"

Orrin looked at the fire and felt a pit in his stomach. "If the fire goes out, we can only feed them jerky, bread, and water. I shouldn't have turned all the rest of the chicken into soup."

"Hen," Madi murmured. She was slowly losing consciousness again.

Orrin turned and saw Brandt and Jude were already out, tossing in their blanket rolls.

"We could pull them back. If we retreat to the safe room instead of sitting in this hallway, we can get those guards to help," he suggested.

"I could go defeat a room and get more monster corpse to burn," Daniel offered. "'More monster corpse to burn' . . . that's a fun sentence I never thought I'd have to say in my life."

"We are not going into another room. That would just be stupid." Orrin tilted Madi's body so she could rest comfortably but wouldn't roll into the fire. "We can wait a few hours. Maybe this is just temporary, whatever it is."

"You sure?" Daniel stood and looked down the hall. "You put one boost on me, and I could have taken out those Elementals. I just didn't want to show off."

"You? Not show off? Please." Orrin picked up a small piece of ice and threw it at his friend. "I need your help taking care of them. With Madi, I can move her. I'm not sure about Brandt or Jude."

"Boost your strength."

"That might be the problem. What if I fall sick, too?"

Jude moaned loudly.

"I'll stay and help, of course." Daniel picked up a second waterskin and moved toward the knights. "I'll keep them watered and fed."

"Let them sleep a few hours in between."

Daniel waved over his head.

Now, we wait, Orrin thought. *Stuck in a dungeon with over half the party down. This isn't looking good.*

The next few hours were drudgery. Feeding the trio, then getting them water was boring and thankless work.

Orrin and Daniel moved the other two closer to the fire after Daniel discovered Brandt's hands were cold as . . . well . . . ice. Daniel was able to manhandle them over with ease, and Orrin set up a circle of all their packs, taking his and Daniel's out of his [Dimension Hole] to finish the circuit.

"It's like a campout, but with dead bodies," Daniel said grimly.

"They aren't dead. Brandt just drank half that water." Orrin had taken the barrel of water out of his storage and was currently refilling all their waterskins.

"I'll take some more of that." A small voice drifted over.

Orrin almost dropped the water and hurried to the fire. "Brandt?"

"Hi, kid. What happened?" The knight tried to sit up and managed to get into a half-sitting, half-bent position over his own pack.

"We don't know for sure, but my money is on Orrin's buffs." Daniel appeared next to Orrin. "Here, eat something."

Brandt took the bread with a shaky hand. "I feel like I was beaten all over."

"And you were having trouble talking earlier. All three of you," Orrin said and waved to the other two sleeping teammates. He looked closer. Madi and Jude were both snoring with a gentler ease than before.

"Thanks for not leaving us," Brandt said between bites. "You two really are honorable."

"Leave you? I just suggested taking a room out without you guys, but Orrin had to be all strict and logical," Daniel quipped.

"I'm not sure I can finish this bread," Brandt said and then handed the bread over quickly. "I feel so wrong."

"Try to get some more sleep," Orrin ordered. "You'll feel better when you wake up."

Brandt nodded gently and passed out with his body still leaning over the bags.

Daniel sighed and got him situated back on the ground.

"They're getting better."

Daniel nodded. "But the fire is starting to sputter."

"That's fine. We don't need it to last forever. A little cold won't kill us, and we can always use the torches I brought."

Daniel slapped his head. "Thank god. I forgot about the torches. I really thought I'd have to sneak off and kill a monster."

Orrin paused. "You are joking, right? You weren't about to go off on your own after I specifically told you not to?"

Daniel smirked at him. "I mean . . . I would have asked for a strength buff first."

"Dumbass."

By the afternoon, Madi and Jude had both come around as well. Madi was able to stay awake and talk, although she could move her body less than either knight.

"It has to be the [Utility Ward] buffs," she agreed with Daniel. "Nothing else would make sense. But why would it not affect you both?"

"Well, I'm a [Hero]," Daniel said as he puffed up. "So, no little stat boost is going to stop me."

"And it's my own spells. It would be weird if it brought me down, right?" Orrin offered.

"This sucks. We were making such good time. Brandt is going to make us turn back as soon as he can get up," she complained.

The three sat in silence, listening to Jude's snores.

Orrin summoned an ice sword and used it to move the broken ice cores around. The giant marbles had remained after the fire had guttered out. Five torches now lined the group, sunk into the ground where Daniel had stabbed the hard floor with his shortsword.

"Madi . . . what do you want to do after you beat a dungeon?" Orrin asked.

She watched him move the cores in circles for a moment before she answered. "Well. Defeating a dungeon is good for Dey and makes the world safer. The extra stats are also amazing. But truly?" She looked at Daniel. "I want to follow the [Hero]."

Orrin kept moving the sword round and round. "Why?"

"Because I'm fucking awesome," Daniel put in. He leaned back and put his hands behind his head.

"I've been kind of going nonstop for a while now. Today is the first time that I was able to really be alone with my thoughts. I mean, Daniel was here, but he's an idiot." Orrin smiled at his friend. Daniel flipped him off. "What I mean is, what's in it for you?"

Madi frowned. "You still don't trust me."

She threw an arm over the bag she was leaning on and grunted in pain as she pulled herself upright.

"Let me tell you something about myself. My father has never allowed me in a dungeon . . . I'm not sure he ever would have, either. My mom was a part-time adventurer. She was damn good, too. Until she wasn't. She died repelling a dungeon break from the Silver Vaults when I was eight. Ever since then, it has been my dream to defeat one. I read all the stories as a little girl, you know, *Elizabeth and the Fallen Crater, Denna and the Sandy Dunes.* The children's stories of great adventurers who overcame the odds to shatter dungeon cores and lead nations."

She used the back of her arm to push tears away from her eyes. "But after my mom died, I became the cloistered princess instead. Begging lessons off Brandt when he could escape his squire training. Reading everything I could so that I could unlock a different class than my father. Because he wants me to be the same as him. Facades and manipulation. But I want to be like Denna and help push my party to the top of that final dune. I want to help the [Hero] complete his main Quest, even if you never share it with me, Daniel. You ask what I want to do after we defeat this dungeon? I want to defeat every single dungeon in this world so nobody ever has to die from one again."

Chapter 38

Orrin sat in silence against the door they'd cleared, watching Madi and the knights sleep. Madi's little speech had taken it out of her, and she'd gone back under quickly.

Orrin threw a [Identify] on her sleeping form.

Madeleine Catanzano
Prism Conjurer Level 14
Status: Fatigued, Dizzy
HP: 110
MP: 170

Strength: 10
Constitution: 11
Dexterity: 10
Will: 17
Intelligence: 16

"Move over." Daniel kicked Orrin's leg. He sat down and pulled a blanket up over them. "It's fucking freezing in here."

Orrin nodded. "Yeah. It is. Two of the abnormal statuses on Madi have disappeared."

Daniel moved around until he was comfortable. "That's great news." He sighed as he settled down. "So . . . are you going to tell me?"

"Tell you what?" Orrin had to move again. His back was in the doorjamb now.

"Why you're being a dick to Madi again. I thought you two made up."

Orrin turned to make sure Daniel was joking. He wasn't.

"You really think I can forget getting stabbed because her father wanted to test if you were a [Hero]? Or that right after we saved her from those bandits, she threatened to kill us? She's a little trigger-happy, don't you think?"

Daniel let the blanket drop to put his hands up defensively. "O. I'm on your side. Don't bite my head off. I know you hold a grudge. I'm not surprised. I just wanted to know . . . why now? We're kind of up the creek."

Orrin mulled it over. *How do you tell someone you are just pissed? Pissed that none of your spells work like you want them to. Pissed that you spend all your time in the back. Pissed that you just almost killed all your new friends, even if one of them is totally a spy and the other is a two-faced bitch who would likely push you off a cliff if she could get away with it.*

"Can I just call it a bad day?"

"You can." Daniel put his arm around Orrin's neck. "I won't believe you, though. I will drop it if I'm being a dick, though. Just remember, she tried to have me killed, too. I have every reason to not trust her as well. But strangely, I do."

"Of course you do." Orrin shrugged his arm off. "They never would have actually killed you. You're the prized ass. I'm just the problem they haven't been able to solve yet."

Daniel got quiet. "You know, I was serious when I threatened them. If they try anything . . . ever again . . . I'll find a way to reduce that house to the ground with them in it."

Orrin stood and let the blanket fall. "If you have to do that, I'm probably dead. I'll play nice, though. She hasn't done anything to break her promise so far. But I'm waiting."

"Should we have a safe word?"

"What?"

"You know, like if we need to get out of town quick. We could figure out a place to meet. Even plan different routes if we get separated."

Orrin stared at Daniel.

"Why are you looking at me like that? It's not a bad idea."

"I know," Orrin responded. "It's actually a good idea. Which is why I'm surprised."

Daniel stood and slugged Orrin in the arm. "Jerk."

"Idiot."

They chuckled.

"How about 'television' or just 'TV'?"

"And just how do you think you could use that word in a normal sentence on this world?" Orrin asked. "That's got to be the dumbes—"

"'You know, all this reminds me of a TV show I watched once,'" Daniel cut in.

"That's not too bad, actually," Orrin admitted. "But I can't exactly go saying that, can I? I'm a local."

"Shit. I forgot. Um . . . I don't know."

Orrin thought for a minute. "What about just mentioning that tree? The one you hollowed out our first night here. It's innocent enough that you could just be telling a story. Same for me. But we'll know."

"Okay. So, like, 'hey, this hallway smells worse than that big tree we spent the night in.'"

"Perfect." Orrin laughed. "And if we need to communicate in a hurry, just yell, 'TV.' If we need to run, who cares if they know I'm from the same planet as you?"

"I'm not sure you actually are from Earth," Daniel said and dodged Orrin's attempted hit.

Orrin leaned back on the wall. "Thanks for not giving me too much shit. If she's for real, maybe I'll come around."

"No, you won't," Daniel said as he rolled the blanket up into a ball. "You still haven't forgiven me for breaking your Spider-Man toy when we were, like, seven."

"It wasn't a toy. It was a collectib—"

"Yeah. Yeah. Come on. Let's go check on the kids." Daniel put the wadded-up blanket under his arm and trudged off to check on Madi. Orrin moved toward the guys.

Brandt was snoring again but sounded much better. Cleaner, somehow. Jude turned when Orrin got close.

"You awake?"

Jude turned over and blinked his eyes. "I think so?"

Orrin grabbed a water and handed it to him. "Drink while you can. You guys have been sweating a lot, even in this cold."

Jude took it and drank greedily. "Thanks." He huffed a few breaths. "I feel a lot better. How long were we out?"

"It's almost night. Daniel and I can take watch and let you guys sleep. Tomorrow we can figure out what to do. Madi thinks Brandt will demand we return."

"Mysterious illness in the middle of the dungeon? Yeah. He's going to be a stick in the mud."

"Sorry." Orrin took the water back and set it against the bags. Another quick identify on Jude showed the fatigued and dizzy statuses were gone. The words *brain fog* were fading, but *nauseous* was still there.

"It's not your fault, kid, even if it is. We all accepted the risks. New magic is dangerous. That's why so many people stick with the tried and true methods. But, hey. We survived. That's how you get better."

"How are you feeling? Most of your statuses are gone, but it still says 'nauseous' and 'brain fog.'"

Jude closed his eyes to concentrate as he spoke. "Sometimes I feel like I'm about to lose the word I'm trying to say, but then I catch it. Closing my eyes helps. I don't really feel nauseous, though."

"Madi upchucked on Daniel earlier. You're not feeling queasy?"

"No. Not at all. Mostly just exhausted and wrung out."

Jude chatted a bit more with Orrin before saying he felt like he'd been up all night and wanted to sleep more. His soft snores joined the chorus around the hallway before long.

Orrin still felt jittery, and Daniel hadn't slept much the night before, so Orrin took first watch.

Why would my spell affect them like that? It was my first time using the level-two [Utility Ward]. I guess my stats had also increased, so it was a much bigger jump. Why did Madi throw up when she cast that spell? I'm never going to figure this out.

He tried to let Daniel sleep through again, just like their first night, but Daniel woke himself up and told him off. After checking on everybody and making sure they seemed okay, Orrin fell back on his blanket and slept.

"Morning, sunshine." A voice penetrated his lovely dream of flying over the ocean. He'd been like a bird, huge wings and . . . he lost it.

"Ugh."

"Brandt busted out a small can of coffee beans he brought," the voice tempted him.

"Coffee," Orrin murmured. "Give me."

"He's awake." Footsteps drifted, and Orrin opened his eyes. Jude was stretching in the corner. Madi was huddled with a blanket over her but sitting upright. Brandt held a small pot over a torch, heating something inside.

"I told you he'd get up for coffee," Daniel, the voice that had woken him up, said to Brandt.

"We all deserve it, even if it's supposed to be for emergencies only."

"Coffee is always an emergency." Orrin crawled his way out of his blanket and made his way over to the godly smell of beans with hints of chocolate. "You were holding out on me?"

Brandt shook his head and poured a small amount of the black brew into a cup with a makeshift filter. Orrin watched it with greedy eyes.

"We bring a little in dungeons. In case we need it on another floor. Staying awake while on watch is important."

He took the filter out and handed the small cup to Orrin. "For keeping us safe."

"If that's all it costs, I'll make sure to keep you all in tip top shape." Orrin drank and sighed. "Yum."

Madi giggled. "How can you drink that without cream or sugar?"

"Like this." Orrin sipped again. "Heaven."

"Now that we're all awake," Brandt started. "It's time to pack up and head back."

Boos and noes echoed from every direction. Jude even threw a piece of jerky at Brandt.

"But you all seem better," Daniel argued. "Sure, Madi might need a piggyback ride—ouch. Don't throw food at me."

While Daniel argued, Orrin used [Identify] to go over everyone. Madi still had a blinking fatigued marker, but every other member of the party was clear.

"Madi's fatigue should pass soon, I think," Orrin chimed in. "Not arguing to keep going. Just pointing it out."

Brandt looked at her. "She said she felt better."

"It's just a little stiffness," Madi played it off. "I'll be fine. Let's at least take a look in the next room. More information for next time, right?"

Brandt seemed torn between wanting to carry her out himself and granting her wish to stay. "We can look. But then we go home to Dey. It's been at least two days since the Horde reached the Wall. It should be taken care of now."

"Do you think a lot of people got hurt?" Orrin asked. He'd been low-key worried the entire dungeon trip that they'd show back up and everyone would be dead. Brandt had painted a pretty grim picture before.

"No. The guard would have mobilized a full response team. Specific traps and surprises would have been set. Some people probably got hurt trying to play the hero—no offense, Daniel—but overall, the extra time we had to prepare most likely made all the difference."

Orrin let out a sigh he hadn't realized he was holding in. "That's good."

Daniel slapped a hand on Orrin's back. "Time for some buffs."

Everyone took a step back.

"Just for me," Daniel said with a smile.

"I'm going to hold off. We can experiment when we get back to Dey and figure out what happened. But until then, no." Orrin put his hands in his pockets.

"But I didn't get sick!" Daniel whined. "Fuck."

Orrin watched as Brant and Jude moved around gingerly. He pushed a sword over to clatter on the ice and watched them both wince at the sound. "Sorry. It slipped."

Hangover-like effects.

Madi tried to put her pack on her shoulder and almost toppled over.

She's lifting that like she did a full-body workout yesterday.

A bunch of little things started to add up and Orrin began to form an idea of what happened and a plan to confirm.

But not now. Get in. See the monster. Run away.

The only person who seemed excited to dash back into danger was Daniel. He was already posted up for first spot by the next door.

"I'm ready whenever you guys are."

"Daniel. We are going to look and leave. Please do not run in." Jude rubbed his temples.

"You guys are no fun. Can I at least hit it around a bit if it's small?"

"No." Three different voices echoed.

Brandt opened the door and looked inside. "Clear so far. Go ahead and enter."

Orrin went in last this time. As he walked through the door frame, the landscape in front of him spread into the distance again. The room was at least as big as the Elemental room, but the floor was rolling blue sand with a gently blazing sun in the sky above.

"It's pretty, but I don't see any monsters," Daniel griped.

Orrin pulled up his [Map]. One red dot circled just at the edge but then disappeared.

"There is something over that way." He pointed.

They took a few steps into the sand. Orrin knelt and scooped a handful of the blue stuff.

"Hey, guys, this is ice. Tiny, tiny ice."

He went back to watching his blue box. Whatever was in here was shy or didn't know they were here.

Brandt and Jude stood on point on either side, with Daniel taking the center. Madi and Orrin stood in the center of them all.

"Should I do a [Gravity Well] shout?" Daniel suggested.

"Let's move back to the door. Then go for it," Brandt said as he started walking backward.

"The door is right there." Daniel complained and waved his sword.

Orrin agreed that they could probably make a jump for the door before anything could sneak up on him but kept his mouth shut.

"Fine. I want to get going." Brandt stood with his arms crossed.

Daniel let out a yell that pulled the sand around him like a magnet. The echoes vibrated and twisted on the ice sand, and, a second later, screeching in the distance let them know something was coming.

"Here they come. Five, no, six dots, moving in fast from over there." Orrin pointed.

"Get a look with [Identify] if you can, and then we leave."

They watched in the direction he had pointed. Orrin kept his eyes glued to his blue box.

"They're close. I don't want to look away in case they circle to the sides. Anyone have eyes on?"

"Nothing," Daniel said.

Orrin frowned.

"Shit. They must be underground," Jude speculated. "Get back. Not worth a fight."

Orrin and Madi turned and ran out. Jude followed behind them. Brandt had to drag Daniel a little, but he accepted defeat with some grace.

"We could have taken whatever it was . . . but probably not smart to fight something that can pop up from underground," he said, but he still looked glum.

"Thanks for listening better, though," Orrin joked. "Brandt only had to pull your ear a little this time."

Daniel smirked. "I did say I would try."

"All right," Brandt cut in. "Let's head back home."

They made their way back to the safe room ice door they'd come through. Brandt pulled it open. It looked like the safe room they'd left the day before. Or was it two days now?

"See you guys out there." He stepped across the threshold, and a flash of bright light hit Orrin's eyes. Brandt had disappeared.

"Magic fuckery," Daniel muttered. He stepped across, too. Jude followed.

Madi turned back to Orrin. "You coming?"

"Yep. Just enjoying the light show."

Madi smiled. "It is pretty. I wouldn't have noticed. See you on the other side." She stepped through.

Orrin looked around at the remnants of the camp they'd set up. "I won't miss this place," he said to the empty hallway. Then he stepped forward and left the dungeon.

Chapter 39

Dust from inside the tent swirled and entered Orrin's nose as he stepped out of the dungeon.

"Achoo."

"Bless you," Daniel said from in front of him. The rest of the party was turned toward him, backs to the flap of the tent.

"Shouldn't we have come out down there?" Orrin turned and pointed to the stairs they'd climbed down when entering the Aqua Chambers.

"No. This is the entrance," Jude said. "Could you imagine how cramped the stairs would be if a few parties left at the same time?"

A voice from outside echoed into the tent. "Are you back already, Brandt? That was a quick little jaunt. Could the kids not make it past the big bad monkeys?"

Laughter sounded from the other guard.

Daniel opened his mouth, probably to say something stupid. Jude put a hand up to stall him.

"Don't respond. They'll just be wanting to report back to the other lords."

Daniel closed his mouth but grumbled as they left the tent.

The same two guards as before were standing on either side of the entrance. Orrin noticed a small one-man lean-to that he had missed off the one side. *How long do they stay out here?*

"You two are still here? What, is this a punishment detail?" Daniel asked in a chipper voice.

The guard that had spoken, Pete, stepped up toward Daniel. "Are you the reason your party is back already? Pissed yourself when you saw the big rock-throwing apes, huh? Had to come crawling home?"

Orrin watched Daniel closely. Back home, Daniel was not used to taking insults from anyone. Thankfully, he only smiled broader as the man strewed spittle on him.

"So it *is* a punishment detail. Good to know." Daniel smiled and wiped his cheek. "Keep up the good work."

Jude smirked as they left. Pete was huffing in indignation as they saddled the horses, still picketed a few yards away. Within a few minutes, they were traveling back down the road toward Dey.

Jude leaned over on his horse. "Kid. I've got to know. How did you know how to handle Pete? He's a right asshole and always down to fight, but you just ignoring his bravado confused him something fierce."

Daniel shrugged as he readjusted in the saddle. "Just didn't seem like it would be a good idea to knock out the guard of another lord. Silas would probably want to give me a talking-to."

Jude and Brandt laughed. Even Madi had to hide a smile.

"How long are they out there, though?" Orrin asked. "Alone in the middle of nowhere . . . that has got to suck."

"Daniel hit it in one. It's a punishment. Usually for falling asleep at your post, getting into a fight, or pissing off the wrong higher-up. Most of the time it's only for a week or two. The guard sends a few supplies, and they always have two people out there." Brandt smirked. "But it is the most boring thing I've ever had to do."

"What did you do to get in trouble?" Daniel asked eagerly.

Brandt blushed, and Orrin caught the glance toward Madi. "I don't remember. It was a long time ago."

Madi chuckled evilly. "Do you want to know? I was there."

"Lady Madeleine, please," Brandt begged.

Madi's eyes flashed. "I thought I told you—"

"We are no longer in the dungeon," Brandt pointed out quickly. "Decorum dictates that I—"

"He got caught putting firesnaps in my father's clothing." Madi rushed to speak over Brandt. "He spent a month on the dungeon watch."

Jude was laughing, but Orrin asked, "What's a firesnap?"

"A red flower. It looks like a little fireball when they release their pollen," Madi explained with a satisfied look on her face. Brandt's head was hung in shame. "If you grind up the petals, it can cause a prickly, burning sensation on the skin. Children use it to prank their parents and friends. It doesn't really hurt, just aggravates you for about an hour."

Orrin smiled at the image of Brandt putting itching powder in Silas's clothes. "Oh, that *is* funny."

Brandt mumbled something about lookout and rode his horse forward, away from the group.

"How did he get caught?" Daniel asked as they watched him ride ahead to scout the road.

"A maid reported she'd seen him leaving the lord's wing afterward," Madi said.

"Afterward? Wait. He actually pulled it off?" Daniel turned on his horse.

"Yes. My father was scratching his back and chest during an audience with some elven emissaries. He had to send them away and take a bath to soothe the burning." Madi was laughing.

"Who knew he had it in him?" Daniel looked back at the small figure in the distance with pride. "Sir Bennett, the prank master."

They made camp near the end of the day. Brandt kept mostly away for the first half but then sent Jude to scout, too. Daniel said he could just make out Dey in the distance, and Orrin had to agree. He could just see some lights.

Orrin had a sudden thought a little later after they'd mostly finished setting up camp.

"Hey, Daniel, come over here." Orrin waved his friend to the fallen logs Jude had rolled out of the underbrush. Not too thick, they offered just a little reprieve from the dewy ground.

"Yeah?" Daniel left the fire alone and sat down. "What's up?"

Orrin turned his [Camouflage] on. Then he slapped Daniel upside the head. His spell ended.

"Nice. It works."

"What the hell?" Daniel rubbed his head. "What did I do?"

"Nothing. I'm just going to power level my camo before I go to sleep." Orrin turned [Camouflage] back on and punched his friend in the arm.

"Damn it, Orrin. Quit it."

Jude and Madi chuckled.

"I only have to do it like twenty more times."

"Can you at least hit me easier?"

Orrin did not hit him easier.

[Camouflage] 10,000/10,000 !

"Nice." Orrin bent over his blue box and opened the prompt.

Unlocked [Camouflage II] melt into your surroundings. Increase ability to remain undetected. 10 Minutes. 10 MP (0/10,000) -2 AP

"Damn. It just doubles the length of time." Orrin pouted and showed the box to Daniel. He had held his hand out to see what was worth getting hit for.

"It doesn't say attack damage breaks the spell, though," Daniel countered.

"Shit. That actually is better. I was hoping for straight invisibility, but I guess staying hard to see after attacking would be better."

"Invisible murderbot," Daniel commented.

Orrin scrolled through his store, searching for anything else that might be worth his remaining two ability points. He scrolled over the tabbed spells he'd saved for later, but everything cost too much.

He still needed to get [Increase Dexterity] and [Increase Will] to level three, get [Heal Small Wounds] to level three, figure out how to get [Lightstrikes], and buy [Merge]. He scrolled back over [Alchemy] in the skills tab.

> [Alchemy] learn the basics of alchemy. -12 AP

Expensive, he thought. *But then maybe it'll increase my potions' effectiveness or something.*

Orrin also pulled up something that every member of his party already had . . . a weapon proficiency.

> [Sword Proficiency] Level 1—You are adept at using swords. -10 AP.

Orrin sighed and bought [Camouflage II].

"At the least, it will make you guys not have to worry about me getting hit."

"You got it?" Daniel was still rubbing his arm. Orrin threw a heal on his friend.

"Yep. Probably should have gotten it in the dungeon, but leveling it kind of slipped my mind."

Brandt returned from gathering firewood. He fed some to the fire and put the rest nearby. "Okay. Daniel and Orrin, get some sleep. You get last shift tonight," he said and shouted down their arguments. "No. You two have babied us long enough. We'll get back early tomorrow. There will be a lot of work to do, I'm sure. Rest up."

Orrin didn't protest. He was too tired. He curled up in his blankets and fell asleep.

"Where's all the traffic?" Daniel asked as they neared the city walls. The road was abandoned.

"The Horde should have hit three days ago at the latest," Brandt responded, standing up in his stirrups to see farther ahead. "Some normalcy should have returned by now."

Jude spurred his horse ahead. "I'll check it out. Wait here."

Brandt pulled his horse in front of the others and stared after Jude anxiously.

"They had more than enough time to set up the defenses," Madi said to herself. "We should be able to see merchants moving again. People should be out and about."

Orrin pulled up his [Map]. They were only a mile out from the Wall. "There's nothing on my map, but we can move closer to—"

"We wait for Sir DeGuis," Brandt interrupted. The finality in his voice was a stark difference from the Brandt in the dungeon.

They waited fifteen minutes before Daniel pointed out the dust storm that was Jude.

Jude pulled his horse up short. His normal affable smile was drawn tight. "There was a second Fogbinder. They just pushed it back this morning. There is no final count on injuries and deaths."

"Just pushed it back? What happened?" Brandt signaled for them to start riding.

Jude turned around and rode close to Brandt. "I only got a small debrief. We're expected back by Lord Catanzano as soon as possible. Dragoon team is being sent to hunt it down. We're to relieve the Wall guard until the all clear is given. The first Fogbinder fell into the traps, but when our men were sent to kill it, the second one appeared. It turned into a bloodbath. At least two thousand dead. Sir Dhommel died and Sir Sinduk lost both arms."

"Shit. Who's leading Chimera?"

They continued to speak of parties and names foreign to Orrin as they neared the gates. A single guard waved them in.

"How can we help?" Daniel asked. "Can we help hunt the Fogbinder?"

"No!" Brandt said emphatically. "We would be of little use in that fight. Leave it to those with more levels. A retreating Fogbinder is a worst-case scenario. If you want to help, go see if the Hospital will let Orrin heal some people. I'm sure there will be a lot of injuries."

"I want to help—"

Brandt turned his horse in front of Daniel's. "Listen closely. You are still a secret. This is a tragedy, but Dey has seen its fair share of days like this. Pull it together and be the man I think you can be." He turned to Madi. "Lady Catanzano, I leave these two in your charge. We ride ahead for your father."

Jude and Brandt left without another word. Madi ushered them back to her house, leaving the horses with a young stable girl.

"If you want, I can show you to where the injured would be taken?"

Orrin nodded.

"I'll just be here. I can't do anything to help," Daniel said and started to stomp off.

"Just being there would help," Orrin called after him. "There's bound to be a lot of small tasks you can help with, too. Come."

Daniel didn't turn but paused. "No. You go and help them. I need some time to . . . I . . . Tell me where it is. I might come later."

Madi gave instructions. Daniel went inside.

"He gets like that when he feels out of control," Orrin explained.

Madi stared at the closed door for a moment more, then turned. "Let's go. You might need to talk with someone from the Hospital but I'm sure they'll let you help."

"Even if they say 'No', I'll be healing." Orrin swore. He finally felt a purpose. Something he could actually do to help.

"No." Madi pulled him along side streets back toward the center of Dey. "If you do unregistered healing, they can bring a petition to the lords. If they don't try to take you themselves."

"I'd like to see them try," Orrin said. He was getting upset at the idea of a group of healers who wouldn't let him heal.

"Not take you out. *Take you.*" Madi turned down another street. "Young healers disappear for a time and come back . . . different. More accepting of the Hospital's teachings. I don't want Daniel crashing down the Hospital doors because you couldn't wait for an official okay."

"I'll be patient and understanding, Madi." Orrin fingered one of the regen potions on his hip. "But I'm going to help any injured people I find."

She sighed and turned back on a main street. "If the roads aren't too clogged, they should be bringing people here . . ."

She trailed off at the sight in front of them.

A large building, Orrin guessed the Hospital itself, dominated the square. Orrin would have described it as a church, but he hadn't seen or heard any mention of gods so far in this world. In front of the ornate building was a large grassy field, with a beautiful fountain, benches, and a few small gazebos. A perfect place for a fair or picnic.

Or to store dead and dying people. The grass was stained with the rust color of dried blood. The benches had been turned into make-shift surgery stations. Cries and screams came from every direction.

"Orrin, wait here, and I'll get permission for you to work on some people. Just enough healing for someone else to come along and finish."

"What does that mean? I can heal a sword through my chest. Why can't I heal these people?" He waved his arm across the field. There had to be five or six hundred civilians here. These were not guards.

"The poison from the Fetid Canines needs a different type of healing—that's not my expertise. Lost limbs and deep enough cuts into the organs take too much mana to waste on saving one person. It's a game of saving the most lives. Just be practical and we can do some good."

Orrin felt rage bubbling inside. He had listened to his mom's complaints of hospital administration and budget cuts for years. He'd seen her come home wrecked after not being able to save someone. He felt powerless at the sight of all the hurt in front of him and terri-fied that somebody was going to get in his way.

"Madi. Do me a favor." Orrin rolled his sleeves up and started walking toward the people in pain. "If you meant anything of what you've said to me, if you really want to be part of Daniel's party and be my friend, get every person you can to remove the poison from everyone on this field and just keep people alive long enough for me to get to them."

"Orrin. No. What are you doing? You can't heal everybody here."

"If I can't, tell Daniel it was fun."

"Orrin, they'll stop you. I'll help you however I can, but they'll stop you."

Orrin smiled. A healing angel walking toward a crowd in need of healing. "Not if they can't see me."

Orrin cast [Camouflage II].

"Sorry, Tony. Sorry, Daniel," he whispered.

Orrin turned on [Mind Bastion]. He drank a regen potion.

And he started blood cycling.

Chapter 40

Orrin analyzed the situation in front of him. He was invisible with an endless amount of mana. He knew that he'd pay for it after, but what were a few days passed out in his own sick compared with helping these people? He was going to heal these people no matter the consequence.

> New Quest!
> Heal 200 people of Dey
> Time Limit: 2 hours
> Reward: Variable
> Failure: Loss of [Heal Small Wounds]

Orrin waved the screen away. *I don't need an incentive to do the right thing*, he thought angrily at the system.

He approached a body lying near the edge of the green. [Identify] told him she was already dead. The girl next to her was bleeding from multiple cuts on her arms and scalp, as if someone taller had slashed down at her with a knife. She wasn't in immediate danger, but Orrin pumped [Heal Small Wounds] into her until the cuts scabbed over. He moved to the next.

He worked tirelessly, body after body. One in ten was dead when he reached them. After finding a mother crying over a boy no older than eight with a torn-open stomach, Orrin spent three pools of mana knitting together the boy's wound. Orrin smiled for the first time when the boy hugged his mother, tears of joy streaming down her face.

That smile was wiped away when he saw a group of men yelling at Madi just a few dozen yards away.

". . . telling you in the name of the Catanzano house to only focus on healing the Fetid poison. A member of my house will heal everybody."

"Young Madeleine," a pious-sounding man with an attractive face and small circular glasses said to her, talking down to the child as he said it, "we do not take our orders from you. The people here will be seen at our discretion, based on what is best for everyone."

Orrin growled but left it to Madi. He would do what he could. He moved to another crying man, holding a limp body in his arms. The body was male and nearly gone, the Fetid poison keeping his wounds seeping.

Orrin cast [Heal Small Wounds] several times until the man's health was better.

"Take him to the group over there. Ask them to rid him of the poison and he'll be fine."

The man looked around frantically at the voice that had spoken to him. He focused his eyes near Orrin's shoulder.

"They said he's too weak to move. Please." The man held out a bag with silver spilling out. "Please, I have more at home. Just help him."

Orrin felt disgust well up in him, even over [Mind Bastion]'s calming presence. The man had the same knife cuts on his arms. They healed up with only two quick heals.

"Save the money. Ask for Madi. Go before he bleeds out again."

The man looked at his arms and scrabbled to pick the man up. He struggled for a minute before Orrin cast the smallest [Increase Strength] he could on the man.

Orrin worked on the next person while watching the scene unfold. Madi waved her hands around yelling. The group of healers moved as a group to different people at random. Small bags exchanged hands, and people who were nearly dead seemed only half-dead.

Orrin cursed.

"I'm sorry, sir. No need to waste your time with me. Please help my granddaughter." The woman under him had white hair and wrinkles so deep he struggled to tell where the cuts were. Luckily, he didn't need to.

"I just did. She'll be fine. You will be, too. Talk to me. What's your name?" Orrin turned on the same voice he'd heard his mom use when he was younger and she'd brought him to visit the terminally ill and elderly.

Most times people just want to have someone to listen to them. His mom's voice echoed in his ears.

"I'm Marene, young lord. Blessings upon you."

The man carrying the one he'd healed had reached the group of healers. Orrin could hear Madi yelling at them.

"I'm not a lord," Orrin responded.

"I may not be able to see you through that spell, but you are a lord to be helping us," she responded. "It is odd, though. I know you are there, but my eyes slide off you like hot oil on a pan."

Orrin finished healing the old woman. "You should be fine now. Just move easily for a bit. Here's your granddaughter."

The tiny girl he'd healed a moment before leaped at her grandma. Orrin caught her and set her down. Her eyes were wide.

"Gran. A ghost just grabbed me."

"He's no ghost. Hush and sit."

Orrin moved on, healing person after person. Madi convinced the healers to look at the man at their feet, and after a moment, he stood. The two men embraced and pointed in Orrin's direction. They'd probably been asked who healed them.

"Shit."

Orrin finished healing a man who had been bitten so many times up his legs that they looked like a sieve. He walked to the edge of the grass and then ran all the way around to the other side. He might miss somebody, but the crowds of people were already starting to thin around him. As they were healed, they wandered about to find family and friends. Some started crying louder than they had while cut to pieces when they found the unmoving bodies of their loved ones.

At the corner farthest from the Hospital steps, Orrin paused for only a moment when he spotted a stout man sitting on a bench, his legs dangling from the low seat.

A dwarf! Orrin shook his head and continued. The man's arm was mangled. Blood dripped slowly down to his fist, pooling under the bench. The meat of his arm had been sliced to the bone in multiple places, and Orrin could see where entire chunks had been ripped out.

"Quite the injury," Orrin whispered as he started pushing healing magic into the dwarf.

"Who's there? What's going on?" The diminutive man's eyes moved around before settling in Orrin's direction. "What's an elven [Windwalker] doing this far out from the forests? And how are you healing me?"

The man's questions were rapid-fire and brash. Orrin smiled behind his [Camouflage]. The man's certainty that Orrin would answer his questions reminded him of Daniel.

"Not an elf, and I'm healing you because you're bleeding out here." Orrin checked his [Identify] again. The dwarf's health was climbing slowly . . . much slower than anyone else's.

"You best stop wasting your mana. Your Elders are going to have your hide for trying to use magic on a dwarf. Just give me some clean cloth and I'll bandage myself up."

Orrin didn't stop. Health points didn't equate exactly to full health. One boy had only eighty points, a small enough number that only two or three casts of [Heal Small Wounds] should have been enough to heal him. Orrin had spent nearly a hundred mana to heal about five hundred actual health. Each injury had an underlying amount of health that needed to be healed before the person's HP would stabilize. He'd been averaging two pools of healing magic per person.

He was on his fifth pool and only now was seeing the cuts on the dwarf's arm start to close up.

"Stone and veins! What kind of monster are you?" The dwarf stared at his arm in awe as the skin grew slowly back over itself.

All in all, it had taken Orrin more mana to heal the dwarf than the last four people combined. He started to move on but felt a hand on his arm.

"How did you see me?" Orrin quickly checked to make sure [Camouflage] was still working. It was.

"Just listened to the ground," the man said, brushing off the question. "Thank you. My name is Broddag Ironspine. If you ever need anything, I'm in your debt. I've never seen anything like that."

"It was just some healing. No debt needed. Just don't make a scene when you leave the square." Orrin tried to pull away again, but Broddag's grip was a vise on his elbow.

"Just some healing? Child, you just healed a dwarf. My constitution is over fifty, and you overhealed me. I won't even have scars from those Kniferunners."

His constitution is over fifty? He must be a high level, Orrin thought to himself. He looked around, but nobody was paying attention to the two of them. Broddag couldn't make out his face, of that Orrin was sure. He'd heard Daniel complain enough about it.

"I'm new to healing. Is it normally that hard to heal such a high-level person?" Orrin tried to keep his voice quiet. There still were a lot of people moaning all around.

"High level? No, I'm level twenty-two, but I am pretty young still. Just had my eighty-second birthday. It was hard for you to heal me because I'm a dwarf. My constitution is higher than a human's, so I would have had a lot of resistance to your spells. Do they not teach that at the Hospital?"

That makes sense. Constitution helps resists magic, not just increases your hit points. I must have only been getting a few points of healing through each [Heal Small Wounds] on him.

"Um . . . I'm still new. Maybe I skipped that class. Please don't tell anyone we talked, though. I've got to go . . . More people to heal."

Broddag raised an eyebrow. "You're healing against their wishes?"

Orrin didn't answer. He tried to pull his arm away again, and Broddag noticed he was still holding fast. He looked up and saw the group of healers looking around for the invisible healer that was creating a stir.

Broddag released Orrin's arm. "I'll go point them in the opposite direction. Don't spend all that mana now. You must be part elf to have that much mana. Good luck, friend to the dwarves."

Broddag hopped off the bench and began to make his way in the opposite direction of the healers. Orrin hoped he wouldn't regret talking with the man.

But I learned a few more things. I really need to spend another week just holed up in Silas's library.

Orrin continued on his way, healing everyone he could. The dead started to be the only ones not moving about, as the gasps of feeling healing magic flowing through them alerted others of a nearby healer. People began to push close and beg.

"Help me, please. I can pay."

"Heal my girl, she's nearly gone."

"Do you know who I am? I demand—"

Orrin finished healing a pregnant woman with cuts on her back and slipped between the yells to search for people who couldn't move. He double-checked the new Quest. Not because he cared about the reward, but because now he had a time limit before he would lose his spell.

> Quest
> Heal 200 people of Dey (179/200)
> Time Limit: 32 minutes
> Reward: Variable
> Failure: Loss of [Heal Small Wounds]

Orrin's regen potion had worn off. All that meant to him was more cycling. The cold, logical part of [Mind Bastion] told him that he'd spent more mana already than he had in those first few days before meeting Tony and going through hell. He knew he couldn't push himself too much more. He'd been spending more time dodging the group of healers, who had recently split into two lines. They slowly moved along the field, healing a few small wounds here and there.

They have to act like this is their doing, he realized. Orrin didn't care about the credit. He just wanted to save as many lives as possible.

He heard the soft ding of the blue box telling him the Quest was complete a few minutes before the time was to run out. Orrin kept moving along. There was only a handful of people he hadn't gotten to, but the Hospital was out in force now. Orrin saw a few healers pass out from mana overuse and be taken back inside on stretchers.

He knelt down by a boy about his age, maybe a year or two older, and used [Identify]. He was surprised to see his health was nearly full, but his mana was at zero.

Orrin almost moved on but turned back at the last moment. He knew how much that feeling sucked, and without [Mind Bastion] and [Blood Mana] he'd have probably ended up passed out in pain a lot more, too. He cast a quick [Increase Will], level one. The boy's eyes flickered open.

"Ugh," he moaned.

"Just relax a minute and you'll be fine. It's probably best to get a mana potion or go get some sleep. You only have about five minutes before that wears off. I have one here, if you can drink another today," Orrin explained gently. He looked around and spotted the next person to heal. He put the small vial in the boy's hand, but before he moved, another healer hurried up and squatted by the woman he'd targeted.

"What? What's going on? Did we heal them all, sir?" The boy tried to sit up, but Orrin held him down by the shoulder.

Heal? Orrin pulled his [Identify] box back up. *Shit.*

Amir Fallah
Healer Acolyte Level 8

HP: 98/100
MP: 30/140

Strength: 12
Constitution: 10
Dexterity: 13
Will: 11
Intelligence: 11

He'd just accidentally healed one of the Hospital workers. The other healer nearby looked up and began walking toward Orrin and Amir.

"Shit," Orrin whispered and looked around for a quick escape. The grassy plaza was thinning out. Madi was still following along behind a middle-aged man who seemed to be in charge.

He almost teleported away when the nearby healer spoke in a voice of disgust. "Amir, you idiot. Did you try healing without permission? You look like you overdrew."

Amir's eyes focused into clarity, and he looked around. He ducked his head when he saw the other healer. "Teacher Dou, I tried to save a life but passed out due to my inexperience. I must have regained some mana while sleeping."

"Well, I knew it couldn't have been you healing everyone. Principal Mangin noticed you were absent from the count. Lucky for you, I found you sleeping, so you won't be punished . . . too severely." Orrin didn't miss the glimmer of joy at the prospect of punishment in Dou's eyes.

Amir's eyes passed over the shimmer of Orrin's [Camouflage]. "Someone has been healing against Principal Mangin's orders? Everyone, you say?"

"Enough people that we will have to come out in force. We can't have some other healer showing up the Hospital, can we? I suggest you stick close to me. I'll teach you the proper protocols as we work."

Amir mouthed "go" as Dou turned his back. He downed the mana potion and left the empty vial on the ground behind him. Orrin grabbed it and crept slowly backward.

Once he was out of range, he looked around and saw that what Dou said was true. More healers were flowing out of the Hospital and even the few targets that Orrin had set for himself now had a healer or two around them.

He sneaked up behind Madi and tugged on her sleeve. She jumped but excused herself from the man Amir had called Principal Mangin.

"I will see myself back to my house now, Principal," Madi said with the slightest tilt of her head.

"I will send someone to your home later for your report," the man said without looking at her. "You will tell me who this healer is that destroyed so much work today."

"If you mean the person who obviously saved lives that the Hospital was willing to sacrifice, then I'm sure I have no idea who that healer is," Madi responded with the same slick attitude that Orrin had seen her father use. "Good luck with your teachings."

The man grunted and left. Madi hurried away, with Orrin on her heels. They rounded the corner, and Orrin, not wanting to wait any longer to get away from the increasing number of eyes of Hospital healers, teleported them across town to the Catanzano house.

Chapter 41

Orrin and Madi appeared near the front gate of her house. Almost nobody was around—just one guard he didn't even recognize.

"Hmm. I guess this is as close as I can get us with your dad's teleport block up," Orrin mused as a single guard opened the door for them. "I should probably tell Daniel I'll be gone for a few days. He's going to be pissed."

Madi dropped her short spear off in a circular grate that Orrin had taken for a trash can but saw was actually for quick storage of weapons. *Sort of like an umbrella stand*, he thought. *Practical*.

"Why? Where are you going?" Madi asked as they headed up the stairs. "We should really all stick around until my father returns from dealing with the Fogbinder."

"I'm using a skill that has really bad backlash," Orrin explained. "I'm probably going to be out sick. Like, incapacitated for a few days. Sorry, I won't be able to help much with reconstruction. But if anyone needs healing before I go, I could probably just push it a bit more."

Madi frowned a bit. "Is this related to your"—she lowered her voice to a whisper—"blood magic?"

"Um. A bit," Orrin hedged. He really didn't want to share much with Madi. She had come through for him in the Hospital's field, and from what he'd heard of the conversations between the healers and her, she'd put herself in the line of fire for him. But one good deed was not going to make up for what she and her father had done to him and Daniel. Not by a long shot.

"Okay, I won't pry," Madi said with a forced smile. "Daniel said he would be in his room, so let's find him and tell him how you single-handedly healed half the workforce of Dey."

"It was only two hundred–ish people. I'm sure Dey has way more people than that."

Madi shook her head and pushed Orrin ahead of her. "You idiot. You healed about how many people a single good healer can take care of in a year. You took care of the people so hurt that their families brought them out during a lockdown. Anyone else who needs help will get it now ... because you took care of the worst of it."

Orrin pushed the door to his room open and stepped inside. "Yeah, well. I'm a cheater." He yelled into the room, "Daniel?"

No response. Nobody was in the room.

"That stupid piece of shit." Orrin kicked a bundle of clothes on the floor.

He pulled up his [Map] as Madi walked in.

"Where is he?" She looked around the mess as if expecting to see his dark curls pop up from under a book. "He said he'd be here waiting for us."

Nothing on the map, Orrin thought. *He definitely went after the Fogbinder, but I have no idea where that would be located. Maybe we can find Brandt or even Silas. They'd know.*

"Madi, where would your father be located? Or Brandt?"

"They'd be at the Wall, the westernmost one overlooking the Pass. Orrin, what is going on?"

Orrin sighed. "Daniel went out to play hero."

Their run through the streets was vastly different from Orrin's last time through the city. Dey was deserted.

Doors to shops and homes were closed tight, windows were shuttered, and even the homeless had found somewhere else to be.

However, the biggest differences were the smell ... and the blood.

Small splashes against a wall told the story of a quick attack. The small drops that trailed to a closed door meant the person probably got away. A pool of congealing gore near another door, with bloody fist prints by the knocker, told a gloomier story. Orrin spotted telltale signs of assaults, death, and the occasional escape as they ran.

"Where are all the bodies?"

"Civilians will bring people inside once they can. Bodies piling up would bring more monsters inside the walls," Madi said between deep breaths. They'd stopped near a leatherworking shop to catch their breath.

They made it to the Wall in short order. *I'm getting better at these terrible runs at least,* Orrin thought.

The guards at the first Wall were watching the Pass and didn't try to stop two armored people from running into the fray. Orrin suddenly remembered the Guild required members to fight in Horde attacks.

"Did your father take care of the Guild when we ran, too?"

"What?"

"Guild members are supposed to help fight in a Horde attack, right? Are we going to be kicked out?" Orrin huffed out the question.

"He's taken care of it. Also, attacking a dungeon counts as our monthly quest, so we should be good for a few weeks."

Orrin had completely forgotten about the monthly quest requirement, too. Maybe after he saved Daniel's bacon again, and spent a few days convalescing at Tony's place, he'd go check out that quest board. He really needed to plan out more spells and skills to buy—

Stop it, Orrin told himself. He noticed that while using [Mind Bastion], he had a tendency to spend a lot of time planning his theoretical future actions. *Just get through today alive.*

As they got closer to the final Wall, Orrin turned them south.

"The main gate is where my father will likely be." Madi pointed back north.

"Brandt is down here," Orrin said as he ran. "He never left the party."

"Why would he leave the party?"

"I don't know how fighting a Horde works," Orrin yelled over his shoulder. "I'm just glad he'll be easy to find."

Orrin and Madi stopped near a smaller gate about a half mile south of the main gate. A door on the inside of the Wall was propped open with a tight stairwell circling up.

"This should lead to the top," Madi said as she got in front of Orrin. "Let me go first. Someone should recognize me."

Orrin didn't argue. Soon his legs were burning from climbing stairs after running so much.

I'm buying [Track Star] as soon as I can find it.

At the top of the stairs, another door opened to a beautiful view of the Pass. Orrin could see the forest spread out in front of him, with the sun beating down against the mountains on either side.

"Stop! You shouldn't be up here," a voice demanded from the side.

"I'm Lady Catanzano, looking for Sir Bennett. Bring me to him," Madi demanded with authority in her voice.

"Glad I brought you along," Orrin joked.

The young guard brought Brandt back less than a minute later.

"Mad—Lady Catanzano? What are you doing on the Wall? It isn't safe here." Brandt pushed them back into the small stairwell.

"We think Daniel went after the Fogbinder. He's not at the house," Madi explained quickly. "Have you seen him?"

"I haven't," Brandt said with a frown. "Are you sure he went after it? Dragoon team should have reached it by now. They had quite the head start."

"He's not showing up on my [Map]. How far out is that team?" Orrin asked.

"I don't know specifics—the only thing I was told was it was a few miles out."

Damn it. I really need to upgrade [Map] to see farther out.

Orrin realized he had never checked the blinking blue box icon for his healing Quest.

Quest Complete
Heal 200 people of Dey
Reward: [Heal Small Wounds], level three—heal
up to 40 HP. 20 MP.

Useless. Orrin discarded the box.

"Would you be able to check who passed the gates?" Orrin asked without hope.

"I can ask, but command structure is pretty shot right now. Give me a few minutes." Brandt stopped as he turned to leave. "Orrin, if he did go out there . . . he might not come back. The lowest-ranked member of Dragoon team is about thirty-nine or forty in level. They have ten people, and the brass are already talking as if they're all dead."

Orrin paused as processed that information. "He'll be fine."

"I hope you're right. For all our sakes."

As Brandt left to investigate, Orrin sat against the wall and closed his eyes. He still felt fine, but he'd gone through more mana pools this morning than in the few days before his first crash.

"Are you going to be all right?" Madi asked as she sat down next to him.

"Yeah."

"You really think Daniel will be okay?"

Orrin let out a dry laugh. "That asshole has more luck than anyone I've ever met. He'll get into trouble and find some way out of it."

Madi sat quietly next to him as they waited.

"Someone at the main gate matching his description passed through an hour ago," Brandt said as he rounded the corner at a run. "Madi, your father has demanded you return home with Orrin. He's sending a team out to find him."

"Sorry, no. I'm going after him. I can teleport him back." Orrin stood up and squinted against the sun.

"Lord Catanzano sent a flyer out for reconnaissance. We'll be able to send out a mage with [Teleport] and grab him. Don't worry. Just go back."

"Brandt, point me in the right direction. I don't want to waste time arguing with you. I'm going to go find him, and then I'm going to kick his ass all the way back to the Wall. He lied to us and did something stupid again."

"And so will you be," Madi cut in. "If you go out there alone, you'll be killed. You just spent so much mana healing all those people. Let's go rest and let the guard do its job."

Orrin felt [Mind Bastion] taking the rational parts of her argument and agreeing. The more time he spent pushing off the effects of his huge mana usage, the worse the backlash would be. But another part of him was remembering one of their first conversations after reaching Dey.

We start with three simple rules. One, survive. Two, we're a team. Three, find a way home.

You really make it hard to survive when you run off alone. Orrin frowned as he readied himself to teleport away.

"Wait!" Brandt yelled and grabbed his arm. "Don't jump away. If you are going to leave anyway . . ."

He turned, still holding Orrin's arm in a vise grip. He pointed to the southern ridgeline of the Pass. "The Fogbinder is sticking to the bottom of the Pass. There are a few caves and forested areas that way. It still has a few hundred Fetid Canines and Kniferunners with it that it didn't try to send over the Walls. Just get in and out. Don't try taking that thing on. Dragoon team is out to keep track of the demon. It'll try to circle back, and they're giving their lives to keep pressure on it until we can regroup and get another strategy in place to deal with it. Promise me, Orrin. Get the [Hero] back safely—and don't engage."

"I'm not the idiot that went out after it," Orrin muttered. "I promise. In and out. I'll keep [Camouflage] up the entire time."

Brandt nodded as he finally released Orrin's arm. "I'd go with you, but . . ."

"You have to stay here. Figure out a way to take it down when it comes back. I understand."

Madi's hand gripped the same spot Brandt had just released. "I'll come with you."

"No," Brandt said immediately.

"Sorry, no way," Orrin agreed. "You need to get to safety, too. I can't keep you safe while I'm looking for Daniel."

Madi opened her mouth to argue, but Brandt pushed between them. He mouthed "go" to Orrin and started talking to Madi. She started to say something else, but Orrin teleported to the tree line he could see inside the Pass, leaving Brandt to deal with her.

He landed on his feet with . . . not with grace, but at least with something approaching it this time. Teleporting was getting easier. Orrin looked out at the open fields next to the spotty forests that dotted the miles around him.

I'm coming, Daniel. Please don't be dead.

Chapter 42

Orrin kept watch on his [Map] as he teleported as far as he could see. He even did something he had always sort of avoided.

He used [Increase Dexterity] on himself.

He ran through the forests he came across, with [Camouflage] running nonstop. If he hadn't still been running [Blood Mana] and [Mind Bastion], he would have run out of mana before the eighth teleport. He ran through the trees, dodging and weaving branches, leaping over roots, and avoiding the red dots of monsters all around him.

At the edge of each clearing, he teleported into the distance, to whatever landmark he could make out. After thirty minutes of nonstop movement and teleporting, he reached the edge of the Pass.

The mountains on either side of Dey were huge. Orrin wasn't the greatest at geography, but he was pretty sure the mountains on this planet dwarfed Mount Everest back home.

Something had cleaved the mountains at the edge of the Pass, creating a sheer cliff of rock that towered into the sky. Fragments had chipped away and fallen, creating craters and smaller hills near the base at points.

Orrin stayed away from the edge of the Pass. He felt tiny and afraid standing any nearer to the towering rock. Not to mention all the red dots that lined the edges.

A few caves, he scoffed. *There have to be hundreds of hidden nooks and crannies on my [Map].*

Orrin had still not seen any trail or ding of Daniel on the [Map]. However, he did notice that more of the red dots were congregating near the cliff face the farther he got from the Wall.

"Are you all hiding from something? I know it's not me . . ."

The next hour saw Orrin grow bored. The mind-numbing nature of running, teleporting, and checking his [Map] became a routine all too quickly. The constant fear of keeping out of reach of monsters, keeping his camouflage running, and finding Daniel in pieces were kept pushed to the back of his mind. [Mind Bastion] was working overtime.

Finally, Orrin spotted a gray dot—a single person out in the Pass. He hurried toward the location, over half a mile to the north, away from the cliff.

A man with one leg missing sat against a large rock in the middle of a field. A small mound of cut-up Fetid Canines was piled up in a ring around the man, maybe a few dozen yards away from him.

Orrin used [Identify] from the shadows of the tree line.

Ira Singh
Steel Ravager Level 52
HP:—
MP:—

Damn. The only other person who blocked my identify spell was Silas. I guess [Identify] only gives me information if their level isn't too much higher than my own.

Orrin searched for any hidden traps or monsters. Nothing.

"Fuck it," Orrin said and walked out of the trees, willing his camo spell to drop away. "Hey, are you part of Dragoon squad?"

The man's eyes snapped open, and he pointed a finger toward Orrin. "Stay there. Guild or guard?"

Orrin put his hands above his head. "I'm a Guild member, but I'm out here on my own. I'm trying to find the Dragoon squad—my teammate ran out here to try and fight the Fogbinder."

The man lowered his hand hesitantly and growled something.

"Sorry? Can I come closer? I can't hear you." Orrin put his hand to his ear to mime the question.

"Dragoon team is about an hour ahead . . . I think. I haven't seen anyone else, but I might have slipped unconscious a time or two. Don't come near. I've got my magic all tied up into traps. I'll take as many as I can with me before I go."

"Before you go back?" Orrin really hoped he was misunderstanding what he was hearing.

"The bastard caught me and had some of his dogs chew my leg clean off. My team left me here at my request. We all knew what we were signing up for." Orrin could hear the man grit his teeth even at the distance.

"I'm a healer. Can you turn off whatever would kill me? I'm going to come through." Orrin took a testing step forward.

"A healer? What in the fiery sea are you doing outside the wall?" The man readjusted on his rock and slipped to the side. He let out a low moan and stayed quiet.

"Um . . . are you okay?"

He didn't answer.

Orrin didn't wait and used [Teleport] to land on the rock. His [Map] had shown no traps, but better safe than sorry. Especially after the man had said he'd cast magical spells. Orrin was ready to pop right back if anything happened, but luck seemed to be on his side.

He started casting the upgraded version of [Heal Small Wounds] on Ira. The man looked to be in his late thirties or early forties and had light-brown skin. His long, dark hair was tied back into a ponytail, and a goatee covered his chin. The man groaned as health flowed into him. Unfortunately, his leg did not regrow.

I bet there's a regenerate spell or something. Maybe . . . no, stop overthinking.

Orrin pulled a waterskin out and poured a little bit out on the man's face. It was covered with dirt and grime. Whatever he'd been doing in this small field with dead monster bodies all around, he'd been working himself hard.

"What—who's there?" Ira looked all around before looking back and up at Orrin sitting cross-legged on the rock at his back. "You're just a kid! How did you get across the field?"

"Teleported. You thirsty?" Orrin handed the man his water.

"I'm dead. Teleporting and healing? What are you?"

Orrin resisted the urge to say something quippy.

I'm just your friendly neighborhood . . . No, focus! His thoughts were getting harder to keep on track the more mana he used. *That can't be good.*

"My name is Orrin. I already told you I'm looking for a friend. Which way did your team go, Ira?"

"How'd you know my name?" Ira raised a finger toward Orrin again.

"[Identify] spell. Please lower your weapon. I'm a friendly, I promise."

Ira kept his hand up. "How do I know you're not a demon?"

"I honestly don't know or care. I healed you. You probably won't bleed out now. If your team really is only an hour out, I'll be going. If you see another guy my age, please beat him up and bring him back to the Wall."

Ira slowly lowered his hand again. "How do you expect me to get to the Wall?" He gestured to his missing leg. "I'll just wait here. If I find your friend, I'll convince him to stay as repayment for the healing."

Orrin's healing had sealed up the bleeding stump, but the man still couldn't run anywhere. Orrin asked, "Will you be okay alone?"

Ira let out a laugh and pointed at the corpse of a Fetid Canine. A spot of something shiny jumped from his finger, and the dog corpse began to shred itself into pieces.

No, it's a small knife or a piece of metal moving around super quick.

"That's impressive," Orrin said. "I'll try and get you on my way back."

"Affirmative. Thank you for the boost. I'll do my best to stay alive."

Orrin took one last look at Ira. The man's level was a testament to his skills, and he was out here risking his life to give the people of Dey a fighting chance against the Fogbinder.

I could teleport with him all the way back, but that would take hours. Daniel left ahead of me, but he can't teleport. Did I miss him? I couldn't have missed him. What if I missed him?

He used [Teleport] and popped away.

Orrin found the Dragoon team thirty minutes later. He'd been lucky and found a long stretch of land with no trees and a bunch of rocks tall enough to count as visual locks for [Teleport] to work.

The nine gray dots on his [Map] told him where they were. They'd fanned out and were slowly surrounding another dot on his [Map].

A blue dot.

Daniel.

Orrin raced through the trees with [Camouflage] up and recast his [Increase Dexterity] spell.

He thought he made it just in time.

"Daniel. Duck. You're surrounded."

Unfortunately, the trained death squad took the attempted alert as a signal. The nine remaining members of the Dragoon team attacked Daniel just as he started to turn.

"Orrin?" Daniel turned back and missed the first Dragoon member tumbling out of the trees ahead. The giant man slammed a fist into Daniel's face.

Daniel went down hard.

"Stop. We're the good guys. Ira's alive," Orrin shouted as he raced toward his downed friend.

The giant of a man who had just clocked Daniel knelt by his body and pulled his fist back to punch him again.

"I said stop!" Orrin cast [Increase Will] on himself and then cast an inversed [Increase Strength] on the man five times.

He stumbled and fell over. Then his head snapped up in the direction of Orrin, and he yelled out a string of words.

"Down. Flank threat. Abnormal unknown."

That should have been over one hundred points of strength. How is he even talking?

Orrin didn't have time to ponder as the man slowly pulled himself with one hand away from the fight.

Because, Orrin realized, he was now in a fight. The eight other members were circling him. They still couldn't see him, and they were flanking him as they'd done to Daniel.

Orrin did the last thing they expected.

"I surrender." He dropped [Camouflage] and raised his hands over his head. "Just don't kill us. I can explain."

Sure, he could have tried to heal Daniel and teleport away, but Orrin had no idea if he had time to heal Daniel or if he could teleport an unconscious body. He might have been able to reduce all their strength or dexterity to zero, but these people were trying to save everyone's lives. They'd just attacked the idiot trying to sneak up on them.

"My friend there is an idiot. He thought he could help fight the Fogbinder and came out here alone. I've been searching for him. I found Ira, and he pointed me toward you all. He's alive, by the way. I healed him up."

Orrin felt a blade settle under his neck. He got ready to teleport just in case.

"What did you do to Bin?" a female voice asked from behind.

"Spell to sap his strength. He'll be fine in twenty minutes." Orrin stood very still.

"How do we know Ira really sent you?"

"Nice guy. He was missing a leg. He can cast really fast-moving blades out of his fingers. I promised I'd give him a lift back. I just came to grab my friend there."

Another man walked out of a tree next to Orrin. Like, actually walked out of a tree.

"Okay, that's cool as hell."

The man smirked a little and came closer. "He's telling the truth."

"His truth or *the* truth?" the woman behind Orrin demanded. "Sof, he's dangerous. We're too close to it. That's why we agreed to take out the other."

"Listen, I can get him out of here. Does anyone know if I can teleport him if he's knocked out?"

"Teleporting and healing? He's lying," another female voice from within the trees hissed down. Orrin couldn't see the owner of the voice.

"No. He still speaks true," the man called Sof said. "As far as I know, he must be awake to teleport. Why did you not run when you could?"

"He's my friend. I came out here to save him from his own dumb self."

"Sounds a lot like Sof and Bin, don't it? Ouch." Another male voice from behind spoke and then was quiet. It sounded like someone else had hit him.

"We can't just let him go, Sof," the woman with the blade at his throat whispered softly. "You know it."

The man sighed and raised his empty hands in a helpless gesture.

"I know, Farah. I'm sorry. If we let you go to heal him, you could attack us. We are too close to the Fogbinder," Sof said as he drew a long stick—a wand—from his pocket. "I can kill you or bind you. Which would you prefer?"

Chapter 43

Orrin kept himself extremely still. With Farah's curved blade at his neck, he didn't want to make any sudden movements.

"I'd prefer you let us go, but I'd also say bind before kill."

Sof nodded and waved his wand at Daniel. Roots entangled him and pulled him against a tree. His head lolled before a branch reached down around his forehead and anchored him still.

"Can I heal him now?"

Sof looked over Orrin's shoulder and asked someone behind him, "Maya, what are their levels and classes?"

Orrin froze even more than he already was. Nobody they'd encountered had been able to [Identify] their actual classes, but this Dragoon team was a higher level than most of the guards around Silas's house.

"They're both only level ten! That one is some sort of fighter, but I can't get a clear read on him. This one . . . It . . . it changes the longer I look . . ." The high and clear voice of Maya drifted over Orrin. "Healer, mage, healer, question marks. I've never heard of this. What are you?"

Sof raised his wand at Orrin and gestured.

"It's rude to just ask like that, right?" Orrin tried to stall. Telling his class to Silas and Madi had been a learning experience. He wanted to keep as much knowledge of his class to himself as he could. Sof's eyebrows bunching together told him that he didn't have much of a choice.

"I've got a few different skills, but I'm not too good at fighting. Like I said, I try to focus on healing. Ira can vouch for me."

"And just how can he do that? Ira was half-dead when we had to leave him behind. The Hospital itself would have had to rotate a few healers around to keep him alive," Farah said from behind him.

Orrin turned his head just the tiniest bit to answer her. The blade was connected to a scythe. A long, curved, deadly sharp blade that represented death connected with a whisper of a touch on his jugular. "I could go and teleport him back. It was only about half an hour, but now that I know where to go, I could probably get there in fifteen or twenty minutes."

"And attack us right after you've left? I think not," Farah responded and pushed the blade ever so slightly against his skin. Orrin felt something warm trickle down to his shirt.

"I can bring someone with me?"

Sof stepped forward and put his wand on Farah's blade. "Don't kill him. I'll go."

"Sof, you can't be—"

"That's a bad idea, mate."

"How about I go instead?"

Every member of Dragoon team chimed in—except Bin. He had pulled himself up against the tree and was watching Orrin with half-closed eyes.

Sof raised a hand, and the murmured voices cut off. "I'm going. Maya is in charge until I get back or Bin can walk again, whichever comes first. If I'm not back in an hour, kill the boy and continue after the target."

No pressure, Orrin thought, but he nodded at Sof. The man showed nothing.

Teleporting back to Ira only took fifteen minutes. Orrin was able to think of the place he'd been and [Teleport] brought him automatically to the closest locations he'd already traveled on the way out. With less time spent searching for another jump point and having to avoid monsters, Orrin and Sof appeared outside Ira's circle of death in no time at all.

"Sof!"

"Ira, I'm glad to see you're alive. We caught ourselves a little problem here," Sof said and gestured with his wand toward Orrin.

"The kid is all right. He healed me up. No idea how he's not passed out, though."

Sof pointed at Orrin's feet and demanded, "Stay here."

He walked up to Ira and crouched on his heels. The two whispered in hushed tones. Ira shook his head a few times and lifted his shoulders in a shrug, but Orrin could not make out anything said.

Sof stood and brushed nonexistent dirt from his robe. He looked back at Orrin.

"Ira has vouched for you. Do you have enough mana to get all three of us back to where we met?"

Orrin groaned internally. He'd used [Increase Intelligence], level three, before they'd started teleporting.

I'm going to be sick and hurting anyway, he'd thought.

His intelligence went up by fifty-five points to sixty-six total for a 44 percent decrease in spell cost.

Nonetheless, with about ten jumps back to Ira, he'd already gone through another few pools of mana. Fifty MP per person was a lot for a spell. Adding Ira to it would mean another 250 MP, roughly.

"I guess. You aren't going to leave him behind again?"

Sof's face soured, but Ira let out a bark of a laugh. "Sof tried to hang me from a branch and carry me. I wouldn't let them waste the time. I can do much more now that you've helped me recover."

"But . . . um . . . what about . . . you know . . ." Orrin pointed. "Your leg?"

Sof waved his wand around the stump of Ira's missing limb and then yanked back and down. A small piece of wood grew out of the leg and rapidly matured into a small sapling. Sof reached down and gently broke the tree into a rough approximation of a prosthetic.

"It's not pretty, but I'll be able to hobble around." Ira stood with Sof's help and began to test out his new limb. He was unsteady and almost fell, but Sof caught him.

"Whenever you are ready. We really shouldn't keep the team waiting. Farah's a stickler for punctuality."

Orrin had to stop and recast his [Increase Intelligence] spell again on the way back when it ran out, but they made it back within the hour.

"Ira!" A girl no older than twenty tackled the man and dropped her scythe. Orrin watched as the rest of the Dragoon team came out of the woods to congratulate Ira on not dying.

Sof and Bin retreated a little and talked with their backs to Orrin as the others approached Ira.

A woman standing over six feet tall and with the stature of a heavy-lifting bodybuilder shook Ira by his shoulder before returning to a large club that she'd rested against a small tree. Orrin mistook the club as a tree itself at first.

Another woman with blond hair and wearing a mottled blue robe pulled Farah off Ira and said a few soft words to him before dragging the girl away. Farah reminded Orrin of one of his favorite K-pop death metal bands. She was wearing a black dress with lots of metal bits; a classic Goth.

The men of Dragoon waited their turn and gave fist bumps and handshakes in a typical manly fashion. A short man with shifty eyes and a bow in his hand climbed back up a tree after welcoming Ira back. Two identical men with the stance of fighters approached Ira from either side. One wore heavier armor and had knives, hand axes, and even a few javelins strapped all over his body. The other had only a rapier and leather armor. If their load-out hadn't been so different, Orrin would never have been able to tell them apart.

The final man to approach gave a grunt at Ira and then retreated to his own corner of the woods. The man was almost as big as the woman with the tree club, but he held only a large tower shield with no visible weapon. He did have a bunch of waterskins strapped all over his body and began to drink right after sitting down again.

"Orrin?"

Orrin sighed and realized Daniel had regained consciousness. He waved to Daniel and then flicked him off.

"What? How?" Daniel stuttered. "Can you ask these guys why I'm tied to a tree?"

Orrin used [Identify] on Daniel and saw that his health was at 50/300.

"Sof," Orrin interrupted the man's talk. "Can I heal my friend and go now?"

"Yes to heal. No to go." Sof didn't elaborate and began talking with Bin again. Orrin noticed he pointed at him a few times.

Orrin walked up to Daniel and healed him back to full health. Then he punched Daniel in the stomach as hard as he could.

"Guh. What the hell?" Daniel asked angrily.

Orrin double-checked Daniel's health. His punch had only done one damage.

"The next time you decide to lie to everyone, remember that I'm on your side. If you'd told me, I could have got us here with [Teleport]. I could have kept you from getting jumped by McFisty over there. I could have buffed you so much that even a Fogbinder would have run from you." Orrin trailed off from his whispered rant. "You're my only friend here. Don't fucking leave me behind."

Daniel's fury at getting hit withered as Orrin spoke.

"I'm sorry. Again." Daniel lowered his eyes as best he could while still strapped to the tree. "I just thought that—"

"You didn't think." Orrin poked him in the chest. "You never do. You think you are invincible, but I can't cast resurrection yet, so stop getting into situations where you can die."

"You found a resurrection spell?" Daniel's eyes lit up.

"No, you fucking idiot. That's not a thing."

Daniel closed his eyes and sighed. "Listen. I know I keep fucking up. I heard this group of high-level guards had been sent out, essentially to die. You know they were sent out here to just harry the Fogbinder so it couldn't regroup and attack the Wall right away? Like, they were sent out to die, Orrin!"

"Yes. We were." Sof sneaked up beside Orrin. "But we also all volunteered. None of us plan to actually die today."

Bin trailed behind Sof with his arms crossed over his impressive chest. The sleeveless leather armor he wore creaked as he stuck his fingers into the opposite edges under his arms.

"Why did you attack me? I was trying to find you to help." Daniel tried to turn his head but only succeeded in scratching his forehead against the small branch holding him down. "Could you at least let me move my neck?"

Sof waved a hand, and the tree dropped Daniel to his knees. The druid stepped forward and put his hand out. "I'll apologize for nearly killing you, but I would do it again. Don't sneak up on a person in the Pass. Ever. But especially when a surprise demon pulled the same stunt and wiped out a few platoons just a few days prior."

Orrin saw Daniel's anger flare as he took the extended hand before standing. He got his face under control quickly, but his friend noticed.

He's not used to not getting his way, Orrin realized. *Everything always came easy to him back home. Even the teachers could be convinced of doing it Daniel's way.*

Orrin hadn't stopped to think about it, but Daniel's proclivity for running into danger shouldn't have been that surprising to him. Daniel was the striker on the soccer team and a wide receiver on the football team. He was popular at school, with both the teachers and the other kids. He usually had a girlfriend. His home life was stable.

He's not used to having an actual problem to deal with.

"Well, now that I'm here . . ." Daniel tried to turn on the charm and smirked at Bin. "That was a great sucker punch. Want to see who can take out more monsters?"

Sof shook his head. "No, I'm afraid you two are going back to the Wall, per our agreement. Ira needs to get to the Hospital. No offense, Orrin, but I'd prefer if someone with the proper . . . credentials took a look at him."

"But I got all the way here on my own. Doesn't that count for something? You haven't even seen all that Orrin can do," Daniel wheedled.

"We're going back, D." Orrin looked around for Ira and caught him talking with Farah again. "Hey, Ira. You ready to go?"

Ira turned to Orrin and nodded his head. As he looked away, a dark shape raced out of the tree line and hit Farah's legs from behind. She bent backward, and Orrin heard a snap as a bone broke.

Another three Fetid Canines dashed out behind the first and grabbed the Goth's dress and arm. They dragged her away from the group.

Daniel started to yell and pulled his shortsword off his back. Sof was screaming orders to the rest of his team. Ira was already pointing toward the first dog, his metal attack jumping off his hand and cutting the monster.

Orrin cast inversed [Increase Dexterity] on the Canines pulling Farah. His intelligence was still boosted, but the will buff had worn off during the teleporting trip. It didn't matter, as the twenty-five dexterity off each beast appeared to be enough.

Bin was next to Ira, both punching the Canine into the dirt. The brothers and the bodybuilder woman were beating and stabbing one of the prone monsters, while the rest of the team took turns breaking the other two into pieces. Farah was holding her arm awkwardly against her body but still was able to let gravity do its work to push her scythe blade into one of the Canines' eyes.

Sof had disappeared.

Orrin pulled up his [Map]. Over fifty red dots were running right toward the party.

"There's got to be fifty more coming from the west," he yelled out. "Daniel and Ira, get over here. We need to leave."

Sof pulled himself out of the tree right next to Orrin. His eyes were a little wide. "There's more than fifty. I counted over twice that coming."

"I can only see a mile out. I can try to teleport everyone away ... but I might need a few trips."

Sof shook his head and pulled his wand back out. "It's a little late for that. You can escape, though. We came out here to buy time for the city. Bring Ira back and make sure to report in."

Sof turned back to his team with a sad smile. "It's been an honor, you failures. Lowest kill count buys the drinks when we get back home."

Chapter 44

[Mind Bastion] was demanding Orrin return to Dey with Ira and Daniel.

Shut up, I'm in charge. I'm not letting these people die.

Orrin felt the logical instance and nagging of his thoughts fall to the back of his mind.

Did I just control the skill?

Orrin didn't have time to ponder long, as another two Fetid Canines appeared nearby. Orrin didn't have time to react before one suddenly looked like a porcupine, with arrows sticking out of it at all angles. The other was hit by two axes, a javelin, and half a dozen knives that disappeared a second after lodging into the dog's flesh.

Howls of pain and anger rent the forest air.

"Orrin, I can help them. You can help them," Daniel pleaded.

"I'm staying." Ira had picked up a large branch and was using it as a half crutch, half walking stick to shuffle around. "I'm more help here than in Dey. Give the report, kid."

He tottered away, using his flowing-metal trick to cut up another Canine that just appeared.

Daniel was still looking at Orrin with fear in his eyes. Fear that Orrin would try to take him back.

"We are going to have a long talk after this," Orrin said as he pulled Gertrude from his [Dimension Hole] and started casting his max-level increase spells on Daniel and himself. "If I survive . . ."

"What do you mean?" Daniel smiled as he picked up the thick slab of metal. "I'm not going to let anything hurt you."

"I'm cycling. I have been for a few hours now. This fight is going to cost me a few days' throwing up and fever if I'm lucky."

"What? No. Why?" Daniel stopped spinning Gerty and looked aghast at his friend. "Orrin, how much mana have you used?"

"Enough that a little more won't hurt," Orrin said and yelled over to Bin. "Big guy, I can make you stronger, too, but you might feel sick after. You want it?"

Bin fought with his fists and pulled a gore-covered hand out of a Fetid that had stumbled in by itself. He nodded once.

Orrin cast [Increase Strength] and [Increase Dexterity] at his highest levels on Bin, who looked into the distance and then took a step forward to punch the side of a tree. He splintered the trunk.

"How many times can you do that?" Sof asked as Bin let out a slow smile.

"As much as needed right now. Which stat do you want?"

"What stats can you do?" Sof responded in kind.

"All of them but constitution."

"Will and intelligence?"

Orrin nodded and cast. *Better they survive and kill this thing than trying to keep my spells secret. Maybe if we all make it through this, I can ask them to keep it quiet. Or get Silas to pull strings.*

"Can you do the whole team?" Sof was staring into the distance, checking his own status with buffed stats.

"Yeah, gather them up."

"Everyone gather, quickly," Sof demanded and nodded at Orrin.

Orrin let loose as they all approached.

A small part of his logic skill kept him from simply using all four stats on every person. Instead, he pulled up a quick [Identify] on each member of Dragoon team and made judgment calls with only a few questions to clarify. Orrin couldn't read anything beyond names and class titles on any member of Dragoon team.

Bin
Fury Fist Level 53

Increase dexterity and strength.

Sof
Arborist Druid Level 55

Increase intelligence and will.

Noah
Pain Drinker Level 49

That sounds absolutely terrible.
"Noah, favorite two stats?"
"Con and strength," Noah replied, hefting his tower shield like it weighed only a few pounds.
"Pick something other than constitution."
"Dexterity."
Orrin cast.

Al
Returner Level 42

What the hell? Can he come back over and over? Have we met before?
"Al, same question."
"Intelligence and dexterity," the twin said before throwing a hand axe into the woods. It reappeared in his hand a second later, and he threw it again.

Gracie
Mauler Level 51

Gustaf
Sword Dancer Level 39

Increase strength and dexterity for both.

Clifford
Trick Shot Level 47

"Clifford?"
"Intelligence and dexterity, please?"

Maya
Wind Singer Level 44

Ira
Steel Ravager Level 52

Increase will and intelligence for both.

"You've all got ten to twenty minutes. I'll try to teleport you out if you get hurt."

"What kind of build gives that much mana?" Orrin heard Maya whisper to Ira.

"And he already healed me today for a few hundred HP at least," Ira whispered back.

Sof walked to a nearby tree and stuck half his body into it. "Dragoon team. Let's thin that bastard's army."

Sof disappeared into the tree.

Bin, Noah, and Gracie started running to the northwest with Ira limping behind.

Al and Gustaf headed southwest, with Farah, Clifford, and Maya trailing behind them.

Daniel ran after Ira and picked the man up under his arm. "I'll carry you until we see something."

"Shit. Fine." Ira relented.

Orrin took a look at his [Map] and then headed after Daniel. The team to the south had fewer red dots anyway.

Fighting Fetid Canines in the trees would be difficult, but Orrin wasn't there to fight. Daniel could get all the XP he wanted, but Orrin just wanted to keep this small family of fighters alive.

Then the first wave hit.

Orrin watched Sof step out of a tree and dance to another. His movements were quick, but his arms moved in a slow rhythm, pulling roots out of the ground toward the sky and tree branches down to touch the earth. Every time he appeared, a Canine was tripped or grappled.

Noah had grabbed two waterskins off his chest and chugged the contents. Orrin smelled the distinct tang of alcohol in the air. When two dogs jumped at the man, he turned his tower shield sideways and batted them both at the same time. A few hundred pounds of moving mass repelled without stopping his run.

Gracie followed behind Noah, crushing skulls with her club. Ira caught any stragglers with his quick-moving metal attacks.

Daniel was using [Shooting Star] and [Gravity Strike] with abandon. Orrin saw [Side Steps] activate once or twice as well . . . until the first Kniferunner appeared.

Just as Brandt had described, the Kniferunner was a spider the size of a small horse. All eight legs ended in sharp, tapered points, and Orrin watched one leg rub against a tree and leave a long gash in the bark.

The monster rushed Gracie. Noah stepped in front and held his shield up. He let out a yell, and a blue bubble surrounded him.

The Kniferunner changed targets and tried to stab Noah with its long spear-like legs. As Noah slapped the attacks to the side with his shield and even once with his hand, Gracie began raining blows down on the monster's back.

Bin dropped two dogs he'd caught by the nape of the neck. The resulting sound of their heads being struck together was still ringing as he ran to help the shield and club wielders. The giant spider never took its eyes off Noah and his blue halo, even as Bin grabbed a leg and, with a heavy twist, pulled the limb clean off.

Orrin didn't attack anything with magic as he tried to reserve using any more mana than he had to. He did take the odd swipe at the Fetid Canines, although most were now running at Noah. The blue bubble skill was like Daniel's aggro skill. Orrin watched as Noah took a few shallow cuts from the Kniferunner that scabbed over quickly. Noah didn't do much damage, but he was soaking up the attacks while Bin and Gracie removed limbs, crushed in the monster's carapace, and generally just destroyed it.

The fight lasted only thirty seconds once all three were on it.

Ira and Daniel kept two Canines occupied until Daniel was able to slip through and decapitate one. A quick step and he batted the second into a tree hard enough that the resulting snap of bones pulled Bin's attention from the dead Kniferunner.

Sof stepped out of a tree a minute later and squatted, taking big breaths of air.

"Sixteen . . . knives . . . and sixty Canines left," he announced.

"Any sign of the Fogbinder?" Gracie asked. Her voice was gentle and soft, which was an odd contrast to her actions. She had grabbed a leg of the dead spider and snapped it off before shoving it into the center mass.

"No, but there's a small clearing a quarter of a mile north of here. I'll draw them in and you four do your thing. Knock a few into the trees for me, too," Sof said and put a hand on Bin's shoulder.

"Careful," the big man mumbled in a voice low enough to make Darth Vader jealous. Orrin realized he hadn't talked in front of him, either.

"You, too." Sof put his hand on Bin's cheek and then walked back into a tree.

"Let's go," Ira said and started to hobble off. Daniel sighed and picked him up again.

They got to the clearing, which was only large enough for them all to swing their weapons without hitting each other, and waited. Two minutes later, they heard the barking of Fetid Canines and saw the trees moving.

Orrin cast [Ward] on the team, himself, and Daniel but didn't announce it. They'd figure it out when they didn't take damage.

Ira stood in the middle of the clearing, with Noah in front of him. Gracie and Bin flanked Noah. Daniel stood guard at the back with Orrin.

Hopefully seeing these guys demolish the monsters so easily gives him some perspective, Orrin hoped.

Fifteen dogs ran into the clearing, frothing and slobbering their poisoned drool as they rushed the targets ahead. Orrin saw a single Canine get dragged up into a tree before the fight began.

Noah started his blue shield up again, and a full dozen of the monsters tried to bite him as Noah and Gracie waded through with death in their swings and punches. Ira sent out his spells, cutting a foot out from under one and slicing into the neck of another. Daniel darted forward to let Gerty crash down, cleaving one in half for every four the Dragoons took out. The fight was quick, with only Gracie taking a scratch to her arm.

"It's fine." She pushed Noah back as he tried to look at it. "Somehow, I didn't even take damage. I must have scratched it on a tree."

Orrin had watched the dog's paw come down on her arm just as she smashed it into the ground. It had scratched her, but [Ward] had stopped the damage.

Daniel smiled over his shoulder and nodded at Orrin. "Good job."

Ira looked between the two. "What? He's just standing there. I appreciate the spell you cast, but at least try and use that sword."

"Oh, that's a terrible idea," Daniel laughed. "He'd probably end up hitting one of us."

"There's about sixteen more coming," Orrin announced. He could see Sof as a small gray dot that disappeared from one spot to pop up at another. The dot darted between the red monsters and then came in a straight line back to the clearing.

Sof fell out of a tree at the edge and ran to the group. "Five more Canines, but we've got eleven Kniferunners coming our way. Two minutes out."

Orrin asked, "How many can you comfortably take out?"

"Canines? We could go all day." Noah slurred his words. "Knives . . . maybe two if we're lucky."

Orrin fumbled his sword and let it fall to the ground as he pulled his bestiary from his [Dimension Hole].

Please be something useful. Please be something useful.

Kniferunners roam the lands beyond the Pass and are found in underground caverns. They grow to enormous sizes for arachnids and subsist on a diet of meat and metal. Their bodies are prized by Alchemists and Weaponsmiths, as they digest the metals to harden their legs into weapons. Kniferunners sharpen these legs into blades, running over enemies, which gives them their name. Five Star (*****)

"Shit," Orrin murmured. "Sof, are *Kniferunners* strong or quick?"

"Both. We need either Bin or Gracie to pierce their armor, too."

Orrin turned to Daniel. "I'm going to try and slow them down. Daniel, use your aggro skill on one side of the clearing."

Orrin glanced over his shoulder to Noah. "Noah, you go over to the other side. Maybe we can make them split up. Bin and Gracie, pick one side each. You both will need to move quickly. Ira and Sof, back them up."

"What are you planning?" Sof asked.

"I'm going to do what I did to Bin and try making them slow. If it works, great. If not, we'll have to run."

Sof shrugged. "It's a better plan than any I have. If we survive, maybe you can explain just what these skills are. I'm getting a bit jealous."

"Or maybe we can all just act like I was never here?" Orrin gave Sof a long look and held eye contact. "I would prefer to keep my life quiet and private."

Sof didn't answer. He didn't have time. The sound of a hundred clicking legs echoed through the forest.

The enemy had arrived.

Chapter 45

Four Kniferunners came from the right, and seven more came from the left. The Canines followed the spiders, split nearly in half with each group. Daniel and Noah activated [Gravity Well] and the blue-shield skill. The two groups of monsters paused and then turned as one toward Noah.

Shit, his skill must be at a higher level than Daniel's.

Orrin started using inversed [Increase Dexterity] on the Kniferunners. Five casts on the front spider slowed it down dramatically, but it still was moving forward.

Orrin spent a second to use [Identify].

Kniferunner
HP: 380/380

The slowed spider fell from the front of the pack to the back. Orrin continued to slow all the monsters. He got six of the Kniferunners before they hit Noah's shield.

The long legs of the spiders reached around Noah's shield and began to hit his arms and chest. Lines of blood little more than paper cuts appeared on his skin.

"What's going on? They're hitting me, but it's barely a scratch," the man slurred and continued to push one spider back with his tower shield.

Orrin checked Noah's status and saw the [Ward] was draining rapidly. Noah's health would have already been taken out if not for Orrin's spell. He cast it again.

"I'll keep Noah up," Orrin yelled. "Everyone else . . . start taking out those spiders."

Orrin continued to cast [Ward] on Noah and inversed [Increase Dexterity] on the Kniferunners, with a [Heal Small Wounds] on Noah when he didn't turn back quickly enough.

Bin and Gracie were dashing around, using skills Orrin could only guess at. Bin's fists were glowing red, and Gracie had actually grown a foot taller, her mace looking like a twig in her big hands.

Daniel was using [Gravity Strike] on one monster's back over and over. On the fifth strike, the spider splayed its legs and went down hard. The next hit broke the hard shell, and Daniel pushed the blade in deep. He gave a grunt as he twisted the handle, ripping a large rent into the Kniferunner's carapace. Sof danced close, pointing his wand at the open hole. His wand rose high, and then he slammed it point down at the gash. A small branch shot from the tip of the wand and speared into the innards of the beast. It gave a small shriek and tried to run, but the branch grew into an upside-down tree, launching the spider into the sky.

Orrin finished slowing the spiders and turned to the Fetid Canines. His spells immobilized them. Orrin held his sword above his head and brought it down, one poison dog at a time.

Experience Gained: 500 XP (100 XP x 5)

I'm close to level eleven, Orrin realized. *I should get a kill with Daniel. I can level my dex and will to level three.*

Daniel was using the same strategy on another slowed Kniferunner. Orrin threw a [Lightstrike] at it and hoped his friend could finish one off alone. He went back to using [Ward] on Noah.

The fight lasted hours in Orrin's mind, but when Daniel brought Gerty down on the last Kniferunner's head with a satisfying splat, all Orrin's buffs were still running. Everything had lasted less than ten minutes.

Experience Gained: 550 XP
Level 11 Obtained!
+10 AP

"How are we alive?" Sof looked around in awe at the piled-up dead spiders and the few Canines leaking blood from stab wounds to the head. "Eleven Kniferunners should have taken us out right away . . ."

Bin and Gracie slumped on the ground, and Noah drank deeply from a new skin.

Orrin pulled up his [Map]. "Nothing within a mile."

Sof sat down next to Bin. "We should check on the others and find a spot to rest. We . . . we did a lot today."

Orrin turned and eased a hand axe out of his [Dimension Hole], out of view of the others. Then he began hacking on the legs of the spiders.

"What are you doing?" Gracie asked as Orrin found the easiest part to cut . . . right above the second joint.

"My book says these legs are worth a lot." Orrin shrugged.

Noah stood up and walked over to a body. He brought the bottom of his shield down hard on a leg. It snapped right off. "How much are we talking?"

"Noah, you can't carry those around while we fight," Sof pointed out.

"I'll carry them all," Orrin volunteered. "We can do an even split for all of us once we make it back."

Gracie's face fell. "If we make it back."

Sof stood back up and helped Bin to his feet. "Let's go find the others. Hopefully they didn't get hit as hard."

They made their way back south. Sof stayed with the party, claiming his mana was nearly out. Orrin kept his [Map] up, but they found no traces of more enemies.

Orrin found one gray spot ahead and signaled to Sof. The druid let out a whistle that was returned in a different pitch a minute later.

Clifford, the bow and arrow guy, jumped down out of a tree a few minutes later.

"Sof, we got hit by two Kniferunners and about twenty Fetids," the man started reporting right away. His voice was quick and a bit spastic. Orrin was reminded of the kids who used fidget spinners in class all day and still got sent to the front office for talking too much. "Me, Al, and Maya took them out slowly by just chipping away from the trees, but Farah got impatient and tried to poison a spider. It cut her up, and we had to retreat back to bravo base."

"Did you come out looking for us?" Sof asked as they turned back east slightly and began walking again.

"No. Actually, I didn't know you were around until I heard your whistle. I'm making sure nothing followed us back. Maya said she spread our scent farther west, but I wanted to double-check."

"Good idea."

Ira had declined Bin's and Daniel's offers to carry him, and they'd made a slower pace than Orrin felt comfortable with. The sun was beginning to set, and the trees made it seem darker already.

"Good job back there," Daniel whispered as they fell to the back of the group. "You saved their lives."

"I'm sure they could have avoided it completely if they weren't worried about dealing with us," Orrin retorted. "I haven't forgiven you yet, Daniel."

"I know, I know. But seriously, great job. You slowed those things down so much I barely had to use my speed-boost skill to catch them. Do you think they'll keep going or try to head back?"

"I don't know." Orrin ducked under a low-hanging branch.

"Are you going to make us teleport back as soon as we get them back?"

"As soon as we get back to their camp, I'm going to have to sit around and help take care of them. Did you forget what that kind of boosting did to Madi and Brandt and Jude?"

Daniel was silent. "Shit, I forgot for a minute."

"Because we distracted them, they had to fight instead of evading the monsters and trying to find the Fogbinder. Because of that, I had to buff them. Now . . . well, maybe I can teleport them back a few at a time."

"And just leave the Fogbinder out here? What happens if it has time to regroup and attack Dey again?"

"What do you want from me, D?" Orrin spun on his friend. "These guys are higher level than us. They know what they're doing. We don't."

Daniel held up his hands in a placating gesture. "I'm just saying, me and you could teleport around at the top of the trees. We could look for the thing. You with [Map] and me with [Telescope]. Only half the team will be out if they even get sick. We could take it out and be back tomorrow."

Orrin sighed and followed the group. He didn't answer Daniel. He didn't want to deal with him right now.

They survived because I buffed them, he told himself. *Even if having to fight in the first place is our fault, everyone survived. Be positive.*

Bravo base was a small cave created from huge sheets of rock that had fallen from the cliff side of the Pass.

Farah was leaning up against a wall, holding a ripped piece of cloth against her side. Orrin saw the darkness of stained blood seeping through and rushed to her side.

"Is it bad? I can heal it if—"

"Get away from me." Farah pushed him away. "We wouldn't have had to fight if you and your friend hadn't shown up."

Orrin stepped back.

"Farah, shut up and take the help." Maya was sitting by the small fire and using little gusts of wind to keep the smoke flowing farther into the cave. "We've had to fight like five times since we started this mission. We probably would have had to fight again anyway."

Sof helped Ira sit and began dragging his wand up and down the fake wooden leg. It twisted and shaped as he played with it, with a small knee joint appearing in the middle. Ira bent it gingerly and smirked.

"That'll help a bit," he said. Sof smiled and went to sit with Bin.

The Dragoon team debriefed informally, and Farah finally allowed Orrin to cast a few healing spells on her. He was sure he could have spent a few extra heals on her, but she just chucked the piece of bloody cloth into the fire and walked away without a thank you.

Daniel scowled after her. "What a b—"

"It's fine," Orrin said and elbowed his friend in the ribs. "How are you? Did you take any more damage?"

Daniel shook his head. "No. Did you get much experience? That fight brought me almost all the way to twelve."

"Just past eleven," Orrin responded. "I was more worried about keeping everybody alive."

"I've been looking at my skills, and I think—"

"Daniel," Orrin interrupted him, "maybe later. I need to make sure they understand that they're going to crash."

Daniel pulled a face but didn't argue. Orrin went and sat in front of Sof and Bin. Bin had an arm around the druid.

"Sof, I kind of told you guys earlier, but when those buff spells I cast wear off, you are all going to get . . . sick."

"Orrin, those spells wore off a while ago. I don't feel anything."

Orrin was surprised but kept at it. "I . . . I don't get it. Last time I used the spells that high, my party went down for almost two days. Would you mind if I checked your status? I can use [Identify]."

Sof hesitated but eventually nodded.

Sof
Arborist Druid Level 55
HP: —
MP: —

It's the same as earlier. No abnormal status effects, but maybe I just can't see them.

"I'm not seeing anything off . . ." Orrin scratched his head. "Please let me know if you feel strange, though."

Orrin made his way back to Daniel. "Sof's fine. Nobody else looks more than tired. I don't get it."

Daniel shrugged. "They are a higher level than Brandt. Maybe it has something to do with that?"

Orrin pulled a bedroll out of his [Dimension Hole] and draped it wide over the both of them.

Sof set up a sleep and watch rotation but left Orrin and Daniel out of it. That was fine by Orrin. He was ready for a full night of sleep.

Orrin pulled up his store and made two quick purchases.

> **Would you like to Upgrade [Increase Dexterity] (5,000/5,000) for 3 AP?**
> **Yes or No?**

Yes.

> **Would you like to Upgrade [Increase Will] (5,000/5,000) for 3 AP?**
> **Yes or No?**

Yes.

> **[Increase Dexterity] Level 3 (0/10,000):**
> **Increase target Dexterity by +4 for 20 minutes. (15 MP).**

> **[Increase Will] Level 3 (0/10,000):**
> **Increase target Will by +4 for 20 minutes. (15 MP).**

Finally, the complete set. Orrin pulled up his status.

> **Orrin**
> **Utility Warder**
> **Level 11 (490/2,000)**
> **HP: 90**
> **MP: 380**

Strength: 9
Constitution: 9
Dexterity: 9
Will: 28
Intelligence: 11

Abilities:
[Mind Bastion]
[Dimension Hole]
[Identify]
[Blood Mana]
[Map], [Party View], [Monster View], [Trap View], [Zoom]
[Side Steps] Level Three (9/300)
[Mana Pool]
[Through the Ages]

Spells:
[Calm Mind] 5 MP
[Heal Small Wounds] Level 1, 5 MP; Level 2, 10 MP; Level 3, 20 MP (740/10,000)
[Camouflage] Level 1, 10 MP; Level 2, 10 MP (210/10,000)
[Lightstrike] 10 MP
[Ward] 20 MP
[Inverse] 5 MP
[Utility Ward] Level 1, 100 MP; Level 2, 200 MP
[Ice Sword] 1 MP per sword
[Teleport] 50 MP per person (4,650/5,000)
[Ice Ward] 20 MP
[Increase Strength] Level 1, 5 MP; Level 2, 10 MP; Level 3, 15 MP (1,530/10,000)
[Increase Dexterity] Level 1, 5 MP; Level 2, 10 MP; Level 3, 15 MP (1,620/10,000)

[Increase Will] Level 1, 5 MP; Level 2, 10 MP; Level 3, 15 MP (660/10,000)
[Increase Intelligence] Level 1, 5 MP; Level 2, 10 MP; Level 3, 15 MP (1,080/10,000)

Orrin looked over his build until his eyes got heavy. The last thing he remembered was Daniel pulling the blanket back over him as he fell asleep.

Chapter 46

Orrin woke to the smell of bacon. He rolled over in his bed and . . .

"Get off me." Daniel pushed him as Orrin sprawled out over his friend.

"What? Sorry." Orrin fully woke up and looked around. The entire Dragoon party was awake, and Al was roasting strips of meat on a small pan over a fire.

"Breakfast? Al took down a Jackadeer earlier." Sof knelt near Orrin with a handful of something between bacon strips and sausages in his hand.

Orrin picked one up gingerly as Daniel turned and pulled the blanket back over his head. "Is it edible?"

"Jackadeer are low-level monsters, so the meat isn't as bad as you'd think. Better than jerky, anyways," Sof said as he put another two down by Daniel's head. "Better eat quick. You two need to be off before we leave."

Daniel finally stuck his head out from under the sleeping bag. "Don't you think it would be better if we came along?"

Sof shook his head. "If those monsters hadn't been all around us yesterday, I would have made you leave then and there. We've already voted, and despite some protests—"

Gracie and Noah let out loud coughs.

"—we are sending you back with Ira. There is no reason for you to be here anymore. Go home."

Sof stood and went back to his friends. Orrin took a bite of the meat stick. It did taste somewhat of bacon but reminded him more of a sausage in consistency. How had Al made these?

Daniel ate in silence.

Orrin watched the party move around. Not one person seemed to have any side effects from his buffing.

Gracie came up and sat down next to the two of them.

"I just wanted to say thank you," she said in her soft voice. "You both did a good job, and we're sorry you couldn't come along. You helped us take out a big chunk of its little army, though, so we have a better chance now."

"A big chunk? Didn't Sof say there were like sixty Canines or something with even more Kniferunners?" Daniel asked as he munched on his breakfast.

Gracie nodded and ran her hand through her short hair. "Yes, but . . . and no offense . . . we can take care of the rest on our own. We try not to go all out like that. We sneak up and take out one or two at a time before retreating. The Fogbinder can only bring so many monsters into the Pass with it, and it would have to release control of all the single type of monster under its control to get more. There aren't usually any Fetid Canines or Kniferunners in the Pass."

"So it's like a control skill for monsters?" Orrin asked, fascinated. "If you kill too many of one type, won't the Fogbinder just switch to another monster type?"

Gracie smiled. "You are a bright one. Yes, in theory, if the Fogbinder wanted to it could. But Bin has fought one before. The plan is to get the numbers low and then strike the head. We'll go after the Fogbinder himself."

"Won't that be dangerous? Could it control you?" Daniel asked. Orrin could see he was remembering Silas's ability to freeze his body.

Gracie's laughter echoed around the small cave. Sof looked over and frowned but didn't say anything.

"No, it's not mind control. We are sure of that. Fogbinders can't control anything but monsters. Other than that, they only have a few magical abilities . . . mostly air attacks."

"So why not attack it right away?" Daniel asked. "Find out where it is and kill it quick."

Gracie's smile turned sad as she spoke. "They always keep the biggest of their army nearby. There are two strategies for killing a Fogbinder."

She leaned in. "When we got the news that there was one coming, we sent out a few thousand of our green recruits and surrounded them with some of our best. A large group of bait but with our best fighters and defenders there to keep the newbies away from the actual danger. When the Horde appeared and the fighting started, a few teams were sent in to dispatch the Fogbinder. It worked perfectly . . . until the second one showed up and hit everyone from behind."

She wiped her eyes and continued, "The other way . . . instead of drawing the army away from the Fogbinder using bait, you rush the Fogbinder with all you have. Friends go down and it's a roll of the dice who lives and who dies, but it only takes a strike or two to take a Fogbinder down. They are mostly intelligence and will, with very little constitution."

"You're going to suicide bomb the thing?" Orrin gasped.

"We are going to take out as many monsters under its control that we feel safe to do first," Gracie said. "But then, yes. Some of us will likely not come back."

Orrin sat quietly as Daniel asked more strategy questions. He got the general idea. If they attacked after taking out too many of the Fogbinder's army, it could just go and restock with something else nearby. But to willingly run to your death without any guarantee that it would work . . .

"Orrin? God, I really hate this skill." Daniel was snapping his fingers in front of Orrin's face. Gracie had gone back to Noah.

"Sorry, what?"

Daniel turned his back to the Dragoon team as they started taking up camp and getting ready to leave. "I think we should help them."

"No."

"Just listen—"

"No."

"Can't you just—"

"If you say one more word, I'll have Sof tie you up again."

Daniel pursed his lips together. Then, in one breath, he coughed out, "You buff them all."

"First off, that wouldn't work. The buffs only last for twenty minutes, tops. Second, I'm still surprised they haven't passed out like everyone else did in the dungeon."

"Use your [Utility Ward]. Just enter and leave the party."

Orrin opened his mouth to argue but couldn't think of any logical comeback. It might work. He'd have to explain yet another skill, but it might save somebody's life.

"It's not a bad idea, huh? Maybe they'll let us stay another day or two, just in case they don't find—"

"I'll buff them once and then we go home." Orrin stood and walked away before Daniel could argue.

He made his way up to Sof.

"Yes? Are you ready? Ira is complaining, but he really should get back to a healer for his leg."

"I want to run something by you," Orrin said, leaning on one foot and then the other. "I want to increase your stats again."

"Thank you for the help yesterday, but we already voted. It's not that the boost didn't help, but we move slower with you and Daniel around. We can't protect you and do our jobs. We need to be able to—"

"I get that. I'm not asking to stay," Orrin cut Sof off. "I can make the buff last all day, but only to people in my party."

Sof raised an eyebrow. "What's the catch?"

"I want your word that you all won't talk about my skills. Or Daniel's. We don't need the attention."

Sof peered into Orrin's eyes, searching for something. "Why? Why protect him?"

Orrin felt the weight of the question. Sof wasn't asking why they didn't want the attention. He wasn't asking why Orrin wanted to help.

He was asking why Orrin had risked his life to protect Daniel. Someone that Sof saw as entitled, reckless, and probably idiotic.

"Daniel is my friend."

Sof waited in silence.

Orrin glanced around. Nobody else was close enough to overhear. "He's a [Hero]."

Sof smiled. "I thought so. His skills. The attitude. The way he's drawn to them."

"You knew?" Orrin scanned nearby again. Bin was helping Gustaf push a blanket into a backpack. Gracie and Maya were chatting near the cave entrance. Everyone else was around the fire, grabbing a few last bites of breakfast.

"I suspected."

"What do you mean, drawn to them?" Orrin asked.

"[Heroes] always are drawn toward demons. It's part of their build. You could say it's in their blood."

Orrin looked back and remembered how fervently Silas had tried to get them out of town before the Fogbinder showed up. The looks and glances at Daniel, as if checking up on him all the time.

He knew. He knew that Daniel might try to go after a demon and sent us away to protect him.

Orrin was conflicted on that. Silas was keeping information to himself again, but this time . . . he might have been doing the right thing.

I'll deal with him later.

"You promise not to tell anyone?"

"I do. I have no need to get involved with a [Hero]. If you are telling the truth about the buffs, as you call them, I would appreciate it. And if my team is able to keep even one extra person alive . . . I will be in your debt. I will never mention you or he came to this side of the Walls," Sof said and stuck out his hand.

Orrin shook it. "I should warn you, there might be side effects."

"You said that about the others. Nobody felt anything different."

"It's a different skill. This is the actual one that knocked most of my party out for a day with nausea and fatigue."

Sof looked up at the ceiling and sighed. "We know where the Fogbinder is. We'll fight him today one way or the other." He looked back down at Orrin and smiled. "What's a little vomit to a dead man?"

Orrin and Sof talked of logistics, and soon enough the time came for goodbyes. They had only met the group the day before, and already, Orrin was going to miss the quiet gentleness of Gracie, Sof's steadfast calmness, and even the pointed looks from Farah.

Sof rounded up the other eight members who would stay and fight.

Sof Has Invited You to a Party
Yes or No?

Orrin hit Yes. He cast [Increase Will] and [Increase Intelligence] on himself—Level two only, but five times. He'd need the decreased costs and increased output for all the magic he planned on using.

He cast [Utility Ward] level two.

"Sof? All my stats went up to a hundred," Gracie yelled with a start. Even Noah looked lucid as he focused on something in front of him.

Holy shit! Stacked together, my stats are at one hundred! Orrin thought but pushed that thought back with all the other things to worry about later.

"Farah, drop out and enter Daniel and Ira's party for now. Maya, invite Orrin," Sof demanded. "Nobody is ever to talk of this. Dragoon team secret."

Al and Gustaf gave each other a look and high-fived. Gustaf saw Orrin staring at them. "Noah told us what happened, and we were hoping to try it out. That many extra points will go a long way."

Maya Has Invited You to a Party
Yes or No?

Yes.

Orrin repeated the spell. With his intelligence so high, the spell cost next to nothing.

Sof then had Orrin join the team with Daniel, Farah, and Ira, using the spell one last time. Orrin cycled back to full MP.

"I guess this is goodbye." Orrin looked around at the joyful faces. Hope was living in the cave with the Dragoon team now.

"Good luck." Daniel waved.

"You better take good care of Ira," Farah threatened. "Straight to the Hospital, do you hear?"

Orrin waved and teleported the three of them out of the cave.

It took two hours to teleport back to the Walls of Dey. Orrin's knowledge of the land was now making it easier to jump around, even with two other people along.

"You'd think I'd get used to it," Ira complained as they landed hard on the top of the Wall near where Orrin had originally left. Daniel was supporting half the man's weight, as each [Teleport] use left them a few inches above the ground. Ira had fallen hard the first time.

"Can we drop you off here at the Wall?" Orrin asked. "I know Farah said right to the Hospital, but I should probably stay away from there for a few days."

Daniel looked up from helping Ira balance. "Why? What did you do?"

Orrin waved a hand. "Nothing. Nothing. I just need to go visit a friend soon. That's all."

"I can help Ira to—"

"And then go running right back out?" Orrin shook his head. "I'm getting you to Madi and handcuffing you to your bed."

Daniel opened his mouth with a smile.

"Yeah, I know. I heard it, too," Orrin said with a smirk. "Come on, let's find a guard to help Ira."

Chapter 47

Orrin had landed them in the same general spot where he had left Madi and Brandt, but neither was nearby. They ended up leaving Ira with a guard, who snapped a salute at the Dragoon member and hurried him off on the back of a small cart.

"Come find what's left of us in a few days," Ira said as they pulled away. He waved, and the metal mage disappeared around a corner.

"Let's get back to Madi's house," Daniel demanded. He'd continued to fidget and turn toward the Pass, but after Orrin had shared the information from Sof—namely, that [Heroes] had a natural urge to fight demons—he seemed to be able to fight it better.

"I'm not going back yet." Orrin shook his head and took a step away. "I'm going back to Tony's."

Daniel stepped with Orrin, keeping without grabbing distance. "No, you don't. I can keep watch over you and clean up your throw-up. It won't be the first time. Remember when we got into my dad's rum?"

Orrin wanted to vomit at the memory. Left alone to play video games all weekend while Daniel's parents were out of town, the two fifteen-year-olds had decided to try liquor for the first time. Orrin had yet to try it again.

"It's more than just keeping me hydrated," Orrin argued. "I have more questions for him, too."

"I'll come," Daniel said. "Show the way."

"He can read minds. I'm not sure how much he already knows," Orrin argued again. "What if he can tell you're a [Hero]?"

Daniel shrugged. "You already told Sof. He probably told the rest of the team. It's only a matter of time before everyone in town knows, too. Why don't you want me to go?"

Orrin was asking himself the same question. He was keeping Daniel away from Tony. But it might actually be easier for Tony if he had some help over the next few days.

Why do I have the feeling it is a bad idea?

"I don't really know," Orrin admitted. "I just don't think you and Tony would get along much."

"From what you told me, nobody would get along with him."

Orrin watched Daniel's eyes drift back to the Wall. "Maybe we should get you back to Madi and Brandt before you do something stupid again."

"Don't change the subject." Daniel's head snapped back to Orrin. "I can control it now that I know what it is. It's like an itch. No ... that's not right. You know when you take a free throw and you just know it's going in as it leaves your hands? Every time I turn toward where I know he is ... the Fogbinder ... I get that feeling. Like this is the perfect and right thing to do." His eyes glazed as he looked back to the Wall. "I bet I would have found him eventually."

"And he would have killed you," Orrin said and slapped the side of Daniel's head. "That's why we should drop you off and then I'll go get better."

Daniel dragged his head away from the direction of the Dragoon team and sighed. "We're both really fucked up, huh?"

"Of course we are." Orrin grinned. "Now, should we walk or use [Teleport]?"

"Walk. Stop being stupid. No more mana use for you," Daniel said and gestured down the street.

Orrin turned and began walking. Something hit him in the back of the head. He stooped and turned in one motion, pulling his sword free.

Daniel was laughing, holding one hand out. "Now we're even."

Getting Daniel to let him leave again after finding their way back to the Catanzano house ended up being easier than he thought. As soon as they got within sight of the house, the single guard at the front door ducked inside, and Madi appeared like a storm.

She told Daniel off, for risking himself and not trusting them, before pulling him into a hug. Madi turned and stepped toward Orrin as well, but he shook his head and took a step back. She smiled and gave him a knowing nod.

"Now get inside before I have Brandt come out here and make you."

Daniel seemed willing to take his lumps. Orrin, however, had other plans.

"I'll meet you both back here in a few days. Madi, keep an eye on him. I guess something in the"—Orrin stopped and noticed the guard standing nearby—"something in Daniel's class makes him seek out dangerous opponents. He'll tell you all about it."

Madi's scowl let him know he wasn't out of the woods. "And where do you think you're going?"

"I'm going to go be sick for a while. All the magic I did really didn't sit well with my stomach. 'Bye." Orrin tried to turn and get out of the anti-[Teleport] spell's range but Madi, was getting quicker at noticing the two boys' tricks. She grabbed his arm and pulled.

"No. I risked my neck for you. Twice. We can help you here or send for whatever you need. Please. Trust us a little."

Orrin looked at her hand on his arm. "It's hard to trust someone when it's demanded."

Madi let go and stepped back. "Sorry. Habit." She put her hands in her pockets. "No more grabbing. No demands. Will you at least tell me where you are going?"

Orrin thought about telling her. With [Mind Bastion] up, he was even able to do it mostly with the rational part of his brain. The problem was even rationally, telling her where he would be, while at his weakest and most vulnerable, seemed like a terrible idea.

"He's going to a mind mage named Tony's place," Daniel said, ratting him out.

"Come on, D," Orrin said with irritation in his voice. "If I wanted everyone to know—"

Orrin stopped at the look on Madi's face. He'd seen her look angry, scared, haughty, and joyful. Terrified and shaking was new.

"Quiet Anthony?" Madi's voice was a whisper.

"I mean, he doesn't talk normally, but I definitely wouldn't call him quiet."

Madi gave a signal, and the guard went inside. She looked up and down the street before gesturing for Orrin and Daniel to step closer. "Anthony was a mind mage. A real one. The kind that even the lords of Dey couldn't control. Even my father is wary of him. They say he can make you do anything he wants. He just walks right into your body and can make you kill yourself if you look at him wrong."

Orrin wanted to laugh. Sure, Tony was a little rough, and maybe he had walked right into Orrin's body . . . but he was a good guy. He'd helped Orrin. Plus, Madi's story didn't line up with Tony's own story about his past.

"Have you met him? He seemed nice enough to me. He helped me get through some skill backlash."

Madi shook her head. "When I was younger, my father would scare me with stories of what Anthony would do if I ever went too close to his house. People don't go to him for help."

Orrin distinctly remembered Tony calling himself the boogeyman. *What a lonely existence if even kids are taught to fear you.*

"Well, that's where I'll be if your dad wants to try taking me out," Orrin said flippantly. It wasn't really fair to Madi. She actually had been trying lately. But Madi's attitude toward the man who had helped him was eliciting feelings Orrin had thought he'd left behind.

She just doesn't know him. She wouldn't be scared of him if she just took the time to talk with him. The thoughts tumbled through his mind, and Orrin realized he'd had the same thoughts a hundred times . . . targeted toward himself. Madi was like all the other kids who ignored him and thought he was a freak for being quiet and a little different.

Madi's eyes were wide at Orrin's accusation, and her mouth opened and closed as she tried to find the words.

"That's not fair, Orrin," Daniel said, coming to her rescue. "They've kept their word. Silas hasn't given you any—"

"Any reason to doubt he'd try sticking another sword in me?" Orrin said. *This is getting out of hand fast. I don't want to have this conversation.* "I'll admit Madi has been on her best behavior. She's been a great teammate and really stepped up, especially yesterday. But I didn't think you'd forget who we work for so easily."

Madi had tears in her eyes, but Orrin could see they were angry tears. She was pissed. "Will you never forgive us for that? They went too far. You were only to be roughed up until Daniel used a skill or two. There was to be no actual danger, and we *did* have a healer nearby in case of—"

"A healer? You saw exactly how much good they are. You took a gamble, Madi. You both did. You've given me some reason to trust you . . . to a degree. But your dad?" Orrin laughed and shook his head. "If I don't come back in a few days, you'll know for sure. Try not to let him know I'm staying at Tony's. He might try to kill two problems with one well-placed assassin."

Orrin turned and walked away, using [Teleport] as soon as he could.

Orrin meant to land outside Tony's house. He meant to walk up to the front door and knock.

Instead, he found himself coming to from unconsciousness on the street a block over.

"Sorry." Tony's voice in his head actually sounded a bit relieved. "It's been a long few days, and I'm a bit jumpy."

Orrin looked around. He was alone. "Tony?"

"Shut it," Tony's voice in his head yelled. "I knocked you out with a proximity spell. Most people know not to teleport so near my house."

Orrin guessed it made sense. A mind mage spook who was worried about being killed probably had some defenses set up against attacks.

"Get up. I didn't hit your mind that hard."

Orrin scrambled to his feet and made his way around the corner. He found Tony's house and went to knock.

Madi's stories filled his head, and he hesitated.

"Oh. Scared of me now?"

Orrin didn't know if he actually heard the hurt and fear of rejection in that voice in his head or if he projected it there himself. Either way, he knocked.

"Now? You're a terrifying dude. I've been scared since you made me walk into your house the first time," Orrin answered the air.

A chuckle turned into a full laugh as Tony opened the door and stepped to the side of his narrow house. "What brings you back?"

Orrin grimaced as he entered. "You can't tell?"

Tony's laughter cut, and he stared at Orrin closely. "You fool. At least it's not as bad as last time."

"Not as bad? I've used more mana in the last two days than—"

Tony waved a hand in Orrin's face and turned to walk back inside. "Not as bad, but still unpleasant. You've increased your levels and, if I'm not mistaken, your will? That was smart."

Orrin followed. "That makes a difference?"

Tony grunted. *How does he grunt in my mind?*

"So, you'll help me again?"

Tony started making tea. "Of course. One gold a night. Same as always. Although I'd love to hear why you went out and did something so stupid. You didn't try and fight the Fogbinder, did you?"

Orrin clenched his teeth at the thought of how close Daniel had gotten to his objective. If the Dragoon team hadn't stopped him . . . Why did the [Hero] class draw the person to demons?

"I was kidding. You did? What's this about the Dragoon team?"

"Hey. I thought you promised to stay out," Orrin said, clamping down on his thoughts.

"That was last time. Besides, you're basically screaming. Angry, mixed-up feelings, betrayal. The emotions are always there. I can only get a few pieces of the thoughts underneath. But I'll stay out as much as I can."

Orrin frowned as Tony poured the tea into two cups. "Thank you. I'm sorry. I wouldn't even know where to begin."

Tony smirked as he took a sip of his tea. "Well, you could always start with why the [Hero] went after the demon."

Chapter 48

"What?" Orrin asked, trying to play stupid and gain some time. He needed any excuse to derail Tony's question but also needed to figure out exactly how much Tony knew.

"You were yelling in your mind. You were doing it last time you were here, too, but I didn't catch much. Somehow your skill seems . . . quieter . . . more controlled this visit," Tony explained. "Except when you thought about the Dragoon team and then something about a [Hero] and a demon. I've been stuck in my house for so long that I know a little about a lot." He waved his hand at the books all around. "[Heroes] and demons go hand in hand. So . . . ?"

Orrin was sweating but trying his best not to form a coherent thought in front of the mind mage.

Tony pushed a plate with small cookies across the tiny table. "You don't have to tell me. Like I said last time, I keep lots of secrets here. If you met a [Hero] out there and they made you promise not to share the information, that's fine. I'm just curious. Everyone loves a good [Hero] story."

Orrin formed a single sentence, doing his absolute best to not let his mind wander. "Can you stop reading my thoughts altogether?"

Tony shrugged. "Like I said, I only pick up stray thoughts unless I'm actually trying. Most of your thoughts are better guarded." He pulled his teacup close and looked down at the liquid steaming below his face. "Imagine my ability like this. Your mind and thoughts are this tea. Most people have some natural protection to their mind, like the cup around it. A low-level mind skill would let someone skim your surface thoughts." He dragged a finger across the top of the tea, watching the ripples hit the porcelain.

Tony looked up from the drink. "Of course, some people have naturally stronger cups—or minds. You can also take precautions and get skills that counteract most mind mages." He turned an empty plate upside down and put it on the cup, covering the tea completely. "Harder to see any thoughts that way."

He removed the plate. "My own ability lets me see into the mind a bit more, shielded or not." Tony took a cookie and dunked it into the tea, swirling it before taking a bite. "It's hard to find specific information, and surface thoughts are easiest." His voice continued his explanation as he chewed and swallowed. "But I hear almost every thought around me within a certain radius. It's loud. I've had to learn to tune most of it out." He popped the rest of the treat in his mouth.

Tony leaned across the table to grab another cookie. "Some words always cut through, though. *Hero. Demon. Dragoon.* I had a friend on that team a long time ago. Usually, the guard puts the odd ducks on Dragoon. The expendable squad. She died violently."

"That doesn't answer my question." Orrin focused on the shortbread cookie, counting the pieces as he crumbled it between two fingers.

"No, I can't turn it off completely. Your skill blocks it better than most, and if you focus you can keep me out, but any lapse and your thoughts will tumble out. I really do try, but it's like walking in the rain and trying to not get wet."

Orrin focused on [Mind Bastion], imaging his thoughts stuck inside a metal box instead of the teacup. An image of Tony sitting on the outside, looking at the shiny steel.

"That's amazing. You went completely quiet on me. You did level up."

Orrin ignored Tony and focused, closing his eyes. *I already told Sof that Daniel was a [Hero], which was probably a mistake. He did say he basically already suspected, though. Tony knows I'm not a [Hero] because he already looked over most of my skills and spells last time. If I stay and don't tell him or I try to lie, he'll figure it out. Now that I know I can't think about it, it'll be all I can think about.*

He put his head in his hands. *I have to tell him or leave. I can't leave because I need to turn off [Mind Bastion] and pay the piper for all my mana use.*

Orrin opened his eyes and sighed. "My friend is a [Hero]. We didn't know that demons would trigger some sort of attack mode, and he ran off after the Fogbinder. I went after him. We ran into the Dragoon team and just got back."

Orrin paused and went for broke. "Oh, and I healed a few hundred people in front of the Hospital, so I'm probably on their shit list. A lord of Dey has already tried to have me killed once and I'm sure he will try again. And his daughter knows I'm here. She's terrified of you, by the way. I hear you're a really scary guy."

Tony's smile was anything but scary. "You decided to trust me. Thank you. That must have been hard. I'll pay you back by telling you a secret."

Tony stood up and walked down the hallway to his front door. He double-checked the front lock and stood still with his head against the wood. Then he came back into the kitchen and sat as if nothing had happened.

"Sorry. I wanted to make sure this conversation stayed private. I'm guessing other than your friend the [Hero], I'm the only one who knows."

"Knows what?" Orrin felt ice forming down his spine.

"You don't have to hide it." Tony smiled. "You're a [Hero], too."

"I'm not a [Hero]," Orrin shot back. "I'm a—"

"Yes. I know. You're selling your class as something else. But I heard a few thoughts here and there the last time I was helping you." Tony's voice in his mind stayed calm and unrushed, keeping Orrin from running away. "You landed here with your friend. That's how [Heroes] arrive. You cried out for your mother when you were sick and begged for 'I-B-proven,' which is not a real word. You also tried distracting yourself by thinking of a small box with moving people inside it. That's not something that exists in this world. So you're a [Hero]."

Orrin sat stunned. His secret was out . . . had been out. *How long has he known and why hasn't he done anything?*

"Why? Why tell me now?"

"You trusted me. I'm not a bad person. I have no desire to go on a Quest or get involved in the politics you're sure to find your-self in. But I can be a friend. You have a good heart and a strong sense of what's right. Something I wish I had more of when I was your age."

Orrin's metal box was shaking. Keeping the cascade of thoughts in his mind safe was seeming more and more pointless. Why had he ever thought that he could hide something from a mind mage? Did Silas have this kind of ability, too? Did he already know Orrin was from another world and was just playing them?

"Silas Catanzano?"

"You said you would try to stay out." Orrin tried not to sneer, but his voice was still low and angry.

"Boy, you're doing admirably with a skill you've had for, what . . . a few weeks? But you are screaming into a pillow while I'm right next to you. Some things are going to get through even if I plug my ears. Is Silas the lord that wants you dead?"

". . . yes," Orrin finally responded.

"Then you have nothing to worry about. If he had no use for you, you would be dead. He's the most pragmatic man I've ever had the misfortune of meeting, but he doesn't kill without reason. If he had a reason, you'd be dead already."

Orrin gave in a little. "I have him backed into a corner. He can't get rid of me so easily."

"So he knows your friend is a [Hero] but not you."

"I'm NOT a [Hero]!" Orrin yelled, a little forcefully.

"Shh!" Tony waved his hands at Orrin, then closed his eyes in concentration. They popped back open a few seconds later. "You're lucky my wards are so good. Don't go shouting about [Heroes]."

"I'm not," Orrin whispered dejectedly. "I have proof. So just move along."

"Proof? No. We'll get back to that." Tony's voice in his mind was speeding up in excitement. "How'd you pull one over on Silas?"

"You know him?" Orrin tried to dodge the question.

"In a previous life. Don't change the topic."

Orrin sighed. "My friend said he wouldn't help his daughter and let her be part of our team if he tried to keep me away again."

"Again?" Tony's eyes were shining.

"Silas . . . and maybe his daughter . . . set some goons after us. One stabbed me right here." Orrin pointed to his chest. "They were testing to see if Daniel was a [Hero] and swore they had healers nearby. Promises and apologies, but they also tried to keep me away from him after the last time you helped me."

Tony leaned back in his chair and stared up at the ceiling. No more questions came at him, and Orrin sipped his tea. Tony had put the right amount of honey in again.

"So Silas sets some low-level gutter shit on you, almost kills you, and tries to break the two of you up . . ." Tony's voice drifted. "Yep. He definitely thinks you are just a nobody. Idiot."

Tony tipped his chair back down and looked at Orrin. "Why did you stay with them? Silas has connections and probably flashed a lot of gold at you, but why trust him?"

Orrin shook his head. "I don't trust him. But I don't know anything about this world. I didn't know if he would just kill us or throw us in a cell. My friend seems to have completely forgiven them, though. We had another little fight before I came here."

Tony nodded. "I guess that's not the worst answer I've heard. If you had run, he likely would have tried to just toss you in prison until you did what he wanted. You could have escaped somewhere else, but I'm guessing you were pulled here. [Hero] Quests usually have a rhyme and reason to them. He's also higher level than you and has guards around, so . . . playing it safe was a little smart, I guess."

"I mean, I did kind of scare him into not using his spells or what-ever on us. So we might have gotten away with just saying no."

"His spells? Oh, that [Command] skill? That's harmless. It wears off after a minute and can't be reused on the same person over and over or they get resistant to it. I'm surprised he even tried that on you."

"Wait. That's all that was? I thought he was a mind mage like you?"

Laugher filled Orrin's head as Tony's mouth made odd gasping noises.

"Silas Catanzano . . . a mind mage. That's hilarious." Tony wiped his eyes. "But to more serious matters. Why are you so adamantly refusing that you are a [Hero]? You've told me more salacious details than that."

"I'm not. I'll admit that I'm from another world. My friend and I both arrived in the forest to the east. He's a [Hero]. My class ended up being [Utility Warder]."

"That's odd." Tony leaned in his chair again. "I know you're telling the truth, but summoned people are always classed as a [Hero]. It just makes no sense . . . You said you had proof you aren't one, though. What's that?"

Orrin realized that Tony had steered the topics easily through to this point—the one thing he'd tried to avoid talking about. The one thing he'd crafted his own answers to avoid. The subject of Administrator Access.

"Can we just say I know and leave it at that?"

"Sure," Tony responded, too cheerfully. "But since you are here and going to be throwing up all over me for the next week or so, I'm sure you'll be telling me eventually."

"That's not fair. The deal is—"

"I'm a man of my word. I don't listen in on purpose, but now the thought is in your mind." He smiled evilly. "So you're more likely to tell me."

"That's underhanded."

Tony shrugged. "I'm a mind mage. Kill me if you're unhappy."

Orrin considered going back and taking his chances surviving with Daniel and Madi.

"You could try going back. But part of what saved you last time is my skills. I'm able to shield your psyche from the backlash and keep you alive when your brain tries to turn off. There's an even chance you survive as a slobbering imbecile or die."

"This is blackmail."

Tony held up his hands. "Whoa. That's harsh. I just like puzzles and gossip. I'm not going to use this against you. I've known this whole time we had a [Hero] in Dey and never told a soul. If you truly need to keep this a secret, I'll show you how to use that box in your mind a little better. You seem to be a quick study. You might even be able to pull it off and keep it quiet. I won't try picking the lock. On my honor."

Orrin grimaced. Tony had him over a barrel, and they both knew it. "Teach me."

"Lessons are five gold, up front."

"All that just to get some extra money?" Orrin pulled the gold pieces out and slid them across the table. "You know, I've got a lot of gold and am in need of a teacher. Someone who can get me caught up on everything about this world that I don't know."

Tony smiled. "Now, that sounds like something that could be fun, but I'm not sure gold would be needed. How about we trade? You tell me more about your class, where you came from, and this big secret you're holding. I'll be your personal guide to Asmea. Deal?"

Orrin knew Tony was going to find out one way or another. Even if the man promised not to go searching in his mind, he was going to tell him in a moment of weakness. *Better to get something out of it.*

Tony's smile grew wider. "Looks like it's a deal."

Chapter 49

Orrin hesitated. *Where do I even begin?*

"Um . . . I'm not sure where to start . . ." Orrin trailed off.

"Where are you from?" Tony's eyes were wide with childlike glee.

"Earth. It's a planet with no magic or system. We don't have monsters or demons," Orrin said. "I mean, some people believe in demons and angels, but nothing like things that actually walk around and harm you in plain sight."

"I've read about other worlds with no magic. We can talk more about that later. How did you get here? Was it a cave you walked into? Or an armoire?"

"What? No. I—we got hit by a truck."

"What's a truck?"

Orrin let Tony go off topic, explaining cars to the best of his limited ability. The topic of transportation brought up trains, planes, and space travel.

"You visited a moon?" Tony's face held complete disbelief.

"Not personally, although I guess if I were rich enough, in a few years I could. A bunch of billionaires are trying to make space travel more accessible."

"What's a billionaire?"

"Someone who has more money than they could ever spend, basically," Orrin said with a shrug.

Tony leaned back from his spot over the table. "You let me get distracted. Tell me more about your class. Summoned otherworlders don't usually change from [Hero]."

"I've told you. I've always been [Utility Warder]. It was the only choice left after—"

"What do you mean, choice?"

Orrin sighed and relented. "When I first arrived, the system gave me a bunch of error messages and then rebooted or something. Then it started to . . . read my mind? No, that's not right. It's like it was responding to my wishes. I got this long list of classes with things like [Wizard] or [Fighter] or even [Farmer]." Orrin let out a laugh. Tony did not laugh back. In fact, his face had gone slightly chalky.

"Go on," the voice in Orrin's head said with a reedy timbre.

"I started thinking of what kind of things I'd like to be, you know? Like, healing and buffing but with the ability to do damage. That part hasn't really been a major focus, I guess, but all the classes disappeared as I thought of different things I wanted. They all disappeared."

"And then?" Tony was leaning back in his chair again, trying to look less interested than his voice sounded in Orrin's head.

"The system created [Utility Warder]."

Tony stared into Orrin's eyes for a moment before asking his question. "What aren't you telling me?"

Orrin shrugged. "I don't know if it's relevant."

"It is."

"Sometimes, the system says I have Administrator Access, whatever that means."

Tony slipped, and his chair tumbled backward. He fell to the ground.

"Tony? Are you okay?" Orrin pushed his chair back and hurried around the small table. Tony was already pushing himself to his feet.

Orrin reached out his hand, and Tony scrambled backward.

"I'm sorry. I'm sorry. No more questions. I'll never say a word and . . ."

Orrin tuned out the rambling in his mind and looked down at the broken shell of a man scooting backward on his hands, his legs scrambling to catch purchase as Tony tried to get away from him.

"Tony? What the hell? Stop."

"Yes, sir." Tony's voice quivered in his mind, and the old man held still. His eyes closed, and Orrin saw tears start to flow. "Please. I'm sorry."

A small and dark part of Orrin's mind calculated how much information he could get from the pale and shaking senior citizen cowering in front of him. Whatever Administrator Access meant, Tony was terrified of it. Terrified of *him*. He could make Tony tell him everything about the world or even use his mind magic to get the information he needed to survive. Maybe even the information needed to get home!

That's not me. Orrin shook his head. He reached out and grabbed Tony's hand, pulling the man to his feet.

"Listen. I don't know what Administrator Access is. Even if I did, you have no reason to be scared of me. You saved my life, and I consider you a friend," Orrin said as he helped the man right his chair and sit back down. "I'll get some more tea. Just relax."

Orrin busied himself in the tiny kitchen, pouring more tea from the kettle and bringing the honey and milk to the table with him. He let Tony mix his own and sat quietly, letting him gather himself.

"You really don't know what you can do?" Tony's eyes flickered up and then back down as he twirled his spoon in the tea. "This isn't just a test? I always thought you were a myth."

"I'm still the same guy who threw up all over your sheets a few weeks ago. I'm learning as I go here," Orrin said.

Tony let out a sigh and sat upright in his chair again. Orrin hadn't noticed how much he'd sunk in on himself. "Administrator Access is a legend. Something that every country and king would try to get their hands on. Only fragments of stories remain, and most people believe it's not a real thing, but what does exist is terrifying. Administrators could change a person's class, grant Quests, and change the course of a person's life! Or they could rip every skill and spell you'd ever learned away and leave you without the system completely. Every story I've ever read with an Administrator has at least one in the role of a bad guy, taking everything away from a person."

"So, are they people or gods?" Orrin asked.

"What's a god?" Tony's face was puzzled at the new word. His entire attitude had changed from five minutes prior.

"Someone who sits in the clouds and either messes with people's lives or does nothing as we screw everything up," Orrin replied. "I guess that's not fair. Some people believe they do good . . . or are good. I'm not explaining this well, am I?"

"I'm not sure," Tony answered. "Administrators were just people. They lived a long time, but they could die. Some records seem to show they lived among us, but others say they ruled. It's a big topic for historians."

"So, an Administrator is just a class? That makes no sense. I'm a [Utility Warder]."

"No. They had their own classes. Usually unique or rare ones. One reputable history book that survived the breaking of the world spoke of a few of them. A group that had led everyone into a golden age of sorts. They each had massive powers and were in the eighties to nineties in level. They just had Administrator Access as well."

"And that's what you're scared of? That I have this power? I barely know what it does."

Tony sipped his tea as he answered. "That's honestly more terrifying. What if you get mad that I basically forced you to tell me and take everything away from me? If you take away my skills and spells, I have enemies that would rain down upon me within the hour. I'm not scared of death, but they wouldn't kill me." He shivered.

Orrin considered his words carefully. "Tony, if I ever accidentally used a skill on you, I'd figure out how to undo it and protect you until I could."

He watched the man slowly unwind a bit more. They sat in silence. Orrin had finished his tea and couldn't drink any more. He stood and put his cup in the sink.

Orrin turned around and leaned on the counter. "What exactly could an Admin—"

Quest Complete
Defend the Wall—Help push back a Horde
Reward: Calculating . . .
Horde Type: Demon Fogbinder x 2
Participation: >1%
Calculating . . .
3,500 XP

Level 12 Obtained!
+10 AP

"Ah, what the fuck?"

Tony paled again. "What's happening?"

"Quest completion? Oh shit, did killing those few Fetid dogs count as repelling a Horde? Shit. I'm going to kill Daniel."

It took a few minutes for Orrin to explain the Quest and everything that had gone into avoiding it, only for the [Hero] to ruin it all.

Tony let out another one of his inaudible laughs using his real voice. The gasping sound made Orrin's skin crawl.

"So . . . after all Silas went through to keep you away until you could gain an actual large amount of participation . . . your friend drags you into a battle and kills a few pups. Oh, that is too good!"

Orrin was scratching the counter, trying to pick a small fleck of paint off. "Yeah. Hilarious. Just a waste of a great opportunity."

"Oh, please tell me that his daughter also helped? You mentioned Daniel shared the Quest with her. I wish I could see his face when she—"

"She didn't go out and help, so she probably still has the Quest," Orrin cut him off. His head snapped up. "I can have her reshare the Quest with us! We can . . ." Orrin trailed off as Tony shook his head.

"It doesn't work like that. Quests are unique things. You can't game the system like that. It's been attempted. Usually, the [Hero] is the only one who can give a Quest. It might actually be that if he completed it, the Quest will disappear from anyone else he shared it with."

"But the level Quests didn't disappear." Orrin started to pace. "If that one didn't, then maybe this one will still be there for the rest of the party."

"Honestly, I don't know. Most of the information on the [Hero] class is locked up tight by the nobility and foreign governments. I'm not sure any one person actually knows even half of what must exist on them."

Tony fell into silence again. Orrin tried to remember what they had been talking about, but the disappointment of getting the Quest dulled his memory. Instead, he asked, "So, are you still willing to tell me more about the world? Or should we wait until after I do my best impression of dying?"

Tony smirked. "If you survive, I'll be your guide to this crap hole. You ready?"

"As ready as I'll ever be." Orrin grabbed the pitcher of water off the counter. "I'm bringing this up with me. I remember how thirsty I was last time."

Tony stood and gestured to the door. "Up the stairs. You remember the way."

Orrin grimaced and climbed the steps to hell.

Orrin's first time detoxing from [Mind Bastion] and [Blood Mana] had taken four full days and most of the last night. The second time lasted five full days.

The only difference was that Orrin remembered every excruciating minute this time.

He cried in pain as lances of fire spread through his veins and screamed as something pierced the backs of his eyes with cold iron. Tony tried to feed him, but for the first three days, Orrin had no appetite and barely could keep water inside before vomiting bile down his chest. When he finally did keep some bread down, each swallow was glass, cutting his throat as the sustenance settled in his empty stomach like a weight.

Never again, he cried to himself, hugging a pillow and wet with sweat. *Never again.*

Daniel never came to check up on him.

One day short of a week later, Orrin woke from his first sleep of more than two hours. He remembered Tony singing to him again, even though the man had stayed downstairs. He'd drifted and dreamed of his mom. She was making him pancakes and yelling at him to come downstairs. He could almost smell them.

His stomach rumbled, and Orrin held the wall for support as he stood.

"Wait for me. I'll help you down the stairs," Tony's voice said in his head.

Orrin let the old man take most of his weight as they made their way to the kitchen. Tony had some boiled eggs and toast smeared with honey on a plate ready for Orrin.

"Thank you. Again," he rasped out as he slumped into the chair. He ate ravenously and downed an entire pitcher of water. Tony just sat quietly and waited.

Orrin finished his plate and wiped his mouth.

"If you do that again, it'll likely kill you," Tony whispered in his mind. "You need to learn to control yourself."

"I survived, didn't I?" Orrin said, feeling a little cocky. *Is this how Daniel feels all the time? Lucky and invincible?*

"Only because I used every trick I have to keep you from going insane or drifting off in your sleep," Tony said. He blinked hard and shook his head. "I'm tired. I'm going to sleep now. I haven't been able to get much, what with watching you. Don't leave. We need to have a long chat."

Orrin nodded and pulled up his status. *I can get a few new—*

Tony stood and put his hand on Orrin's shoulder. "And don't buy anything. If you have extra ability points, you're going to need them." He stumbled up the stairs, leaving Orrin alone in the kitchen.

"What should I do, then? I'm not tired anymore," he yelled up the stairs.

The response came back crisp with condescension in his ears. "Clean up your mess."

Orrin groaned and grabbed a mop.

Chapter 50

A few hours later and Orrin had cleaned the sickroom, the kitchen, and even tried sweeping the hallway to the front of the house; however, the door was magically locked and he couldn't get it open. He left the small pile of dirt pushed to the side.

Tony's kitchen had a long counter, a sink, and a small ice chest. Orrin helped himself to some slices of meat that looked like steak and made something that he was hesitant to call dinner.

Tony clomped down the stairs just as Orrin finished.

"What did you do to that?" His face scrunched up as he gestured at the charred exterior.

"I tried to cook." Orrin grimaced and pushed the other chair out with his foot. "I can cut it in half if you want."

"Why not?" Tony said as he sat down.

Orrin cut the meat in two, finding it well-done all the way through. He grabbed another plate and transferred half, giving Tony the bigger piece.

They both took a bite.

"Bleh." Tony spat the meat back out. "If you wanted to kill me, you could have just stabbed me in my sleep."

Orrin chewed and chewed. The meat did not break down. "What is this?"

"It was supposed to be cold cuts for a sandwich. It's Alnursteer."

"Steer? Like a cow?"

"Sort of. Alnursteer have ten legs and are the size of a barn. They are raised specifically for the meat, but you eat it raw. I didn't know what it tastes like cooked . . . Now I know why."

Tony stood and dumped both plates into the trash bin. "You didn't use any ability points, did you? You'll need one at least, and we can talk about some others."

Orrin glanced at his status. "I have fourteen points."

"That's more than we'll need. I've been doing a little research since the last time you were here." Tony grabbed a book with multiple papers bulging out between pages. "I have a few theories, but first you should open up your skill store. You really need to buy [Obscure]. It should only be one ability point. It'll be faster if you just read it."

Orrin pulled up the skill in his store.

[Obscure] Erase skills and spells from your Status. Prevents closer inspection from [Identify], [Detect], and similar skills. 1 AP.

Would you like to purchase for 1 AP?
Yes or No?

"So it lets me hide specific skills? Doesn't [Hide Status] already do that?"

"[Hide Status] lets you block most scrying spells against your specific class. [Obscure] won't ever show up on your list for others. Nobody will ever know you have it unless you tell them. You can hide skills or spells. It's one of the first skills an aspiring mind mage takes, because if a guard catches you with the wrong skill . . ."

Orrin trusted Tony enough to hit Yes. [Obscure] appeared on his status.

"So I just concentrate on the skill and—" As Orrin did what he said, [Obscure] grayed out on his status. "Oh, that's cool. So I'm guessing I should hide [Blood Mana]?"

"And [Mind Bastion]. It's unique. It'll raise a lot of questions." Tony started pulling papers out of his book and spreading them around the table. "Tell me when you're done. I'm not sure where to start here."

Orrin grayed out [Blood Mana] and [Mind Bastion]. "I'll still be able to use them, right?"

"Yes. [Obscure] does nothing but create a barrier that other scrying spells can't pierce. You wanted information on the world, right? What do you know?"

"What we've learned from the books we bought is that the world is called Asmea. There are a few different countries, named Odrana, Veskar, and Dey. There was a [Hero] who ended the world a long time ago and put everyone together on this one landmass, and through the Pass is monster land."

Tony nodded along and waited when Orrin stopped talking. "That's it?"

"I've been kind of busy. I didn't exactly go in for a history lesson."

"How has nobody else figured out you're not from here?"

"Hey! I've done a good job keeping my mouth shut . . . and I've had Daniel to distract them," Orrin said, his voice trailing off quietly at the end.

Tony pulled a blank piece of paper out of his stack and wrote something, then begin to fill in Orrin's lacking knowledge of the world.

"Odrana is Dey's closest neighbor, and while not an ally, they would never attack Dey. No country would, as they'd then have to fund and maintain the Wall and Pass. Dealing with the Hordes for all of civilization is not an easy or cheap task."

"What does Dey produce for money, then? I haven't seen large farms or mines or anything, really."

"The Guild," Tony responded. "It started off the remnants of whatever Guild was from before, but turned into a powerhouse of its own. In the time before Odrana and Veskar rose up, they helped set up different merchant lines safely, explored areas and staked claims to different resources, and escorted large groups of people to the unexplored parts of our new home. They have a presence in every city but consider Dey the main base. They pay taxes to keep the city running, as does everyone else."

Tony held up a finger. "Hold your other questions for now. Odrana is ruled by a family of exceptionally talented mages, and they are usually pacifists. The family's oldest son recently ousted his mother as the leader, though. I'm sure you've heard of the war?"

"With the elves, right?" Orrin gestured for a piece of paper, and Tony handed one over, along with a small, primitive pencil. He started to take notes. *Daniel needs this information, too. I still can't believe he didn't visit me.*

Tony sighed in Orrin's head. "Yes. Although rumors abound on who started what, anyone who knows the elves knows they would not leave their forest. A few hundred years of persecution and they almost all retreated to their last bastion. I believe the new mage lord is trying to expand his own power by taking the elven forest homelands as his own."

Orrin considered his Quest

> **Stop the War in Odrana**
> **Reward: 200,000 XP and Variable.**
> **Failure: Loss of 10 levels.**

I need to figure out the best way to stop the war. Orrin wrote down a bullet point of things to do. He used [Through the Ages] to keep it private.

"What's that you're doing?" Tony peered at the paper. "A hidden writing skill? Useful."

Orrin finished writing and looked up. "So, hypothetically, how would one stop the war?"

"Short of killing the mage lord and placing another pacifist at the head of the family? Destroy the elven forest. They'd have to relocate and spend the next hundred or so years setting up in the forests south of Dey. Is that the [Hero] Quest?" Tony's eyes shone as he asked.

"Yep," Orrin said. "Here, take a look." He gave a blue box to Tony without actually sharing the Quest.

"Stop the war in Odrana. That's the Quest." Orrin told the truth and lied at the same time. Luckily, Tony was distracted and reading the Quest box.

"Amazing!" Tony's hands held the air to the sides of the box like it was a physical thing. "I guess you could also try to just stop the fighting. An announced [Hero] holds a lot of weight in the politics of this world."

"What's an announced [Hero]?"

Tony gave Orrin a look that screamed "stupid" without actually saying anything.

"Just someone who isn't hiding and announced it, huh?" Orrin asked sheepishly.

Tony put another piece of paper over the first. "Odrana covers the most land area of the populated world. It produces most of the food we import and is split into a few different territories that all answer to the Sanerris family. That's the mage lord's family. Each territory also has its own specialty products or commodities, but Mistlight is the crown jewel. It's the only port town that survives the monsters of the sea and that can actually send out ships. Nobody has ever returned with proof of other lands, but they still have merchants that can travel the coastline and the deeper rivers. I've heard they are taking most of the army by boat to the coast of the elven forest to attack. Mistlight also is home to the Sanerris School for Spells, one of the most sought-after education locations for magic users."

Tony continued and pulled out a small, less detailed map than the one Silas kept. "This entire area is Odrana." He dragged a finger along the top half of the map. "This is the elven forest." A small circle above Dey, abutting the sea above.

"And the forest next to Dey? Is that under Odrana's or Dey's control?" Orrin pointed out where he and Daniel had first arrived.

"Technically, it belongs to Veskar, but nobody lives there. The lords of Dey sent out teams to keep it clear of dungeons. I'm sure they could send a bill, but Veskar is . . . well . . . Veskar."

"Guy from another planet here," Orrin said, pointing to himself. "I don't know what that means."

Tony rocked in his chair in thought. "Veskar is the land that nobody else wanted. It isn't as fertile, it doesn't have much in the way of resources, and there are a lot of swamps. People who come from there are usually a little rougher and more ready to fight. It's not so much an actual country as a loose collection of groups that have agreed not to kill each other. A lot of them end up joining the Guild. Some of the best fighters in the Guild are from Veskar, but there is the odd magic user or even healer.

"Veskar is also where the orcs ended up after the dwarf and orc wars."

"What about the dwarves? I've seen a few around."

Tony shook his head. "Nobody actually knows. Well, we know they hollowed out a mountain, but nobody knows which one. They have an entire network of [Teleportation Sites] set up in the major countries. They trade for food and keep away from the other races for the most part. They bring weird things back sometimes, too, like monster hides and parts. So a few of the higher-ups think they have another way through the mountains."

Orrin wrote more notes. "That reminds me, I have some Kniferunner legs I need to sell."

"I know a few people who would be interested in that. I'll give you their names. What else do you want to know?"

"So much." Orrin organized his thoughts. "I've got three big ones related to my skills and spells . . . if that's okay."

Tony gestured for Orrin to continue.

"Obviously the first thing is my [Blood Mana]. Is there a way to use it and not get hit with the consequences?"

Tony pulled a few more papers and slid them across the table. "Maybe."

"What? That's it?" Orrin pulled the papers close and browsed them. Some were notes from the same [Vampire] book he had bought already. A few seemed promising, though. Most of it was terrifying.

"So if I use my own mana, then use [Blood Mana] to refill it using a living thing's mana, this will definitely happen?"

"Every time. I couldn't find a hard number for how much or how long it takes, but your class would change to [Vampire]."

Tony's notes were a study of multiple books. In short, using [Blood Mana] on others was how a person could "earn" the new class change. Draining a person of their mana could also kill a person if overdrawn, and the descriptions in Tony's notes were graphic.

Eyes shriveled in her head . . . veins standing up against the mottled skin . . . hair dry and brittle . . . rigor mortis of the face, set into a broken-jawed scream . . .

Orrin pushed the notes away. "I just stopped throwing up. Why?"

Tony leaned across the table and waited for Orrin to look him in the eyes. "I wanted you to understand just how dangerous that skill can be."

He pushed a single piece of paper to Orrin.

After studying the [Vampire] for several months, I made a fascinating discovery. He could drain his own health for more mana. After I had tapped him dry, the subject cast his [Hypnotic Gaze] on my assistant. The boy died, but I was able to keep the subject contained. I began watching his intake with greater care and was able to create an [Analyze] subskill that monitored his mana and health distribution during the use of his blood skill. After this, the experiment was—

"What experiment? What happened?"

Tony waved a hand over the papers. "That doesn't matter. If I recall, the [Vampire] broke out and killed dozens before being put down. Did you notice the [Analyze] subskill? If he created something to monitor the intake and outtake of [Blood Mana], you can, too. Maybe even a way to track how much you can use a day before taking backlash."

"How would I even know what to monitor, though? Sure, I know how much mana I've got, and I know how many times I cycle to get to full, but I don't actually know what that means."

Tony pulled out another stack of papers and smiled. "How much do you know about mana?"

Chapter 51

"What do I know about mana? I know how much I have and that I have to use it to cast a spell. I know I can only drink two or three potions a day and most people don't reset their mana until after they sleep, although I don't know why," Orrin said. He stretched out in his chair.

Tony noticed the stretch. "I'd say let's go for a walk, but this conversation should be as private as possible. A lot of what I'm going to tell you isn't exactly common knowledge. Sorry."

Orrin shrugged.

"Mana is your life force or will. It's the mental energy of your body. When you cast a spell, you are exerting your will upon the world and changing it. To do so, you use a part of yourself. If you choose to increase your will, you expand your life force and are able to use more as a result. On the other hand, your intelligence is how well you can utilize that life force and tap into the neutral mana all around, which is why the price of spells is cheaper with a higher intelligence. When a person sleeps, they are recharging their own mana pool. There are a few ways to refill your pool, but that is different than recharging. Mana potions and [Blood Mana], for instance."

"That makes sense. I guess [Meditate] just allows a slow recharge, though?"

"[Meditate] is an outlier. It recharges your mana pool like sleep, so any recovered life force, or mana, won't count as refilled mana. Refilling your mana pool with potions is different. You are using somebody else's mana, and that creates some instability in your life force. Drink too many and your body prevents your life force from recovering. This manifests in different ways for different people. Some lose the ability to ever do magic again, some go insane, and some just die."

"The same with health potions, right?" Orrin stopped himself from picking at a loose splinter in the table.

"Not at all. Health and skill activations are separate topics. Well, maybe not completely. What you are doing with [Blood Mana] is converting your own health into mana, so I guess I should step back and explain that before going any farther."

Tony stood and walked around the small kitchen, windmilling his arms. "I'm going to start at the basics, so bear with it. Strength is, in general, how strong you are. Dexterity is how fast you can move or react. But neither is completely just physical."

"But I—"

"Don't interrupt or I'll lose my train of thought," Tony said, pointing a finger in Orrin's direction. "A person with high dexterity moves faster, yes. But it also lets them process and think a bit faster. A lot of people miss that. It's why keeping your stats level is so important, but every generation thinks they can find a way around it. If you dump straight into one stat, it always backfires. You create your own weakness. But that's only half of it. You also have to deal with constitution."

Tony continued talking as he walked in circles around the table. Orrin stood and leaned back on the wall, creating more space around the small room for Tony to pace. "Constitution dictates how much health you have, but it also is so much more. It's how well you can take a hit or survive a spell. It reduces the damage you take and lets you survive longer without food. Constitution is the most overlooked stat we have, and people never give it the credit it's due. Your health is just a construct. A single hit can kill a person with one health or one hundred. I'm sure you know about critical hits?"

Orrin nodded.

"Your health is just a representation of how much damage your body can take before you go down. Even at zero health, a person might be able to survive if somebody is around to keep them stable. It's slipping into the negatives that kills you."

Tony turned to Orrin. "Do you know why your mana, your life force, will reset when you sleep, but your health can take days or weeks to fully recover without a healing spell or potion?"

Orrin shook his head. "But I'm guessing you'll tell me."

"Don't be an ass," Tony said as he stuck the stump of his tongue out at Orrin. "Your strength and dexterity are your life energy. The physical part of you that makes you . . . you—the meat sack that walks around and does what your mind tells it to do. Your will and intelligence are your life force, the intangible pieces—your thoughts, your dreams, your mind."

"So the physical stats are my body and the magic stats are my mind?"

"In general, yes. But also no. Because remember I said dexterity has some mental aspects? Well, so do will and intelligence. Even strength to an extent. I'm not going to go down that rabbit hole, but suffice it to say, the two sets have a small piece of the other in each other. Does that make sense?"

"Like yin and yang?"

"What's that?" Tony stopped and looked at Orrin.

Orrin walked over to the table and drew a circle. He separated it into two sides with a curvy S and doodled a yin and yang symbol, complete with shading and two smaller inversed circles inside.

"It represents dark and light, I think. How the two need each other and are actually part of each other," Orrin explained.

Tony stood over the paper for a long silent minute. "This is the best explanation for stats I have ever seen. Do you know what the circle is? The two halves connected into one?"

"Yeah, I told you. It's a yin and yang symb—"

Tony slapped Orrin upside the head. "This side here, the darker one. It's your strength and dexterity. The other is your intelligence and will. What is missing?"

"Constitution?"

"Constitution. Your life energy and life force working together. Constitution is your health, but it's also your life energy and life force. Without constitution, you have neither strength nor will. Without the others, you don't have constitution. It's more than just your HP. It builds a buffer for all your other stats." Tony drew his finger in the circle around Orrin's drawing. "It encapsulates and protects everything."

Orrin stared at his sketch. "Huh?"

Tony looked down at the ground and took a deep breath. "When a fighter uses a skill, what do you think he's doing?"

"Huh?" Orrin was feeling more and more stupid.

"When your friend uses a skill, not a spell or something that uses mana, what do you think is generating that energy?" Tony pushed.

"I . . . hadn't really thought about it, to be honest," Orrin replied.

"Some skills, like weapon-fighting skills, are innate. They just become part of a person. Others use mana, but most fighting skills don't have a cost to them. They can just be activated . . . but only so many times close together." Tony looked Orrin in the eye. "This is a secret that a lot of organizations keep very close and dear. Constitution is the important stat. Strength lets a person hit harder and dexterity lets them swing faster, but constitution is how strong their body is. It's how quickly the skill can recharge and how many times a person's body can take the damage of using a skill. Have you ever seen a fighter type overuse a skill? They can't. They get tired and run out of energy. That's constitution protecting them. It's the same when you use too much mana—your body shuts you down."

"But why does it only take sleeping to regain your . . . life force, but life energy takes so much longer?" Orrin finally felt like the wheel was turning in his head again.

"Good question." Tony's eyes glimmered. "What do you think?"

"Please don't play teacher like that. Just tell me."

Tony frowned. "You really are no fun. Remember what I said about will and intelligence earlier? You are using your own life force to exert change on the world around you? There is life everywhere. When you sleep, your body simply absorbs it. It's like how plants absorb sunlight for nutrients. You do the same when you sleep. Some part of the brain shuts down and you can convert that neutral life force into your own. But health is more than just life force, right?"

"It's life force and life energy," Orrin said, peering down at his circle.

"Mostly, yes. There's a lot more technical stuff, but that's the main idea. You can't create life energy without healing spells, which is really just a fancy conversion of life force into life energy. Otherwise, you have to let your body's natural processes work and restore whatever you lost."

Orrin stood silent and then began to scribble notes under the yin and yang doodle. Then he had a thought.

"When we were all in the dungeon, I used a spell to boost everybody's stats by a lot. But not constitution. Everybody but me and Daniel got sick. Like passed-out-on-the-floor sick. They had all these status effects like fatigue and dizziness and . . ." He tried to remember the others.

"Brain fog and nausea?"

"Yes. Wait, how do you know?"

"Just because you are unique in being able to boost another person's stats doesn't mean people can't do it to themselves. There are a few classes—the one that comes to mind is [Berserker]. The person can use a strength-increase skill for a time at the cost of being able to tell friend from foe. They destroy nearly everything in their path. But if their constitution is too low, they pay the price on the other side of the skill use."

"So the entire reason they got sick was a low constitution score?"

Tony shrugged. "That's my theory. I have no idea why you or the [Hero] didn't also have the same backlash. Maybe he has a skill that stops the effects. Maybe [Mind Bastion] protected you. We have no way of knowing."

Orrin sat back down. Tony joined him.

"So if they just increased their constitution, I could buff them again without worrying about them getting sick? Wait. Dragoon team didn't get sick, either, from one of my buffs. Maybe they didn't get sick."

"Finding out would be a good idea. The more information we have, the better we can plan. But there's another thing you haven't thought of or asked. What do you think cycling, as you call it, does?"

Orrin thought. *[Blood Mana] lets me turn health or life energy into life force. [Heal Small Wounds] lets me turn life force, or mana, into life energy.*

"I'm just turning life energy into life force and back again," Orrin said aloud. "But the cost isn't the same. I'm doing an even exchange from health to mana, but it's cheaper to heal up again."

"And because you are using less life force . . ." Tony trailed off.

Orrin imagined the dark and light sections of his drawing moving back and forth. "The extra has to come from somewhere. Even exchange and all that."

Tony looked surprised. "I didn't realize you knew that."

"I barely remember it. Something about a law of physics."

"What's physics?" Tony's eyes shone with his natural curiosity. His hair seemed to stick out even more.

"Later. So, when I'm healing, I'm actually using some of my mana but also some of that neutral mana in the air you mentioned?"

"Got it in one." Tony beamed. "Top marks for you."

"So that's why I get sick if I cycle too much."

"Half-right. You also use [Mind Bastion] to ignore what your body is saying. You could probably get away with cycling a bit more if your constitution was higher as well. Or . . ."

"Or what?"

"You can buy [Analyze] and we can try to create a subskill that lets you know exactly how much cycling you can do without long-term effects. Then you'll know when to stop and I won't have to clean vomit out of my hair again."

Orrin pulled up his store.

[Analyze] Monitor target. 5 AP.

Would you like to purchase for 5 AP?
Yes or No?

"Monitor target? That's it?"

"It's one of those skills that grows. It doesn't cost more ability points, and I've heard of some very impressive things it can do."

"You don't even have it?"

"I haven't leveled in years. You think I have ability points left over?"

Orrin considered. *Five ability points is a lot for a gamble. It might not even work.*

He sighed.

Yes. Purchase.

[Analyze] was added to his list of skills.

"What's next?"

Chapter 52

Tony smirked. "You just use your new skill."

Orrin waited. "What else?"

Tony shook his head. "Nothing else. Try it on this." He pushed the half-empty cup of tea sitting on the table toward Orrin.

Orrin used [Analyze].

Black Tea

"You just had me spend five ability points on this?" Orrin nearly yelled. "What good is this?"

Tony laughed with his halting choking sound. "Boy, did you really think it would be so easy? Do it again."

Orrin used the skill.

Black Tea from Veskar

"It says 'from Veskar' now," Orrin muttered. "Why did it give more information?"

"The more you monitor something, the more you learn. You could keep using that on this swill and eventually it would tell you what region it was grown in and how long it's been since the tea leaves were harvested. But that's not the point. Do it again."

Orrin complied, but nothing new appeared in the box. He tried again and again and again.

"I did it five times," Orrin complained. "Nothing new is happening."

Tony pointed to the counter behind them. "Can you grab those two canisters of tea there?"

Orrin stood. "Why?"

Tony waited for Orrin to grab the canisters and sit back down. He turned one container around so Orrin could read the handwriting on the dark glass jar. *Veskarian Black Tea.*

"I don't get it."

"A lesson within a lesson. Use your eyes before you use your skill. You might pick up something." Tony turned the second canister around. *Veskarian Green Tea.*

Tony smiled and rolled his hand. "Again."

Orrin used [Analyze] on the green tea.

Green Tea from Veskar, Spalril Territory

"I still don't get it."

Tony sighed in Orrin's mind. "If you know something about the item you're analyzing, you don't have to waste time learning the basics. Keep going."

Orrin used [Analyze] another twenty times or so before it happened—the skill stopped working. "It didn't activate. Why did the skill stop working?"

"You've used up your ability for now," Tony responded.

"How?"

Tony shrugged. "Same way you use up your mana. I told you already, skills have to recharge just like spells. I'm actually surprised you were able to activate it so many times. You definitely have something affecting your constitution."

"What was the point of doing that?"

Tony reached across the table and patted Orrin's hand. "Kid. You are an impatient ass. You need to slow down. You are still recovering from your last attempt to off yourself. There's no rush, and I'm trying to teach you the best I can. I've never had a student before, so be patient."

Orrin swallowed the words in his mouth and tried a different route. "Can you at least tell me what I should be doing with [Analyze]?"

Tony nodded and put the two canisters of tea back on the shelf. "Every day, preferably before you go to sleep, use the skill on yourself. Try to do it while using spells and while using [Mind Bastion]. Try it with [Blood Mana], but no more than one cycle a day. It might take a few weeks or months, but you—"

"Months? Tony, I don't want to be here another few months. I have to—"

Tony slammed his hand on the counter. "Listen!" His voice echoed in Orrin's head. "You need to get a handle on yourself. Do you realize how advanced your spells are? You've broken into higher magics already. A normal mage gets a hundred mana a day if they're lucky to practice, and you've used that much in five minutes, only to do it again and again. You need to understand what you are doing to yourself or you could die. You have to put in the work and be careful or you'll kill yourself, Reed!"

Orrin waited and watched Tony breathing hard. When the man seemed to catch his breath after his tirade, Orrin asked, "Who's Reed?"

Tony's eyes flickered. "Who?"

"You called me Reed."

Tony waved his hand. "No, I didn't. Wait half an hour and try to use [Analyze] again. Use it on yourself this time. I'm going out to get some more food—you've cleaned me out." His voice continued as he walked down the hall to the front door. "Don't let anyone inside."

The door slammed closed.

Orrin was left alone.

He waited about half an hour and started using [Analyze] on himself. Instead of the status that [Identify] gave, he received a weird amalgamation of information.

Orrin. Age 17. Heart rate 68 bpm. Weight 130 pounds. Height 5 foot, 10 inches.

After half an hour of nothing, Orrin got bored and started looking through his other spells. He noticed a blinking cursor on his status. *I must have leveled [Teleport] when I was coming back from the Dragoon party.*

Orrin
Utility Warder
Level 12 (1,990/3,000)
HP: 90
MP: 380

Strength: 9
Constitution: 9
Dexterity: 9
Will: 28
Intelligence: 11

Abilities:
[Mind Bastion]
[Dimension Hole]
[Identify]
[Blood Mana]
[Map] [Party View], [Monster View], [Trap View],
[Zoom]
[Side Steps] Level 3 (9/300)
[Mana Pool]
[Through the Ages]
[Analyze]

Spells:
[Calm Mind] 5 MP
[Heal Small Wounds] Level 1, 5 MP; Level 2, 10 MP;

Level 3, 20 MP (740/10,000)
[Camouflage] Level 1, 10 MP; Level 2, 10 MP
(210/10,000)
[Lightstrike] 10 MP
[Ward] 20 MP
[Inverse] 5 MP
[Utility Ward] Level 1, 100 MP; Level 2, 200 MP
[Ice Sword] 1 MP per sword
[Teleport] 50 MP per person (5,000/5,000)!
[Ice Ward] 20 MP
[Increase Strength] Level 1 5 MP; Level 2 10 MP;
Level 3 15 MP (1,530/10,000)
[Increase Dexterity] Level 1 5 MP; Level 2 10 MP;
Level 3 15 MP (1,620/10,000)
[Increase Will] Level 1 5 MP; Level 2 10 MP;
Level 3 15 MP (735/10,000)
[Increase Intelligence] Level 1 5 MP; Level 2 10
MP; Level 3 15 MP (1,155/10,000)

Would you like to upgrade [Teleport] for 10 AP?
Yes or No?

"Fuck," Orrin whispered. He only had eight points left after buying [Analyze]. Every few minutes he used the skill again, but nothing had changed.

I could buy a few low-level spells and create more wards, but I'm not sure what would be best. With Tony storming out, Orrin felt more alone. He'd been sick for a week and hadn't seen anybody but the crazed old man. *Why didn't Daniel visit?*

Orrin spent an hour going through different interesting-sounding spells and skills in the store and even considered buying the [Alchemy] skill again. In the end, he saved his ability points for now. *I might need to create a new ward on whatever mission we do next—or maybe I can save a lot of time if I just level [Teleport] . . . I'll ask Daniel.*

Orrin used a few buffs to decrease his mana and then started using [Analyze] again.

On the third try, something new came up.

Mana Regeneration: 1 MP/min

Well, that's promising, he thought. *Only another million hours of doing this and I'll be able to rebuild my [Identify] ability.*

He blood cycled a little health and tried again. Nothing.

Orrin sighed.

Three hours later, Tony returned. It was dark outside, and he brought back no groceries, but Orrin was smart enough to not say anything. Tony made some cold-cut sandwiches and told Orrin he could leave after dinner.

"Why? I'm just now learning and—"

Tony waved a hand to silence him. "This isn't a punishment. You can keep practicing [Analyze] on your own. In a few weeks, come back. If you have questions, come back. But you should go tell your friends that you're alive. They were worried, so you should probably—"

"What do you mean, they were worried? Did Daniel come?" Tony stared at Orrin until he hung his head. "Sorry."

Tony harrumphed and ran his hand through his hair. "The boy came with the young Catanzano girl. She stayed well back but seemed inclined to attack me if I did anything spooky." He smiled at the nice memory. "I resisted the urge to yell 'boo' in her mind . . . It was close."

Orrin chuckled, and Tony seemed to lighten a bit. "Your friend Daniel . . . he's hurting." Tony pushed a few crumbs around the table. "I don't get involved, and I rarely speak on what I hear to others . . . you know this." He looked up at Orrin. "He's lost, and I don't just mean in this world. He truly was worried for you. Not that he fully knows what you went through, but the worry was there. He loves you like a brother." Tony turned his head quickly.

Orrin put his sandwich down. "He's got a funny way of showing it. We keep getting into fights and he doesn't care about the backlash from my skills."

Surprising Orrin, Tony smiled. "Yeah. Brothers are like that. Nobody fights with you like a brother." He looked up with shining eyes. "Daniel might be an asshole sometimes, but he's your friend. Don't let him forget it. He's feeling the pressure of being the [Hero], and I think something happened while you were out. He showed up here two days after you started your recovery and again two days before you were up. I wouldn't let him in and sent him on his way . . . Don't give me that face, I told him you were doing fine without him. I don't need the whole town in my house. But the second time, he looked haggard. I'm not sure what happened, but he seemed desperate for you to wake up."

Orrin listened and smushed some of his bread with his finger. He opened his mouth but couldn't find the words.

Tony reached over the table and ruffled his hair. "I know. I'm the best and you'll miss all our talks. You can come back tomorrow if you want. We still have lots to talk about. I still have questions, too. I'm not sure I believe in your flying buildings."

"Airplanes." Orrin laughed.

"Mmm-hmm, sure."

"Thanks, Tony."

The man grunted and stood, turning his back to the table. He busied himself at the counter. "Get on out now. Don't forget to keep practicing [Analyze]."

Orrin used [Camouflage] through the streets. He could have used [Teleport], but after being cooped up in Tony's house for so long, the night breeze felt great.

He passed by the square in front of the Hospital, taking care to not bump into anyone. Somebody had already scrubbed the cobblestones of blood, and the few areas of grass that seemed darker were difficult to make out in the half-moon light.

Orrin had almost made it out of the square when he noticed the sounds of a fight. *It's not your problem, Orrin. You don't have to play hero tonight. Just go home and chat with Daniel.*

Orrin kept walking for a dozen steps and then heard a wheeze of pain. He stopped and balled his fists, trembling.

That wasn't the sound of a fight. Somebody was being beaten.

Orrin wasn't a stranger to being bullied. Even with Daniel as his friend, the occasional mouth breather thought Orrin would make a great punching bag. Daniel wasn't able to be around all the time, and Orrin had taken his fair share of beatdowns.

A wicked smile lit up his face. *Mugger or bully, I can do magic now.*

Orrin turned back and swiftly made his way to the alley one street over. He was surprised to find two boys and a girl, all his age, standing over another form. All four were in the white garb of the Hospital.

Orrin almost left then, but one of the standing boys lifted a foot and kicked the still form on the ground. Orrin recognized Amir, the [Acolyte] he'd healed.

"You think you're better than us, Fallah?" the girl hissed and used a walking stick to jab at his ribs. "You think you can question Teacher Dou and get away with it?"

The second boy stepped on Amir's hand and twisted his foot. Amir let out a stifled yell, and Orrin realized they'd stuffed a rag in his mouth. This was more than simple bullying.

"First you tried to heal those peasants without permission, and then you have the audacity to ask questions about the Elder's choices?" The girl was talking again, egging on the two boys to continue. "You know, I'm not sure anybody would miss you if you just went home. What do you think, Jed?"

The boy stepping on Amir's hand spat. "The little peasant prodigy running off sounds like a good idea."

Orrin had seen enough. He couldn't risk scanning all three with [Identify], remembering Daniel's earlier warning that healers could sense that. Instead, he pulled the strongest inversed [Increase Dexterity] he could and cast it on all three.

Jed lifted his foot to stomp and fell over in an uncoordinated mess of limbs. The girl turned and laughed at her friend. She took a step toward him and fell flat on her face. Orrin heard bone hit the ground, and a wail filled the air.

"Mha teef," she cried. Orrin could see her hands on her mouth. "What happeneth?"

The third boy must have had a higher constitution. He stumbled but caught himself. Orrin watched as Amir, forgotten by the trio, started to crawl to the side of the alley. The one standing conspirator was able to get his friends up. They drunkenly tottered back toward the Hospital.

Orrin listened to them throw curses back at Amir. Once they were out of sight, he crept closer. "Do you need a heal?"

Amir looked at the empty alley. "Who's there?"

Orrin dropped his [Camouflage] spell. "Hi again."

Amir paled. "It's you! You were real."

"If you don't need a heal, I'll be going." Orrin scanned Amir and noticed that his health, while halved, wasn't critical.

"Wait. Please. Tell me how you did it?" Amir scrambled to his feet, holding his left hand to his side and trying not to grimace.

Orrin stopped. "Do what? That? I just made them stumble a bit."

Amir shook his head. "Not that. You healed half the city. You helped more people in an hour than the Elders do in a year. Please, take me as your student. I'll do anything."

Chapter 53

Orrin started laughing. The absurdity of the situation was too much.

Amir stepped closer and put his hands together. "Please, take me as your student. I'll leave the Hospital. I'll place my points however you recommend. I want to help people like you do."

Orrin felt the wall hit his back. He hadn't noticed backing away from the young man as he pressed closer.

"Listen, man, I'm sorry to tell you, but I have no idea what I'd even teach you. I've just got a lot of mana. You're already in the Hospital. Just let them teach you." Orrin looked over his shoulder. "And maybe find some better friends."

Amir's shoulders slumped, and his head hung low. "Thank you for stopping them. I think the teachers will suspend me soon and the protections I had will be gone."

Orrin wanted to walk away, but he'd seen that look before . . . on himself. "Hey, why would they suspend you? You're an acolyte, right?"

Amir shrugged. "I was a [Healer Acolyte], but I was demoted for helping before I was given clearance."

Orrin scanned Amir and saw his class had changed to [Healer Initiate].

"Wait, what? They can change your class?" Orrin had never heard of that. "I thought the Hospital just helped you gain the class. How do they do that?"

Amir crossed his arms and rubbed them. Orrin realized it was chilly out and Amir's dirtied and ripped white robe had lost a sleeve. He pulled a blanket out of his [Dimension Hole] and handed it over.

Amir pulled it over his shoulders and thanked him. "After the invisible healer . . . you . . . healed all those people, my teacher was angry. The Principal was angry. I had already broken one of the tenets set by the Hospital, so I was punished."

Amir raised a hand to his neck. "I was shown true pain for two days for my failure to follow orders. I thought that would be it, but then the city began whispering about you and what you did. They came a week ago and took my healing away."

Orrin was pissed. He'd already had a pretty bad image of the Hospital from the research he and Daniel had done. This was something darker. Amir was describing torture and holding people back from actually helping.

"How do they take away your healing?"

Amir frowned. "What do you mean? They took away my amulet."

It was Orrin's turn to frown. "What amulet?"

Amir's face moved from confusion to surprise to elation. "You're not from another healer group, are you? You're a natural [Healer]! There are rumors, but I've never met one."

Orrin realized they were still standing in the middle of an alley a few hundred yards from the Hospital. "I'm not . . . whatever that is, but we shouldn't keep talking out here. Those idiots might come back."

Amir nodded his head and pointed down the street. "We can go to my da's café. It's only a short walk."

Orrin perked up. "Café? Like with coffee?"

Amir lit up. "Do you like coffee?"

Amir's father had established a small shop at the end of a street that Amir described as full of lawyers, officials, and bureaucrats. "The type of people who always need a good pick-me-up."

The shop itself had two small tables outside and a window to order from. Amir used a key to open the side door and practically pushed Orrin into a chair inside.

The interior was as tiny as it looked from the outside. Behind the small closed window was an elaborate contraption of silvered pipes and large glass jars of different sizes of coffee beans. A small tray sat next to the window. "For pastries."

The rest of the small room was filled with bags of different beans and sugar. A single chair rested behind the door, which Orrin was currently sitting in.

Amir came alive as he twisted knobs and filled hoppers. He explained to an interested Orrin what each pipe did and even pointed out the different types of coffee.

"This one is from a tiny village in Odrana that all other beans are said to originate from. This one is from the elven forest—nobody knows how they actually grow, because the climate there is all wrong. We've got a variety from Odrana and a few from Veskar. The difference is really in the notes you get. Odrana coffee is usually more nutty and fruity. Veskarian coffee has more citrus and floral notes."

Orrin let the man work his nervous energy off. He'd been accosted, saved, and found himself face-to-face with the legendary invisible healer! *What a shitty superhero name.*

Amir turned knobs, and water fell from one pipe into a metal container. He placed it on a small stove device. While the flames licked the metal and heated the water, he put a handful of beans into a mortar.

"This is Odrana coffee, but it's actually a newer bean. It isn't as strong as some of the others but has a beautiful smoothness. It's my favorite, and my da always keeps some on hand in case I'm having a rough week."

He used a small filter in an inverted-triangle holder and poured in the ground-up beans, then the water on top. Orrin watched the barista work in silence.

A few minutes later, Amir handed Orrin a small, plain cup. "Cream? Sugar?"

Orrin shook his head and sipped.

He had had a lot of amazing moments since landing in Asmea. He'd learned magic, fought monsters, and met some cool people. But every moment so far paled in comparison to the first cup of coffee made by someone who didn't mangle the process.

"Mmm."

The coffee was hot and smooth, just as Amir had said. The flavor had some spice and nutty undertones but kicked in a little chocolate toward the end.

"You like?" A hopeful Amir rolled forward and backward on the balls of his feet.

"Amir. If I had anything to teach you, I would, just for this cup of coffee."

Amir grinned. "I'm glad you enjoy it."

Orrin slurped up some more. "Okay. So now that we're not standing outside the stronghold of the crazies who tried to beat you up . . . tell me about the amulet?"

Amir leaned against the wall, planting one foot and resting the other behind him. Casually cool.

"It is common knowledge, so I'm not breaking any rules. When you join the Hospital, you join as an Initiate. You run errands and take classes. You learn the rules and how to follow orders. You are taught about the theories of healing and how not to overdraw or do more harm than good. You following so far?"

Orrin tilted his cup up as he drained the last bit of nectar. "Yep."

"Becoming an [Acolyte] is a great honor. One I worked three years to achieve. I was given an amulet that let me use the healer spell [Heal Small Wounds]."

"Yeah, that's the one I've got."

Amir's eyes flashed with desire and a tint of jealousy. "You just have it? You didn't have to use an amulet for years?"

Orrin shook his head.

"The Hospital loans an [Acolyte] an amulet until we understand the spell enough to buy it ourselves. When it appears in our system store, we become full members of the Hospital. Our lives and class are tied to them."

Orrin set the empty mug on the counter for pastries. "So that's why healers never leave the Hospital. Your class is connected to the entire group. Interesting."

Amir scowled. "That's one word for it. I want to become a healer to actually help people. I can't stand them, charging so much and healing so little. Their reasons may have started off meaning well, but it's all politics inside the walls of the Hospital."

Orrin watched Amir get worked up. The man had been so calm, but talking about the corruption he'd seen fired him up in a way that reminded Orrin of his own dad. Before he'd left, he'd been an activist outside work. He organized, marched, and protested anything he thought unfair or unjust. He'd even brought Orrin along for a few before . . .

Orrin realized Amir was nearly crying. "—Mom died, I swore I would never let something like that happen again."

Orrin stood up and clapped the man on his shoulder. "Hey, I have no idea how to teach you or what I could offer, but if you need a friend, you've got one."

The weight of the day—or probably weeks—hit Amir, and the man hugged Orrin and started to cry in earnest. Orrin awkwardly patted his back and waited for him to stop crying.

Amir pulled back and wiped his face with his one remaining sleeve. "Sorry. It's just been a lot."

Orrin smiled kindly. "Yeah. I get it. My life has been so crazy the last few weeks, you wouldn't believe me if I told you."

Amir noticed the empty cup and pointed. "You want another?"

Orrin grinned stupidly. "Friends forever."

The two stayed talking for a few hours. Orrin could tell Amir was nervous to go back to the Hospital dorms where he lived. So, he let him tell his life story. His parents had traveled to Dey as merchants from Odrana and found themselves having a baby along the way. His mom and dad had started the coffee shop after finding no real competitors around. With the family connections back home, they had a steady supply of product. His mom had gotten sick, and the costs of continued healings had grown too much. She'd hidden how bad she really was but had died five years ago. Amir had joined the Hospital shortly after in an attempt to never let the same happen to anyone else.

The boy, who had started quiet and timid, turned out to be a deeply kind and intelligent man. Amir had done well in his classes and risen quickly, but he hadn't noticed that by doing so, he'd ruffled some feathers. He wasn't adept at the politics and movement needed within the Hospital, and all his smarts had been wasted.

"Teacher Dou enjoys punishing me. His son was passed over for promotion for a year because I was elevated to [Acolyte]. Of course, I only found this out after I was assigned to him. He rarely lets me do actual healing and keeps track . . . kept track of how much I did. Now it'll be years before I can heal again, if ever. You're sure you don't know how you learned [Heal Small Wounds]?"

Orrin shook his head again. He'd told Amir that he had gotten the spell with his class. A rare class only possible to people from his small village. Amir had just accepted the excuse and moved on.

Orrin put down his third cup of coffee. "I better get going soon. It's late."

Amir looked out the small window. "Yep, it's past midnight. Sorry for talking your ear off. My da listens, but he's family and that's different, you know?"

Orrin nodded but didn't say that he didn't know. He hadn't had a real conversation with his family in years. After his dad left, his mom had tried for a while, but Orrin had pulled back. Once she started working more and he was ready to talk, she wasn't around.

The anger from his past and disgust at all the secrets and plotting Amir had described filled Orrin's chest, and he felt like punching something. The excessive amount of caffeine wasn't helping.

I hate this. This guy should be doing what he wants and helping people. If more of the healers had tried to help like he did, maybe more would have survived.

Orrin clenched his fists until his knuckles popped. *Tony said Administrators could do all sorts of stuff. I should be able to give Amir a new class or maybe a healing spell.*

In a caffeine-fueled daze, Orrin concentrated hard, staring at Amir. He felt the room around him shaking and waited for the ding of a blue box.

"Um, Orrin? Are you okay?"

Orrin stopped. "What?"

Amir was looking at him with concern. "You said you've had coffee before, right? You look a little hyped up. You were looking at me really weird."

"Sorry," Orrin said and forced a laugh. "I was just thinking how much shit you've gone through and got lost for a minute."

Amir put a hand to his chest. "Thank you. That means a lot." He grabbed a small bag of beans off the counter. "Here, take this and visit. I'll probably be working here again soon."

Orrin thanked Amir and tried to pay. Amir's frown told him to not push it. He started walking back to the Catanzanos', the smell of coffee beans in his nose and his thoughts on questions to ask Tony about Administrator Access. He really wanted to help Amir.

Orrin was so engrossed in his own thoughts, he missed the two people shadowing him.

Chapter 54

The sound of footsteps running up behind him was the only warning Orrin got before he was tackled from behind. Orrin was lifted into the air, and the oxygen was crushed from his lungs as two strong arms squeezed him. He gasped and clawed at the armored forearms but couldn't get a good purchase on his attacker.

"I'm so glad you're okay!"

The attacker dropped Orrin from the hug and spun him around. Daniel stood in the moonlight with a grin on his face. Madi was standing a few feet away looking slightly concerned at Orrin's hard breathing.

"Daniel! You scared him," Madi chastised. "He's shaking like a leaf."

"Oh shit," Daniel said and took a step back. "I'm so sorry! We got lucky on our way back from that asshole's house and found you. I didn't even think, I just ran at you. I'm so sorry."

Orrin heaved in deep breaths as his friend apologized over and over. "You just surprised me. I thought someone was attacking me. I'm a little jittery."

Daniel's look of concern and apprehension faded back into his normal smile. "It's good to see you. We tried to come and visit, but Anthony wouldn't let us inside."

"Wouldn't let *you* inside. I never would have willingly gone into that madman's house," Madi chimed in behind Daniel. "No offense meant to you, Orrin."

Orrin waved her comment off. "So you did try to visit." He felt conflicted. On one hand, his friend had actually tried to come through for him. Orrin realized it must have taken a lot for Daniel to try and visit, even after the little fight he'd picked. Madi had even gone as far as visiting the outside of Tony's house . . . her equivalent of facing a nightmare in real life.

On the other hand, Daniel had let Tony drive him off. Orrin understood the reason Tony had given him for not letting his friends inside—Tony needed to be focused completely on keeping Orrin alive. The internal magic trying to rip him apart after turning off [Mind Bastion] was not something he could turn from for long, and he'd been annoyed enough at having to drive Daniel away the two times he'd visited.

"Of course we did," Daniel said with a frown. "I wanted to push in anyway, but he promised you would be fine. He said he needed to focus on keeping your mind in one piece and to go away. Madi convinced me he was probably telling the truth."

Orrin looked over Daniel's shoulder at Madi standing a few steps back. She seemed gloomy standing in the dark shadow of a building.

"Thank you for talking some sense into him," Orrin said. "And I have no right to ask for it, but I hope you'll forgive me what I said before I left. Tony thinks me turning into an asshole might be a side effect of too much mana use."

Part of their conversations had been about ways to monitor how much he overused cycling. Tony had him go over as many details as Orrin could remember, from how many times he used the bathroom to how hungry he was and any odd behaviors. Tony saw the pattern from both overuse periods right away—Orrin became a bigger prick the more time he spent cycling.

Madi hesitated but stepped forward and put her hand out. "I'm not sure you need to ask my forgiveness. As I already told you, I know I'll be in your debt for a long while. I promise not to do anything that makes you question me."

Orrin took her outstretched hand. He noticed her wince slightly as he squeezed, and she turned her hand over. The inside of her hand was raw.

"What happened? Do you want me to heal your hands?"

Madi pulled her hand back. "No, thank you. I'm supposed to let them heal naturally. So they'll callus."

Daniel stepped close and put an arm around Madi's shoulder. "We've been practicing our teamwork and our skills. Madi can take on Brandt now nine times out of ten."

"It's more like two out of ten, but I am improving. Brandt said it's because Daniel has a higher [Spear Proficiency] than me. Someone with a higher-level proficiency can help you move your own skill up faster."

Orrin tucked that nugget away for later.

"So tell us everything!" Daniel grabbed Orrin and threw his other arm around his shoulder. He held both Orrin and Madi close. "We left Anthony's hours ago. He said you left an hour before we got there, and we searched forever trying to find you."

"I made a friend." Orrin ducked out from under Daniel's arm and gave him a light push. "Let's go back home, and I'll tell you guys all about it. Most of the week was just pain and puke, but Tony and I had a good conversation, and we think there might be a way to regulate my cycling . . . as long as I can create a skill."

Madi frowned again. "Creating a skill is really difficult, Orrin. It can take years of study and focused research." She looked at him and quickly continued, "But I'm sure you'll be fine. Maybe just don't use your mana skills for a while. We don't want to lose you."

Daniel let his arm fall off Madi and turned back toward the street. "Okay, then. Let's head back." He started walking, leaving Madi and Orrin behind.

Orrin watched his back and sighed.

"Don't judge him too harshly," Madi whispered as they followed. "He's been a wreck all week. He blames himself for you being sick, and rightly so."

"I had already used a lot of mana to heal that crowd of people," Orrin hedged for his friend. "It's not completely his fault."

Orrin could feel Madi's glower darken. "True, and he didn't know he would have such a strong pull to fight demons. Something my father failed to mention to us."

The way she said "father" made it obvious that Silas was in the doghouse with Madi.

"I figured he knew," Orrin admitted. "At first, I thought he was trying to protect you, because sending us away to avoid the Wall Quest seemed a little thin. But when Sof—the leader of the Dragoon team—mentioned it, I realized your dad had to have known."

Madi crossed her arms in a tight hug. "I'm sorry."

Orrin sighed. "Listen, I was an asshole to you before I left. I can't keep blaming you and your dad for everything. I think we have just been terrible at communicating."

Madi put up a finger and started counting. "I threatened to kill you because I thought you were a [Vampire]. That was my fault. I should have asked more questions and not jumped to conclusions."

Orrin laughed. "I forgot about that one. I probably should have tried explaining my skill better."

She put up another finger. "My dad testing Daniel with a bunch of low-rent thugs. It never should have been more than a light rough-up, and they took it over the line."

Orrin rubbed his chest. His healing had taken away the damage, but a slight scar still puckered between two ribs. He kept quiet.

Madi put up a third and fourth finger. "Trying to push you away when we thought we struck gold with finding a [Hero] all for ourselves. Trying to strong-arm you into leaving."

"Luckily, I was able to fight back that time," Orrin half joked.

Madi shook her head. "My father saw an opportunity. He told me whatever spell you used weakened him a bit, but he still felt confident he could have taken you. He just rearranged his goals to include you." She made her hand into a fist. "That's all he ever does. He plots and plans and moves pieces on the board."

Orrin and Madi walked behind Daniel. He kept looking back but sensed the mood and stayed ahead.

"You mentioned your mom was an adventurer when we were in the dungeon," Orrin said. "When she was around, did your dad do the same stuff?"

Madi turned her head toward the sky. The flame from a lamp-post winked off her eyebrow piercing . . . or maybe it was a tear. "She grounded him. He's always been about the end, no matter the means. She just wanted to protect people, no matter the end. I . . . I think they balanced each other well. He's not a bad man, Orrin. He's responsible for thousands of lives and makes decisions daily that I never want to make. He sends guards to their deaths so that the people of Dey can sleep in peace. I know that in my head. He makes choices for our future that keep him up at night . . . and I love him . . . but . . ."

"You can love somebody and still not like their choices."

Daniel waved at them to hurry up. They were approaching the Catanzano house.

Madi waved back. "I'm telling him tomorrow that I'm going to reject becoming the next Lady of Dey. I have cousins. It's been done before. I want to follow my mother's path—No—I want to follow my own path, and it's well past the time I've told him that."

Orrin didn't know what to say. Turning down the role of being in charge, of doing the work she'd been groomed for, wasn't a small thing. "Are you sure?"

Madi nodded. "He'll tell me I'll change my mind and be back in a year's time, but I'm committed. Not just to Daniel as the . . . well, you know . . . but also to our team. To you."

She stopped within a stone's throw of her house and turned to Orrin. Daniel was talking to the one guard stationed outside the house. "I'd like to start over and be your friend. Just like Daniel has become."

Her sincerity in the entire talk hadn't wavered, and Orrin knew the right words to say, but as he opened his mouth . . . all hell broke loose.

Out of the corner of his eye, Orrin watched as the guard waved back to Daniel and then fell as if in slow motion. A small feather puff sprouted from the side of his neck.

Two dark-cloaked figures fell from the rooftops on either side of the street and raced toward Daniel, even as he rushed to catch the falling body of the Catanzano guard. One took something long and thin and put it to his face. Daniel reached back and grabbed his neck. He turned and saw his attackers, took two steps, and collapsed facedown.

Orrin realized he was moving. He pulled down every spell in his arsenal. He boosted his dexterity, strength, intelligence, and will; he inversed the same and tried hitting each of the figures. One of them stumbled, but the other kept moving, barely casting a glance at Orrin.

Madi was screaming. Not yelling in panic, but screaming orders at the Catanzano house. The front doors slammed open, and three guards rushed out. The assailant that Orrin had tripped cast a spell, and icy bars grew in the door frame, blocking the rest of the house. Orrin saw Brandt start hacking at the ice, yelling orders at the men around him.

The three guards who had cleared the door sprang into action. One grabbed Daniel and started dragging him back toward the house, while the other two ran at the closer cloaked attacker. The figure swirled and raised their arms into the air, with two vine-like whips that lashed out. Each guard took a single hit from the whips and went down.

Orrin's practice with [Increase Dexterity] finally paid off, as the burst of speed didn't trip him up. He reached into his pocket and plucked his sword out just in time to run through the one he'd made stumble. They were just pulling their arm back to cast another spell, and Orrin heard the shock of air leave their lungs. The third guard raised a spear to meet the closer attacker. Orrin tried casting inversed debuffs on the figure again, but other than another look back, they didn't stop spinning the dual whips.

Orrin tried to pull his sword out of the dying attacker. He'd run them through the back with all his strength. The blade was caught on something and stuck.

Brandt was yelling at Orrin to leave the sword, but he needed something to attack with. The third guard was holding off the whips. Brandt wasn't hitting the ice bars anymore. A guard on the inside was holding his hands close to the bars, letting off a bright flame that looked like a blowtorch at high power.

After another tug, Orrin let go and moved as if in a dream. He looked over his shoulder. Madi had her spear extended and was fighting a third figure. His head snapped back, and he watched one of the whips move around the guard's spear, yanking it from his planted position. The second slipped through and wrapped around the man's neck. He let go of his spear and started grabbing his throat, but to no avail. The guard was out in seconds.

Orrin used [Ice Sword] and then threw a [Lightstrike] at the whip wielder. They just ignored the hit and grabbed Daniel's leg. Then they turned and started dragging him back toward Orrin.

Orrin continued to pelt the figure with debuffs. He cycled and didn't care. He screamed in frustration and held the sword up.

"Orrin, they're going to kidnap him. Don't let them tel—" Madi's voice was cut off as she was knocked back into a wall.

"Orrin . . . You are the friend?" A feminine voice came from under the dark hood. "Move aside."

"You're not getting by me," Orrin growled, planting his feet in the stance Brandt had taught him. He held the point of the ice sword at the person trying to take his friend. "Let him go now and I'll let you live."

A small laugh escaped from under the hood. "Don't be absurd. You're so below me, I shouldn't have even brought the others. I only need a few steps to be outside this pathetic [Hold] field."

Orrin cast another round of debuffs and threw a [Lightstrike] for good measure. He also focused on something else behind him and waited.

The attacker sighed. "That is getting annoying. I'm not sure what that is, but please stop. I quite like my stats right where they are, thank you." She flicked her free wrist and snapped the whip near Orrin's face.

Orrin saw what he was waiting for and quickly applied a few [Wards] and [Utility Ward] at level one.

"Where are you taking him?"

"A [Hero] is rather valuable. He'll be much more useful elsewhere. Don't worry, you can visit in a few months."

Orrin threw his sword at her and summoned another. She easily parried it with a flick of her whip.

"You know you can't hurt me. Don't make me ask again. Move."

"Madi, now!" Orrin yelled and threw himself to the side, landing heavily on his arm.

Orrin had sent an invite to her to join his party and then boosted her stats. The sounds of battle behind him had faded, and Orrin had noted the annoyance in the attacker's voice as she watched over his shoulder.

He cheered as the easily recognized streak of light blasted past him and raced toward the figure holding his friend.

Then Orrin's heart dropped as another cloaked figure with a sword stuck in their chest jumped into the line of fire and dropped.

The female tsked and stepped over the still body of her comrade, dragging Daniel's body over him. Orrin had time to see Daniel's wide and scared eyes begging for help right before she teleported them both away.

Chapter 55

"No!" Orrin yelled and grabbed at the empty air a few feet from him. He was too late. His friend had been kidnapped.

Orrin opened his [Map], but the only party member he saw was Madi. Daniel hadn't responded to the invite request he'd sent. He probably wasn't able to. His eyes had been open, so he was conscious. But he hadn't been able to move or even speak.

Madi ran up beside him and started tugging at Orrin's arm. She was yelling something about getting inside the house, where it was safe. The ringing in his ears made it hard to understand.

A small cough from the ground caught his attention.

"We need to get inside in case they try to come back," Madi was saying. Orrin ignored her and pulled his arm from her grip. He walked over to the crawling form with a sword stuck through his back. The blade scraped along the ground under his body as he pulled himself forward. The man's hood had fallen back, and blond hair was matted in sweat. He reached out toward the spot Daniel had been teleported away and let out a moan of despair.

Orrin used [Identify].

Tymon Depin
Ice Shadow Level 23

HP: 9/100
MP: 150/200

Strength: 10

Constitution: 19
Dexterity: 14
Will: 20
Intelligence: 22

Orrin scanned through the man's spells and skills. No [Teleport], just a bunch of stealth skills and ice magic.

"I'm going back to Tony's house," Orrin said quietly. He grabbed the handle of his sword and pulled. Tymon let out a scream as the sword jostled inside him. Orrin put a foot on the man's shoulder and pulled harder, sending a healing spell down to keep the man from dying.

The sword came out with a disgusting, wet slurp, and Tymon passed out. Orrin checked the man's health, which had stabilized at about half. He turned to Madi. "Are you coming with me?"

Madi looked back at the safety of her house, her father, and the life she'd always known. Orrin saw Madi steel her shoulders and knew her choice.

"Let's go."

Orrin couldn't teleport the man when he was unconscious, so he simply picked him up and threw him over his shoulder. With his strength buff still active, it was easy. He imagined he looked comical, carrying the larger man through the town. *Except for all the blood.*

"What are you planning to do?" Madi whispered as they walked the same path that Orrin had taken a few hours before. "Just ask Anthony to break all the rules set up for his kind?"

"He'll tell me how to get to Daniel," Orrin answered stoically. He had [Mind Bastion] up still. He'd activated it so quickly during the fight that he couldn't turn it off yet. "And if he won't, there are other ways of making a person talk."

Tymon's low groans echoed down the street.

Tony was already standing on his small stoop as they approached. "What in the fiery pit are you doing back so soon? You can't even go one day without . . . Who is that with you?"

"Tony, this is Madi. Madi, Tony. You can yell at me all you want later, but somebody just kidnapped Daniel. I need your help making this one tell me where he is." Orrin flipped the man bodily to the ground in front of Tony's steps. "Quickly."

Tony's eyes darted between Orrin, Madi, and the groaning man at his feet. "You don't know what you are asking."

"I don't care," Orrin nearly yelled. "Drag the information out of his head or I'll spend my points on skills that'll let me do it myself. You know I'm not bluffing."

Madi was looking back and forth with a puzzled look on her face, and Orrin realized Tony had not been talking in her mind. To Madi, Orrin was having a one-sided conversation with the mind mage.

Tony's face softened, and he shook his head. "Young Catanzano, please talk some sense into your friend."

Madi flinched. She breathed out slowly and talked to the ground. "By the power of the Catanzano house, I release you for any crimes you may commit in the aiding of this request."

She turned her eyes up to look Tony in the face. "Please help us find Daniel."

Tony sighed and waved for them to come inside.

Orrin felt silly having to pick up Tymon's body again as Tony ushered them into the house. Madi made sure to stand with Orrin between her and Tony as they entered. Orrin could feel her trembling as they walked down the long hallway into the kitchen.

"I promise I will not eat your eyes or attack you while you are in my home." Tony grabbed the extra chair and spun it against the wall.

"What?" Orrin asked.

"He was talking to me," Madi said in a quivering voice. "He's listening to my thoughts."

Orrin slumped Tymon in the seat and pulled out some rope he'd stored what felt like forever ago in his [Dimension Hole]. He looped it around Tymon a few times before Madi hip-checked him out of the way and did it correctly.

"He does that. Just ignore it. He's really not that scary," Orrin said as he stepped out of the way. He checked the man's HP again, but, without the sword stuck through a lung, he seemed to be stabilized.

"Please stop misinforming the next Lady of Dey. I am quite scary and not to be trifled with."

Tony was pouring tea into three cups and setting cookies out. "Now, young Catanzano, would you like one or two cubes of sugar?"

"Tony! This is not the time for tea," Orrin chided. "Get in his mind and find out where they took Daniel."

Tony raised an eyebrow as he looked at Orrin. "He's unconscious. If I jolt him awake, his thoughts will be scrambled. I'll do my work as fast as I can, but don't assume to tell me how to do it." He turned back to Madi. "Two sugar and a dash of cream?"

Madi cinched the rope tight and wiped her hands on her pants. After a pause and an audible gulp, she responded. "Yes, thank you."

"Tell me what happened while we wait for our friend to wake." Tony pushed a cup into Madi's hands. He took a sip of his own and looked up expectantly.

"Daniel was ahead of us walking toward the house when he went down. Some people appeared and took out the guards. There was a fight, and someone got Daniel and teleported him away. How long before he wakes up?" Orrin explained in a rush, ignoring the smell of chamomile next to him. He paced in the tiny room and pointed to the unconscious man.

"He'll wake when he wakes." Tony ignored Orrin. "How did Daniel go down? A toxin of some sort? That has to be it. You can't teleport an unconscious body. I wonder—"

Orrin tuned out Tony's rambling. He'd already learned that talking only with his mind led to his conversations sometimes taking a stream-of-consciousness path.

Orrin pulled up the [Map] again and tried inviting Daniel to his party of two. No response, and [Map] still showed nothing.

Tony snapped his fingers in front of Orrin. "I'm over here strategizing and you're ignoring me?"

Orrin sat heavily in the remaining chair. Madi stood holding her tea politely and eyeing the front door.

"Sorry. I'm distracted."

"He had to have been hit with some sort of poison or biotoxin. You said he went down. Did he move or seem awake at all?"

Orrin could still see the pain and fear in Daniel's eyes. "He was awake. He knew what was about to happen and couldn't do a thing about it."

Madi shivered in the corner.

"So a neurotoxin, something that froze up his ability to move or even resist the pull of being teleported away." Tony tapped his chin. "You don't have any healing spell except [Heal Small Wounds], right? I'll be right back."

Tony stood up and headed upstairs, passing Madi. "I promise it isn't poisoned. It's actually quite good." He looked down at her full cup of tea.

Once he left, Madi sat down quickly in the empty chair and pushed the cup away from her. "How do you react so calmly around him, knowing he can read all your thoughts?"

Orrin shrugged and watched Tymon's breathing. Had it become more shallow? "I just figure if he's going to read my thoughts anyways, I should imagine he's a nice guy and hope he reacts well to that."

Madi squirmed in her chair.

"He can probably still hear your thoughts upstairs," Orrin added. "You can wait outside if you want."

"I'm not going anywhere, and you better not leave me behind." Madi grabbed the tea and took a big gulp of the hot liquid. "Ahh. It's scalding."

"It's tea—what did you expect?"

Tony's footsteps down the stairs alerted them to his return. He was carrying two books as he walked back into the kitchen. He slapped one down next to Orrin.

"I can't remember which one has the information, but check in there."

"What are you talking about?" Orrin asked. He had to wipe a layer of dust off the book to make out the title. "*A Healer's Field Guide?*"

Tony slipped a finger behind a page and flipped through his own book. "Look for the chapter on antitoxins. There's a skill for it, and if you're going off on a rescue mission, I'm assuming having your [Hero] up and about might be preferable."

"[H-hero]? We . . . we are trying to find our party member Daniel, not a [Hero]," Madi stammered out.

Tony did his eyebrow thing and shook his head. "You need to get better at lying, young Catanzano."

"Leave it, Madi," Orrin whispered and opened the book.

No table of contents, but each chapter has its own heading, at least. He flipped through the few hundred pages quickly but saw nothing on toxins.

"Found it." Tony turned his book around and pushed it close to Orrin. "That's the one. It's usually only unlocked in higher-level healers, but you shouldn't have a problem with that."

"What does that mean?" Madi questioned, but Orrin was reading.

After the seventh conduit is unlocked, a new branch can be explored, including those dealing with toxins. While the fourth conduit has remedies for particular toxins, not all can be covered by the lesser paths. Along this higher path is a skill, [Remetabolize]. This ingenious skill allows the healer to change the very structure of the toxin until it is benign. While this author posits the skill is duplicative of the fourth conduit remedies found in Chapter Sixteen, others have theorized—

"Tony, you're a genius. This will let me get rid of the toxin keeping him prone."

Tony beamed. "Exactly."

Orrin opened his store and searched.

> [Remetabolize] change the toxicity and structure
> of a toxin. 50 MP. 4 AP
> Would you like to purchase for 4 AP?
> Yes or No?

Orrin hesitated. "I don't need this, though. If you can find out where he is, I can teleport in invisible and just pop back with him."

Tony frowned. "True. However, think about this: once they've got him secured, they'll likely have him drugged up so nobody can attempt a rescue." He scratched at the stubble on his chin. "But they'll also have antiteleport precautions. You should bring all this information to Silas—I mean, your father. He'll be able to help. But that can all wait."

"Why?" Madi asked.

Orrin would have sworn the lights dimmed and the shadows ran along the walls. Tony's face became more angular in the dim light, and his mouth changed from his playful smile to a downright evil-looking grin.

"Our guest has joined us."

Orrin turned with Tony to see Tymon's eyes fluttering open.

Chapter 56

Tymon opened his eyes and tried to move his arms. Madi's knots held tight, and he started to struggle in the chair.

"Tymon. Tymon. Tymon." Tony's voice echoed in the room. Orrin glanced at the mind mage, but the frail old man had disappeared.

Instead, Orrin saw the Tony of Madi's nightmares. Shadows began to pour from his mouth every time he spoke. His eyes were black coals, shattered by fiery crevices. The wispy white hair had thickened into a mane of dark-brown hair that hung down to his shoulders. The colors of the rest of the room were drowned out, and Tony shone in his vision with a deathly light that made him appear gaunt.

"Try not to stare at me." Tony's voice whispered in Orrin's mind. "I can't direct this skill, and I'd rather not see it in your eyes every time you look at me in the future."

Tymon was whimpering in his chair. His eyes were wide with recognition. "Quiet Anthony? What? Why?"

Tymon tried to turn his face away, but Tony reached out a hand and gently pushed Tymon's chin back to the front.

Tony's hand was covered in dark blood that dripped slowly from his fingers. A smear was left across Tymon's face.

"No. You should only be looking at me. I'm your problem for the rest of your poor, pathetic life." Tony's voice lost some of its rich timbre and began to deepen with a gravelly quality that made Orrin's skin crawl. "Don't worry about that. Nobody knows you're here. Nobody is coming for you. Nobody is going to save you."

Orrin smelled the ammonia before he noticed the darkening spot down Tymon's pant leg. He heard Madi take in a gasp of air behind him.

"Now, Tymon, should I send these children out of the room before I begin, or should I let them watch? You did kidnap their friend. It might be . . . therapeutic for them to see you in pieces."

Orrin's [Mind Bastion] kept his logic churning, but he could still feel waves of pure terror emanating from Tony's spell. Tony was forcing terror into Tymon, and even the peripheral hits of the skill were almost overriding Orrin's own ability.

Madi had no such protection. She gagged and threw up. Orrin heard her take a few steps outside the room and breathe heavily.

"Sorry, young Catanzano. It's been a while. You should be fine where you are."

"Please!" Tymon wailed, tears streaking through the dirt on his face. "Please don't do this. I'll tell you whatever you want."

A small carving knife appeared in Tony's bloody hand, and he stepped forward. "Oh, Tymon. Of course you'll tell me everything. I already know that. But this isn't just about getting information."

Orrin couldn't help it—he looked at Tony.

His friend was gone. A towering figure of fire, blood, and death stood with a slight hunch to avoid the ceiling. The smoke from his mouth now covered most of his body. Each time Tony moved, Orrin caught a glimpse of underneath. His skin had peeled off in long ribbons down his naked chest, and blood ran to his feet. His eyes continued to glow, but with a blackness that squeezed Orrin's heart. The knife in his hand appeared rusted but still sharp enough to cut.

"This is about revenge for your sins in my city." Tony stepped forward and shaved the knife along Tymon's forearm, skinning the man.

Tymon's screams echoed in Orrin's ears.

"Tony! We need him—"

Tony turned and winked an eye. For a fraction of a second, Orrin saw the room clearly. Tony was still an old man. He was holding a butter knife and was rubbing jelly on Tymon's arm. Then the nightmare was back.

"Please! Ahhh. Noo!" Tymon continued to cry and buck against the ropes. Orrin heard Madi heaving again in the other room.

Tony stepped back. Or the huge smoke monster did.

"Who do you work for? What was your mission? Where are you supposed to meet after?"

Tymon was shaking his head and staring down at his bloody arm. The long strip of skin had been pulled back, and red muscle throbbed underneath.

"Focus, Tymon . . ." Tony gently stroked Tymon's hair.

The captured man's head snapped up. He was hyperventilating but managed to squeak out a few sentences. "We were hired by Odrana. They want the [Hero] for their war effor—"

Tony slammed the knife down into Tymon's leg. The man screamed again.

"So Lord Wendeln hired you. Don't lie to me, Tymon. I really don't appreciate being lied to in my own home."

"Lord Wendeln? He wouldn't dare to do something like that!" Madi cried out from behind them.

"Oh. That's interesting. Why was Wendeln scared? Tymon. I can see into your mind. Don't try to hide the thoughts—just let them out and the pain can stop."

"F-fuck you," Tymon stammered.

Tony's teeth shimmered into a smile. "Some resistance? Oh, what a treat. You are going to be so much fun."

Tymon let out a scream and started to shake in his bonds. With a jerk, he tried to bite into his own shoulder and kept crunching his teeth together in a grinding clatter.

Tony stood still, stared straight at Tymon for a moment, and then sighed. His monster-demon facade faded.

"What is happening to him?" Madi asked hesitantly from the hallway. She wiped something away from her chin.

"Currently, Tymon is in his own dream. He'll be there for a few minutes." Tony clapped his hands and bustled over to the small closet that kept his cleaning supplies. He grabbed a bucket and the mop that Orrin had grown to hate. "Be a dear and clean up after yourself?"

Madi took the bucket and shook her head in disbelief as the screams continued. "What kind of dream did you put him in?"

Tony shrugged. "Honestly, I don't bother watching them anymore. You'd be amazed what people come up with on their own. Do you want to see?"

Madi glanced at Orrin. He shook his head no. She squared her shoulders. "Yes."

Tony pulled a half smile and quirked his head. Madi's eyes opened wide, and then she vomited again.

"At least this time you got it in the bucket." Tony took a large step over something into the hallway. "I'm going to get a map. I caught a glimpse of a rendezvous point."

"What if he stops screaming?" Orrin shouted down the hall. "How long is this going to last? We don't want the neighbors to call the guard."

"Sound barriers throughout the house, my boy. If he stops screaming before I get back, stab him again. He's terrified of you."

Madi was on her knees, hugging the small metal pail. Orrin patted her back as she emptied her stomach of her dinner. They cleaned her mess out and then filled the bucket with water. Madi took hold of the mop and began pushing the mess across the floor, making an even bigger mess. Orrin sighed and grabbed the mop from her.

"What did you see?" Orrin asked as he slopped the water on the ground and cleaned up someone else's throw-up in Tony's house for a change. "The nightmare that Tymon is in . . . what was it?"

Madi was holding her arms tight and staying close to Orrin. She opened her mouth twice before she muttered, "Spiders. He's got thousands of spiders crawling over his body. They're going into his nose and eyes. They got under the skin where Tony cut his arm, and you can see them moving around under the skin. He's screaming and chewing them up, but more keep appearing."

"That's disgusting," Orrin agreed. "Are you all right?"

Madi choked out a laugh. "I'm in Quiet Anthony's house while he uses all the magic that's outlawed in Dey. One friend was just kidnapped immediately after another one recovered from almost dying. My father is going to have me killed for what I'm doing. What do you think?"

Orrin watched the mop's head push the dirty water around for a minute. He dunked it in the fresh water and turned it tight, letting the sediment rinse off.

She just called me her friend. Say something, you idiot. Orrin looked up from the floor. "Sorry. We're going to get him back."

Madi smiled faintly.

"And I consider you my friend, too."

Orrin blushed and hurried to mop up more of the vomit, the echoes of crying, teeth grinding, and screams in the air.

Tony clumped back down the stairs, holding the tube that Orrin knew he kept his map in. "What happened? Why is Orrin so red?"

"No reason," Madi said. "What kind of map is that? Did you get it at Pierre's or Rubenstein's?"

Tony pursed his lips. "It's from Jacques. The one who trained Pierre. Nice dodge, by the way. You must have had some mental training."

Orrin watched the two go back and forth, then pushed the mop and bucket to the side. "Can we try again? Maybe he'll answer our questions now."

Tony's smirk at Madi softened, and he tousled Orrin's hair as he passed. "Sure. Sure. Maybe he'll offer to guide us to him, too."

Orrin went to follow, but Madi grabbed onto his sleeve. "Can we . . . stand back here? We can see from the doorway."

Orrin didn't need to see what was going on. He nodded and let Madi stand close behind him.

Tony shook his head and rolled his eyes. He smoothed a map of Dey down on the table. "Okay, Tymon, let's see if you want to cooperate."

Tony's shape morphed into the beastly visage quicker this time. His body stilled for a moment as he glared at Tymon, and the man coughed three times before his eyes stopped spinning.

"Please. Please, no more. Get them out. Get them out of my eyes," Tymon pleaded. His eyes were red with tears, and snot had made a path down to his chin.

"I think I want to watch your little friends lay some eggs in one of your eyes. Would you like to watch, too? I could remove one for you. I could place it on this table, and we could watch together. How does that sound, Tymon?" Tony's voice was once again rocks grating against steel. Each word sent goose bumps up Orrin's arms. "Or . . ."

Tymon cowered and shook as Tony spoke. But at the *or* and the inflection of that word, hinting at something better, the attacker's nose flared and his eyes widened. "Anything. You wanted to know about Lord Wendeln, right? He's made a deal for something. I don't know the details, but we are selling the [Hero]. In the morning. We have enough bellton root extract to keep him dosed until then. Longer, even. I stored it myself in an icebox. We're to keep our hoods up the whole time. Please don't feed me to the spiders again."

Tony's form didn't move during Tymon's diatribe. When he finally stopped, Tony nodded once. "All true. Where were you taking the boy? Where would they keep him overnight?"

Orrin watched Tony move the rusting dagger over his map as Tymon gave directions. Tony pulled a pencil from behind an ear—a ridiculous place for a demon smoke monster to be hiding something—and marked a spot on his map. He held it up for Tymon.

"Yes. Yes. That's where we were supposed to meet up after."

Tony snapped his fingers, and Tymon's head lolled.

"Is he sleeping?" Orrin asked as he moved into the room. Tony had already changed back to his normal self.

"No, he's dead." Tony didn't take his eyes off the map. "This is only about twenty miles outside the city. If what I saw in his head was right . . ."

"Dead?" Madi entered the room.

Tony looked up at the anger in her voice. "No, I was being sarcastic. He's sleeping. I'm sure you and your father will want his head for attacking your precious house." He turned to Orrin. "Does nobody here have a sense of humor?"

"It's just not a good night for jokes," Orrin replied. He studied the map and Tony's mark. Northeast. It was in the same direction that he and Daniel had taken that big rat–killing quest for the Guild. So long ago.

"I'd think a shitty night like tonight would be the perfect time for jokes." Tony scratched the top of his head. "So, kids. Should we go save the [Hero]?"

Chapter 57

Orrin made sure the straps on his armor were tight and remembered to belt on his sword this time.

"I'm not saying Tony shouldn't come," Madi argued again. "I'm saying we should get reinforcements. My father can have half the guard out there tonight."

Orrin checked to make sure the sword could still be drawn. He'd nicked it a bit on Tymon's ribs. It grated a bit toward the end but otherwise came out fine.

"I'm going to drop Tymon off with your dad," Orrin answered her finally. "I'll ask Jude and Brandt to come. I have no chance against the teleporter. She just shrugged my spells off."

Tony returned from upstairs with a crossbow nestled in his arms and a satchel across his shoulder. "Did you get a read on her?"

Orrin slammed the sword back into the hilt. "No. It happened too fast—I didn't even try to [Identify] her."

Tony grunted as he hit the first-floor landing. "Learn from the mistake. Knowing her name could give old Silas a lead."

"But he'll have one. When we tell him what Tymon said. Another lord of Dey kidnapped Daniel right out from Silas's protection," Orrin said as they traipsed back into Tony's kitchen. "He'll be able to tell the others and—"

"And do what, exactly? How much power do you think Silas has? Without all four working in concert, nothing gets done in the entire city, and even then, it's only half-assed."

"My father does the best he can with—"

Tony waved a hand. "I'm not saying he doesn't try. Think, girl. What exactly can he do with the word of one small fish like this one?"

Tony gestured at the sleeping body of Tymon.

Madi hung her head in defeat. "Not much. He could wake a magistrate, but without witnesses . . ."

Orrin looked back and forth at the two. "Are you telling me that Silas can't do shit against another lord kidnapping and attacking someone right at his own front door?"

Madi silently began undoing the knots on Tymon's bonds.

"That's the dumbest thing I've ever heard!" Orrin continued. "Isn't he supposed to rule this city? What dumb person set up the city so the lords could act without repercussions?"

Tony was rummaging in drawers and pulling out crossbow bolts a few at a time. "If one lord could just accuse another of something and have him thrown in prison, Dey would have fallen a long time ago. It's no secret all four houses have their share of skeletons in the closet. Shit, a few generations back, the Timpe house tried a coup d'état. Only the family members directly caught were executed, and the Timpe lord continued his rule for another three years before a family member took him out."

Orrin helped Madi pick Tymon up off the chair. Between the two of them, they could just lift the man. "Oh, Tony. I'll invite you to our party and use [Utility Ward]."

Orrin sent an invite to the man, but Tony shook his head. "You better not use any spells except [Teleport]. You are still recovering. Leave the rescue mission to us."

Orrin clenched his teeth to stop a retort. He knew he had already cycled a few times, but from Tony's earlier assessment, he was still within normal parameters . . . for him.

Madi turned to go through the front door first, doing a side shuffle to keep Tymon from falling over. Once they got down the front steps, Tony put a hand on Orrin's shoulder and gave the all clear.

Orrin cast [Teleport] and moved all four of them to the Catanzano estate.

The area was chaos incarnate.

Guards ran up to them as soon as they appeared and tried to push them back. Silas's personal guards appeared and attempted to pull Madi inside. A bystander caught sight of Tony and screamed. All the while, men with axes chopped down the frozen gate still standing in front of the house. Enough had been cut away that people could duck through, but the work was still far from done.

"What is going on here?" Silas's voice pierced the darkness, and Orrin sighed in relief as the man wheeled himself over. "Release them at once. That's my daught—"

Silas stopped talking at the sight of Tony. His usually stoic face went through so many emotions at once that Orrin couldn't get a read on the man.

"Hi there, Sly-lus. Your daughter has asked for my help cleaning up a little mess. We brought you a present." Tony smirked, projecting his voice into the minds of all those nearby. Orrin heard a few more screams, and most of the locals left quickly for their homes.

"Anthony. Whatever you were thinking of doing, you can crawl back to your little hidey-hole now. We don't need your kind of help." Silas pointed at two guards and gestured. "Please take this man inside for questioning. He was one of those who attacked here tonight."

The guards looked at each other, and one paled. "Begging your pardon, sire, but Mr. Anthony doesn't fit the description of—"

"Not him, you incompetent fool. The knocked-out man my daughter is carrying. The one with blood all over his clothing. I'm assuming you retrieved your sword, Orrin?"

Orrin grunted as the men took Tymon off his hands and nodded. "Tony helped us find the people who took Daniel. We know where they—"

"I think this conversation can wait until we get inside," Silas cut him off. "Thank you for the help, Anthony. You may go now." Silas turned and pushed his wheels toward the house.

Orrin stepped forward and grabbed the back of Silas's seat. With a burst of anger, he twirled the man around and bent close, getting into Silas's face. Orrin ignored the sound of steel being drawn and whispered quietly to Madi's father, "Tony has helped find my friend, who you promised to keep safe. You failed in your task. He's with me. Get the stick out of your ass."

Silas held up a hand to his guards without breaking eye contact with Orrin. "Be careful, Orrin. My patience only goes so far. Quiet Anthony will not enter my home."

Orrin nodded slowly and backed away. "Fine. I only came for Brandt and Jude anyway. If you want Tymon, the man I caught while you were inside, to talk, just mention spiders. He'll tell you who orchestrated all this."

Orrin looked around and spotted both the men he'd just named. "You two coming or what?" He sent a party invite to both.

Jude accepted immediately.

Brandt turned to Silas, who waved a hand. "Bring the woman back alive if possible. Take eight more of your own choosing. Rescue is priority."

Brandt accepted the invite.

"I can't teleport that many men," Orrin mumbled, surprised at the elder Catanzano's orders. "I can only take a few at a time."

"Coordinate with Brandt. Come along, Madeleine." Silas pivoted his chair and didn't look back.

"I'll be going with them to save my party member," Madi called out in a strong and loud voice.

The chair lurched to a stop. Silas peered over his shoulder and glanced at the dozens of witnesses around. He exchanged another look with Brandt, who nodded again. With a sigh, Madi's father said, "As you wish. Please be home by morning. We're having those little pancakes you adore."

Orrin watched the lord of Dey move slowly back inside his home. "Well, that could have gone better."

Tony laughed in his head. "Boy, you have no idea how close you came to being killed in a spectacular fashion just now."

Tony obviously hadn't said that to anyone but him, because Madi said at almost the same time, "He is such an ass."

Orrin pursed his lips and then waved everyone over. He spread out a map on the ground and pointed. "So, here's the plan. I'll take Tony and scout ahead at where we think they've got Daniel. If it's only the woman and we can take her, I'll jump in and grab him and come right back. If there are more people, I'll need your help figuring out what to do, Brandt."

Brandt raised a hand. "We have two [Locationists] we can use. Both can only move ten miles in a jump but can take four men each. We can't bring horses, though. That's at least twenty miles out, if not more. It'll take a few hours to get close enough to be of help."

Orrin closed his eyes and started running figures. *I've still got [Utility Ward] running. If I cycle and cast max buffs, I can [Telepo—*

Tony slapped him upside the head. "No. You turn it off right now."

Brandt and Jude moved their hands to their weapons, but Madi waved them off. "Is he thinking of playing hero again?"

The other guards looked at each other and began to whisper.

"I'm not a [Hero]. I just want to get my friend back. I can teleport us all there now. It'll take a few jumps, but we can all be there right away."

Brandt gave a small smile. "We want to get to Daniel, too. But that bitch that took him couldn't have jumped him twice. She'll have needed to travel by foot. And I'm sure our boy spent every minute making that a pain for her."

Orrin took a deep breath and steadied himself. "It's worth getting there faster. I can do it."

"You'll die." Tony spoke into everyone's heads. The certainty of the words spoken into their minds made it real. Everybody gave Orrin a disapproving look.

"Daniel wouldn't want you to be reckless," Madi said softly. "He's already going to be pissed off enough when we save his butt."

Jude chuckled. "Come on, Orrin. Have a little faith in us. We'll find their camp easy enough."

Orrin closed his eyes and let go of [Mind Bastion]. His MP was nearly full from his last cycle, but he felt the beginnings of a headache.

"Well done," Tony whispered to Orrin alone. "True growth is hard, but self-discipline pays dividends. I'm proud of you."

Orrin pushed away the tears of anger and sadness as his emotions flooded back in full force. "So I can cast [Teleport] eight times and have enough mana to still fight. Madi, Tony, Jude, and two of you can come with me. Brandt, you get the other eight and your teleporters to meet us here." He pointed to the map, halfway between Dey and the jelly-stained mark on the map. "I'll find you and we can find Daniel."

"Sir, if I may?" One of the guards Brandt had called over spoke quickly. "What is going on? Who are we going after?"

Brandt responded in a gruff, military clip. "Someone kidnapped while under our protection. That's all you need to know, Jenson."

Another guard rubbed her foot on the back of her leg. "I think what Jenson is asking, sir, is who are we up against? Is this Daniel kid someone's bastard? Is this a house dispute or does it have something to do with the war with the elves? We just want to know what we're walking into."

Brandt's eyes narrowed. "Does it matter? We had the honor of House Catanzano stained tonight by three attackers, and you care who did it? Whether it's the elven army or a Demon Lord, we will go in there and knock them out cold. Within two days, I want every-one in Dey talking about the corpses hanging over the gates, not the attack and embarrassment we suffered tonight. Is that understood?"

"Yes, sir," a chorus of guards answered.

"Get your gear. We're traveling light and we're moving out in five minutes."

The guards all ran, leaving only Brandt and Jude with Madi and Tony. Orrin rolled up the map and handed it back to Tony.

"Do you have any idea who it is?" Brandt whispered once the last guard was clear of sight. "Who took Daniel?"

"Lord Wendeln, but he's working for or with someone else, we think," Orrin answered.

Brandt's intake of breath was his only response. Jude was staring at the ground and shaking his head. "No way would he go that far."

"I don't care who it is," Orrin said, his eyes flickering in the light of the torches all around. "I'm going to get Daniel back, and then we are going to make somebody pay for this."

Chapter 58

The guards returned carrying an array of weapons and small packs. One even brought extra packs for Orrin and Madi. Orrin declined his. [Dimension Hole] held all he would need.

Brandt helped Madi strap the quick-drop harness over her shoulders. The entire bag could be released in an instant for greater mobility in a fight.

Jude introduced Orrin to everyone. The guards coming with them were a strange group. There were three women, each wearing contrastingly different styles of armor. Alysha stood in half plate and a tower shield, a longsword at her side. Leigh wore ring mail and held a longbow. Hetdt twirled a short wand in her fingers, wearing padded armor under a long robe. They all nodded at the introduction and went back to stuffing their packs.

The other five guards were men. Two mages in robes only, Efraim and Brooks, shook Orrin's hand. Charlie, Shiu, and Ryland were in the Catanzano colors. Each had a shortsword and a long dagger strapped at his side.

"You're the one who got in her way while we were trapped inside," Shiu said with a look. "You couldn't have stopped her from getting away?"

Jude growled low and took a step toward the man, but Orrin stuck out his arm and blocked him.

"I did my best, but I'm only level twelve. My spells bounced off her. Tony thinks she must have a high constitution. Is that going to be a problem for you all?"

Shiu let out his breath in a huff. "Sorry. I didn't mean to sound like an asshole. We all felt useless stuck behind the door. Except for Ryland here, who got a chance and blew it."

Orrin recognized him as one of the two who had charged the kidnapper. The tall man scowled. "She got lucky with that whip. I didn't know her reach, but I'll get her this time."

The other two members of the expedition held the uncommon class of [Locationist]. Orrin knew that teleporting wasn't rare but to have a class dedicated to it was. A man and woman stood arguing a few steps away from everyone else. They wore normal clothing and would have been indistinguishable from any other citizen of Dey.

As Jude explained, teleporting yourself was easy enough, but most people didn't build out to have the mana needed to move groups of people. These two worked for the Guild and made a decent living making quick jumps around town. They plied their trade in anything from an alarm to a letter.

Orrin and Jude wandered over to the couple just as the man pushed the woman hard. She stumbled back only a bit.

"Open your ears. Do you realize what they're asking? We are going to be stuck ten miles away from the gates and have to walk back alone," the man spat.

"Orrin, meet Jack and Jillian, the worst siblings you'll ever see." Jude interrupted the fight. "Jack, you've already agreed to the terms. Are you trying to squeeze more pay out of a rescue mission?"

When Jack's eyes left his sister to glance at Jude, Jillian took the opportunity and sucker punched him in the stomach. The man doubled over.

"Nah, Jude," Jillian said with a laugh. "We're ready to go when you are. We can always sleep under the stars tonight."

"Are you two not coming with us?" Orrin asked.

Jack spat on the ground and straightened. "The contract is to ferry you lot as close to Doc Haven's fields as we can. You can all find your own way back."

"But you could help us. I could buy you mana potions. I've only got a few hundred-MP mana potions, but I'd share. You could get us closer and . . ." Orrin trailed off. His fingers had rested along his potion belt and he'd realized he still had a regen potion.

"Tony!" Orrin turned away, ignoring the [Locationists].

The man appeared behind him. "I was hoping you wouldn't think of that."

Orrin yelped and twisted. "Fuck. You're too quiet for an old man."

Tony smirked. "Yes, you could probably teleport the group closer after the first jump. But then you'd be asking a dozen people to wait on their hands while you spent, what . . . ten minutes refilling your mana pool?"

"Eight minutes with the potion," Orrin countered. "But I could only get about half the group each jump. I'd have to wait with the first group then jump back and jump again . . ."

Orrin ran the numbers. "The first half would need to wait for about fifteen minutes for me to get everyone there and recharge."

Tony nodded. "And do you think these people who were just insulted are going to wait around? Use your potion when we get to our destination. You're going to need it."

Orrin talked with the teleporters some more. They told him where the teleport point would be, roughly. Orrin and Tony were able to find a spot only half a mile away that Orrin knew—he couldn't teleport somewhere he hadn't been. They settled for a spot not far from where Orrin and Daniel had helped Toby the farmer with his giant rat problem so long ago. Toby's farm was only four miles from Dey, but they'd traveled farther out in search of those monsters. Orrin's group would catch up with the others and then they'd all start running.

Brandt gave the all clear. The groups split up, with Tony and Madi sticking close to Orrin. Brandt and Jude were in charge of three soldiers each. Hetdt and Ryland joined Orrin's group.

With a final nod, Jack and Jillian popped each group of five away. Orrin rolled his shoulders and did the same.

Hold on, Daniel. We're coming for you.

Landing in a field with rotting animal corpses was not a pleasant experience. *At least I wasn't as unlucky as Madi.*

She'd landed after the [Teleport] with both feet stuck through a maggot-ridden corpse of a Dire Rat.

While she yelled at Orrin, he ignored her and used [Map] to find the other members of his party. Jude and Brandt were closer than they'd thought.

"This way," Orrin said, not seeing Madi's hand slapping his head until [Side Steps] triggered. He jerked to the side, and she fell down, nearly missing another pile of rat bodies.

"Nice!" Orrin muttered sarcastically. "Maybe you should hit me some more. I haven't leveled that up all the way."

Hetdt let out a single chuckle but quickly stifled it. They moved on and connected with the group.

"The siblings left already?" Madi asked distastefully.

Brandt nodded. "They took a potion and teleported right back. Everyone, gather up. We run in twos, side by side, and staggered. Keep another group in sight at all times. Orrin and I will take point. If you need a break, hand signals only. We don't know how far out they'll have scouts, but you can bet we aren't going to sneak all the way in. Full engagement upon contact. Lord Catanzano requested the one who attacked his house be taken alive, but the rest are fair game."

Jude looked up at the starry sky. "I won't be pointing fingers if she doesn't make it."

Brandt gave Jude a stern look. "Move out, people."

Running. It always ends up being running, Orrin thought as he kept one eye looking forward and another on his [Map]. Brandt had set the pace at first but had to slow down for Orrin and Tony. The man was ages older than anyone else on the team.

"Still nothing," Orrin whispered in his head to Tony. Tony then pinged the report to everyone. Keeping quiet and unnoticed for as long as possible was paramount.

Thirty minutes turned into an hour, and Orrin started to flag. He waved at Brandt and the convoy slowed to a stop.

"Did you find them already?" Jude whispered as they huddled. "What's the plan? Can you give us all those boosts?"

Brandt shushed Jude and turned to Orrin. "Needed a break?"

"Just a few minutes," Orrin responded. He didn't mention that Tony had groaned in delight when they stopped, too.

Tony shot Orrin a rude gesture with his finger.

I guess the middle finger crosses dimensional borders. Orrin chuckled to himself.

As everyone else stood waiting, Orrin, Tony, and Madi squatted and tried to catch their breath.

"Do you think I should buff everyone?" Orrin asked the other two. "It might be the difference we need."

Madi had been quiet for the entire trip and simply looked to the mind mage.

"If we get the chance, then yes," Tony responded. "If we get attacked, try and teleport Daniel away."

"You don't think we are going to get the drop on these kidnappers, do you?" Madi asked in a whisper.

Tony shook his head. "Something is off about all this. How did they know Daniel was out of the house? Tymon knew where they planned to escape to but had no [Teleport] ability of his own. Did they think he would just show up later?"

Orrin pondered Tony's words until the stitch in his side subsided. "You both ready?"

Madi pulled a smile on. "I didn't need the break. That was for you."

Tony winked at Orrin. "She was nearly falling over, too."

"I was not," Madi said and put her hand on her hip.

Orrin let out a low laugh. "Let's go."

After two full hours of running, Orrin held up a fist and stopped. Brandt gave a few hand signals, and the party spread out.

"I've got movement up ahead. Someone is sitting in that small cluster of trees at the foot of that small hill," Orrin explained to Tony.

"Brandt wants to attack," Tony responded a minute later. "I suggested you and I go for a walk. I can make the scout's eyes pass off me. You can use [Camouflage]. We can take him out quietly. Brandt said it's up to you."

Orrin didn't hesitate. "Let's go. I'm going to cast [Utility Ward] on everybody, though."

Tony grunted and began telling the rest of the group what was happening.

Orrin's party consisted of Brandt, Jude, Tony, and Madi. He wanted all five of them to be in the best shape if it came down to a full-on brawl. With his promise not to mana cycle, he cast the spell without prebuffing himself.

Casting [Utility Ward] at level one on his party, as he didn't want to risk level two and the negative effects, Orrin glanced at his mana.

MP: 431/530

Luckily, his stats had already gone up dramatically from the first cast. That base 28 in will was really coming in handy, though.

Tony missed a step and turned to Orrin. "Hearing about it and witnessing it firsthand are two very distinct things. I feel younger than I have in a decade."

Madi waved and looked at Tony. Tony shrugged and gestured for Orrin to follow. Orrin cast [Camouflage] and tried to stay close to Tony.

"What was that?" Orrin thought at Tony.

The mind mage shook his head. "She told me to keep you safe. Now, let me concentrate—I have to cast this without knowing where the person is. Not exactly the easiest thing to do."

Orrin watched as Tony shimmered and flickered before coming back into view.

"That should work," he said and continued his earlier conversation. "She's scared to let you out of her sight. It's sweet but also self-serving. She's new to having a friend. She's worried that if you get hurt, she'll have to go back to being completely under Silas's control. She's also mad at herself for thinking of you as a pawn. Her thoughts are at war with each other—*is Orrin a friend first or someone to use?*"

Orrin didn't like that one bit. He was just starting to trust Madi more.

"Don't think like that. She's been raised to view the world in a different way than most. Her instinct is to weigh a person's use first. She's fighting that inbred training hard. She truly cares for you and Daniel."

Orrin nodded and tossed a thank-you at the man before pulling his [Map] back up. He kept an eye on his party member dot. Tony wasn't gone, but Orrin felt a headache start the longer he tried looking at him.

They'd made it halfway up the old path they'd been following. The enemy spot on his [Map] still hadn't moved, but now that they were closer . . .

"There are four more white dots just over the hill."

"Five total? Or four and Daniel?"

Orrin shook his head in frustration. "I don't know."

"Same plan—take this one out. Do you need me to do it?" Tony drew a long stiletto dagger from his hip.

Orrin swallowed hard. He wasn't running [Mind Bastion] to keep out the fear and revulsion of what he was about to do.

"I'll get close and try to drop his dexterity. Then I'll finish him off if we can't take him prisoner." Orrin tried to sound confident.

"Good luck. I'm not sure the guard is going to take any prisoners, though."

Orrin gritted his teeth and drew his sword. "One thing at a time, Tony."

He stepped off into the night, hoping the old man followed.

Chapter 59

Orrin weighed his options as he crept along the tall grass. Clouds moved across the moon, darkening the way even more. Using his [Map], he continued toward the lone guard in the tree line. He also reset [Camouflage].

I'll use [Identify] first and then hit him with a few inversed dexterity debuffs, he thought. Tony's comment continued to nag at him. Orrin had killed already in this world, but always with [Mind Bastion] running. He doubted whether he could do it without the logical blanket of the skill covering his feelings.

"For Daniel," Orrin muttered to himself.

"Shut up," Tony demanded in his head.

Orrin kicked himself and checked the [Map]. No movement.

Moving slowly, so as to minimize the chance of getting caught, Orrin steeled himself. He would do what he needed to protect his friend.

After ten minutes, Orrin could make out the trees and pinpointed where the scout stood. He was crouched on his heels, two trees in from where the tall grass began. Something glinted by his feet.

They had taken so long that Orrin needed to cast [Camouflage] again. He was using the upgraded version, but it still only lasted ten minutes. He checked his mana.

MP: 427/530

Orrin checked the regen potion on his belt with his left hand and rolled the hilt of his shortsword in his right. He moved around the man's right side, keeping a few trees between them. As he got within a few dozen yards, he tried using [Identify].

Wayne Mivren
Toxic Rogue Level 24

HP: 146/180
MP: 135/200

Strength: 12
Constitution: 16
Dexterity: 21
Will: 20
Intelligence: 12

Orrin readied his inversed spells and waited, but Wayne didn't seem to notice.

"What do you see, Orrin?" Tony asked.

"He's a [Toxic Rogue], level twenty-four," Orrin thought back at Tony. "Down on his health and mana a bit. I think he's the one Madi fought off."

"If he is, he's got [Teleport]," Tony responded after a minute. "Madi said he popped away after she got a few hits on him."

So he's a runner, Orrin thought. *I can't just hit him with a few debuffs. I can't drain his mana, so even paralyzed with no dexterity, he'd be able to teleport.*

Orrin squinted and tried to make out the weapon at the man's feet. His hands were between his legs and holding something long. A spear? A staff?

"What did Madi say he fought with?"

Tony gave the impression of a shrug. *So creepy when he does that.* "She didn't say."

Orrin closed his eyes and took a steadying breath. "I'm going to knock his dexterity out, or at least try. Can you keep him occupied so he won't jump?"

"On your mark."

Orrin sprang forward, throwing five inversed [Increase Dexterity] spells at level three that should cost fifteen MP a pop but with his increased intelligence only cost thirteen MP each. His mana drained by sixty-five.

MP: 363/530

Wayne fell to the ground. A moment later, he started crying. "No! No! Stay away! I promise I'll be good."

The kidnapper curled into a ball and started to shake.

Orrin hesitated as he got near the shuddering man. Luckily, Tony did not.

As Orrin slowed, Wayne pointed a finger, and a tiny ball of green liquid shot at him. Tony's arm shot out and pushed Orrin over. Even with his increased strength and dexterity, the old man's stiff-arm was enough to send him reeling. When Orrin sat up, Tony was pulling his punch dagger from Wayne's skull.

The rogue's body slumped to the forest floor.

"Unable to move does not mean unarmed," Tony projected into Orrin's head as he wiped the triangular dagger off. "Grab his staff. We need to get rid of the body."

Tony grabbed a leg and motioned to the other.

"We can just leave it, right?" Orrin swallowed hard, the coffee from earlier threatening to come up.

Tony shook his head. "If they send someone to check on him and his body is gone, they might think he went out to piss. If they find a body, we have no surprise. How close are the rest?"

Orrin shakily pulled up the [Map]. "The others are on the other side of the ridge there. Maybe five minutes?"

"Then let's go. I need to go about halfway back to signal the group. We should hit them as the sun comes up."

Orrin stared at the blood draining from the puncture wound. "I thought I could do this . . ."

Tony dropped the leg. He moved slowly toward Orrin and put his hands on his shoulders. "Look at me. You can do this. You will. I've seen your heart and mind, boy. You hesitated not out of weakness or fear but because you care. You wanted to give him a chance." Tony sighed. "That is an admirable trait, and you should hold on to it dearly."

Tony slapped Orrin. "But right now, your friend needs you to kill all the bastards who are trying to take him. Deal with the body. Carry it into the grass and make sure it can't be seen from here. Try not to leave any drag marks and scuff up the ground around his blood. You won't be able to get rid of it all, but do your best. Okay?"

The slap jolted Orrin back to the present. "Yes. Thanks. Sorry. I got it."

Tony turned and shimmered away again. "I should be able to keep in touch with you the whole way. Don't do anything stupid."

As Tony left, Orrin knelt by Wayne. A man whose life was over so quickly. He ran his hand over the dead man's eyes to close them.

"You shouldn't have taken my friend. I'm sorry."

Orrin stood and grabbed a leg. He took the man's arm and started to pull him up when he had another thought.

"If this works . . ."

Twenty-five minutes later, the entire party arrived. Orrin heard them before he saw them.

"Quiet," Tony ordered, and the guards stepped more lightly as they neared the small, forested area.

"There are four people on the other side of the ridge here," Tony explained, drawing a rough map in the dirt. Having already gleaned what he needed from Orrin, Tony continued, "We're going to go in fast. Orrin and half the group should figure out which person is Daniel and get him out. Orrin will teleport both of them away at the first sign of danger. If we start getting our asses handed to us, run. Don't be cute and try anything stupid."

"Why are you looking right at me?" Orrin whispered, barely making a sound.

"What did you do with the body?"

Orrin pointed to his pants.

"I don't get it," Jude muttered. His voice was a little loud, and he adjusted the volume. "What did you do?"

Tony rolled his eyes. "He put the corpse in his dimensional storage."

Half the guards frowned, and one paled. "That's disgusting."

"I'm going to bury him later," Orrin defended himself. "I just didn't know how far out to put him and thought this would be faster."

Brandt waved a hand. "Later. Let's go."

The group of guards, Brandt, Jude, Madi, Tony, and Orrin made their way up the small path that had been created through the trees. It was evident enough that Orrin didn't have a hard time finding it. As they traveled up the hill, the trees thinned. Two large rocks created a narrow opening, wide enough for Orrin and Madi but small enough that most of the guards had to squeeze through.

On the other side, more large boulders blocked the view, but the trail continued to the left.

"Be careful," Tony whispered in their minds. "They're alert and something's wrong. Their thoughts are muffled to me. Trained."

Orrin didn't understand what "trained" meant but assumed they were walking into a trap. He put [Camouflage] back on.

Brandt and Tony stayed at the front of the guard formation, with Jude hanging back near Madi and Orrin. As Brandt rounded a stone, Orrin saw something dark and fast streak toward the man.

"Look out," Orrin yelled and cast a [Ward] on his friend. The arrow bounced off the man.

The guards roared and ran ahead. Madi and Orrin ran after them with Jude.

As Orrin rounded the granite rock, the small valley opened up in front of him. Three small tents had been erected with a small fire burning merrily in the center. Two hooded figures stood near the fire. One held a bow, and the second had a set of whips out in hand.

A third male, hood down, was swinging a battle-ax that rivaled Jude's hammer. It was at least ten feet long, and he swept it in wide arcs to keep the guards back. The hooded figure with the bow was shooting arrow after arrow, and Orrin watched in horror as two of the mages, Hetdt and Brooks, went down screaming with an arrow that hissed into their limbs.

He stepped forward to heal them.

"Orrin, you better be gone already. Go find him. Jude and I will pull the wounded back around for cover," Madi said, looking around. She couldn't get her eyes to land on him.

Orrin gritted his teeth and looked at his [Map]. A fourth dot was in one of the tents—the one the whip lady was standing in front of.

Orrin sidled along the edge of the battle. Brandt and Ryland were harrying the big man with the axe, while Alysha used her tower shield to deflect the blows into the air. Leigh stood with Efraim as both took shots over the field at the bowman. The other kidnapper's whips lashed out and found each missile.

I need to stop calling her "whip lady."

Orrin used [Identify] and sucked in a breath.

> **Samara Jako**
> **Flower Whip Level 45**
> **HP: —**
> **MP: —**

Fuck. That's no help. Orrin watched as two of the guards in Catanzano livery rushed forward, only to get smacked backward by an arrow and axe strike. *They've all worked together before. That's great teamwork.*

Orrin shook his head and continued his way around the fight, doing his best to ignore the sounds.

He was so close. *Maybe I should teleport into the tent.*

Samara darted forward and joined the fight. Tony had cast something, making the fighter with the axe swing wildly in circles.

Orrin looked back and forth. He was so close to the tent. Now that he was close, he could tell the bowman was a male. He reached over his shoulder, and an arrow appeared in his hand as if summoned. It gave off a dark light, and as he pulled the arrow into his bow, the man giggled.

Orrin debuffed his dexterity at the same moment he stabbed his neck. The man's eyes went wide, and he flailed, dropping his bow. He pulled a long dagger and started swiping left and right. Orrin yanked the blade to the right and watched in slow motion as the man's head was nearly separated from his shoulders.

Orrin spared a quick glance at the battle and stepped into the tent. He nearly tripped over his friend.

Daniel was tied up with vines and had a glazed look to his eyes. He was on his side and had been stripped of his clothes. His armor and sword were in a wooden crate toward the back, with Gerty creating an indent in the dirt beside it.

Orrin swiped everything into his [Dimension Hole].

Orrin yelled out in his mind as loudly as he could, "Found him. I'm going to teleport us out. Get out of here." He grabbed Daniel in his arms and used [Teleport].

Nothing happened.

"Fuck." Orrin thought fast and cut the bindings off Daniel.

"Tony, I can't teleport out." Hopefully, the old man was listening.

Daniel groaned as he turned him over. Orrin pulled a set of clothes out and tugged a shirt over his friend's chest. He'd need to put his own pants on.

"Daniel, can you stand?" Orrin propped him up into a standing position, and Daniel's knees gave way. Orrin caught him.

He's still drugged. Fuck.

Orrin turned and let Daniel fall on his back, carrying him piggyback. His increased strength made him feel stronger than ever before.

"Let's get you out of here, buddy," Orrin said and stepped through the tent flap. "I got you."

As the tent flap closed behind him, Orrin looked into the face of a dehooded Samara. "I'll take that for you."

The guards and Brandt were all down. Orrin couldn't see Tony, Madi, or Jude, but the big axeman was walking around the perimeter, peering into the darkness.

"Please don't make me kill you." Samara took a step forward. "Everybody down there should be fine in a week or so, but you are holding something that does not belong to you."

"He's more mine than yours," Orrin spat in retort. "I know who you work for, and when I get Daniel back to Dey, we are going to kick in his face, too."

Orrin really hoped the system responded to his thoughts alone. He'd never tried buying something without watching the boxes, but he couldn't take his eyes off Samara now.

Samara's face darkened. "That's unfortunate. I had hoped to keep casualties to a minimum." She approached menacingly.

Orrin felt the tickle in his mind of a new skill and immediately cast it.

[Remetabolize].

He cast it three times before he felt the change in breathing. Orrin let Daniel's body slide down his back. Orrin put his hand into his pocket.

"Hands up and drop the [Hero]. Unfortunately for you, this is your end."

Daniel grabbed the handle of Gertrude sticking out from Orrin's pocket and held her high.

"Hey, bitch. Stop threatening my friend."

Chapter 60

Samara scowled. "Child, go back to your tent. You are no match for me, even if you are a [Hero]."

Daniel took a gentle step forward and nudged Orrin behind him. "We'll see. You had to use poison to take me down last time. What, were you scared of me?"

Daniel darted forward and hit Samara with his sword.

Or at least he tried. She dodged under his swing and punched him twice in rapid succession. One fist struck his chest, and the second lifted him from the stomach. He staggered back quickly.

Orrin checked his friend's HP.

HP: 250/300

Two hits and she knocked off a sixth of his health. Orrin grabbed his regen potion and downed it in a shot. He reached forward and grabbed Daniel's shoulder, pulling him farther back.

"Maybe we work together on this one?" Orrin asked.

Orrin couldn't see his friend smile, but he knew it was there. Daniel nodded. "Oh, you are in trouble now."

Orrin cast his highest [Increase Dexterity] and [Increase Strength] on Daniel. He felt a sudden light-headedness and checked his status.

MP: 28–29/530

He watched the numbers ticking up, but he was dangerously low on mana. *Fuck, [Remetabolize] costs a lot!*

Orrin checked Daniel's stats. His dexterity had gone up by eighty-five points. His strength . . .

Daniel
Hero Level 12

HP: 250/300
MP: 80/80

Strength: 100
Constitution: 15
Dexterity: 98
Will: 8
Intelligence: 10

I guess the cap really is a hundred?

"Hey, O. I didn't get a chance to tell you earlier because some assholes decided to drug and kidnap me," Daniel said, cutting into Orrin's thought and loud enough for the woman in front of them to hear. "I got another level while you were sick and some cool new skills that stack. Want to see?"

Orrin didn't have time to answer. Daniel simply disappeared and reappeared a step past Samara. The woman herself was flying through the air away from them. Gertrude was lightly vibrating.

"Holy shit!" Daniel cheered and looked at his sword. "How high did you . . . One hundred freaking strength? Way to go, Orrin!"

Samara hit the ground twenty yards away and rolled backward twice. She stood up and snapped her whips out with a flick of her wrists. "You little fucker. How did you do that?"

Daniel threw a smile over his shoulder at Orrin. "[White Dwarf] lets me increase my mass, so I hit things like a truck. Couple that with [Gravity Strike] and . . ."

Daniel laughed and lifted his foot. He appeared behind Samara. She had time to turn halfway around. Daniel swung Gerty like a bat and launched her into the air with the flat of the sword. Somehow, she kept hold of her weapons.

"[Shooting Star] isn't quite as good as your [Teleport], but I only have to activate it once and I can hop all over the battlefield," Daniel said loudly.

The other kidnapper with the axe was running at Daniel. Orrin checked his mana but didn't have enough to do more than a single debuff or two. He yelled, "Daniel, watch out for the other one."

Daniel turned and did his hovering-foot thing again. As he stepped, he launched at the man. The only problem was, Daniel hadn't quite gotten used to his new strength yet.

His sword cut cleanly through the axe first and then continued through the man's chest. Daniel was moving fast enough that the spray forward didn't hit him, but the part of the man's body that Gertrude had ripped out flew up in an arc.

Blood and gore rained onto the battlefield.

"Oh, shit. That's fucking gross." Daniel stuck his sword in the ground and tried to wipe something meaty from his eyes. "He's dead, right?"

Orrin didn't respond but heard a scream from where Samara had landed.

"You bastards! We didn't kill anyone!" Samara pushed herself from the ground. "I'll kill you!"

Orrin watched as Samara's face went wild with anger. She snapped her whips out in an increasing cadence. With every flick, the whips grew longer, and Orrin could just make out spikes beginning to grow out of the weapons.

"You kidnap me and attack everyone trying to rescue me . . ." Daniel started as he wiped his hands on his pants. He picked up his sword. "You threaten Orrin . . . and you're mad when we fight back?"

Samara charged at Daniel, bent on taking her revenge. Orrin scanned her again but still couldn't see her health.

The entire fight hadn't been a minute. Orrin felt useless to do anything.

Samara ran at Daniel. Daniel lifted a foot.

"Stop!" Jude's voice rang out.

Samara looked beyond Daniel and smiled evilly. She slowed her charge. Daniel stopped himself from checking over his shoulder and glanced at Orrin.

Orrin tried to process what he was seeing.

Jude was dragging an unconscious Madi from behind a tree with one hand. His hammer was strapped to his back, and he held a knife. "The deal was nobody died."

"He killed Argyle," Samara spat. "He at least needs to learn a lesson."

Jude shook his head. "I may not be a match for you, but if you attack Daniel, I won't stand by."

Samara threw her head back and laughed. "This is when you grow a spine? You realize I'll kill your family. You'll throw away all the goodwill you've gained. Why would you even lead them here?"

Jude let go of Madi's foot and sheathed his knife. He pulled his hammer from his back. "I didn't. They found out somehow, and luckily I was able to join. I was able to take out Quiet Anthony for you, or did you think you won this fight on your own?"

"Jude? What the hell are you talking about?" Daniel yelled and turned so he could see both Samara and Jude. "This is a bad joke."

Jude's usually playful face was twisted in a sorrowful grimace. "I'm sorry, Daniel. I really like you. They found out Silas had a [Hero] under his roof and took my family. My sister-in-law and niece are all I have."

"And they'll be dead if you don't help. Tell me how he's so strong? My constitution is too high to be knocked around so easily by someone under level thirty." Samara held her whips to the side, and Orrin could see them more clearly. The vine protrusions had sharp spikes every few feet that pulsed with a life of their own. The tip of the weapons had a small mouthlike appendage that reminded him of a Venus flytrap.

Orrin was shaken when Jude said he'd taken out Tony. He checked his [Map] and saw an unmoving dot in the woods where Jude had come from. *Would a dead body still register as part of my team?*

Daniel shook his head. "Jude, don't. We'll help find your family. You're our friend."

Jude watched his feet as he answered. "I know where they are, Daniel. They're locked up in Lord Wendeln's dungeon. He promised to release them once you were captured."

"I *was* captured. Did he release them? I'm guessing not, because you're here," Daniel argued. "The three of us can take her. Help us."

Orrin checked his mana.

MP: 103/530

I'm going to have to cycle.

The faintest whisper entered his mind. "No."

Tony?

There was no response.

Orrin looked around at all the unconscious members of the guard. Samara had told the truth. They all were knocked out and low on health, but nobody was dead. Small puncture wounds on each of them appeared to be from her whips.

I wonder . . .

Orrin began to cast spells at Brandt.

"I'm dead either way. But if I don't help her, they are, too. Please understand." Orrin watched in horror as Jude lifted his hammer into a readied position and turned his feet toward Daniel. "The other one, Samara. He casts magic that increases strength or dexterity."

"So that's what he was doing to me. It's been years since a spell got through and did something," she said, turning her gaze on Orrin. "What an interesting ability. It's too bad I have to kill you to teach the little [Hero] a lesson."

"Samara, no. Just knock him out. We can take Daniel away and still—"

"Don't give me orders, traitor," Samara cut him off.

Orrin and Daniel waited.

What are they waiting for?

"Hey, O? I'm going to need your help. My quick runner skill is almost up. Did you get anything else that can help here?"

They're running out the clock on his skills. Fuck. Orrin tried one more time on Brandt.

The man moaned low.

Yes!

Orrin had first tried a [Heal Small Wounds], but that hadn't done much. Brandt's health wasn't even that low. His new spell, [Remetabolize], had been the key. But it had taken three attempts to neutralize whatever was in those spikes.

"Brandt, Jude sold us out. Get up," Orrin yelled.

"All your guards are down for at least an hour. My attacks aren't so easy to shrug . . . What?" Samara stepped back as Brandt pushed himself to his feet.

The man turned and surveyed the area. He was between Orrin and Jude. His face darkened as he saw Madi's limp body behind his coworker and friend. His eyes closed tight, and a single tear rolled down his cheek. "Daniel, you take her. I'll stop Jude and then join you. Leave a piece for me."

Brandt opened his eyes, and his crystal gaze pierced Jude. The hammer-wielding friend turned foe shook and tried to avert his eyes.

That's when Brandt attacked.

Orrin remembered watching the two duel before. They were evenly matched, with Brandt focusing mostly on defensive fighting and Jude on offensive styles. The sparring usually ended when one of them tired.

This fight was over in seconds.

Brandt ducked under a wild, last-minute swing and stabbed his sword through Jude's side. His hand moved fluidly, releasing the handle from his striking stance and reversing his grip. He punched his sword to the side, ripping the blade through Jude's armor and stomach.

Jude whispered something and fell to the side.

"Useless," Samara muttered and brought her hand up over her head. She sent her right whip down at Brandt's back, still kneeling over his downed friend.

Orrin jumped forward and used an overhand chop with his own sword to throw the whip off course. It kicked up dust next to the two guards.

Samara's left arm was already coming down with the second attack. But she'd taken her eyes off Daniel.

He must have had a few seconds left in his dash attack, because Daniel appeared where Samara had just stood. He launched her back into a tree that Orrin would be hard-pressed to wrap his arms around. She hit with a glancing blow, and her body broke the base of the tree. It slowly toppled to the side, catching on a few limbs around it and hanging precariously over the woman.

Orrin stood by helplessly as the fight unfolded around him. The quickness with which Samara stood showed she was still in the fight, and Brandt's small stumble as he stood indicated how hurt he still was. Daniel's skill was over. He was stomping his foot repeatedly until he realized nothing was going to happen. He held up Gerty at a side angle. Brandt fell into place next to him.

Orrin's mana was not coming in as fast as he needed. He needed to stop Samara. His debuff spells didn't do much, but he could shave something off. She'd implied enough that just a little might happen. Or should he [Ward] both Daniel and Brandt?

What he really needed was some way to knock out Samara's constitution. She was taking hits from a one hundred–strength sword strike and still walking. If only he had some ability that could take out her constitution, then maybe he could—

Administrator Access Engaged:
Reset Target Constitution.
Yes or No?

Chapter 61

"No way," Orrin gasped as he quickly pressed the Yes button.

Confirm: Decrease Target's Constitution by 10
Yes or No?

Yes!

Orrin felt a rush of power surge through his body and out toward Samara. She stumbled, and her eyes went wide in fear.

"What have you done to me?" she screamed and looked between the two standing members of the rescue squad and Daniel.

Daniel and Brandt exchanged a quizzical look and attacked. Not missing a chance to get within her guard, Brandt slashed at one whip as it fell at him. He pushed that cut into a pirouette, spinning and stabbing at the leader of the kidnappers. Daniel tried to do the same, but his larger sword was easier for Samara's whip to grab. Luckily, with his increased strength, Daniel was able to rip the entire whip from her hand.

Brandt's backstroke hit Samara and broke the skin, slicing a narrow rent in her armor. The smallest trickle of blood stained her outfit. Brandt spun again, but Samara used her empty hand to swat the man's shoulder. His controlled spin careened into a windmill, and Brandt landed hard on his ass.

Daniel thrashed his sword in the air twice to dislodge the stolen whip and came in too late to stop the hit on Brandt. He swung Gertrude with the blade horizontal to the group and connected with Samara's stomach.

She didn't fall in two pieces like her comrade had but was buffeted backward against another tree. Unlike the first time, she was slow to push herself out of the dented wood. Her free hand held her side, and she coughed blood.

Orrin missed it all.

When the rush of power had left his body, darting toward Samara in a blaze, it also rebounded on the caster. Orrin felt like he'd been kicked in the balls, stabbed behind the eyes, and sucker punched in the stomach all at once. He didn't need to open his status to realize what had happened. He could feel it in his bones. After he raised his head off the ground where he had fallen over, he pulled his status up anyway.

Orrin
Utility Warder

HP: 80/80
MP: 28/380 (+150)

Strength: 9 (+15)
Constitution: 8
Dexterity: 9 (+15)
Will: 28 (+15)
Intelligence: 11 (+15)

What the fuck? Why did my health go down to eighty? Wait, why did my constitution go down to eight? Orrin panicked and stared at his status, ignoring the battle raging around him.

"You did this," Samara growled and pointed at Orrin with a bloodstained hand. Daniel's hit had done some actual damage. "Give it back. I worked too hard to give up my stats. That wasn't some measly spell to lock down my strength. That did something to me. Undo it now!"

"Honey, I think you're forgetting about me," Daniel chided and pointed the length of his massive sword at her. "Care to go again?"

Samara reached her hand slightly down and between Orrin and Daniel. Daniel didn't take his eyes off her, but Orrin noticed the fallen whip began to wiggle on the ground.

"D! The whip! Look—" Orrin had time to get out before the vine levitated and struck Daniel from behind, wrapping around his neck and pulling him back toward the still-stunned form of Brandt. "—out," Orrin finished weakly.

Samara advanced on him. Orrin scrambled backward and got to his feet. His sword had fallen farther forward when he'd momentarily blacked out from whatever he'd done, and he quickly summoned an icy sword.

"Stay back or I'll do it again," he threatened. Samara's steps faltered.

"Undo what you did and I'll let you leave here alive." Her voice was hard, and Orrin didn't believe her for a second. "Or I'll take my chance at the spell being broken by your death."

"It's no spell," a familiar voice said into Orrin's mind. He sighed with relief. Tony continued, "Leave now, Samara Jako, hidden Agent of Lord Wendeln, or Orrin will reduce you to dust. You've lost."

Orrin couldn't see Tony and pulled up his [Map]. *There.* Orrin peered toward the tree line and could just make out the old man leaning his back against a tree.

Unfortunately, Samara had the presence of mind to follow Orrin's gaze. "I've always told my lord you should have been killed ages ago." She snapped her final whip, and it straightened like a spear. With a two-step lunge, Samara launched the vine whip-spear at Tony.

"No." Orrin tried to dash forward and hit the spear with his sword, but Samara reached out and grabbed him around the neck. He hacked down with his sword, but he didn't have Daniel's strength. The ice chipped and cracked as he hit her again and again.

Orrin watched the whip sail through the air, twisting with a life of its own. It hit the tree Tony stood behind and broke the bark in a shower of splinters and earth. The impaled figure of his friend stood straight for only a moment as the dust settled, and then he slumped over.

Orrin's screams turned into a gargle as Samara squeezed. Daniel was clawing at his neck, too. He was strong enough to rip the whip off, but it was quickly looping around him over and over. Brandt was up and trying to get to him, but Samara was already cocking her right hand back. Orrin held no doubt that a single punch from her would go through his skull.

"Again," he croaked.

Confirm: Decrease Target's Constitution by 10
Yes or No?

Yes.

The pain was worse this time. He'd landed on his own broken ice sword, and it had cut his arm. But Samara had dropped him. The second decrease in her constitution had dropped her already-low health to her breaking point. She gagged on blood as it bubbled from her lips.

"Give it back," she murmured. "Please. I can't die like this." She reached out toward Orrin. He couldn't tell if she meant to hurt him or if the gesture was in supplication.

Brandt's sword cut into her face as he swung in an upward strike, taking off half her head in the motion.

The fight was done. Daniel was safe.

Orrin watched leaves fall as he closed his eyes.

"What did he do to her?"

"I don't know. That wasn't the normal debuffs. Mr. Anthony, do you have any idea?"

"Ask him, he's waking up now." Tony's gentle whisper helped Orrin open his eyes. "Welcome back. How are you feeling?"

"I'm starving," Orrin muttered and tried to sit up. He got one hand underneath himself and then toppled back over. "What the hell?"

"Orrin," Tony's voice said delicately. "Open your status."

Orrin went to open his status but then remembered.

"You died! I saw her throw a spear-vine thing right through the tree and kill you," Orrin almost shouted. His ears rang with the loudness of his voice.

"I let her see what she wanted to see." Tony's calm voice entered his head again. Orrin felt a twinge of something else in the words.

"Are you casting something on me?"

Tony's smirk, like a kid caught with his hand in the cookie jar, told Orrin everything he needed to know. "Quit it."

Tony shrugged and stood up. "I'll go help the rest wake up. That whip attack had a strong tranquilizer in it. We might have to call for help bringing them back if I can't get them all out."

He dusted his hands on his pants and walked away. Brandt and Daniel stayed crouched near Orrin.

"Orrin, that whip bitch—"

"Samara," Orrin interrupted.

"Sure," Daniel continued. "Samara. She started yelling at you right before you went down. What did you do? New spell?"

Orrin opened his mouth and closed it again. He glanced at Brandt. "Where's Jude? Is he alive still?"

Daniel waved a hand to his right. "His body is over there somewhere. He's probably dead. Tell me what happened."

Orrin shook his head and crawled to his feet. His balance was off, so he summoned a sword. He used the icy weapon as a cane and balanced as he hobbled toward the bodies all around. Most of the guards that had come with them had small growths on their arms or chests.

"What are those?" he asked as he made his way through the battlefield.

Brandt stuck close while Daniel went to pester Tony for answers instead. "When Samara used her whip, those struck would go down after a few seconds. Anthony says it's some sort of seed that she planted inside them. It was the same for those struck at the Catanzano house. They'll wake up when their bodies fight it off, or sooner if we can dig them out."

At the mention of Catanzano, Orrin's head jerked around. "Where's Madi? Is she okay?"

Brandt nodded and pointed. Madi was holding a wad of white cloth to her head as she sat against a tree. "Jude hit her from behind. Luckily, not hard enough for any permanent damage. Just enough to knock her out."

Orrin almost went to Madi first, but he continued to his other target. Jude.

The man's body hadn't been touched. His side was split open, and viscera oozed out. The final grimace on his face still displayed traces of his cocky smile, but Orrin could see a deeper pain there as well.

"I'm sorry," Orrin whispered.

"I had to. He was a traitor," Brandt said stoically. Orrin didn't mention the tears in the man's eyes.

"I meant I'm sorry we didn't figure it out. Sorry we couldn't save him, too," Orrin explained. "I'm sorry to you, too. Can we save his family?"

Brandt stood straight. "I'm . . . not sure. Politics are in play now. Lord Catanzano will need to know as soon as possible."

Orrin frowned.

"But I'll do everything in my power, even if I have to storm Wendeln's house myself."

Orrin smiled and thumped the taller man on his shoulder. "You won't be alone."

He finally pulled up his status.

Orrin
Utility Warder

HP: 66/70
MP: 184/380

Strength: 9
Constitution: 7

Dexterity: 9
Will: 28
Intelligence: 11

Fuck. Okay. So, that's something I never want to use again. Orrin shivered at the phantom pain running through his body. *[Utility Ward] stopped while I was out.* He used his makeshift cane to hobble back to Madi. Checking her over as he approached, he sighed in relief. She'd be fine.

She glared at him as he got close. "I heard you did something stupid and dangerous again. You took out Wendeln's Agent?"

Orrin's confused look made Madi laugh. "You have no idea who she was, do you?"

"You did?" Orrin slumped down next to her and moved her hand. The little blood on the bandages seemed old. The bleeding had stopped.

"Not until Tony shouted it out. Each lord can appoint an Agent as part of the power contract with the city. It's sort of a . . . Brandt? Help me?"

"An Agent is a spymaster, bodyguard, hit man, and enforcer all rolled into one. They are given a portion of the lord's powers to impose the lord's orders."

"Does Silas have one?" Orrin asked.

Brandt and Madi didn't respond. The silence had the awkward feel of a stupid question.

"What?"

Brandt tossed a sympathetic glance at Madi and answered. "Lady Catanzano was his only Agent. He never appointed another."

"Oh. Sorry."

"Can you lot stop dithering about and help?" Tony's voice came back with his normal demanding tone. "The longer these seeds stay in this lot, the harder it'll be for them to walk back unaided."

Orrin glanced over just as Tony dug a dagger into the leg of one of the mages and pulled out a glowing green stone. No, it was a seed about the size of an acorn. "Unless you all want to carry them back."

Orrin's dizziness was fading as he made his way to another guard. He spotted his sword on the way and let the icy sword fall to the side. Brandt stayed by Madi.

Daniel joined him. "Anthony said to just cut an X and pick out the seed with the tip of a knife. Most of the guards should be able to heal without a scar."

Orrin nodded and looked at his friend. Daniel was practically dancing in his attempt to not ask the questions on his mind. "I'll tell you about it later. I promise."

He found the first raised wound on Alysha, the fighter with the big shield. The whip had struck her on the top of her unprotected head.

Fighting sucks, but this is worse. Orrin made the cut and flicked the small seed out. Alysha's breathing grew less ragged. *Who's next?*

Chapter 62

It took about twenty minutes to get the rest of the party relatively taken care of, but Tony hinted it would be a few hours before some of them were able to fight off the toxic side effects and wake up.

"I could try healing them," Orrin offered.

Tony shook his head. "You need to rest. Stop pushing yourself. A little sleep will do them good."

Brandt had carried every guard to a small part of the clearing that hadn't been covered in blood. When Orrin offered blankets from his [Dimension Hole], he'd gladly accepted and covered each separately.

Brandt rubbed the fabric of the last blanket between his fingers. "This is good cloth and looks familiar."

Orrin laughed and slapped the man's armored back. "Good thing I've got it, huh? No need to look closer."

Tony and Orrin sat down next to Brandt. Madi was checking over the guards, making sure they were all comfortably positioned. Daniel had pulled Samara, the huge warrior, and the archer over to their tents and was going through their belongings. At a cough from Tony, he left the bodies alone and began to get firewood.

It's so weird watching Tony mindspeak to just one person, Orrin thought as he scratched his arm. He had healed the slight cut he'd gotten from falling on his own sword, but the skin felt fresh and itched.

Brandt frowned and covered his own shoulders with the last blanket. "I still don't get how we took down Wendeln's Agent. I was able to knock her attacks away, but any hits I landed did nothing at all."

Daniel dropped a pile of small twigs and sticks he'd collected between them. "I'd also be interested in that. Mind you, I was doing damage with everything I had turned up to one hundred, but that lady could take a hit. What did you do to her?"

Madi wandered over as the discussion turned to the new topic.

Orrin hesitated. "I'm not sure I should just say it out loud. Especially after Jude . . . you know."

Jude's betrayal was fresh on his mind.

"If it is any consolation, Sir DeGuis kept his thoughts so well cloaked I never suspected, either. He didn't let a single stray thought through until he let Brandt take him out."

"What?" Orrin turned and stared at Tony.

"Did you lose intelligence as well?" Tony furrowed his brow. "You think Brandt could take out a close friend that quickly? Or that Jude would open up his own weak spot to a sparring partner of years? He acted with honor at the end. He couldn't fight Brandt. Not truly. He knew that his death was the only hope that his family had of not being killed immediately."

Daniel sat close to Brandt and put a hand on his shoulder. "Is that true?"

Brandt kept his head down as he answered in a quiet voice, "I've made that same attack against Jude in practice for years and never landed it. I helped him come up with a counter. When he was a kid, he got in lots of fights due to his smart mouth. He learned to fight, run quickly, or take his lumps. But he took a punch to his stomach once, just to the side, here." Brandt pointed at his own side, just above the hip. "He said it was the worst pain he'd ever felt. It was his critical spot. Like when Madi got hit in the head during the dungeon run?"

Daniel and Orrin nodded at the memory. Madi shuddered.

"When he joined the Catanzano house, he was a good fighter but always too open. I got a good hit in during practice and knew right away. You learn to figure out where to hit a person when your life revolves around protecting others from danger, but you don't hit a sparring partner there. So I went to Jude later and helped him correct his guard. He always kept his hammer's head too high. I thought if I attacked him there, he would use the feint I'd shown him. I'd be able to avoid that but be close enough to try and disarm him."

The dirt under Brandt was wet. "The bastard didn't move." Brandt looked up with haunted eyes and a stricken face. "Why didn't he move?"

Orrin couldn't find any words. Madi wrapped an arm around her protector.

"His last thoughts were about imagining you beating Samara and saving his niece." Tony's voice held both gentleness and strength at once. "He knew you'd find a way. There was no anger when he went quiet."

Brandt stood abruptly, fists held at his sides. "Anthony, do not lie to me. That man was a traitor who knocked you and Madi out. He was a danger to—"

Tony cut him off. "Sir Jude DeGuis gave his life to keep his family safe. Do not sully his memory. We all make the wrong choices, but what we are, who we are when we get the chance to fix our mistakes is what defines us. He made the best of his situation, just as we all would."

The stars in the sky reflected off Brandt's cheeks as he turned and screamed into the night. The wounded howl of a beast . . . or a man who had lost a brother he loved.

". . . Orrin. Daniel. Will you watch over Madi for a while? I need a minute to breathe. I'll check the perimeter again."

Daniel made a shooing motion, and Orrin nodded. Brandt slunk off into the forest. Madi watched him walk away forlornly.

"So now that he's gone . . ." Daniel leaned in conspiratorially. "You got [Increase Constitution], didn't you?"

Orrin shook his head. "Madi, could you give us some privacy?"

Madi looked hurt. "You'll let Anthony know but not me?"

"I'm sorry. Please?"

Madi stood and brushed her knees. "I'll just go try and get some water into the group of men and women who risked their lives to save Daniel."

She stomped off.

Orrin waited for her to be out of earshot. "Remember Administrator Access?"

Daniel blinked and glanced at Tony in shock.

"Don't worry, he knows more about it than we did. Tony's good people," Orrin said, ignoring Daniel's doubtful looks. "When Samara was going on a rampage, I got a prompt to use Administrator Access to reset her constitution."

"So just like [Increase Constitution], right?" Daniel asked confused.

"No, I think it was permanent, and she didn't have a chance to block it. She just lost ten points of Constitution right away."

"That is fucking wild!" Daniel nearly hopped up from the ground. "You can permanently take away stats now, too? Is there a limit? Can you increase them, too?"

Tony reached out swiftly and tried to yank Daniel back down. Daniel jerked back and swatted his hand. "Don't touch me. Orrin might trust you, but I don't yet."

Oh, how the tables have turned, Orrin laughed to himself.

"Sit down, child, and lower your voice. There's a reason I drove Brandt away and Orrin asked Madi to leave. This is more dangerous than you being a [Hero]."

Daniel crossed his arms and scowled but sat back into a crossed-leg position. "Spill, Orrin."

Orrin sighed. "I spent one of my own points to decrease hers. It took twenty points before you guys were doing real damage."

"You spent two points? Like two con points that are gone now? Didn't you start off really low?" Daniel uncrossed his arms and pulled Orrin close, looking him all over for some sort of damage. "Are you okay?"

Tony chuckled. Daniel let Orrin go and glared at the man. "I'm allowed to worry about my friend."

Tony held his hands up in mock surrender. "By all means. I said nothing."

"I'm fine," Orrin interjected, rubbing his shoulders. Daniel's grip hurt a little. "I'm just a little more squishy now."

"Squishy?" Tony asked.

"It's a word we use to describe someone who is weak, mostly in a tabletop game," Orrin explained.

"I've never heard of a dragon in a dungeon before." Tony quirked an eyebrow. "Usually, they stick to the seas and islands, only coming in for the occasional sheep or cow."

"No, no," Orrin laughed. "It's *and*, not *in*, and stop reading my thoughts. Wait, dragons are real?"

"Of course." Tony shivered. Daniel held up Brandt's abandoned blanket, and Tony accepted, wrapping his frail frame up. His hair still stuck out at the top. "Since the world was broken, they avoid nearly everyone, though. The last sighting was years ago. The dead body of a red one washed ashore."

"I want to see a dragon," Orrin whispered wistfully.

"Do they give good experience?" Daniel asked.

Tony sneered. "Good experience? Dragons are an intelligent species. Like humans or dwarves. You get no experience for that."

"But don't we get experience for killing demons? Aren't they intelligent?" Orrin chimed in. He'd been wondering about the experience discrepancy for a while.

"How much do you actually know about demons?"

"They're bad," Daniel answered. "And killing them is kind of my job now."

Tony rolled his eyes and shook his head. "Demons are just another race. Some have horns or different-color skin, but others look the same as you and me. At some point in history, they broke from civilization and did something to the system. They can kill each other, monsters, or even us, and gain experience. However, we also got the ability to gain experience from them. The history books talk of centuries of bloodshed between the two groups until the world was broken and remade."

"But Daniel's right, too, right?" Orrin asked. "They're bad. They attack the Walls of Dey and try to kill people still."

Tony shrugged. "And Dey sends expeditions into the Pass and beyond to kill indiscriminately and find any major cities to destroy. It's a matter of perspective, but if you're asking if I would make friends with a demon, the answer is a firm 'No'. Semantics and logic puzzles aside, I believe anyone who tries to kill me should be in the ground."

Daniel just nodded at the conclusion of Tony's little speech, but Orrin got stuck. "What about a treaty of some sort? Surely, somebody has tried talking with them. Maybe—"

"Orrin, I know what you're thinking . . . literally. It's never been done. They kill anyone they find. You *just* barely evaded one."

Orrin let it rest, but only because the sound of footsteps approaching ended the conversation.

"Perimeter is clear. The sun should be fully up within the hour. How are they?" Brandt asked as he came back from his walk. He put on a professional air, but Orrin could see the streaks in the dirt on his face.

"They really should sleep for a few hours, but if we travel slowly, they could be woken now," Tony answered.

Brandt nodded and turned to the sun. "Let's get to it. I have some unfinished business in Dey. Hey, Daniel and Madi, do you want to help me strip the bodies? Orrin, can you carry a few extra things in your spatial storage?"

Daniel stood and nodded, running back to the task he'd already started. The few times that Orrin had gotten Daniel to play tabletop role-playing games with him, he'd always been a murderhobo. *No surprise he wants to loot.*

"I'll carry what I can. I'm not totally sure what the limit is, but I'm guessing I'll find out soon enough." Orrin stood also. He stretched his arms over his head and bent. "I'm guessing we are going to have to travel on foot?"

Brandt's smile peeked out for just a brief moment as Madi headed to help with the plundering. "Yes and no. They had a cart and a few horses. I think we can let the injured sit in shifts."

"But I'm not hurt."

"Exactly. You get to walk with us. Isn't that great?" Brandt smacked Orrin's shoulder as he passed.

Orrin fell hard on his butt.

Brandt was on his knee immediately, helping Orrin back up. "I'm so sorry. You are hurt, aren't you? I'm putting you on the cart. That was barely a love tap."

Tony stepped in and grabbed Orrin's other arm. "He's just a little mana-tired. So many spells. Go help the [Hero] and young Catanzano."

Brandt hesitated at being directed by Tony but quietly conceded. The two men and Madi were soon breaking down tents and pulling boots off dead bodies.

Murderhobos.

Chapter 63

After taking a few hours to get a catnap in, they loaded up and moved out. Nobody felt fully rested, but only two of the guards were hurt enough to need the cart, so Madi and Orrin were able to ride and rest as well. Tony blamed his old age and crawled up, too, but Orrin suspected the man was just being lazy.

Everybody else walked.

Other than Brandt, all the guards had been soundly defeated, and as they traveled back to Dey, they licked their wounds and grumbled. Two even started a scuffle that ended in moments, as Brandt leaped from one of the newly obtained horses and swiftly solved the dispute by yelling and pulling rank. It was the first time that Orrin had seen the man lose his temper.

"Is he going to be okay?" Orrin whispered to Madi. She sat next to him on the back of the cart, their legs dangling from the edge.

Madi glanced over her shoulder toward the front of the progression. Despite the victory of the mission, a shadow of defeat still loomed over them all.

"I'm not sure," she answered with a sigh. "Jude and Brandt were close. You heard him when Jenson suggested burning Jude's body with the kidnappers' bodies. His decision to bring Jude back with us is questionable and the others know it."

Charlie Jenson's idea to dispose of the traitor had been met with more than Brandt's harsh tongue. Although he was still a bit wounded, the man was limping along behind the cart. Orrin had cast two [Heal Small Wounds] on the man when Brandt's back was turned.

Orrin glanced back at Tony. The man had closed his eyes and fallen asleep between Efraim, one of the mages, and Ryland. From what he'd been able to gather, the two were a couple. While Orrin was grabbing Daniel from the tent, Samara had taken out Efraim. The mage's wind magic had been one of the few things able to slow the big berserker down. Samara's whip had hit his neck, and he'd gone down hard. The mage's naturally lower constitution hadn't helped when his head bounced off a rock.

Ryland had reacted poorly to seeing his partner go down and charged ahead. He'd gotten a few good hits in before Samara had also turned her whips on him. Unfortunately, he'd also taken a hit from the berserker's axe. The two were the most severely injured. Orrin had cast his healing on them a few times over the last hour. Ryland's wound to his side had solidified into a puckered scar, and Efraim's goose egg had reduced to a red bump.

Orrin didn't press the issue with Madi. Her fingers clenched on the back end of the cart gave evidence of her own swirling emotions. *Jude was her guard and friend, too. Mine as well.*

He spent the first hour traveling back to Dey entertaining dark thoughts about the other lord of Dey that had let this happen. After daydreaming up a half dozen plans, ranging from storming the house of Lord Wendeln to kidnapping his imaginary children, Orrin had enough and jumped off the back of the cart. He made his way up to Daniel and Brandt, riding two horses near the front of the little procession.

"Brandt, what are the chances Silas does anything in retaliation?"

Daniel pulled his horse a little closer to hear the man's answer. Gertrude was strapped to his back. During Orrin's sabbatical with Tony, Daniel had gained another level and taken a page from Jude's book. [Light Weapon] allowed him to heft Gerty as if it was the weight of an aluminum baseball bat. The decreased weight only affected him, not anyone who got hit by the few-hundred-pound weapon.

"He'll kill anyone we can uncover, but there won't be any solid proof linking Wendeln to this," Brandt spoke in a clipped voice. "DeGuis's family will likely be found in an alley dead. No witnesses."

"But that whip chick, Sam, said—" Daniel started.

"Samara," Orrin interrupted him.

"Whatever," Daniel said with an annoyed glance. "She admitted to working for him. We all heard it."

Brandt closed his eyes and took a deep breath. "Daniel. I know you are from another world, but you can't be so naive as to think that matters. This is a lord of Dey. Wendeln isn't some merchant or guard. He's a high-level, higher-ranking member of the ruling class of one of the, if not *the*, most important cities in the world."

He huffed. "That doesn't mean I'm not furious. I want to get revenge. I want to save J—DeGuis's family, too. But our best bet is to get back and let Lord Catanzano think of something. Maybe he can at least save the child for an unofficial pardon."

While Daniel continued to argue with Brandt, Orrin retreated back to the cart. It was exactly like he thought it would be—Lord Wendeln was going to get away with everything. Kidnapping Jude's family and turning him would be a footnote in Silas's mind. Stealing the [Hero] and almost killing a dozen guards would be swept under the rug. All because of who the man was. His family protected the Wall from Horde attacks, so he could do anything he wanted with impunity.

He walked behind the wagon, not realizing Tony and Madi were watching him. They exchanged a rare glance, and Tony shrugged.

"No." Orrin made up his mind. "Brandt, stop!"

Daniel was still arguing with him, but Brandt turned over his shoulder and raised an eyebrow.

"We're not going back yet," Orrin announced. He grabbed Madi's hand and pulled her off the edge of the wagon. Dragging her by her arm, Orrin marched toward the two fighters up front. "I've got an idea."

Daniel groaned. "Your ideas are the worst."

Orrin smirked. "But you'll get to have a hundred strength again."

Daniel ground a fist into his open palm. "I'm listening."

The plan was simple: The main party would continue back and report they'd lost Daniel and Orrin to the kidnappers. The guards would travel back with Madi and Brandt, who would keep a close eye on everyone. Orrin wasn't about to risk one of them slipping away and warning Wendeln of what was coming. They'd been burned by a traitor in their midst before and were not going to risk it again.

Orrin and Daniel would teleport to the Wendeln keep, a small fortress built near the westernmost Wall. Each family had a keep they'd live in during their Wall rotation, but the Wendelns usually used their minicastle as a permanent home. The two friends would sneak inside, rescue the DeGuises, and get back to Madi's home and her father's protection as quickly as possible.

Hopefully, the decoy would give them time and the element of surprise to complete the rescue mission.

"I still think I should come with you," Brandt argued for the tenth time. "How will you know what they look like?"

"We'll bring Tony," Orrin said with a smile. "They'll never expect that, and he'll be able to find them easily."

The mind mage shook his head. "I'm sorry, but I can't."

Orrin's plan crashed and burned. "Why? Without you, how can we figure out where to go? You have to come, Tony."

The grizzled man scratched the back of his head and turned away. "As much history as I have with Silas, I have more baggage with Wendeln. I have to stay far away. I know myself. It won't end well."

Orrin floundered.

"Brandt can still come with us," Daniel suggested.

"If Brandt is going, I am, too," Madi added. She'd crossed her arms and glared when Orrin revealed his plan.

"If anyone sees either of you near the keep, they'll know something is up." Orrin shook his head. "Plus, Wendeln could use that against your father. If we get caught, he can just say we acted on our own. Plus, I can teleport us away from any danger."

"They'll have the keep warded against [Teleport]," Brandt said, poking yet another hole in Orrin's plan.

"Well, I guess I'll have to figure out how to destroy a ward, too." Orrin threw up his hands. "Does anyone have anything helpful to add?"

"Why not use misdirection?" Tony suggested. He peered back at the guards milling about behind the cart waiting for the group to finish talking. "While Daniel goes in loud, Orrin can sneak in. Daniel can always run, especially with such a high strength, but Wendeln likes to talk. He'll brag and monologue and tell you all his plans if he thinks he's in a position of power. He's a decent fighter but focused more on large groups, like a Horde of monsters. I think Daniel could hold his own for a few minutes, despite the level disparity."

Brandt was nodding along. "If we time it right, we can get Lord Catanzano and do a routine patrol. If we hear a disturbance, we can investigate. If Orrin can find and free the DeGuises, we might have enough actual evidence to have Wendeln removed as a lord and prosecuted."

The party turned to him as one, with excited looks on their faces. *How did my simple plan get so twisted up?*

Once the group could see the Wall of Dey rising in the distance, Orrin used [Teleport] to move himself and Daniel. They'd picked the spot near the Wall they'd teleported to with Ira. They wouldn't try for the Wall itself, but just inside the city. Luckily, with no current Horde coming, the Wall's guard would be running on a skeleton crew. The chances of running into a guard were low.

Orrin's luck held as they landed right next to the Wall. Nobody else was around.

"So once we get close, I'll buff us both, go into [Camouflage], and try to find the teleport ward to destroy it. Then I'll find Jude's family and get them out. Madi said the entire keep is only twenty rooms and a cellar, which is where I'm guessing the prisoners are." Orrin didn't need to go over the plan again, but without [Mind Bastion], his nerves were flaring once more.

"Orrin, I've got it," Daniel said peevishly. "You don't have to keep going over it with me. I know what you have to do. I know what I have to do. Let's get this done. I want to sleep in a real bed and eat something other than the jerky they kept feeding me."

Daniel spat on the ground and started walking. The Wendeln keep was located about six hundred feet from the north gate. Orrin scrambled to keep up.

"I'm sorry. I wasn't going over it for you; I'm nervous. Tony has made me stop using [Mind Bastion], and all these emotions I've been keeping down bubble up a lot faster," Orrin tried to explain. "It's like everything hits twice as hard now. I was so scared attacking that camp to find you that I almost froze right outside the tent. I kept thinking, *what if he's hurt or not there?*"

Daniel's angry stroll softened, and he turned back with a sigh. "I'm sorry, too. I'm still pissed off I was taken out so easily. After we kick ass and save the day, we are going to start leveling for real. Maybe get back into that dungeon?"

Daniel held his fist out, and Orrin rapped his knuckles against his friend's. They smirked at each other.

"The house is right around the corner," Orrin noted. "You ready?"

Daniel nodded. Orrin cast [Increase Will] at level three on himself once and then slapped a [Utility Ward] at level two down as well.

The two stood there for a moment, basking in the morning sun and going over their heightened stats.

"You are such a cheat—I love it." Daniel chuckled and reached over his shoulder. He pulled Gertrude off his back and tossed it once, spinning the sword. "Let's go fuck up this guy's life."

Chapter 64

The Wendeln keep made Silas's house look like a small beach bunga-low. Three stories tall, the plastered brick shone in the morning sun. Towers pierced higher at three of the corners, with the last side left bare toward the Wall.

So he can watch for a Horde breaking over the Wall, Orrin realized. *This guy takes guarding the city pretty seriously.*

"He's got a goddamned moat," Daniel complained. "There is a flipping drawbridge. This is inside the city. Just how pretentious can you get?"

"Maybe you can break the bridge," Orrin suggested. "That should get everybody's attention. I'm going invisible. Good luck."

Orrin cast [Camouflage].

"Don't do anything stupid. Get in and out." Daniel glanced back and sighed. "And he's gone."

Orrin slapped Daniel on the back of the head. "Not yet. Same advice to you. Get out if you need to."

Daniel rolled his shoulders and started to jog toward the mini-castle ahead. One of the two guards standing at the foot of the bridge, near the front gate, yelled and took a step forward.

Daniel accelerated.

The first guard pulled a mace from his hip while the second turned and knocked on a small door set into the heavy wooden gate. Then he turned also, and a small crossbow appeared in his hands.

A bolt jumped out at Daniel. Orrin almost yelled, but his friend swatted the arrow from the air with a casual flick of his wrist. With a small plop in the shallow water below, Daniel had survived first contact.

Orrin tried to teleport but felt the growingly familiar sense of a ward. He stepped lightly on the drawbridge and crossed slowly, watching Daniel bat the first guard's mace out of his hand. Daniel followed up with a flat-edge love tap to the man's helmet. His bell rung, the first guard went down in a slump of limps.

Another bolt leaped at Daniel, but he slapped it away. The increased [Dexterity] and [Strength] made him into a one-man wrecking crew. Two swings and the guard's crossbow was in pieces at his feet and his arms were in the air.

"Open the gate," Daniel growled.

"It only opens from the inside," the man said with a far calmer voice than Orrin would have expected. He was near enough to see the man's green eyes under his helmet. "You're not getting in, and you obviously aren't going to kill us. You could have taken Jorgen's head off but knocked him unconscious. Who are you and what do you want?"

Daniel also seemed to be taken aback by the composure of the guard. "I'm here to get revenge. Lord Wendeln had me kidnapped, and I'm here to even the score. He'll beg for mercy before I kill him."

Orrin cringed at Daniel's hokey speech.

The guard shrugged. "Like I said, the gate only opens from the inside. Guard change is in two hours if you want to wait. Although if Jorgen wakes up, he's going to be mighty pissed."

"I'm not waiting," Daniel announced. "I'll just break it down."

"It'll take you all day and you'll blunt your blade."

Daniel pushed the guard to the side with the flat of Gertrude and then held his sword over his head. He glanced at the hefty crossbeams of wood with panels of darker wood behind and then at the small door. Daniel took two deep breaths and jumped forward, bringing his oversize sword down at an angle in a two-handed chop.

The blade struck the door just a few inches inside the gate proper. Gertrude punched the thick wood and knocked a hole a few inches thick and a foot long through the door. Daniel backed up to do it again.

The guard pulled a knife and rushed forward to stab Daniel in the back. Orrin raced to stop him but didn't need to bother. Daniel had sensed the movement and twisted, letting the man lunge by him. He swung Gerty in a full arc, slapping the man in his ass and accelerating his forward dive. The guard bounced hard off the gate and fell unconscious at Daniel's feet.

"Nice one," Orrin whispered.

"Fuck. Don't do that."

Daniel had to hit the door five more times before the wood cracked enough that he could kick the wood in half. He stepped through the gate.

Orrin made to follow but heard Daniel mutter, "Oh, fuck."

The sudden flurry of metal on metal from the other side of the busted door let Orrin know that backup had arrived. He gingerly stepped through the broken door. His jaw dropped.

Daniel was facing off against three knights in full plate waving swords, three more guards with swords or axes, and six guards with pikes or spears. *I can never tell the difference between a pike or a spear. One is longer, right?*

Directly inside the gate was a small courtyard. Grotesque monster statues lined a dozen stairs leading up to a double arched door to the main house.

The guards were not playing nice. Instead of attacking once at a time, they attacked as one. Two went in from different directions, while a few spears pierced Daniel's legs. When he stumbled backward, another pushed him into the circle again. Despite all his increased stats, Daniel was losing terribly. Orrin checked his friend's health and saw it was already halfway down.

This is not the plan, this is not the plan, this is not the plan, Orrin chanted in his head as he ran forward. One of the pikemen had stood slightly back from the group. Orrin put a sword into the man's back and pushed.

His sword must have nicked the man's kidney, because his scream of pain stopped most of the other guards from attacking. The wound gushed as the man tried to grab his back. He quickly turned to find his attacker but saw no one there. In his haste to turn, he hadn't lowered his spear (*pike?*), and it slashed against one of the other guards' legs.

In the confusion, Daniel struck back. His [Shooting Star] activated, and Orrin tried to keep an eye on his friend as he became a human pinball, bouncing between guards. Daniel had played nice with the guards outside the gate, but these men had tried to hurt him.

The guards not wearing plate were in pieces within seconds. Arms and legs were strewn across the small courtyard. Some men went down in shock, passing out quickly. Others were screaming.

"Why is that door still closed?" Daniel yelled as he blocked a strike from a still-standing guard. "Shouldn't Lord Wendeln have come out for a chat?"

None of the guards seemed up for chatting. One guard who had only lost a hand raced away, slamming the door open as he ran for help.

Orrin knew the words were for him, though. *Get going, numbskull. Daniel can handle it from here.*

Orrin took the steps two at a time and made it through the rebounding door just in time. As he slipped through the door, he saw people coming from down the hall. He threw himself to the side and stood behind a banner, holding his body flat against the wall.

"What do you mean, a single man? You need me for this?" A rush of bodies funneled toward the door from the long hallway leading farther inside. In the center of the group walked a man dressed in rich clothes with a chain shirt that glimmered like an opal underneath. He complained and gave orders as he strapped a dagger to one side and buckled a sword to his other hip. Lord Wendeln.

He was shorter than Orrin would have thought, barely taller than Madi and well under Daniel's height. His silver hair was short, and his beard was trimmed and oiled. Despite his well-manicured appearance, Orrin felt the power and danger flowing off the man in waves. He didn't dare to use [Identify].

"I think it's the [Hero], sire," the man holding a stump of an arm said, looking as if he'd pass out any second. "He's taken down most of us. I had to come for rein—"

"Enough," Lord Wendeln ordered. "If it's just him, we can capture him again. I thought we'd gotten word he'd been lost."

"We must have been fed a lie." The man who responded looked like he should be in armor, wielding a great axe. Instead, he wore the robes of a mage and held a small book in his hand. "I'm getting word that Lord Catanzano is out on patrol nearby. This may all be a ruse. We should send someone to take care of the guests. If the other lords were to—"

"Hold your tongue, Nicholas. You can go take care of the problem yourself. The rest of you, strike to wound, not to kill. We must take him alive, but quickly. Rodney and Winston, go secure the bridge and raise it. Do not let Silas in my home. Go."

The men funneled out, with the buff mage turning and sweeping back up the hall. Orrin waited for the door to slam shut and followed.

Nicholas strolled unhurriedly down the hallways, Orrin shadowing him the entire way. After two turns, he opened a door and stepped inside.

Orrin waited for a few seconds before he cracked the door open. Stairs led down into darkness, with only a flickering light at the bottom. He braced himself and crept down the stairs, listening for any noise.

"Please, you don't have to do this. Just let us go and we'll stay quiet. We can move away. My brother-in-law is a guard as well. He'll pay you."

"Shut up." Nicholas's voice drifted up the stairs. As well as the sound of somebody being hit.

"Don't you hit her! Uncle Jude is going to kill you dead."

Orrin's heart dropped. Jude's niece sounded much younger than he'd imagined. He crept down the stairs as quickly as he could. The basement opened up into a long storage area, with multiple pillars supporting the weight of the house above. One wall had rows of weapons, while another had sacks of some sort of food and barrels that Orrin didn't have time to investigate, because, in the far corner, a young woman was chained to a wall. Both her wrists were manacled above her head, which lolled from the blow she'd just received. An even younger girl, maybe seven or eight, was pulling on the long chain tied to her ankle, trying to get at Nicholas. The mage held his small book in front of him and began to mutter gibberish. He held his hand outstretched pointing toward Jude's sister-in-law.

Orrin chanced [Identify] and scanned the man's status quickly. He let out a sigh of relief. Nicholas was only a few levels higher than Brandt. His class of [Beastmaster] also made Orrin feel more at ease. He saw no beasts in the room. Nicholas might be an easy mark.

He crept forward and prepared to strike. He needed to save his mana to be able to teleport everyone out. *I hope Brandt gets to Daniel in time.*

Orrin raised his sword to swing. However, he'd misjudged a nearby pillar, and his sword clanged against the stone before he started his downstroke.

Nicholas reacted quickly, ducking and rolling backward. His head darted back and forth, looking for an enemy, but he saw no one. He turned a few pages in his book and pointed at a spot a few feet from Orrin, muttering his gibberish again.

Orrin kept his sword down and close as he circled to get on the other side of Nicholas.

"I know you're in here," Nicholas spat out quickly and then continued his mutters. "You should leave now while you still can."

Orrin didn't answer but ran forward and struck. His sword hit the man's chest, but the robes hid high-quality chain mail underneath. Chain mail that looked similar to Lord Wendeln's. It turned Orrin's blade to the side.

Orrin glanced at the man's status with more care.

Nicholas Wendeln

Damn it.

Chapter 65

Nicholas swung a fist through the air, almost striking Orrin. He felt the air rush by his cheek. [Camouflage] was still running, but after he'd hit the younger Wendeln, the man had an idea of where Orrin was.

Orrin backed away and put his back against one of the pillars holding up the house. He checked his mana.

He'd cast [Increase Will] at level three, with a base of twenty-eight. Two point eight times the plus-four of a level three [Increase Will] gave Orrin an extra eleven will per cast. He'd only increased it once, trying to save his mana for the needed getaway [Teleport].

He'd also cast [Utility Ward] at level two. That had increased his will by another 3.9 times the plus-two of a level-two spell, or an extra eight will points. Except [Utility Ward] was for the maximum possible increase. Five casts for the price of one. An extra forty will, strength, dexterity, and intelligence had been added to Orrin's stats.

Seventy-nine will gave him a lot of mana—890 MP to be exact. Of course, the initial costs of casting a few spells had driven his overall amount down, but with a quick math check, he didn't need too much to get the DeGuises and himself out of here using [Teleport].

My intelligence is up to fifty-one, so my spells should cost about 40 percent of the normal cost. Orrin hoped his on-the-fly math skills would hold up, because he was planning on doing some heavy lifting with [Inverse] to debuff this goon.

Nicholas hadn't followed up after his single swing, instead focusing on his book and low chanting. Orrin knew he was casting a spell of some sort, but Nicholas wasn't even looking at him. He was focusing on a spot in front of the little girl.

Orrin peered around the corner and almost used [Inverse] with [Increase Dexterity], as he'd done before against others, but switched it to [Increase Intelligence] on a hunch. It was Nicholas's highest stat, after all.

Nicholas had finally finished his long, drawn-out casting. A section of the floor between him and the huddled women had turned inky black. A darkness so deep, Orrin's mind saw it more as purple with streaks of murky blue. Nicholas smirked and rounded in the general direction of where Orrin stood, preening in triumph.

A three-clawed red arm reached out of the growing hole and scrambled for purchase on the stone tiles. The room was filled with the sound of nails grating as the claws scratched for a grip. The silence when the arm found a hold on a small crack in the tile was deafening.

A second arm reached through the dark chasm, followed by a third.

With a name like [Beastmaster], Orrin had thought the man would control wolves or horses. He'd had a slight idea that Nicholas was trying to summon something, but what crawled from the pit was more terrible than anything he could have imagined.

More arms joined the first two, as an insect-like red form pushed its body out of the ground and stood tall. Two legs held wide over the gaping hole that was slowly disappearing supported the main body. It would almost look human, except it turned at the wrong angles. Three sets of arms situated evenly up the torso broke at two points before ending in the three-clawed hands that it had used to pull itself from hell. It stood stooped slightly, too tall for the room. The multi-jointed monsterlike monstrosity moved its head around slowly, taking in every detail around it.

Orrin couldn't look away from its face. An open gash split vertically where a mouth and nose should be. Hundreds of tiny pincerlike teeth slid in and out of the hole. Arranged around the top of the head in a halo, eyes opened and blinked against the few lights in the basement.

Orrin cast his debuff spells five times, ripping away large chunks of Wendeln's son's intelligence. Orrin expected curses. He waited for threats. He didn't anticipate fear. Nicholas paled with the first decrease of his intelligence, and his face morphed to terror as his stat continued to plummet.

"What did you do?" Nicholas asked quietly as he flipped frantically through the pages of his book. "Stop! I won't be able to control it anymore. You'll kill us all. It only responds to me."

Nicholas stopped on a page and began whisper-muttering again. A second, smaller hole began to appear a few feet from the first.

Orrin weighed his options. He'd taken away Nicholas's intelligence, probably the stat he needed to control whatever he'd just summoned. The man did seem terrified and shook as he tried to talk faster than before.

I could increase his stats back up . . .

The Beast didn't give Orrin a chance to react. It darted at Nicholas in a flash. The man screamed and tripped backward. A flurry of striking claws in a rushing crescendo that felt vindictive sent blood flying with every slice. The walls were covered with dripping blood in seconds.

"No. No! You are mine to command. Stop! . . . Please, no . . . I am your master!" Screams and pleas came from under the carapace. It bent back on two sets of limbs and screeched into the air, its mouth opening and sending an image into Orrin's mind that he knew would haunt his dreams. The pincer teeth wiggled in sync with its upper arms. Three forked lizard tongues flicked out before the Beast struck down over and over, biting Nicholas on his chest, his neck, and finally his face.

Orrin stood frozen. He raised his sword to strike at the distracted Beast but paused. Instead, he tried [Identify].

[Level 39, Summoned Beast] HP 300/300

Nope. I can't even read what stat to debuff. Running time. Orrin scurried around the side and up to the women. Jude's niece had stretched her body to hold on to her mother.

"Shh. It'll be all right, sweetheart," Jude's sister-in-law whispered to the child.

Orrin dropped [Camouflage]. "I'm here to save you. Let's go, quickly and quietly, while it's distracted."

His increased strength pulsed as he grabbed the metal manacles about her head and yanked them out of the stone. He quickly did the same to the girl's chain.

They hugged fiercely, and then the mother pushed her daughter behind her. "Who are you?"

Orrin's stomach turned as he answered. "Jude sent me. Do you know where the teleportation ward is?"

She shook her head. "I'm Joyce. This is Mira. Where is Jude?"

"Later." Orrin sidestepped that minefield. "We need to get out of here first."

Orrin needed more time to find the ward. They were not going to be able to fight their way out of the keep.

A chittering scream sent chills down his spine. Orrin turned and saw the summoned Beast was done with Nicholas. All that was left of his body was a red sludge and the hints of a chest. The Beast had eaten its summoner.

Orrin had no plan ready for this fight. He held his sword up and placed himself between the girls and the red spider monstrosity.

The monster's eyes blinked. Every eye in the circle opened and closed one at a time in a perfect circuit. Orrin felt his nerve fading and fingered that switch in his mind for [Mind Bastion], ready to start cycling if he needed it.

Instead, the Beast clicked its teeth and scuttled out of the room. Orrin listened to the fading sound of its multiple limbs hitting the steps.

"What was that thing?" the little girl behind him asked.

"Nothing good," Orrin replied. "Do either of you know what a teleport ward looks like?"

Joyce shook her head again, but Mira nodded. "I heard one of the men who brought us food talk about turning it on. There's a real-life [Hero] in Dey! They were worried about him for some reason."

Orrin began to kneel but saw that Nicholas's blood was seeping into the grout in every direction. He squatted instead. "Please tell me you heard where they keep it?"

Her toothy grin was full of Jude's mischief. "Of course."

Orrin spent a single [Heal Small Wounds] on Joyce and Mira. While not physically hurt beyond the single slap that Nicholas had thrown at Joyce, both were a little malnourished. Joyce had picked up a few different hand axes and tested their weight before settling on two she liked. She'd gently taken a hammer out of Mira's hands.

"I need to protect you," the child had cried. "It's my job."

Joyce rolled her eyes. "Your job is to stay behind us and run if there is danger."

Orrin coughed and pointed. "Behind her back."

Joyce spun her child and tutted as she pulled a small dagger from her other hand.

Mira threw a look of betrayal at Orrin. "Now I'm not going to help you."

Orrin groaned.

After some negotiation, Mira led the way up the stairs, holding a training sword. It was wooden and held some weight, but at least the kid wouldn't cut herself with it.

Orrin felt like a fool letting a little girl of eight take the lead, but she'd smooth talked her way through rapid-fire concessions with both him and her own mother. Joyce mouthed "sorry" as the child climbed the stairs.

As they entered the ground floor again, Orrin could just make out the sounds of an ongoing battle outside. Daniel was still holding up well, hopefully. Maybe Brandt had arrived with reinforcements.

With the distraction at the front gate, they ran into no guards or even staff. *Likely all the cooks have run or gotten themselves to safety.*

Mira walked the halls as if she knew exactly where she was.

"You do know where you are going, right?" Orrin whispered.

He received a disdainful and uninterested face in response. "Of course. The guard said he had to go back to his room to set the ward. Guards sleep on the ground floor nearest the door for quick response time. What kind of adventurer are you?"

Orrin raised a hand in defeat. "Not as good as you are going to be."

Mira smiled. "Damn right."

"Mira! Language," Joyce chastised from behind Orrin. Mira ignored her.

Orrin followed them back to the exact hallway where he had started to follow Nicholas.

Mira pointed across the hall at a door Orrin had missed when he came in. "There."

"Stay here," Orrin commanded. "I'm going to disappear and break the ward. I'll be right back."

He turned on [Camouflage], and Mira gasped.

"Shit. What's the ward look like?"

Mira and Joyce shrugged in unison.

He shook his head and crossed the hall, catching a glimpse of more than one person fighting outside. A full-out brawl was happening.

Orrin slipped into the room and looked around. A half dozen bunks were set up down the left side, with racks for storing weapons and armor on the right. The room was empty, and the racks were bare.

Nothing stood out. There was no magical box or stone. No big switch or magic writing on an item he could see. Each bed had a small footlocker, but he didn't have time to search every one.

Orrin pulled up his [Map]. He tried to ignore the dashing colors and focus on the room he was in. *Surely they have some protection for something so impor— Yes! There.*

[Trap View] pinged off a table at the end of the room. He hadn't even given the simple wooden circle a second look. Now he approached it carefully. Orrin crouched and found what he was looking for almost instantly.

Without knowing to look, he would have passed over the slight outcropping that was just a bit thicker than the rest of the table. He found the keyhole on the back of the small block and did the most expedient thing he could—he slammed his sword down on the table as hard as he could. The wood splintered and the box fell. Orrin cheered just as the box let off a click and several small darts sprang out in random directions.

[Side Steps] activated, and Orrin's leg moved an inch to the side.

Too close. Orrin stomped on the box until it broke and a small metal circle fell out. He picked it up and inspected it. Runes ran in small curls around the edge of the bracelet-like device. *This has to be it.*

Orrin ran back to the door and opened it slowly. Mira and Joyce looked at the door opening, and Mira waved.

He hurried back across to them. "I think I've got it," he said, dropping his spell and holding the metal circle up.

"If you can teleport, break it and get Mira out," Joyce said quickly. "Please!"

"I'm getting us all out of here," Orrin responded and tried to bend the metal with his hands. It barely moved, but small flecks started to appear in the runes. "This is strong."

"Here, hit it with this." Mira pulled a small hammer, not even a real weapon, out of her boot.

Orrin shook his head but took the tool. He placed it on the floor and brought down the hammer.

The circle bent at one end, and the metal shimmered once before blackening. For good measure, Orrin hit it again and then snapped the circle open with his hands.

"Okay. Let's get you out of here." Orrin sheathed his sword and took a hand in each of his.

We did it, he thought as they teleported away.

Chapter 66

Orrin caught Joyce as she stumbled out of [Teleport]. Mira landed like a cat and smiled around her.

"This is where Uncle Jude works," the young girl said, running ahead to the Catanzano house. "Hi, Jefferson." She waved to the guard on duty.

Orrin dragged Joyce as they followed the child. The guard smiled and waved back before turning and yelling into the front door. Madi appeared at the door and ushered the group inside.

"Brandt and my father went to help—did you see them?" Madi asked. She was still dressed in her traveling outfit, her spear in hand.

"Was Sir Brandt fighting the bad men who kidnapped us? Is Uncle Jude with him?" Mira asked in response. Madi gave a stricken look to Orrin, who shook his head.

"We didn't see anyone, but Daniel was keeping all of Wendeln's guards occupied," Orrin said. "I did make out a few people fighting but couldn't tell who it was."

Madi nodded and helped push Jude's family inside. She set two guards outside their door and spent five minutes using her social training to calm them down. She answered questions with dodges and gave assurances without promises. Madi closed the door on them as Mira helped her mother get into a big, comfortable bed. Joyce had been standing for days, and her legs wobbled as she finally let them rest.

"They'll be fine with some sleep," Madi whispered as they backed away. "I'll make sure my father keeps them protected. Although with their testimony, I can't see a way that Lord Wendeln gets away with this. Kidnapping a guard's family, attacking my father's house, trying to kidnap Daniel . . . the list goes on."

Orrin let Madi ramble. She was worried about her father, Brandt, and Daniel. He was, too.

Orrin's buffs wore off, except [Utility Warder]. He still had a lot of mana and itched to get back to help but knew he needed to trust Daniel. He could wait a bit longer. *Right?*

"Of course you can." Tony's voice entered his mind. "Yes, I'm still here. I'm warding the surrounding area. Silas can throw a fit all he wants, but I'll be damned if that bastard Wendeln takes those women back."

The feeling Orrin experienced was new. A group of people helping him, taking care of problems before he even thought of them. *Competency in a team?*

"What's the plan?" Madi asked. "Should we stay here? Or . . . ?" She trailed off.

"Daniel was going to escape back here as soon as possible. He should be back by now. The plan was to get out once your dad and Brandt showed up. There's no way he's fully recovered from being kidnapped," Orrin answered, feeling the stress he had been pushing down start to rise up. "I hope he's okay."

Madi stood next to him and put her arm on Orrin's shoulder. "Our boy gets into trouble a lot, doesn't he?"

Orrin's lips pulled into a grin. "I don't know if he's just dumb and runs into trouble or if he's unlucky and trouble finds him."

They waited together, watching the sun rise firmly into the sky.

Daniel and Brandt popped out of the air and fell a few feet from where Orrin had teleported. Daniel had used his [Home Base] skill.

Madi let out a sigh of relief.

Brandt had Daniel's arm over his neck and was keeping him up. Both were alive but also hurt.

Orrin started throwing healing spells on him as they ran to their friends.

"Are you both all right?" Madi asked, beating Orrin to the question.

"Daniel took a few hits from the monster's claws, but he saved my life," Brandt said between gasps for air. He also had multiple triple cuts along his leg and one across his back. The metal of his armor had been torn like cloth. "It was about to bite into the back of my head when he activated his teleport skill."

Orrin paused in his casting of [Heal Small Wounds] between the two fighters, feeling his blood run cold. "The monster?"

"Something that Wendeln did, I'm sure," Brandt continued, handing Daniel off to Madi. "But it went wild and started trying to kill him. Half his men went down trying to contain it as he retreated."

"It wasn't a red spider-armed monster, was it?"

Daniel groaned. "I knew it. What did you do?"

As Orrin explained the fight with Nicholas and the summoned monster he'd accidentally freed in his attempt to free Joyce and Mira, Brandt and Madi helped get the healing Daniel into the house. Brandt's wounds had closed quicker, with Daniel having sustained the majority of the damage. They pushed into Silas's office and asked questions as Orrin did his best to answer.

Brandt left twice to send messages to Silas. A few minutes after he left the second time, he slowly reentered.

"The lords of Dey are convening to handle the [Hero]'s summoned monster together," he said woodenly. "The others have placed Lord Wendeln in charge. The guards of all the houses are searching for Daniel as we speak."

Orrin's emotions flared. Without the normal comfort of [Mind Bastion], he raged. "Silas just went along with this?"

Brandt's head snapped up. "Lord Catanzano was outvoted. His allegations were waved aside until the monster inside the city walls is put down. But he coded his message. We need to get Daniel out of the city until he can get a handle on everything. He'll send for you when it's safe to return."

Daniel pushed himself to a standing position from his chair. He leaned heavily on Gertrude. [Heal Small Wounds] took some time to fully restock his lost blood. "Where am I supposed to go, Brandt? What about Jude's family?"

Brandt shook his head. "I'm going to stay with them. I owe Jude that much. If they die, I'll be cold first."

Madi began running around Silas's office, collecting items and pulling open hidden compartments. She tossed rolls of coins covered in cloth into a small bag, along with other small trinkets of precious metals. She stopped and looked up sheepishly. "We're going to need money for supplies. We can travel east to Veskar because, obviously, we can't go to Odrana. They want Daniel. I don't really know anybody there. We probably shouldn't use my family name, either. We—"

"Madi." Brandt stopped her rambling. "You can't leave. If you do, Wendeln will say Daniel kidnapped you. Your father will have no choice but to order everyone to hunt you all down."

Orrin stayed quiet, listening to another voice.

"If you think for one second that I am going to abandon Daniel— Orrin, back me up here. You're going with him, right?"

Orrin didn't respond, looking out the window that overlooked the front of the house. "Wendeln just arrived. Your dad is not with him."

"Brandt, turn off the teleport ward," Madi pleaded. "Orrin can get us out of here."

"No." Orrin touched the curtain, moving it out of the way. "He's not here for Daniel. He doesn't know he's here. He tracked Jude's family."

"What? How?" Brandt checked the window in a more professional manner, peering from the corner instead of the middle of the window like Orrin had. "Damn it."

"Tony's out there. He wants to know . . . he wants to know if we want to take down a lord of Dey with him."

The room was silent as the group decided their next move. One by one they nodded, and Orrin began to explain.

Daniel walked out of the Catanzano house holding a white sheet on an unlit torch. The surrender symbol apparently traversed both worlds.

"I've come to talk with Lord Wendeln," he called out. "I'm Daniel."

Lord Wendeln still wore his opal chain shirt, but his golden and blue clothes were stained with blood. Likely his own men's blood that had been spilled as he ran away from his son's creation. He held his sword naked at his side, and his well-trimmed beard was stained with sweat.

"The [Hero] at Silas's house? What sort of treachery has that man gotten our fair city into?" Wendeln shouted. "Did you summon a Beast into the heart of my keep at his bequest? If you admit to your misdeeds, I'm sure an arrangement can be found."

Come quietly and we'll only crucify Silas, Orrin interpreted. He heard Tony's low growl in his mind. *I hope he keeps it together.*

"I will," Tony said in his mind, but with the kind of anger Orrin had never felt in his life. The man was aching to attack Wendeln.

Daniel played his part beautifully. "You know I didn't summon the monster, Wendeln. But I am tired of playing politics with Lord Catanzano and Tarris. They are so boring, keeping me locked up and leveling when all I want is to get out there and finish my Quests."

Orrin didn't have Tony's mind skills, but he could see Wendeln's face go through multiple emotions: Hope that the [Hero] would come with him quietly. Confusion and fear at the mention of the Tarris family being involved as well. Something he couldn't know, as it was a misdirection and false. And the greed at the mention of Quests.

"I can help you with that. You seem a smart young man. I'm sure we have much to discuss. Would you accompany me to—"

"I am a smart young man," Daniel talked over the man, earning a scornful look. "And I know my value here. I also know that you already tried to kidnap me once. Why should I trust you not to do that again?"

Lord Wendeln smirked and pulled his beard into a point between two fingers. "If I wanted to kidnap you, I would have. What lies have people been feeding you?"

Orrin had been slowly creeping toward Daniel during the exchange. He took Daniel's hand and placed it gently in a bag he was holding. [Camouflage] was up, and Orrin stood a foot behind Daniel.

"Please let this work," he muttered.

Orrin watched as Daniel's hand pulled the item from his [Dimension Hole]. The body of Wayne the Toxic Rogue and kidnapper fell at their feet.

"This little birdie confessed it was you who tried to kidnap me," Daniel challenged the silver-haired man, who was beginning to look a little more worried. He put his hand back into what looked like an invisible bag and pulled out a long flower whip. Daniel gave it a quick snap in the air.

"Samara sends her regards. She really tried to fulfill your orders." Daniel dropped the whip to the side and pulled out Gerty. "I know who you are and who you work for. Get the fuck out of this city or I'll beat you down just like I did your Agent."

Lord Wendeln laughed. The dozen men around him chuckled nervously. "So you took down little Sammy. I was wondering how you got back into the city. That must have been quite the feat for you. From my reports, you've barely reached level ten. Don't be an idiot. Come with me and no one needs to die."

"You'll kill Jude's family the first chance you get," Daniel responded. Orrin moved away into position. He really hoped everything worked as they'd planned. "You already attacked Lord Catanzano's house to kidnap me—you'll probably do the same to the other lords."

"I don't need to kill them if I have you," Wendeln answered, sheathing his sword. "I don't need to do anything to the other 'lords' of this small city. If you work with us, we can have so much more than the meager scraps of a wasteland guardhouse. Do you know the kind of power the elves hold? What kind of power you can hold?"

Daniel shrugged. "I think I have enough. I don't work with people who kidnap children and threaten my friends. You admitted to kidnapping me and Jude's family. You admitted to breaking your own laws. And yet you still expect me to trust you? What kind of idiot do you take me for?"

The feeling in Lord Wendeln's eyes dimmed. "One that I didn't want to dirty my own hands over. I guess that time has passed." Wendeln folded his arms and nodded at Daniel. "Take him."

"No, Shaw. That won't be happening today," Silas Catanzano, lord of Dey, announced as he dropped the magical veil he'd been hiding behind. Two others stood beside him.

Wendeln choked and tried to figure out what was going on.

Orrin smiled. Tony's plan had worked. While Brandt had turned off the teleport ward, Orrin and Madi had teleported to her father. He had been able to locate the other lords, and Orrin had used the last of his daily mana to get all five of them to a street one away from the front of Silas's house.

Silas had covered the rest. His class of [Allure Sorcerer] gave him the ability to use minor illusion spells, including a powerful veil or magical screen to hide behind. He'd muttered something about not using it in a long time when Orrin had asked him to use it.

Tony's plan had been simple: Let the man brag and talk, thinking he was confessing only to the [Hero]. Silas would get a front seat to the admission. Lord Tarris and Lady Timpe, as well.

"Shaw . . ." Lady Timpe started to talk but turned her head. "I vote that Shaw Wendeln be stripped of his title of Lord of Dey."

Lord Tarris, a tall man in a robe with thinning hair and glasses, shook his head. "Seconded."

Silas rolled his wheelchair forward. "Carried. Lord Wendeln, you are hereby stripped of your title and lands. Your men will be removed from your command, and you will be banished from Dey. If you are not gone within the hour, your life is forfeit."

Wendeln cried out and moved his hands in a similar fashion to his son. He began to chant, and a small black hole appeared in the center of the street, growing bigger by the second.

Chapter 67

As the dark circle grew, the bricks that made up the street fell into the middle, swallowed up into the blackness below. A scream of thousands of voices welled up into the city, and the flapping of wings could be heard churning beneath. Lord Wendeln's men balked at the sight. One was standing too close and started to slip in before another caught his belt and pulled him back.

"You fool," Lord Tarris yelled. "You would use [Harvest] within the city? You'll kill everyone here."

Lady Timpe didn't try to reason with the fallen lord. Instead, she twisted in her half plate armor, pulled a dagger from her belt, and threw it at Wendeln. The man flinched and batted it out of the air with his hand; however, Lady Timpe had drawn her longsword and was rushing the man as he turned back.

Each swing of Lady Timpe's sword hit hardened air right before striking Wendeln. Lord Tarris began throwing spells at the man as well. Flashes of what looked like lightning were deflected off Wendeln's defensive skill. Each strike smashed against the Catanzano house behind, leaving gouges in the brick inches deep.

Silas began twisting his hands in the air before him, looking to Orrin like he was raving. Ripples of air passed over Lady Timpe as she swung in overhand chops that came on faster and faster with each strike. The wavy air hit Wendeln, and he stumbled back. Timpe was able to strike down and severed an arm with one hit.

The pit trembled, and the circle broke. A single scaly hand reaching up was cut as the summon was canceled. Its green fingers twitched twice before it melted into sludge on the dirt. Where the road had been split, a perfect circle of dirt rested. The stones that had been swallowed up were gone.

Orrin watched as Lady Timpe took two more quick swings, striking down to cut off the other arm that reached up with a wand, then crossing from left to right. Lord Wendeln's head rolled across the street.

The fight between the four lords lasted two in-breaths and one out-breath. Orrin counted. They had moved with purpose and speed that even Samara hadn't matched. A true fight between titans.

I've got a long way to go.

Lord Wendeln's men hadn't had the chance to move. Brandt and Madi moved in from behind them, yelling orders to toss down their weapons.

The men did not resist. Weapons hit the dirt. Their lord was in pieces, and he'd tried to destroy Dey. Most looked confused. Orrin noticed one or two were crying.

Lady Timpe was breathing fast but not from exertion. She was staring down at the body of a man she'd worked with for years. Lord Tarris walked forward and rested a hand on her armored shoulder. Orrin couldn't hear the words said, but she stiffened and nodded once.

Silas turned in his chair and nodded once at Daniel. His eyes traveled to where Orrin had dropped his [Camouflage], and a small smile played across his lips. He mouthed, "Good job."

Orrin smiled back. If only Silas knew this had been Tony's plan.

The three remaining lords of Dey ordered the group about, but Orrin was thankful that he didn't have to think for a bit. *When is the last time I slept?*

As more troops arrived in the area, Silas let them go back to the house. They'd earned a rest. It was firmly morning now, and Lady Timpe and Lord Tarris had left with a large contingent of soldiers to box in the now correctly termed Wendeln summon.

Orrin made sure Daniel got into bed first, not trusting him after the last few weeks. He took off his armor and boots and fell on his bed. Sleep took him quickly.

Orrin woke once more to the glorious smell of coffee in the room.

"Wake up, sleepyhead," a voice singsonged. "You've slept almost an entire day."

"Go away," Orrin murmured into his pillow. "Leave the coffee."

Daniel chuckled and sat on Orrin's bed. He waited for Orrin to turn and growl.

"I brought the entire carafe and a cup for you." Daniel offered the cup in one hand and placed the pot of godly fluid down on the nightstand. "They took down that monster. Only minor injuries that the Hospital was able to heal up."

Orrin grunted and took the cup. He slurped some into his mouth and sighed. "That's good."

"Everybody in the city knows I'm the [Hero] now."

Orrin flinched. "Not as good."

Daniel shrugged. "It was going to happen sooner or later. At least now I can practice more. Silas told me the other lords—" He paused. "—and lady?" He shook his head. "The powers in charge granted me and my party access to the dungeons. Of course, I've been invited to like a hundred dinner parties, training sessions, and even a poetry reading."

"I guess the cat's out of the bag now," Orrin said, starting to feel the fuel hit his veins. "What do you think we should do first?"

Daniel smirked and threw a blue box at Orrin.

"The war Quest? Why? We don't know even know where to start for that—"

Daniel cut him off. "Revenge."

Orrin thought it through. The name of the aggressor country, Odrana, had come up a few times. They'd apparently paid for the [Hero], leading to all the recent trouble and the downfall of a lord of Dey.

And leading to the death of a friend.

"How is his family?"

Daniel didn't need more clarification. "Silas has them protected. He's promised they'll be taken care of for life, even after what Jude did. He even said thank you to Tony." Daniel smiled wide again. "You have no idea how funny that was to watch. Tony kept mouthing 'what' and cupping his ear. But Lady Timpe was there, and Silas had to play it cool."

Orrin laughed with his friend. Daniel hadn't slept as long and filled him in on everything he'd missed overnight.

"Knock, knock. I heard somebody finally woke up?" Madi peered around the corner of the open door. "You boys decent?"

"Daniel's never decent, but come on in," Orrin said, sitting up and pouring a second cup. "He was just filling me in on what's next."

Madi pulled a chair over and sat by the two of them. As they chatted, laughing and planning, Orrin felt a knot loosen in his chest. He'd spent so many days in a row saving Daniel, running from problem to problem, and battling, that he'd forgotten to rest.

"What is that face he's making?" Madi whispered. "Is that a smile?"

"Shut up," Orrin said and tossed a pillow at Madi.

"Yes! [Side Steps] triggered."

Two days later, Orrin, Madi, and Daniel trained alone. Brandt had requested some leave, and Silas had been happy to grant it. Brandt had apologized to all three of them repeatedly until Daniel had told him to shut up.

"Take all the time you need," he said, hugging the man. Brandt stood stiff. "We'll be waiting."

Madi kicked off the wall and swung her spear at Daniel, who dodged under her attack. He swung Gertrude at her but slowed at the last minute. Orrin had debuffed his dexterity.

"Not fair, I almost had her." Daniel laughed and ran after Orrin. Orrin threw [Lightstrikes] at both of them and threw a fist in the air.

"I won. You're both dead."

Daniel laughed and then hit Orrin with a wide swing, knocking him back. [Ward] protected all of them from taking too much damage, and Orrin was maxing out all of his spells each day. The quiet of the practice was enough to distract them all from the riots in the streets. Some of Lord Wendeln's men had started rumors that the [Hero] had killed him. The lords of Dey put out the truth, but when the news spread that the heir to the Wendeln seat was missing and presumed dead, the city had turned.

Madi had not been able to even speak with her father. He was out of the house, putting down looting and burning attempts. She'd quietly put back the money she'd stolen from his office.

"You are both getting better," Madi said with a laugh, throwing a towel at Daniel. Orrin walked over and took another towel from her.

"Thanks," he said. The city of Dey, which had once felt so grand and peaceful, was beginning to feel like a cage. "Do you guys think we should wait for everything to die down? I'm not sure how Silas is going to feel about it if we just leave."

Daniel wiped sweat off his face. "We're going to write a letter. Besides, you know he'd refuse to let Madi go, too."

The three had begun planning a trip north, toward the elven forest. Orrin had no idea what Daniel planned to find, but Madi seemed primed for an adventure and backed all his ideas.

"And we'll have the [Hero] with us," Madi chimed in. "What could possibly go wrong?"

Orrin groaned.

Daniel laughed. "Don't worry so much, Orrin. We still plan to level a bit before we head out. It's not like we're leaving tomorrow."

Orrin shook his head and looked toward the setting sun. Something inside still felt off to him. He just couldn't put a finger on it.

In a small house, tucked away far from others, a shadow knocked on the door.

"You summoned me, illustrious one?"

The figure in the chair sat by one of the many windows, looking out at the view. He waved his right hand at the single guard, gesturing for him to approach.

"Leanthun, my nephew." His voice was smooth, if old. "I would send you to Dey to find this new [Hero]. Learn everything you can about his powers. Something old and new is stirring in that area. Something I've not felt in a long time. Change has come to our world."

Leanthun saluted with crossed arms across his chest and bowed. "As you wish, sir." He paused before asking, "Is there anything else you can tell me? Will I need to take care of him?"

The figure smiled and stood from his chair, stretching his back. The sunlight flitted through the open window and lit up the face of the old man with pointed ears. A small circlet of wood ran around his head, and his eyes were pale blue with a deepness that made even Leanthun hesitate to look too long.

"No, nephew. You will not need to harm him. I fear not the [Hero]. I've seen countless of them come and go."

"I don't understand." The younger elf's face was puzzled. Why send him to learn about another [Hero] if there was nothing to fear from him?

"I don't fully understand, either," the old elf chuckled and waved his nephew out the door. "That's why you have to investigate for me. A [Hero] has been summoned, but something more powerful has arrived on Asmea as well. Find it."

The old elf stood on his porch, watching one of the last members of his family climb down his tree. His small house was usually ignored, and he'd spent hundreds of years living away from the bustle of society. He was normally at peace with his life.

Yet, something inside felt off. Hopefully, Leanthun would find an answer.

About the Author

What am I supposed to write here?

Should I tell you how I made the name SourpatchHero? (At the last minute before hitting publish on RoyalRoad.com because a name was required and I couldn't think of anything better.)

Maybe how I came up with the idea for *I'm Not the Hero?* (I read everything ever written and still couldn't find the story about the hero's best friend/sidekick that I wanted and thought . . . I can try . . . what's the worst that can happen?)

What is the worst that can happen? (Get published and have to write an "about the author" section . . .)

Should I write about my life? (Lawyer by day, dad to two sons, and happy husband by night.)

Ok . . . maybe I should expand that one.

I grew up in Florida, a magically hot and humid state, which fortunately also has beaches.

Somehow, I rolled high on my luck and met a cute girl in high school who could stand being around me for longer than a day and I never let her go. We moved all over, going to school, and living a fun life before settling in Virginia.

After having one son and then forgetting how small children don't allow their parents to sleep, we decided to have another one. When the wife started falling asleep earlier and earlier each night, I pulled out my trusty old laptop and started writing a story that had been building in my head. I knew the beginning and how I wanted to end it. I knew a few basic plot points and people I wanted to introduce.

What I didn't know was exactly how little the story would care about any of that. Writing and finding out who each character is and what they want to do has became a passion, and somehow I finished the first book just a few weeks before our second son was born.

Now I have two kids, a wife, a dog, a full-time job, and a published book. I don't know, I think life is going pretty well.

But really, I'm just a guy who started writing a story for myself. That anybody actually read it is amazing. That I've been published is a literal dream come true. Thank you all for believing in this story and continuing to let me make up silly adventures.

Made in United States
North Haven, CT
11 April 2024

51192883R00343